Henry Temple, Cordelia M. Ottley

The Model Book of Dreams

fortune teller, and epitome of parlor entertainments

Henry Temple, Cordelia M. Ottley

The Model Book of Dreams
fortune teller, and epitome of parlor entertainments

ISBN/EAN: 9783337370664

Printed in Europe, USA, Canada, Australia, Japan

Cover: Foto ©Andreas Hilbeck / pixelio.de

More available books at **www.hansebooks.com**

THE
MODEL BOOK OF DREAMS,
FORTUNE TELLER,

AND

Epitome of Parlor Entertainments,

COMPRISING

TERPRETATION OF DREAMS, FORTUNE TELLING, CHARADES,
TABLEAUX VIVANTS, PARLOR GAMES, PARLOR MAGIC,
SCIENTIFIC AMUSEMENTS, ETC., ETC.

BY

HENRY TEMPLL
AND
CORDELIA M. OTTLEY.

CINCINNATI:
J. R. HAWLEY & CO., 164 VINE STREET.
1864.

A DREAM OF ANGELS.

CONTENTS.

(5)

PREFACE.

Nothing which is natural is entirely useless. Dreams must be intended for some purpose. About one-third of our existence is passed in sleep; and during sleep we often dream. Why is this? Does the mind naturally and irresistibly act in a certain way, while we sleep, and this without any possible useful purpose? Certainly not. Common sense, philosophy, and history will contradict this supposition. Mankind, in all ages and countries, have agreed in believing that dreams have a spiritual origin, and to a certain extent, a useful purpose.

We know by the sacred Scriptures, and by ancient history, that dreams of a prophetic character took place in many instances in the early ages of the world; and that the courts of the Oriental sovereigns were attended by learned men, whose business it was to interpret dreams. In modern times innumerable instances have been recorded of dreams, whose symbolic or prophetic character has been attested by their fulfillment.

The popular belief that dreams are sometimes prophetic, is shared by many scientific and intelligent writers in various parts of the world.

Considering the wide prevalence of this belief, it is by no means surprising to find that persons have undertaken to trace the connection between dreams and the events to which they are supposed to predict. They have published books in which the whole matter is reduced to system ; and have enunciated the laws of Oneirology as authoritatively as others have set forth those of Physics or Mental Philosophy. The first part of this volume affords a specimen of these "Dream Books." If the reader cannot bring himself to assent to these interpretations of dreams, he will at least find a great deal of entertainment in reading them.

They afford a specimen of those theories which have entered very largely into the popular belief—a belief which, to a certain extent, is undoubtedly founded on observation of facts, and a comparison of dreams with the events which follow them.

The succeeding parts of this volume hardly require a word of explanation, The Fortune Teller affords a delightful amusement for evening parties. The Charades form a species of entertainment, which has recently acquired an immense popularity; and the specimens of Legerdemain, Tricks with Cards, Parlor Games, and Scientific Amusements are every day coming into more extensive use, giving a greatly increased store of delightful entertainments for evening parties, and combining instruction with amusement.

DREAMS,

AND THEIR INTERPRETATIONS.

Acquaintance.—To dream that you fight with them signifies distraction, especially if the person so dreaming be sick.

Adversary.—To dream that you receive obstruction from him, shows that you will dispatch your business speedily.

Almonds.—To dream one sees or eats almonds, signifies difficulties and trouble.

Alms.—To dream that they are begged of you, and you deny to give them, shows want and misery to the dreamer; but to dream you give them freely is a sign of joy and long life.

Altar.—To dream you uncover or discover an altar, betokens joy and gladness.

Anchor.—To dream you see one, signifies great assurance and certain hope.

Angel.—To dream you see an angel is good, but to speak with or call upon them is evil.

Anger.—To dream that you have been provoked to anger, shows that you have powerful enemies.

Angling.—To dream that you are angling, betokens much affliction and trouble in something which you desire to get.

Animals.—Dreaming of domestic animals signifies the happy return of absent friends, peaceful domestic relations, and reconciliation of quarrels. Wild animals signify secret enemies, of whom beware, as to dream thus, will bring trouble from them.

Apes.—To dream you have seen or had anything to do with them, signifies malicious, weak, strange, and secret enemies; also a malefactor and deceiver.

Apparition.—To dream you see an apparition, or spirit, clothed in white, signifies deceit and temptation to sin.

Appetite.—To dream of unsatisfied hunger, signifies disappointment in your favorite plans. Satisfied hunger, if the imaginary repast be bountiful, signifies that you will inherit a large fortune.

Adam.—To dream you see this father of men, this inhabitant of Paradise, who was betrayed by Eve into sin, is a happy omen. If he looks pleasant, be sure you will succeed in whatever you undertake.

If he looks displeased and angry, then you must use great caution in all your dealings, for some mischief is intended you, but you will get the better of it. Be careful, if he speaks to you, to mind what he says, and observe it as faithfully as you possibly can.

Absence.—

> To dream of any absent friends,
> Good news of them, or ill, portends;
> But if at thy bedside they seem,
> Their deaths, perhaps, may solve thy dream.

Abuse.—To dream that you are abused and insulted, is a certain sign that some dispute will happen between you and some person with whom you have business; therefore, after such a dream you should be particularly careful of yourself, and be as gentle and mild as possible, that you may not give those with whom you have dealings any advantage over you.

Acorns.—

> The dreams of acorns do not slight,
> It promises both strength and might.

Ague.—To dream you have an ague, denotes nothing very particular, more than that you are in danger of becoming a drunkard and a glutton. To dream your sweetheart has an ague, is a lucky omen: it shows you are beloved, and that you will be happy with the object of your wishes, but never very rich.

Alone.—

> 'Tis good to dream thou'rt left alone,
> A friend thou hast on the highest throne.

Apparel.—Nothing more demonstrates the events that are about to happen to you, than dreaming of wearing apparel; but almost every color has a different interpretation, and must depend on its appearing new or old, its fitting you, or being too big or too little. To dream you are dressed in white, is a sure token of success in the first object you undertake, and that you will be successful in love, and that your beloved is of a good temper and amiable disposition. To dream you are dressed in green, denotes that you are about to take a journey to your advantage, and that your beloved prefers you to all other lovers. To dream that you are dressed in black is an unlucky omen. To dream that you are dressed in blue, denotes happiness. If you dream you are dressed in scarlet, you are thereby warned of some very heavy calamity. To dream you are dressed in yellow, is rather lucky than otherwise. To dream you are dressed in crimson, denotes that you will live to a good old age, and neither very fortunate or unfortunate through life; it denotes a small dispute between a landlord and his tenant, which will be settled amicably to the advantage of the latter. To dream that you are dressed in a variety of colors, denotes a variety of fortunes are about to attend you. To dream you are fashionably dressed and in good company, is very good for the dreamer·

he will rise considerably above his present condition. To dream your clothes fit you well, and are conformable to the season of the year, is favorable and denotes success. To dream your clothes do not fit you, and that they are not suitable to the season, denotes the death of some friend, and a loss by fire. To dream you see another dressed in any of the modes above described, forebodes to the person dreamt of the same fortunes, and, in a much smaller degree, the same events to yourself. To dream you are dressed in new clothes, is a very favorable omen; it portends honors and success to your undertakings.

Apparitions.—To dream you see a ghost, hobgoblin, spectre, and such kind of things, is of a very unfortunate nature; it denotes vexation and disappointment; if you are in love, it is a certain sign of your not being beloved in return; depend upon it, some one is about to deceive you, and that you are in habits of friendship with one who is your most inveterate enemy.

Arms.—To dream your arms are withered is a certain sign that you will decay in health and fortune. To dream they are grown strong, signifies that some unexpected success will attend you. To dream your right arm is cut off, denotes you will lose some near male relation; to dream your left arm is cut off, denotes you will lose some near female relative. For a married woman to dream her arms have grown lusty and strong, denotes that she will have many male children, that her husband will arrive at public honors, and will grow rich and make many friends.

Apples.—To dream of apples betokens long life and success, faithfulness in your lover, and riches by trade.

Apricots.—To dream of apricots denotes health and prosperity, a speedy marriage, dutiful children and success in love.

Asses.—To dream you see jackasses, is a good sign. To

dream you are riding on an ass, is the forerunner of some foolish quarrel. To dream that you are driving an ass, denotes that you will fall into some tronble, of which you will get the better. To dream an ass runs after you, denotes that some slander will be raised against you by some foolish persons who will become themselves the victims of the scandal raised against you. To dream you see an ass full loaded, is of very good import, and shows that you will be the founder of your own fortune.

Attorney.—To dream you are speaking with them, shows hindrance of business, and that a man shall have little success in his affairs.

Anchor.—To dream of this emblem of hope, denotes some good to the dreamer; it forebodes very unexpected news.

Armed Men.—To see them in your dream is a good sign, and denotes one void of fear; to dream you see an armed man fly is a sign of victory; to see men come in arms against you, signifies sadness.

Action.—To dream that you are sent of an errand, signifies great loss to the married; to the lover it denotes success in his pursuits, and that he will shortly marry a very amiable and accomplished maiden. For a maiden to dream that she was sent on an errand, denotes that she will shortly marry the object of her affections and be very happy; to the sick, it denotes a speedy recovery.

Ascend.—For one to dream they ascend toward the skies is favorable; particularly so, if the clouds appear bright.

Air.—To dream of the atmosphere has a variety of interpretations, and depends entirely on the different appearances it has. If you dream the sky is clear, of a fine blue, calm and serene, then it is a good omen. To dream it is streaked with white, denotes that many severe difficulties will befall you, over which you will eventually triumph. To dream that it was full of thick, dark and heavy clouds, is an unfavorable token; disappointments will attend you. To dream that the sky is streaked with red and looks fiery, denotes that in love you will be successful, in business not so; it also forewarns you that sickness and trouble will attend your family.

Altar.—To dream you are at the altar and receiving the holy sacrament, is a very unfavorable omen, and denotes many heavy and severe afflictions.

> To dream thou dost an altar see,
> Will joy and gladness bring to thee.

Ants.—To dream of these industrious little insects, hath a variety of interpretations, and depends upon the manner in which you dream of them; if you see them running about, it denotes that you will be a great loser by some plan that you will undertake for gain. If you dream you see them busily employed laying in their winter stores, it is a good omen— things will prosper with you. If they appeared to be devoured by other animals, and otherwise injured and trodden upon, then it is a bad omen. If you dream of these insects when you are sick, you must expect to recover very slowly, and to be a long time before you are able to be about.

Ball.—

> Dream you join the festive round
> And joy and pleasure will abound.

Bear.—

> To dream a bear thy steps pursues,
> A cruel foe some mischief brews.

Beggars.—To dream of beggars is rather unfavorable, especially to lovers, and persons in business. To dream they beg alms of you, and that you refuse it, denotes misery, want, and a prison; if you are in love, some scandalous person will ruin you with your sweetheart. To dream that you give them alms, indicates success in business, and that you will obtain, after much difficulty, the object of your affections, your children will be sickly, and narrowly escape many dangers.

Bleeding.—To dream you are bleeding, denotes loss of

goods and character, and that your sweetheart will not marry you. To dream you see another bleeding, indicates that some person who pretends to be your friend is about to take some great advantage of you. To dream you draw blood of another, denotes that you will recover a law-suit, and be successful in love and in business. To dream another draws blood of you, is a certain prognostic that you will be unsuccessful in love and in business, and in every thing you undertake.

Blind.—To dream of being blind is a certain sign that you repose your confidence in some person who is your bitter enemy; it denotes also that your sweet-heart is unfaithful, and prefers another; in business, it denotes that you will lose money, and that your servants want fidelity.

Boat.—To dream that you are on the water in a boat, provided you are in company, denotes prosperity and success in your undertaking. If you dream you are in a boat alone, it is a bad omen. To dream the boat oversets, is the most fatal of all omens.

Bridge.—To dream you are crossing over a bridge is a good omen—it denotes prosperity through life, and success in love. To dream you are passing under a bridge, indicates that you will never be perfectly at ease. If you meet with any obstruction on the bridge, it foretells a fit of sickness; are you a lover, it denotes that your sweet-heart will be afflicted with illness. To dream a bridge breaks down with you, denotes sudden death.

Bread.—To dream you see a great quantity of loaves of bread, denotes success in life. To dream you are eating good bread, denotes that you will be shortly married. To dream the bread is musty and bad, denotes the loss of friends, and that some near relation will shortly die.

Brother.—To dream you see your brother, denotes a speedy marriage in your family, and that the dreamer will be long-lived; if you are in love, it is a favorable omen.

2

Buildings.—To dream of being amongst buildings, denotes that you will change your present place of residence, and that you will make many new friends in life; if you are in love, it foretells your sweetheart is about to remove at a distance from you, and that you will be in danger of losing the affections of your lover by new faces.

Bulls.—To dream you are pursued by a bull, denotes that many injurious reports will be spread of your character. If you dream the bull gores you, or tosses you, then expect shortly to lose your liberty; it denotes that some person high in power will do you an injury.

Burning.—

> To dream of burning doth imply
> A sudden danger ripe and nigh;
> Of all escapes, you then beware,
> For though fate threatens, it may spare.

Butchers.—To dream of seeing butchers, is in general a very unlucky omen; it always foretells some injury to the dreamer. If you see them cutting up meat, some of your friends will be hanged, and you will experience much misery and poverty.

Blowing the Fire.—To dream you are blowing the fire, indicates to the lover, that your sweet-heart is very angry with you.

Barn.—To dream of a barn, and that you see it well stored with corn, denotes much good; it foretells to a man that he will marry some rich woman; to a maid, that she will marry a man who will grow very rich by his industry, and be promoted in the State. If you dream you see an empty barn, the reverse will happen.

Bathing.—To dream of a bath is a very unpropitious omen; expect after it to experience many hardships and much sorrow. If you are in love, your sweet-heart will experience many crosses and losses; but to dream you are bathing yourself in clear water, denotes happiness, prosperity and success in love—if the water is dirty, then it foretells shame and sorrow, and a disappointment in love.

Beheading.—To dream you see any one beheaded, is a good omen—if you are in love, you will marry the object of your affections—if you are in prison, you will speedily gain your liberty.

Bells.—To dream you hear the bells ringing denotes a speedy marriage, and that you will receive some very good news.

Bees.—To dream they sting you, denotes loss of good character; and if you are in love, of your sweetheart. To dream you see them at work, is a very lucky dream—it forebodes great success by your own industry. To dream you see them making their honey under your own roof, is the best omen in the world. For the rich to dream of bees is rather unlucky; but to the poor they denote comfort, affluence and success.

Beard.—For a man to dream he has a long beard, denotes good fortune; if he is in trade, he will thrive; if he is in love, he will marry the present object of his affections, who will bring him some money; if he is a farmer, it denotes good crops, and an addition to his farm. If a married woman dreams of a beard, it is unlucky—it foretells the loss of her husband, and that she will fall into great distress. If a maid dreams of a beard, it denotes that she will be quickly married. For a woman to dream that she has a beard, is a very lucky omen, and denotes that she will speedily attain her most sanguine desires.

Battle.—To dream you see a battle in the streets forewarns you against secret enemies, who will endeavor to harm you—if you are in love, your sweetheart is false to you.

Bacon.—To dream of bacon denotes the death of some friend or relation, and that enemies will endeavor to do you mischief—in love, it denotes disappointment and discontent.

Back.—To dream you see your back, betokens some uneasiness; for the back to be broken or hurt, shows you will be scoffed at by your enemies; yet to dream of the back bone, signifies health and success in love, marriage and business.

Basin.—To dream of a basin, signifies a good maid; and to dream you eat or drink therein, shows you have a love to the servant maid.

Beans.—To dream you are eating beans, always signifies trouble and dissension.

Bereavement.—To dream of the death of near relatives betokens a wealthy and desirable marriage in the family. If you are present at the deathbed and suffer great sorrow, you will soon marry; if already married, it means a new partnership in business, which will lead to fortune.

Beets.—To dream of eating beets, signifies freedom from trouble, and expedition of business; because they make the body soluble.

Burial.—

> To dream a burial passes by,
> News of the living doth imply.

Briars and Brambles.—If you dream you are passing through places covered with these things, it portends troubles; if they prick you, secret enemies will do you an injury with your friends, and unfavorable tales will make your sweet-heart shy of you; if they draw blood of you, expect heavy losses in trade.   If you dream you pass through them without injury, then you will at last triumph over all your enemies and become happy.

Bells.—To dream one hears ringing of bells, if of a sanguine complexion, brings them good news; but to others, it shows alarms, murmurings, disturbances, and commotions.

Birding.—To dream you catch birds, signifies profit and pleasure.

Bird's Nest.—To dream you find one is a good sign. To dream you find one without eggs or birds, shows you will meet great disappointments.

Birth.—To dream of one's birth is good for him that is poor; but to him that is rich, this dream signifies that others shall rule over him against his will.

Bishop.—To dream of a bishop denotes some coming important event in your religious life. Communion signifies fame. To be denounced signifies misfortune in love. Confession signifies the exposure of some secret which will ruin you.

Blindman's Buff.—To dream that one plays blindman's buff, signifies joy and pleasure.

Blossoming of Trees.—To dream you see all sorts of trees blossoming, is a sign of joy, comfort, and recreation.

Brewing and Baking.—To dream of brewing and baking is the sign of an ill housewife, who lies dreaming in bed, when she should be at work and doing her business.

Burning Fire.—To dream of a burning fire denotes great anger and contention. If you succeed in extinguishing the fire you will triumph over your enemies. If you are not successful in extinguishing it, they will triumph over you.

Broth.—To dream of eating broth is a good sign, and signifies profit and gain.

Burdens.—Heavy burdens signify that you will have to labor for another person's support; if you cannot bear the burden, many persons will depend upon you; if it is supportable, you will be able to sustain the additional care with honor and credit.

Burned.—For a man to dream he is burned, signifies (according to the interpretations of the Persians and Egyptians) that he shall be rich, honored and respected; but if he imagines that he was burned by a fire that did not quite consume him, he will inevitably perish in the end.

Basket --For a man to dream of baskets is evil—it de-notes decay of business to a merchant, and want of employ-ment to a mechanic, and loss, of place to a servant;—but if a woman dreams she receives a number of baskets, is good, and especially so if well filled;—to a maiden it denotes that she will have many new lovers; to the wife that she will have an increase in her family; and to the widow that she will soon marry again.

Bonnet.—For a maiden to dream she gets a new bonnet, gives promise of a new lover, but Mother Shipton says that much depends on the color;—if green, he will be deceitful; if blue, he will prove affectionate; if pink, his love will not be lasting; if yellow or white, he will quickly improve marriage.

Business.—To dream of business signifies that an unknown friend desires to enter into partnership with you. After such a dream, marriage is sure to be happy.

Buttons.—To dream of bright buttons is always good; if rusty, it portends to misfortune; if covered, sadness; if a man dreams he has lost all the buttons off his clothes, it is a sign he will not live long.

Cards.—To dream you are playing at cards, is a sure prognostic that you will be in love, and speedily married. If you hold a great many picture cards, your marriage will be the means of making you rich and happy. If your cards are mostly diamonds, the person you marry will be of a sour and disagreeable temper; if they are mostly hearts, your marriage will cement love, and you will be very happy and have many children; if they are mostly clubs, you will get money by your marriage; if they are mostly spades, your marriage will turn out very unhappy, and your children will be undutiful, and subject to many hardships; if you are in expectation of a place, you will get it; and if you are in business, you will be successful.

Castle.—To dream of being in one signifies that you will receive a legacy. To leave a castle signifies desertion of friends and heavy loss. To view a castle from a distance signifies that after expecting a legacy for years you will be disappointed about receiving it. If an unmarried-person dream of a castle, he or she will remain single. To see a castle fall or besieged, signifies that you will suffer great losses from lawsuits.

Cats.—To dream of these domestic animals, is indicative of much trouble and vexation—it denotes to the lover, that your sweet-heart is treacherous; if you keep servants, they are unfaithful and will rob you. To dream you kill a cat, denotes that you will discover a thief, and prosecute him to conviction; expect also to lose your own liberty through some pretended friend.

Cattle.—To dream you see cattle feeding, denotes great prosperity, and unexpected success; to a lover it foretells a happy marriage, with many children, and to the man it shows that his wife will receive some unexpected legacy. To dream you are driving cattle denotes that you will become rich by industry; if you are in love, it shows that you have many rivals, but that you will distance them all. To dream you see fat cattle, also denotes a plentiful year. To dream you see lean and hungry cattle, denotes scarcity and famine.

Cave.—To walk in one, signifies to fall in the estimation of friends, and suffer from scandal. To meet a friend in a cave, signifies that you will marry beneath you, and be unhealthy. To meet loathsome animals signifies, trouble with your children. To come out from a cave into sunshine, signifies to rise from some great affliction.

Clock.—To dream you hear the clock strike, denotes that you will be speedily married, and that you will be moderately successful in life. To dream you are counting the hours, if in the forenoon, shows much happiness, and that your sweet-heart is true to you; but if in the afternoon, that misfortune and danger will attend you, and that your sweet-heart is false and loves another.

Coach.—To dream you are riding in a coach is a very unlucky omen; it foretells poverty and disgrace; if you are in love, your sweet-heart will be idle and bad-tempered; if you are in trade, you will become bankrupt; if you are a farmer, your goods will be seized for rent; it also denotes that the dreamer will shortly be in prison.

Coals.—To dream of coals is a very unlucky omen; it denotes much affliction and trouble. To dream you see coals burning, if they are very clear and bright, is a good sign. To dream you see the coals extinguished and reduced to cinders, denotes death, either to yourself or some near relation or friend; it also indicates great losses, and forewarns you of beggary and of prison.

Comets.—To dream you see one of these extraordinary ethereal substances, is ominous of war, plague, famine, and death; to the lover it forebodes an entire frustration of his hopes; to the farmer, failure of crops; and to the seaman, storms and shipwrecks. After such a dream, change, if possible, your present place of residence.

Cook.—

> Dream you're busy with a cook,
> And for a wedding shortly look.

Corn.—To dream you see fields of corn, or that you are among unthreshed corn, is a very favorable omen; it denotes success in business; to the lover it announces that you will marry, have many children, and become rich and happy. If you are a sailor, it denotes a lucrative voyage and fine weather, and that you will be near marrying in the next port you touch at. If you dream you are gathering ripe corn, it is the most fortunate dream you can have.

Crowns.—To dream you see these emblems of royalty, portends success and elevation to dignities, either in the church or State. For a maid to dream of a crown, shows she will marry a very industrious man, or one who is rich.

Crutches.—To dream you are walking on crutches, is a very unfavorable omen; to dream you see another walking on crutches, denotes that these things will happen to some friend.

Currants.—To dream of currants prefigures happiness in life, success in undertakings, constancy in your sweet-heart, handsome children to the married, riches to the farmer and tradesman.

Church.—To dream of a church is portentous of evil. If you are in a church during divine service, you will be engaged in a lawsuit, or some quarrel that will go very near to ruin you. If you are in love, your sweet-heart is unfaithful, and prefers another; if you expect a place, it forebodes disappointment; if you are in trade, you will never thrive in your present situation

Cage.—To dream of letting birds out of a cage, denotes a speedy marriage. To a person in business it denotes success, and to a farmer it denotes good crops.

Cain.—To dream of this first-born son of man, who was Adam's eldest son, is a very unfavorable omen. After such a dream, let the dreamer travel into another part of the country, and form new connections.

Cakes.—To dream you are eating cakes, denotes happiness and prosperity.

> Dream that cakes you knead and make,
> You'll thrive and many profits take.

Candles.—To dream you can see candles burning, denotes, if they burn clear and bright, that you will be speedily married. To dream that new candles are brought in, denotes that, by the interference of friends, all your disputes will be amicably adjusted, and that your sweet-heart will recover from a fit of sickness.

> A light that burns both bright and clear,
> Denotes some pleasant letter near;
> But if dull the candle grows,
> It certain disappointment shows.

Cheese.—

> To dream of cheese is not in vain,
> In trade you will a profit gain.

Chickens.—To dream of a hen and chickens is the fore-runner of ill-luck; your sweet-heart will betray you, and marry another. If you are a farmer, you will have a bad crop, and lose many of your poultry: if you are in trade, some sharper will defraud you; if you go to sea, you will lose your goods, and narrowly escape shipwreck.

Chess.—If any one dreams that he plays at chess with an acquaintance, it is a sign that he will fall out with somebody he knows; and if he imagines in his dream he wins, he shall be over his enemies. And on the contrary, if he dream that he loses, he will be overcome and worsted in the combat.

Clouds.—To dream of white clouds, signifies prosperity; clouds mounting high from the earth, denote voyages, the return of the absent, and revealing of secrets; clouds red and inflamed, show an ill issue of affairs; to dream of dark and obscure clouds, shows an ill time of anger.

Caterpillars.—To dream you see caterpillars, signifies ill luck and misfortune by secret enemies.

Chains, Pearls, Precious Stones, Ear-rings, &c., and all adornings of the heads and necks of women, are good dreams to the fair sex; to widows and maids they signify marriage; to those that have no children, that they shall have children; and to those that have husbands and children, purchases and riches; for as women are provided with these deckings, so shall they be stored with husbands, children, and goods.

Chariot.—To dream of guiding a chariot drawn by wolves, leopards, dogs, tigers, or such like beast, is only good to such as have great enemies. To dream to be drawn in a chair by men, is good.

Cheeks.—To dream one hath cheeks plump, fat, and of vermilion tincture, is good to all, especially to women; but to dream that you are lean, pale, and full of wrinkles, signifies grief and heaviness.

Capon.—To dream that a capon crows, signifies sadness and trouble.

Carrion.—To dream of carrion, signifies sadness.

Carrots.—To dream of carrots, signifies profit and strength to them that are at law for inheritance: for we pluck them out of the ground with our hands—branches, strings, and veins.

Cart.—To dream of being tied in a cart, to draw like an horse or an ox, denotes servitude and pain to everybody; but to dream that you are carried in a cart or coach, the contrary.

Coal-pit.—To dream of being in the bottom of coal-pits, signifies marrying with a widow; for he that marries her, shall never sound the depths of her policy.

Combing.—For any person to dream of combing him or herself, is good, both for man or woman, for it signifies to get out of evil times or affairs.

Comfort.—To dream you have comforts of any one, betokens to the rich and happy, injury and mishap; but to the poor and afflicted, aid and comfort.

Command.—To dream you command any one, signifies troubles; to dream you see one command, signifies anger and authority.

Complexion.—To dream one sees an unknown person of a brown complexion, is a sign of glory, honor, success, and dispatch of business. If one dreams he sees a woman of a very brown complexion, it signifies a very dangerous disease. If you see a woman unknown in your dream with long and comely hair, with clear complexion, it is a very good sign.

Corns.—For a man to dream his flesh is full of corns, shows he will grow rich proportionably to his corns.

Crocodile.—To dream of a crocodile signifies pirates or robbers at sea, or wicked persons of any sort like the crocodile.

Cross.—To dream you see a cross carried along, signifies sadness.

Cross Purposes.—To dream that one plays at cross purposes, signifies prosperity, joy, pleasure, health, and concord among friends and relations.

Crow.—To dream you see a crow, signifies expedition of business. To dream you see a crow flying, is ill luck; and if you hear them croaking unpleasantly, the dream is so much the worse. If you dream the crow flies on the head of a child, it will be in great danger of some misfortune.

Cypress Trees.—To dream you see a cypress tree, denotes affliction and obstruction in business.

Crowing.—To dream that you are crowing, or that you hear others crowing, denotes ill luck, especially to lovers; but to dream that you hear pigeons crowing, is good, especially to the newly married, as it denotes happiness.

Crawl.—To dream that you are crawling on the floor is bad; but to dream that you are crawling on the roof of a house is good, particularly to the lovers, as it is a sure sign they will be married.

Children.—To dream you see children, denotes success in your undertakings. To dream you see a child born, denotes a speedy marriage, and that you will be very happy with your family. To dream you see a child die, imports that you will experience some heavy misfortune, and that your sweet-heart will marry another. To dream you see children dirty and ragged, denotes that some friend will endeavor to prevail on you to commit an act by which your reputation will be endangered; it also denotes that you will be in prison and experience poverty.

Climbing.—To dream that you are climbing up a tree, denotes that you will be successful in life. To dream you are climbing up a very steep hill or place, foretells many difficulties in life, and much sickness. If you reach the top, you will get over all your difficulties, and recover from your illness; but if you awake before you have attained the top, you will be disappointed in love and all other projects, and die in your next illness.

Cherries.—To dream of cherries, indicates disappointments in life, vexation in the married state, and slight in love.

Cucumbers.—To dream of cucumbers, denotes recovery to the sick, and that you will speedily fall in love, or that if you are in love, you will marry the present object of your affection. It also denotes moderate success in trade; to the sailor it foretells a pleasant voyage, and a sweet-heart in a distant climate.

Dancing.—To dream that you are dancing at a ball, wake, or entertainment, foretells that you will shortly receive some joyful news from a long absent friend, and that you are about to inherit some unexpected legacy: for it foretells success and happiness in love; that your sweet-heart is kind.

Deer.—To dream you see deer in a park, denotes war and famine; to the lover it foretells some very unpleasant dispute with his sweet-heart.

Dice.—To dream that you are playing at dice or backgammon, denotes much good to the dreamer, in either love, marriage, or trade.

Dirt.—To dream of dirt signifies sickness and dishonor To dream you fall in the dirt, signifies that you will be treacherously dealt with.

Ditches.—To dream of deep ditches, steep mountains, rocks and other eminences, surely foretells danger and misfortune: expect thieves to rob your dwelling; that your children will be undutiful, and bring you into trouble. If you are in love, it foretells unhappiness if you marry your present sweet-heart; if you are in trade, it denotes loss of goods, if not of liberty.

Dogs.—To dream of these faithful and domestic animals has very different significations, according to the manner in which you see them. If they fawn and fondle upon you, then it is a lucky omen; if you are in love, your sweet-heart will marry you, and render you happy; if they are barking and snarling at you, then depend that enemies are secretly endeavoring to destroy your reputation and happiness; if you are in love, be careful of your sweet-heart.

Drowning.—To dream you are drowning, or that you see another drowned or drowning, portends good to the dreamer. To the lover it denotes that your sweet-heart is good tempered and inclined to marry you.

Dead.—To dream of talking with dead folks is a good auspicious dream, and signifies a boldness of courage, and a very clear conscience. To dream a man is dead that is alive and in health, signifies great trouble, and being overthrown at law.

Darkness.—To dream you are in a very dark place, or that you are in the dark, is a very unfavorable omen. To dream you get out of darkness into light, denotes good to the dreamer. Expect also to hear some glad tidings from a far distant country.

Death.—To dream you see this grim-looking bundle of bones, denotes that you will either be speedily married yourself, or else assist at a wedding. To dream that you are dead, also denotes a speedy marriage, and that you will be successful in all your undertakings. To dream you see another person dead, denotes unkind usage from your friends.

Drunkenness.—To dream you are drunk, is one of those dreams by which the dreamer is forewarned of that of which at present he knows nothing. It denotes that some person whom yet you do not know, will become a very good friend, and promote your welfare. To a woman it denotes that she will be beloved by an excellent man whom yet she has not seen; and to a man it denotes that he is tenderly beloved by a woman whom he does not at present think of, who will make him extremely happy, and bring him money.

Dairy.—To dream you are in a dairy busy at work, is a very favorable omen; but to the maid it indicates that her lover will be of an industrious turn, and that if she marries, she will have children, and her husband will become rich and rise to honor. To the farmer it denotes that his crops will be abundant, but that he will lose some of his live stock by thieves.

Devil.—To dream of this professed enemy to the human race, denotes that many dangers will threaten you, all of which you will overcome; if you are in love, it forebodes that some one is endeavoring to alienate the affection of your sweet-heart, but will be unsuccessful.

Dolphin.—To dream of a dolphin, shows to seafaring men, a wind from the place whence you dream he cometh. But to dream you see the dolphin out of water, signifies the death of friends.

Drink.—To dream you drink cold water is good; but hot signifies sickness and hindrance of affairs. To dream you drink wine with moderation, is good; to drink oil, signifies poison. To dream you are drinking, when you are dry, from a stream or fountain, is a sign of sickness. If a man dreams he is drunk with some sweet and pleasant drink, it is a sign he will be loved by some lady and grow rich thereby.

Dunghill.—To dream you stand on a dunghill is a favorable omen. It is a sure forerunner of success in every thing undertaken at this time. For a maiden to dream she is on a dunghill is a sign that she will marry the choice of her affections, who will be a man of some importance.

Daisy.—It is good to dream of daisies in spring or summer; but bad in fall or winter.

Dandelion.—To dream of gathering dandelions is ominous of one—to dream you see a large bed of them denotes that you have many new enemies forming, who will do you much injury in secret. If one in love dreams of dandelions, be sure his sweet-heart is playing him false.

Eagles.—To dream you see an eagle soaring very high in the air, denotes prosperity, riches, and honor: to the lover it foretells success in love—and a happy marriage. To dream you see an eagle perched on the steeple of a church, or on any other high eminence, is a very good omen: it denotes that in some arduous undertaking you will be successful, and thereby arrive at riches and honor; it also denotes that the dreamer will make his fortune beyond the sea.

Eden.—To dream of being in the Garden of Eden, signifies that every happiness will be yours, and you will become selfish and indifferent to the wants of others. If you pluck fruit, you will divide your pleasures with one in every way worthy to enjoy them.

Eels.—To dream of eels, signifies to beware of slippery pursuits and uncertain speculations. If the eel escapes you, you will be jilted in love; if you hold it, honor and married happiness will be in store for you.

Effigy.—If you dream of seeing any friend portrayed in effigy, he is a hypocrite, carrying a fair face over a false heart. Beware of him, especially in love matters.

Eggs.—To dream you are buying or selling eggs, is a very favorable omen: whatever you are then about will succeed, whether it be love, trade, or getting a place. To dream that you are eating eggs, denotes that you will shortly have a child and that your affairs will go well. To dream your eggs are broken, denotes loss of goods, quarrels and poverty; if you are in love, it forebodes a separation between you and your sweet-heart.

To dream of eggs will profit give,
And show that thou shalt thrive and live.

Elderberries.—To dream of elderberries augurs content and riches; to a maiden, they bespeak a speedy marriage; to the tradesman, success in business; to the farmer, good crops.

Elephants.—To dream of an elephant is a very fortunate dream; it denotes acquirement of riches. If you are in love, it denotes a speedy marriage with your sweet-heart, and many children, chiefly boys, who will distinguish themselves by their learning.

Elf.—To dream of an elf signifies a happy return of one long absent; presents of value may be expected after this dream, which also signifies marriage, with wealth, position and happiness.

Elk.—To dream of one elk, signifies loss of property and danger to your life. To dream of a drove of them, signifies that you will be forced to abandon your favorite projects in a matrimonial connection.

Eclipse of the Moon.—To dream you see an eclipse of the moon, denotes that you will lose some female friend—your mother, if she be living. You will experience great uneasiness on account of a woman; your sweet-heart will be unfaithful; poverty will overtake you, and misery end your days.

Eclipse of the Sun.—To dream you see an eclipse of the sun, denotes that you will lose some male friend—your father, if he be alive; and that you will experience some uneasiness by the means of some treacherous friend; to a woman *enciente*, it foretells a son who will be a great man.

Elopement.—To dream of a friend's elopement, signifies marriage against the wishes of your friends, and unhappy. To dream of your own elopement, betokens entering into ruinous speculations in love or business

Earthquake.—To dream of an earthquake, warns you that your affairs are about to take a very great change. If you see many houses tumbled into ruins, then it will be much for the better; should the houses appear to stand, then for worse.

Eyes.—To dream you lose your eyes, is a very unfavorable omen; it denotes decay of circumstances, loss of friends, death of relations and miscarriage in love.

Execution.—To dream of the execution of offenders, shows that you will be suddenly sought after for relief, by some that are in very great want and extremity.

Earthworms.—To dream of earthworms, signifies secret enemies that endeavor to ruin and destroy us.

Ear.—If a man dreams his ears be fair and well-shaped, it shows he shall come to great renown; but if he dreams his ears are ill-favored and deformed, it shows the contrary. This dream is ill to a servant, and those who have a lawsuit, if he be the plaintiff or the defendant; but it is good to an artificer or one that worketh with his hands, for he shall have many that will employ him. To dream one picks or cleans his ears, betokens that good news shall come forth one side or other. But to dream that the ears have been beaten or chafed, signifies we shall hear ill news. If any one dreams his ear is hurt or split, he will be offended by some one that belongs to him; or by some friend. If he dream that his ear is quite off, he shall be utterly deprived of their friendship.

Epitaph.—To read or write an epitaph in your dream, signifies much good to come from a secret friend. To read your own epitaph, signifies marriage with one now an entire stranger, of great wealth and position.

Equipage.—To dream of possessing one, signifies complete happiness, with the gratification of every wish, however extravagant.

Ermine.—If you dream of new, unspotted ermine, look for a union with one possessing every good and virtue. If your ermine be soiled or spotted, you will commit some contemptible and degrading act.

Eucharist.—To dream of giving thanks or partaking of the sacrament, signifies a rigid examination before some high tribunal. If you escape clear of reproach, look for happiness.

Eve.—To dream you see the mother of all men, is a favorable omen; it denotes great happiness to the lover.

Eye-brows.—To dream the eye-brows are hairy and of a good grace, is good, especially to woman. But if either men or women dream their eye-brows are more large and comely than they used to be, it is a sign they will succeed in the matrimonial way.

Evil Spirits.—To dream evil spirits obstruct your doing good under a show of devotion, denotes obstruction in your affairs by a hypocrite; and if you dream that you see hideous physiognomies, something more than vulgar shall be revealed to you.

Eating.—To dream that you are eating, is a very unfavorable omen; it portends disunion amongst your family, losses in trade, and disappointment in love; storms and shipwrecks by sea.

Enemy.—To dream you talk to an enemy, is a caution to have a care of him. To dream you fight with, and are worsted by him, denotes that you will meet with some misfortune, which has threatened you for some time.

Face.—To dream your face is swelled, shows that you will accumulate wealth; if you are in love, it denotes that your sweet-heart will receive an unexpected legacy and marry you.

Fall.—To dream you fall from any high place, or from a tree, denotes loss of place and goods; if you are in love, it surely indicates that you will never marry the present object of your affections.

Feet.—To dream you are near a river or fountain, and that you wash your feet, signifies molestation and trouble; to dream of one scratching the soles of your feet, signifies loss by flattery.

Fan.—If a maiden dreams she has been fanned by a man, she will soon make a new conquest, or else marry the present object of her affections. For a man to dream that he is fanning a person, signifies that he will soon meet with many changes in his affairs.

Fence.—To dream of climbing a high fence, signifies a sudden rise in life. To dream of creeping under a fence, signifies that you will commit a degrading act.

Furniture.—To dream of getting new furniture that pleases you, is good; if it seems not to please, the dream is a bad one. To be pleased with furniture, denotes health, happiness, and prosperity; to display furniture, denotes trouble, perhaps a death or a funeral.

Faction.—To dream of being engaged in faction or sedition, denotes wealth by indirect ways.

Fashion.—To dream of being a fashionable person, signifies that your associates look down upon you. To dream of being amongst fashionable people, signifies that your dearest friends will ruin you.

Father-in-Law.—To dream one sees his father-in-law, either dead or alive, is ill; especially if he dreams that he use violence or threatening.

Fish-Ponds.—To dream of fish-ponds, denotes thriving

Flageolet.—To dream that you play or hear playing on a flageolet, denotes trouble and contention, and being overthrown at law.

Flesh.—If any one dreams he is increased in flesh, he will gain wealth. On the contrary, if he dreams he is grown lean and thin, if he be rich, he will grow poor, or at least conceal his wealth, and he will be in a mean condition. To dream of eating all sorts of meat, whether flesh or fish, signifies either neglect of business, or anger and sickness.

Flies—To dream of a swarm of flies, denotes that you have many enemies; it also denotes that your sweet-heart is not sincere, and cares but little about you; to dream you kill them is a very good omen.

Flute.—To dream you play or hear playing on a flute, signifies trouble and contention.

Fool.—For a man to dream he is a fool, is good for those who would govern and teach children.

Folly.—For a woman to dream she is become foolish and is publicly guilty of folly, it is a sign she will have a boy, who in time will grow great; if a maid, she will be speedily married, and that to an honest man.

Forest.—To dream that you are walking in a forest, signifies trouble.

Fields.—To dream you are in green fields is a very favorable omen. To dream you are in plowed fields, forbodes some severe disputes that will be brought upon you by some person who has no children. To the lover, it denotes disappointment: to the married, unhappiness and undutiful children: to the tradesman, loss of business and a prison. To dream you are in a meadow covered with flowers, is a very favorable omen; if you are soliciting a place or favor, it portends you will surely obtain it.

Figs.—To dream of figs, is the forerunner of prosperity and happiness; to the lover, they denote the accomplishment of your wishes; to the tradesman, increase of trade: they are also indicative of a legacy.

Fighting.—To dream you are fighting, denotes to the lover that you will lose the object of your affections through a foolish quarrel; it also forbodes much opposition to your wishes, with loss of character and property. After such a dream, you are urgently recommended to quit your present situation, because such a dream indicates that you will not prosper in it: to the sailor, it denotes storms and shipwreck, with disappointment in love.

Fire.—To dream of this subtle element, denotes health and happiness to the lover, marriage with the object of your affections, and many children; it also denotes that you will be very angry with some one on a trifling occasion. To dream you see burning lights descending as it were from heaven, is a very bad sign indeed. It portends some dreadful accident to the dreamer, such as being hanged, losing your head, having your brains dashed out, breaking your legs, getting into prison, or other strange accidents. To the lover, it also denotes the loss of the affections of your sweet-heart; to the tradesman, bad success in business. To dream that you are burnt by fire, denotes great danger, and that enemies will injure you; to the sailor, storms and shipwreck.

Fishing.—To dream you are fishing, is a sure sign of sorrow and trouble. If you catch any fish, you will be successful in love and business; if you catch none, you will never marry your present sweet-heart, nor succeed in your present undertakings: if they slip out of your hands after you have caught them, the person you marry will be of a roving disposition, and some pretended friend will deceive you.

Filberts.—To dream of filberts forebodes much trouble and anger from friends; to the tradesman they denote a prison and decay of trade; to the lover, a complete disappointment; to the married, care and undutiful children.

Fingers.—To dream you cut your fingers, if they bleed, is a very good omen; you will be successful in love, and your sweet-heart will prove kind and true; you will get money from a quarter that you least expect, and be successful in your enterprises. If you dream they do not bleed, then it denotes damage by a variety of accidents; that lawsuits will attend you, and that you will be unsuccessful in most of your pursuits; in love, you will not succeed with your present sweet-heart, who prefers another. To dream you lose your fingers, denotes the loss of friends, servants, goods, trade, and sweet-hearts.

Feasting.—To dream you are at a feast, denotes that you will meet with many disappointments, particularly in the thing which you are the most anxious about. In love it forbodes much uneasiness between sweet-hearts; and to them which are married it foretells undutiful children, with many heavy losses.

Fleas.—To dream you are tormented with these little insects is unfavorable.

Floods.—To dream of a flood, shows that you will meet with great opposition from rich neighbors, and that a rich rival will attempt to alienate the affections of your mistress. To the tradesman, it denotes lawsuits, loss of business, and a prison; to the sailor, it denotes much success by sea, but danger on shore; to the farmer, it indicates loss of cattle and a dispute with his landlord. To dream you are drowned in a flood, denotes that you will quit your native land, and after many hardships and perils, return to it rich and happy: that you will marry a pretty woman and have fine children.

Flowers.—To dream you are gathering flowers, is a very favorable omen: expect to thrive in every thing you undertake, and that you will be successful in love, marry happily, and have beautiful children. Should they wither under your hands, then expect heavy losses in trade; that your sweetheart will die; or, if you are married, that you will lose your husband or wife, and also your favorite child.

Flying.—To dream you are flying, is a very excellent omen: it foretells elevation of fortune; that you will arrive at dignity in the State, and be happy. If you are in love, your sweet-heart will be true to you; and if you marry, you will have many children, who will all do well, and be very happy. It indicates that you will take a long journey, which will turn out advantageous to you.

Forge.—To dream of working a smith's forge, denotes a brain full of projects; the blowing with the bellows signifies the getting of a wife, and the hammering on the anvil, her scolding tongue.

Fortune.—If any man having become poor after he hath been rich, dreams he hath the same land and possessions he had before, signifies that his good fortune will return.

Fountain.—To dream you are at a fountain, is a very favorable omen. If the waters are clear, it denotes riches and honors; and in love, it foretells great happiness in the marriage state, and that your sweet-heart is of an amiable disposition, and true to you: but if the waters appear muddy, then it denotes vexation and trouble, disappointment in business, inconstancy in your sweet-heart, and misery in the marriage state.

Fox.—To dream of this crafty animal is the forerunner of much difficulty. If you are in love, your sweet-heart will turn out of a sour, disagreeable, ill-natured disposition; if you are in trade, sharpers will endeavor to defraud you, and over-reach you in bargains.

Fragrance.—To dream of sweet perfumes signifies that you will in a moment of trouble, receive an anonymous gift of money; to dream of offensive odors signifies that you will be called upon to contribute largely to some new charity.

Friend.—To dream you see a friend dead, betokens hasty news of a joyous nature. If you are in love, it foretells a speedy marriage with the object of your affections.

Frogs.—To dream of frogs is a very favorable omen. To the farmer, it foretells good crops and an increase of his live stock; to the tradesman, it denotes success in business; to the lover, a faithful sweet-heart; to the married an increase of children, who will be very happy; to the sailor, pleasant and prosperous voyages, with a wife in a distant country.

Fruits.—If you dream of fruits when out of season, or that you are gathering them when green, it denotes sickness; if you dream they are rotten, it foretells poverty. To dream of gathering ripe fruit, when there is plenty, betokens happiness and riches, and the speedy receipt of money: if you gather fruit from an old, withered tree, it is a sign that you will unexpectedly inherit the effects of some aged person. To dream you have made yourself sick by eating fruit, is a sorrowful omen.

Funeral.—To dream of a burial, denotes speedy marriage, and that you will hear of the death or imprisonment of some near relation or esteemed friend; it also foretells the acquisition of wealth, and that an estate will fall to you from a distant relation by your mother's side; if you see any particular person attending the funeral, either that person, or some friend of his, will die and leave you something. If there is a hearse with feathers on it, you will marry some rich person yourself, or assist at some relation's wedding, who will marry well, and be a friend to you.

Fairy.—For a maiden to dream she sees a fairy, shows she will soon change her present state, by becoming the wife of a good husband. It is good for women under any circumstances to dream of fairies; but it denotes evil to men, and no man should undertake any important matter for several days after, or it will surely end in his being disappointed.

Flag.—To dream of raising a flag signifies that your name will be widely known; to dream of seeing a flag floating signifies good news.

Files.—To dream of dealing in files prognosticates activity. To purchase files, shows you will have many applications to attend to business; to sell files, shows you will have others to work for you, yielding profitably.

Flambeau.—To dream of flambeaus is a sign of trouble, excitement, and distress: to the merchant, losses at sea; to the mechanic, want of employment; to lovers, deceit and treachery.

Furnace.—To dream of seeing a furnace indicates a quarrel which will cost you dear friends. If you heat the furnace, you will be the only sufferer.

Ferry.—To dream of crossing a ferry signifies that indecision in an important matter will make you the laughing stock of your friends.

Fortress.—If you are confined in a fortress in your dream, your plans in life will suffer from undue influence of others. If you dream of placing others in confinement, look for valuable goods, which will enrich you.

Gallows.—To dream of the gallows is a most fortunate omen : it shows that the dreamer will become rich, and arrive at great honors. To the lover, it shows the consummation of his most sanguine wishes, and that by marriage he will become rich and happy, have many children, particularly a son, who will become a great man, and be the founder of his family's honor.

Garden.—To dream you are walking in a garden, is of a very favorable nature : it portends elevation in fortune and dignity. To the lover, it denotes great success, and an advantageous marriage ; to the tradesman, it promises increase of business ; to the farmer, plentiful crops ; and to the sailor, pleasant and prosperous voyages.

Geese.—To dream of geese is the forerunner of good : expect soon to see a long-absent friend. They denote success and riches to the dreamer in the furtherance of his pursuits : in love they augur speedy marriage and fidelity in your sweetheart.

Giants.—To dream of seeing giants is ominous of good.

Gifts.—To dream you have any thing given you, is a sign that some good is about to happen to you. It also denotes that a speedy marriage will take place between you and your sweet-heart. To dream you have given any thing away, is the forerunner of adversity ; and in love, denotes sickness and inconstancy in your sweet-heart or partner.

Glass.—To dream of glass, marks inconstancy in your sweet-heart ; and is ominous of bad success in your undertakings in life. To dream you break glass, shows that your sweet-heart will forsake you, and that you will unexpectedly meet with misfortunes and troubles. To dream you receive a glassful of water, is indicative of speedy marriage, and that you will have many children, who will all do well. If the glass appears broken, the death of your sweet-heart; or, if married, of your spouse, is predicted.

Globe.—To dream that you are looking at a globe, foretells much good, and that you will become a great traveler.

Gloves.—To dream of receiving a gift of a pair of gloves, signifies an offer of friendship. If the gloves are light, the connection will be pleasant; if dark, it is doubtful. To receive a package of gloves, signifies much good offered to you at one time. To present gloves in a dream, signifies a gift in charity. To dream of old, ragged gloves, signifies disappointment and deceit from your dearest friends.

Ghost.—To dream of seeing it, signifies a marriage in the family. If you dream it speaks, prepare to die.

Gold.—To dream of gold, is a very good omen; it denotes success in your present undertakings, after experiencing some little difficulties. If you receive gold in bars, you will inherit an estate in a far distant country, and have some trouble in getting possession of it: if you receive eagles or any other gold coin, your affairs will prosper, your sweet-heart will be true and marry you; you will have many children, and be very happy. If you pay gold, it betokens an increase of friends and business; if you let gold fall, it denotes an attack from thieves; if you are in trade, some swindler will attempt to defraud you. If you pick up gold, it denotes that some quarrel will be settled to your advantage: if you are in prison, it shows you will speedily be enlarged: it also denotes the death of a husband or wife if you are married; if single, of your sweet-heart.

Good.—To dream that we do good to any one, signifies

jollity and pleasure; and to dream that others do us good, is profit and gain.

Gooseberries.—To dream of gooseberries indicates many children, chiefly sons, and an accomplishment of your present pursuits. To the sailor, they declare dangers in his next voyage; to the maiden, a roving husband.

Grapes.—To dream of grapes, foretells to the maiden that her husband will be a cheerful companion, and a great songster. They denote much happiness in marriage, and success in trade. If you are in love, they augur a speedy union between you and your sweet-heart.

Grave.—To dream you see a grave, foretells sickness and disappointment: if you are in love, you will surely never marry your present sweet-heart. If you go into the grave, it shows you will experience a loss of property, and that false friends will defame you; if you come out of the grave, it denotes success in your undertakings, that you will rise in the world, become rich, and if you are in love, that you will speedily marry your sweet-heart. If you take another out of the grave, you will be the means of saving the life of a person, who will be a very great friend to you, and receive some unexpected legacy.

Grain.—To dream you see any kind of grain, and that one gathers it, signifies profit and gain.

Games.—To dream one plays at ball or top, signifies travail and pains, and to gain wealth by contention and injury. To leap, run, or dance, signifies prosperity in affairs; but to dance without music, foretells want of money.

Garlic.—For a man to dream he eats garlic, signifies he shall discover hidden secrets, and meet with some domestic jar: yet to dream he has it in the house, is good.

Gibbet.—To dream you see a person hanging on a gibbet, is a sign of damage and great affliction.

Girdle.—To dream that you are girt with an old girdle, signifies labor and pains. A new girdle signifies nonor.

Gin.—To dream of drinking gin, forebodes short life, and that many changes will happen very suddenly, which will be chiefly very pleasant, but that they end with dissatisfaction.

Gondola.—If a female dream she is sailing in a gondola, she will speedily marry a person who will make her happy. If a man dream he is in a gondola, in smooth water, it is an excellent dream; and if the water be muddy or troubled, it denotes much strife.

Guns.—To dream you see people firing off guns or cannon, augurs that the dreamer will experience much adversity. To dream that they are firing at you, shows that you will be exposed to many perilous dangers, such as shipwreck, assassination or loss of liberty. If you are firing at them yourself, it foretells that you will be involved in a lawsuit that will prove very prejudicial to you.

Hail.—To dream you are in a hail-storm, presages great sorrow in life. If you are in love, it forewarns you against marrying your present sweet-heart, who will prove of a very bad temper and make you miserable.

Hair.—For a man to dream his hair is long like a woman's signifies cowardice and effeminacy, and that the person dreaming will be deceived by a woman. To dream one sees a woman without hair, signifies famine, poverty, and sickness. To see a man bald and without hair, signifies to the contrary.

Hands.—If any one dreams that his hands are comelier and stronger than ordinary, he will be employed in some important affairs, which he will bring to a happy issue. If one dreams that his hand is cut off, or that it has grown lean and dry, or hath been burnt, he will grow poor. If a woman dreams thus, she will lose her husband, or her eldest son, or fall into a decay. If any one dreams that he works with his right hand, it is a sign of good fortune to him and his family; if with the left hand, that denotes bad luck. To dream the hand is hairy, signifies trouble and imprisonment.

Hanged.—To dream of seeing people hanged, or that you are going to be hanged yourself, denotes that you will rise above your present condition by marriage.

Hat.—To dream your hat is torn or dirty, signifies damage or dishonor; but to dream you have a hat on that pleases you, signifies joy, profit, and good success in business.

Hills.—To dream of climbing and traveling over hills, signifies good, in your own age, and to carry your name to posterity, as a patron of arts, or architects. To descend hills in sleep, denotes illness. Green hills foretell happiness.

Heart.—To dream of your own heart, signifies trouble in love. To see the heart of another, denotes that as they seem to you, their characters really are. Bleeding hearts foretell trouble.

Hay.—To dream you cut it, signifies that you will have great influence in society. To dream of raking it together, denotes that you will stand at the head of assemblies.

Hog's Bristles.—To dream that you have hog's bristles, signifies great and violent dangers.

Horns.—To dream one hath horns on his head, signifies dominion, grandeur, and royalty. To dream you see a man with horns on his head, signifies he is in danger both of the loss of his person and estate.

Horses.—To dream of horses is a particularly good sign; inasmuch that if any one dreams that he saw, took, or mounted a horse, is a happy omen to the dreamer. If any one dreams he is mounted on a stately horse, full of mettle, nimble and well harnessed, he will have a handsome, noble, and rich wife, provided the horse be his own. To dream one sees a horse running, signifies prosperity and the accomplishment of one's desires. To dream of riding on a tired horse, shows one shall fall desperately in love. To dream you see a horse dead, is a sign a stagnation will take place in your business with some losses, but these may be overcome if the horse be well in flesh, and has not died a natural death.

Hunger.—To dream one is unusually hungry, and that his appetite craves sustenance, shows he will be ingenious, laborious, and eager in getting an estate, and will grow rich.

Husbandmen.—To see yourself become a husbandman in your dream, shows you shall meet with great toil, yet after awhile become rich. If you dream you are plowing, it denotes success, and to single persons, speedy marriage : and if the fields be full of flowers, it is a sign of much happiness.

Hatred.—To dream of hatred or being hated, whether of friends or enemies, is ill.

Heaven.—To dream of heaven, and that you are there, signifies grandeur and glory.

Head.—To dream you have a great head or a head bigger than ordinary, and very highly raised, that signifies dignity, esteem. If a sick person dreams thus, it prognosticates both the headache and violent fever. If one dreams his head is cut off by robbers and murderers, that signifies loss of children, relations, estate, or wife; and to the wife so dreaming, the loss of her husband. To dream that one cuts off another's head, signifies assurance of effecting business, or revenge upon your enemies. To dream you cut off the head of a pullet, or a green goose, signifies joy and recreation. To dream one hath the head of a lion or wolf, or some other cruel beast, it is a good sign to the dreamer. To dream one hath the head of a dog, horse or ass, or such four-footed beast, is servitude, pain and misery to the dreamer. To dream one hath a bird's head, argues one shall not stay long in his country. If one dreams that he is careful to comb and trim his head, it is a sign he shall dispose well of his business. To dream you wash your head, signifies deliverance from danger.

Hen.—To dream that you hear hens cackle, or that you catch them, signifies joy, profit and assurance of the dispatch of business. To dream that you are turned into a hen, signifies disquiet. To dream that you see a hen lay eggs, signifies gain. To see a hen with her chickens, signifies loss and damage. To dream that a hen crows, signifies sadness and trouble.

Hornet.—To dream of hornets, shows you will have to do with people who will assault and discredit you.

House.—To dream of building a house is a good omen; in love, that your sweet-heart is good-tempered and faithful, and will make you very happy; to dream you see a house on fire, foretells hasty news. If it be your own house that is destroyed, the news will be bad; if your enemy's house, it will be good.

Hunting.—To dream you are hunting, and that the game is killed, shows much trouble through the pretensions of false friends, but that you will discover them, and overcome all their machinations.

Ice.—To dream of ice is a favorable omen; to the lover it shows your sweet-heart is of an amiable temper, and faithful. To dream you are sliding or skating on the ice, denotes that you will pursue some unprofitable concern, and be much worried by your engagements.

Incendiary.—To dream of an incendiary, signifies that a false friend is trying to ruin you by spreading false reports. If you dream of securing an incendiary, do not fear troubles that threaten you—they will pass over.

Invasion.—For a maiden to dream of invasion is a sign that some evil-disposed person will endeavor to lead her astray. To a man in business, it denotes much competition; to the mechanic, loss of his situation.

Intrigue.—To dream that you are connected in an intrigue, is ominous of evil.

Ivy.—To dream of ivy, betokens constancy in love, success in life.

Incense.—To dream of incense is good, as it betokens success in matrimony and business, to the envy and annoyance of others.

Indigence.—To dream of relieving others, denotes that

you will only rise to power or wealth by your own exertions. If you dream you are yourself in poverty, signifies that you will fall into an unexpected difficulty, and lose the confidence of those you most love.

Infant.—If an unmarried woman dreams of an infant, it prognosticates that she will go through some trouble; but for a man to dream of infants, is good.

Inn.—To dream of being in an inn, is a very unfavorable dream; it denotes poverty and want of success in undertakings; expect soon to be yourself, or some of your family, committed to prison. If you are sick, it denotes you will never recover. To the tradesman it shows loss of trade and bad servants.

Injury.—To dream you receive an injury signifies that you have many friends—no enemies. If you dream of inflicting injury, you will both receive and dispense blessings.

Ink.—If you dream of black ink, you will become involved in some disgraceful scheme. If you dream of red ink, good news awaits you.

Inquest.—To dream of being at an inquest, denotes prosperity. To dream that you are the subject on which the inquest is held, prognosticates that you will come into prosperity by the death of some rich person. To dream an inquest is held on the body of a friend, is also good to the dreamer.

Idiot.—If any one dreams he is turned idiot, or mad, and is guilty of public extravagancies, he shall be long lived, a favorite, and gain pleasure and profit by the people.

Image.—To dream of an image, or statue, signifies children, and the will and affections of the dreamer.

Infernal Things.—If any one dreams that he sees the devil, or any other infernal spirits or representations, it is a very bad dream, bringing along with it, to them that are sick, death; and to the healthy, melancholy, anger and violent sickness.

4

Iron.—For one to dream that he is hurt with iron, signifies that he shall receive some damage; to dream that one trades with a stranger in iron, signifies losses and misfortunes.

Idol.—To dream you see persons worshiping at an idol, betokens a change of affairs, and much for the better; to dream you worship an idol is a sign of merriment: such as going to balls, parties, or excursions, pleasant journeys and the like. If a sick person has this dream, he will have a speedy recovery.

Ignominy.—For any one to dream they suffer ignominy, shows he will be unjustly accused of having done wrong, and that he will after a little take a sudden rise in the world.

Illumination.—It is a certain sign of war, when persons dream of seeing a city illuminated. To dream your own house is illuminated, betokens much quarreling among relatives.

Jail.—If you dream of seeing others in jail, you will be deprived of your own liberty. If you dream of being imprisoned, you will be elevated to a high station in life, and increase your number of friends.

Jollity.—To dream of a jollity, feasts, and merry-making, is a good and prosperous dream, and promiseth to the dreamer great preferment.

Jewels.—To dream of possessing jewels, signifies that you are on the road to happiness.

Jessamine.—To dream of this beautiful flower, foretells good luck; to lovers, it is a sure sign they will be speedily married.

Jeopardy.—If you dream that you are in jeopardy it will be very fortunate for you; if a person so dreaming be in business, it foretells success and great profit.

Jubilee.—To dream that you are at a jubilee, is a sure sign that you will have a fortune left you by some rich relations.

Jockey.—If a female dreams she sees a jockey riding at full speed, she will have an offer of marriage made her very unexpectedly; for a man to dream he rides with, or sees a jockey riding a race, denotes a sudden good turn in his affairs.

Jug.—For one to dream of drinking out of a jug, is a sign of going on a journey; if the jug be large, the journey will be long; if small, the journey will be short; and so, if the liquid drank be pleasant, so will the journey; and if unpleasant, the journey will be full of troubles.

Juniper.—It is unlucky to dream of the juniper, especially if the person who so dreams be sick. But to dream of gathering juniper berries, if it be in winter, denotes prosperity.

Jury.—If you dream of being tried by a jury, you will lose your sweet-heart, and gain the affections of another on a voyage. If you dream of being acquitted by a jury, you will shortly meet with interesting and romantic adventures.

Joy.—To dream of joy and festivity is a token of good for such as would marry, or it betokens enjoyment for those fond of society; to the sad and fearful, it announces absence of heaviness and fear.

Juniper Berries.—To dream of these, signifies that the person so dreaming will shortly arrive at great honors, and become a great person; to the married, it foretells the birth of a male child.

Keys.—To dream of keys is favorable to a person in trade; and to a sailor, they denote some gift, and that the dreamer will become rich. To dream of finding a key, denotes an addition to your estate; if you are married, it foretells the birth of a child. If you give another a key you will be speedily married; in love, keys betoken faithfulness, and a good-tempered sweet-heart.

> To dream your keys are gone or lost,
> Denotes that you'll be vexed or crossed.

King.—To dream of a king, denotes strife and slavery of the mind.

Knives.—To dream of knives is a very unpropitious omen; it betokens lawsuits, poverty, disgrace, strife, and a general failure in your projects: in love, it shows that your sweet-heart is of a bad temper, and unfaithful, and that if you marry you will live in enmity and misery.

Kissing.—For a man to dream of kissing a young maid, and that she vanishes away before he can accomplish his desire, denotes that the next day he shall see great store of good cheer. To dream you kiss a person deceased, signifies long life.

Kite.—To dream of your seeing a kite, showeth you shall be in danger of thieves and robbers.

Ladder.—To dream that you ascend a ladder, signifies honor; but to dream that you descend a ladder, betokens damage.

Lake.—To dream of a peaceful lake, denotes content. To dream of gazing into a lake, denotes an access of fortune from an unexpected source. To dream of floating on a lake, signifies to glide through life without trouble and with many friends.

Lamb.—To dream that you feed or bring a lamb to the slaughter, signifies torment. To dream you see a lamb, or young kid, signifies extraordinary comfort.

Larks.—To dream of hearing a lark, denotes cheerfulness, health, from good habits, riches by industry, and happy wedded life.

Leaping.—To dream you are leaping over walls, doors or gates, is a sign that you will encounter many difficulties in your present pursuits, and that your sweet-heart will not marry you.

Legs.—To dream your legs are scabby or itchy, signifies fruitless perplexity and care. To dream one hath a wooden leg, signifies the alteration of your condition from good to bad, and from bad to worse.

Lent.—To dream of Lent, denotes that you will attain a

high and responsible position, but be surrounded by false and envious friends, who will endeavor to lower you by counseling mean actions.

Legacy.—To dream of receiving one, denotes losing whatever you own that is in the hands of another, involving you in litigation, debt, unhappiness and trouble.

Letters.—To dream you receive letters, is demonstrative of your being beloved by a person of the opposite sex, who is very much your friend ; to dream of writing letters, shows success in enterprises.

Leopards.—Dreaming of leopards foretells honor.

Lettuce.—To dream that one eats salads made of lettuce, and other herbs that may be eaten raw, signifies trouble and difficulty in the management of affairs.

Lemons.—To dream of lemons, denotes contentions in your family and uneasiness on account of children; they announce the death of some relation, and disappointment in love.

Lion.—To dream of seeing this king of beasts, denotes that you will appear before your betters, and that you will be promoted to some lucrative office, accumulate riches, and marry a woman of great spirit; it argues success in trade, and prosperity from a voyage by sea.

Looking-glass.—To dream of looking in a glass, denotes children to the married, and to the unmarried it promises a lover speedily.

Leap-frog.—For a man to dream he plays at leap-frog, is bad; from many causes, troubles and vexations will soon overtake him. If a maiden has this dream, it signifies that her lover is inconstant.

Leap-Year.—To dream of leap-year, is one of the best and most lucky dreams : every thing you undertake about this time will prosper; and your efforts will be four-fold successful. It is alike good to male and female.

Leeward.—For a captain or seafaring man to dream his vessel drifts to leeward, is ominous of a storm.

Land.—If a man dreams he hath good lands well enclosed with pleasant pastures, bestowed upon him, he will have a handsome wife. But if the land seem spacious, and not enclosed, that denotes pleasure, joy and riches. If he dreamed that the said unenclosed lands had fair gardens and fountains, fields, pleasant groves and orchards adjoining thereto, that signifies he will marry a discreet, chaste, and beautiful wife, and that she will bear him handsome children. If he dreamed the land was sown with wheat, that signifies money and profit, with care and industry. But if he dreamed it was sown with any kind of pulse, that denotes affliction and trouble.

Love.—To dream of being in love, denotes that you are not susceptible. If you dream of another loving you, you will pass through life alone and unsought.

Lamp.—To dream of a burning lamp, signifies prosperity. To dream of a lamp suddenly extinguished, signifies the death of a near friend.

Lantern.—He that dreams he sees a lantern with a light in it, extinguished, that signifies unto him sadness, sickness, and poverty.

Laurel.—To dream you see a laurel tree is a token of victory and pleasure ; and if you be married, it denotes the inheritance of possessions by your wife. To dream one sees or smells laurel, if it be a woman, she shall bear children ; if a maid, she will be suddenly married.

Law.—As to matter of law, to dream of places, of pleading, judges, attorneys, &c., signifies trouble, expense, and revealing of secrets ; if a sick man dreameth he obtains a suit, he shall come to a better estate.

Lizard.—To dream that one sees a lizard, signifies ill-luck and misfortune by secret enemies.

Laughing.—To dream of laughing violently, betokens

sorrow and weeping. It also denotes change of circumstances and friends.

Lobsters.—To dream of eating lobsters, foretells a new love affair. If they are highly seasoned, your new flame will be hot-tempered but generous, capricious but warm-hearted; at times moody but affectionate.

Labor.—To dream you labor, denotes a life of luxurious indolence. To dream you watch others toil, denotes wealth gained by manufactures.

Logs.—To dream that one is cleaving logs, is a sign that strangers shall come to the party dreaming.

Light.—To dream you see a great light is a happy presage: it denotes that you will attain great honors, and become very rich; in love, it shows a sweet-heart of an amiable disposition, that you will marry well, have children and be very happy.

Lightning.—To dream of lightning without tempest, and falling near without touching the body, signifies change of place. If a man dreams he see lightning fall before him, it will hinder his traveling. But if you dream that you are all burned and consumed with lightning, it is death to the dreamer.

Lilies.—To dream that one sees, holds, or smells lilies out of their season, it signifies that the hope of the thing desired will be frustrated. But the same dream of lilies in their season is good.

Linen.—To dream you are dressed in clean linen, denotes that you will shortly receive some glad tidings; that your sweet-heart is faithful and will marry; if it is dirty, then denotes poverty, and disappointment in love.

Lioness.—Dreaming of seeing a lioness is good to the rich or poor; marriage is also hereby signified; those that have children, upon this dream, shall lose them; but if you dream that she destroys you, it is death to the dreamer;

for persons at sea to dream of this animal, is a sign of a storm.

Lean.—If one dreams he is growing lean and wasted, he will be disturbed, and have suits at law, or some other ill business, that will occasion the loss of his estate, or else he is in danger of falling sick. Nevertheless, if a woman dreams the tongue grows less, it signifies unto her honors, wisdom, prudence and discretion.

Lice.—To dream that you are lousy, and that you are killing a great number of them, is a very good omen; it denotes great riches to the dreamer; they also portend deliverance from enemies, and that you will overcome much slander and malice.

Lips.—To dream that one hath red, handsome lips, is a good sign that your friends enjoy their health; and to have them dry and chapped, the contrary.

Lying.—To tell a lie in a dream is not good, except by players and jesters, who practice it, and deceive people.

Maid.—To dream you obtain a young maid, signifies joy. To dream you take away a maid by force, signifies sorrow.

Markets.—To dream of markets filled with goods and people, is a good dream to those that traffic; but riding to market, signifies a short voyage: if in a storm, the voyage will be difficult and the success of your object doubtful; if in fair weather, the result will be the contrary.

Marriage.—To dream you are married, is ominous of death, and very unfavorable to the dreamer; it denotes poverty, a prison, and misfortunes. To dream you assist at a wedding, is the forerunner of some pleasing news and great success. To dream of being with your newly-married husband or wife, threatens danger and sudden misfortunes, and also that you will lose a part of your property; to the sailor, it argues storms and shipwrecks, with a narrow escape from death.

Milk.—To dream you drink milk is an extraordinary good sign ; and to dream you see breasts of milk, signifies profit. To dream you are carrying milk is a good sign, but if you fall and spill it, misfortunes will befall you, from which it would be difficult to extricate yourself.

Mad.—To dream you are mad, and that you are in company with mad people, is very good to the dreamer ; it promises long life, riches, happy marriage, success in trade, and good children ; if you are a farmer, some accident will happen to a part of your live stock, but you will have plentiful crops ; if you have a lawsuit, it will be determined greatly in your favor.

Mice.—To dream of mice denotes prosperity, success in love, and a happy marriage.

Midwife.—To dream you see a midwife, is a revealing of secrets, and signifies hurt. To those who are kept by force, to dream of a midwife, signifies liberty. If an unmarried woman dream often of seeing her, it forebodes a fit of sickness, which will be of long continuance.

Minister.—If a minister dreams he gives his people clear water to drink, it signifies that he will teach them the word of God faithfully ; if the water be troubled, he will preach heretical and false doctrines.

Martyr.—If one dreams he dies for religion, that man will arrive at great honor. It signifies also that his soul will be happy hereafter.

Meat.—To dream that you see the meat you have eaten, signifies loss and damage.

Measles.—If any one dreams he hath the measles, it denotes he shall gain profit and wealth, but it shall be with infamy.

Mire.—

> To dream you wade in mire and stubble,
> Foretelleth surely toil and trouble,
> Yet perseverance will not fail
> O'er toil and trouble to prevail.

Monkeys.—To dream of these mischievous creatures, is ominous of evil; they announce deceit in love, undutiful children, malicious enemies, and an attack by thieves.

Mountains.—To dream you see steep and craggy mountains, presages difficulties in accomplishing your designs: if you ascend them and gain the top, you will be successful in whatever you undertake, become very rich, and arrive at great honors in the State. To a maid, they denote that she will marry a man who will become rich and powerful, and that her children will be people of consequence.

Mulberries.—To dream of mulberries is of good import: to the maiden, they foretell a speedy and happy marriage; to the lover, constancy and affection in his mistress; they also denote wealth, honors, and many children; they are particularly favorable to sailors and farmers.

Music.—To dream you hear delicious music is a very favorable omen, promising joyful news from a long absent friend; to married people it denotes sweet-tempered children; in love it shows that your sweet-heart is very fond of you, is good-tempered, sincere, and constant. Rough and discordant music foretells trouble, vexation, and disappointment.

Monster.—To see a monster in the sea, is not good; but out of the sea, every fish and great monster is good.

Money.—To dream of receiving money, is a good omen; in love, it foretells a speedy marriage and many children. If you dream you lose money, it is a proof you will be deceived in love, and will be unsuccessful in some favorite pursuit. To dream you are paying money, foretells the birth of a son destined to cut a great figure in life.

Moon.—To dream of the moon is a very favorable omen; it denotes sudden joy, and great success in love.

Mother.—To dream you see your own mother living, signifies joy. To see your mother dead, signifies misfortune.

Melons.—To dream of melons, to sick persons is a prognostic of recovery, by reason of their humidity or juicy substance.

Monuments.—If a sick person dreams of seeing monuments, he or she so dreaming will quickly recover. For the healthy to dream of monuments, is a sign of good-luck.

Nakedness.—To dream you see a man naked signifies fear and terror. To dream you see a woman naked signifies honor and joy, provided she be fair-skinned and handsome. But if crooked, old, wrinkled, or otherwise ill made, and black withal, it signifies shame, repentance, and ill-luck.

Night-mare.—To dream of being ridden by the night-mare, is a sign that a woman so dreaming shall be domineered over by a fool.

Night Walks.—To dream of walking in the night signifies trouble and melancholy.

Nutmegs.—To dream of nutmegs is a sign that many changes will soon overtake you.

Navigation.—If any one dreams that he is sailing in a boat, and recreating himself without fear, he will have comfort and success in his affairs, but if the water be tempestuous, it falleth out contrarily. To dream of being in a ship or a boat, and in danger of oversetting or shipwreck, is a sign of danger, unless the party be a prisoner or captive, and in that case it denotes liberty and freedom.

Night.—To dream of a dark night, signifies trouble and perplexity ; but if you have some light from the moon in your dream, you will come safely out of your annoyance.

Night Birds.—To dream of any kind of night birds, as the owl, bittern, and bat, is ominous, and those who have such dreams should undertake no business on the day following. He that travels by sea or land, and sees in his dream any of these birds, will fall into a great tempest or into the hands of thieves.

Nightingale.—To dream of the nightingale signifieth good works, and principally weddings.

Nest.—To dream of finding a nest signifies domestic bliss with one whose acquaintance you will form suddenly. If there are young in the nest, you will have a large family; if eggs only, enemies are around you; if broken eggs, they will cause you great woe.

Nine-pins.—To dream of playing at nine-pins, is a sign of quarreling; if successful, you will get the better of your adversary; if the reverse, you will be worsted.

Nation.—To dream of being in another nation denotes wonderful news from abroad; to dream of receiving friends from other nations, denotes that you will make an important scientific discovery.

Nymph.—To dream of seeing a nymph, denotes a marriage with one of rustic, poetic, and romantic tastes. You may also expect to live in the country.

Nuptials.—To dream of being present at a friend's wedding, denotes that you will aid in an elopement, which will bring misfortune; to dream of your own marriage signifies that your first love will jilt you; you will marry your second, but repent it.

Night-hag.—For a woman to dream of a night-hag denotes that she will be much slandered by some one she deems her friend. For a man to dream of this nonentity, is a sign that some woman is endeavoring to do him an injury.

Neigh.—To dream you hear horses neigh, augurs that you will have new and powerful friends, who will do you much service.

Negroes.—It is not good to dream of negroes, unless they be singers or dancers, or otherwise making merry. To dream of seeing negroes in a church, is ominous of evil.

Nose.—To dream one has a fair and great nose is good to all, for it denotes prosperity in affairs, and acquaintance with rich persons.

Nosegays.—To dream of gathering and making nosegays

is unlucky, showing that our hope shall wither as flowers do in a nosegay.

Nut Tree.—Dreaming that you see nut trees, and that you crack and eat their fruit, signifies riches and content gained with labor and pain. Dreaming that you find nuts that have been hid, signifies that you will find treasure.

Nails.—To dream your nails are growing long is very good, and denotes riches, prosperity, and happiness; great success in love; a good, industrious husband or wife, with dutiful children; it also foretells that you will suddenly receive a sum of money that will be of great use to you.

Nectarines.—To dream of nectarines is ominous of strife between friends, of riches to the farmer and tradesman, of infidelity in lovers, of children to the married, of bad weather to the sailor, and to the poor they announce plenty and increase of wages.

Nuts.—To dream you see clusters of them denotes riches and happiness; to the lover, success and a good-tempered sweet-heart. If you are gathering them, it is not a good omen, for you will pursue some matter that will not turn out to your advantage. If you crack them, the person who courts you, or to whom you pay your addresses, will treat you with indifference, or be very unfaithful.

Oak.—To dream of an oak covered with verdure, signifies a long and happy life; if it waves, look for many changes; if it is stripped of foliage, look for poverty in old age. To see many young oaks thriving, foretells male children, who will reap distinction by bravery. Oaks bearing acorns betoken unlimited wealth.

Olives.—To dream you see olives denotes happiness, and that you will be successful in all your present undertakings; to the lover, they foretell a speedy marriage with the object of your affections. If you are gathering them off the trees, they then announce much trouble and vexation through friends and children; to the lover, they show your sweet-heart is un-faithful.

Onions.—

To dream of eating onions, means
Much strife in thy domestic scenes;
Secrets found out or else betrayed,
And many falsehoods made and said.

Oysters.—To dream you are eating oysters is a very favorable omen.

Ocean.—To dream that you are on the ocean with a woman, is a sign some female acquaintance is deceitful, or that you are deceived in some friends. It is unlucky to dream you swim, walk on, or catch fish in the ocean; but it is neverthe-less lucky to dream of the ocean to any person about to go on a journey, unless, indeed, it be very tempestuous.

Overturned.—If a woman dreams she be overturned while riding, it is ominous that she shall be greatly distressed for a short time. For a man to have this dream, denotes that some animal to which he is attached will sicken and perhaps die.

Orphans.—Whoever dreams of orphans will receive profits or riches by the hand of a stranger : for a man to dream of a female orphan denotes that his wife will be rich. To dream about orphans in any way, is an excellent dream to both sexes.

Office.—To dream you are turned out of your office fore-tells death and loss of property. It you are in love, it indi-cates want of affection in your sweet-heart, and misery if you marry the present object of your affection.

Offices.—Dreaming that one is deposed and put out of his office, estate, place, or dignity, is bad.

Oil.—Dreaming that you are anointed with oil is good for women, but for men, denotes shame.

Olive Trees.—Dreaming that you see an olive tree with olives, denotes peace, delight, concord, liberty, dignity, and fruition of your desires; to dream that you beat the olives down is good for all but servants.

Oven.—If you dream that you see an oven burning hot, it signifies change of place.

Owl.—To dream of this bird at night is a very bad omen; it foretells sickness, poverty, and imprisonment; it also fore-warns you that some male friend will turn out perfidious.

Oxen.—Dreaming of oxen denotes a year of plenty and fruitfulness; but, if they appear poor and lean, it threatens a year of scarcity and famine. To dream that you feed oxen is a good sign, but to see oxen go to water is a bad sign.

Old Man.—For a woman to dream she is courted by an old man, is a sure prognostic that she will receive a sum of money and be successful in her undertakings. For a maid to dream of it, shows that she will marry a rich young fellow, and have many children by him, who will all become rich.

Old Woman.—For a man to dream he is courting an old woman, and that she returns his love, is a very fortunate omen; it prefigures success in worldly concerns, that he will marry a beautiful young woman, have lovely children, and be very happy.

Oranges.—Dreaming that you see and eat oranges signifies wounds, grief, and vexation, whether they be ripe or not.

Organ.—Dreaming that you hear the sound of an organ, signifies joy.

Orchard.—To dream that you are in an orchard denotes that you will become rich, that you will marry much to your advantage. For a married person to dream of being in an orchard, shows an increase of children, who will become rich, and live happy; in love it denotes affection and constancy in your sweet-heart.

Packet.—To dream of a packet coming toward you denotes joyful return of friends; if, on the contrary, it sails from you, look for loss of friends and confidence.

Pale Face.—To dream of seeing in a mirror your own face very pallid, denotes the sudden and dangerous illness of a friend.

Palsy.—To dream of suffering yourself, or seeing others suffer from palsy, signifies great uneasiness from your present engagements, causing nervous excitement and doubt. To dream of a recovery from palsy, denotes a sudden rise to great eminence.

Pantomime.—To dream of witnessing pantomime, signifies low pursuits; if you enter, after this dream, upon a theatrical profession, it will be without honor, and you will end life an outcast.

Paper Hangings.—To dream of seeing the walls of another newly papered, betokens grief to him; to see your own walls newly hung, foretells a death in your own family. If you dream of new papering with your own hands, you will be widowed in early life.

Paradise.—To dream of paradise betokens a clear conscience, pure spirit, and Christian disposition.

Parrot.—To dream of a parrot signifies that when you are away from home, slanders will attack you and circumstances confirm unfavorable reports, but eventually, you will live down these false troubles and rise above them.

Pastor.—To dream of a pastor signifies that you are yourself insincere, or are surrounded by insincere friends. If he is performing the marriage ceremony, prepare for your own nuptials.

Pail.—To dream of milking in a dirty pail, is not a good sign.

Paper.—To dream of paper is a good omen; but if it appears rumpled, it will give you much pain.

Peaches.—Dreaming of peaches in season, denotes content, health, and pleasure.

Pears.—Dreaming of pears well-baked, denotes great success and expedition in business.

Pies.—Dreaming of making pies is joy and profit.

Pigeons.—Dreaming you see pigeons is good.

Pine Trees.—Dreaming that you see a pine tree denotes idleness and remissness.

Pile.—Dreaming that you pile any thing against the wall, denotes assistance in business.

Poverty.—To dream of being in poverty signifies good to some, but cross fortune to those that make commodity of their tongue and fair speech.

Prayers.—To dream you offer up prayers and supplications to God signifies happiness.

Pedestrian.—To dream of making a long journey on foot, betokens great hardships, false friends, loss of money, unhappy marriage connections, and final retirement from the world.

Pedlar.—To dream of a pedlar, signifies that you have a false estimate of your friends' value, and that time will show them to be hypocrites.

Physician.—To dream of a physician, signifies good in many forms; if he is relieving you, you have made a favorable impression where you most desire it; if, as a friend you meet him in society, look for true, happy love.

Pope.—To dream of a pope, signifies to look up and expect a sudden accession of power.

Predecessors.—To dream of your predecessors, as grandfather, and other ancestors, signifies care.

Pit.—To dream of falling into a deep pit, shows that some very heavy misfortune is about to attend you; that your sweetheart is false, and prefers another; to a sailor it forebodes some sad disaster at the next port he touches at. To dream that you are in a pit, and that you climb out of it, foreshows that you will have many enemies and experience many troubles, but that you will overcome them, marry well and become rich: to a sailor, it denotes that he will experience ship-

5

wreck, and be cast on a foreign shore, where he will be hospitably received, and marry a rich and handsome wife and live at ease.

Plays.—To dream you are at play is the forerunner of great good luck. It betokens great happiness in the marriage state, and success in business : to a maid, it shows speedy marriage with a young man who will be very successful in life, and acquire riches and honors and make her happy.

Purse.—To dream of finding a purse, is a very favorable omen ; it denotes great happiness and unlooked-for prosperity ; in love, it is the sure token of a speedy marriage, and of being dearly beloved by the object of your affections. To dream you lose your purse shows the loss of a friend ; in other respects it denotes some pleasant adventure is about to happen to you, by which you will be the gainer : to the sailor, it denotes the loss of his sweet-heart while at sea.

Plums.—To dream of plums, augurs but little good to the dreamer : they are the forerunners of ill-luck, and show loss of goods and reputation. They are indicative of infidelity in lovers, and much vexation in the married state.

Palm.—If one dreams that he see or smells the palm, it signifies prosperity. If it be a woman that dreams so, she shall bear children ; if it be a maid, she will be suddenly married.

Partridges.—Dreaming of partridges is a sign that a man shall form the acquaintance of women that are malicious, ungrateful, and void of conscience.

Plague.—If any one dreams he has the plague, it signifies his hidden store will be discovered, and he will run the risk of losing it.

Plant.—Dreaming that you see a plant come out of your body, is death ; to dream of plants quick of growth, as the vine and the peach tree, denotes that the good and evil portended shall quickly happen ; but trees that are slow of growing, as the oak, olive, &c., shows that the good or evil that shall happen to us shall be long in coming.

Plow.—To dream of a plow is good for marriage, and such like affairs; but it requires some time to bring it to perfection.

Pole-cat.—If a man dreams he has a pole-cat, it shows he shall have an ill-natured wife.

Pond.—Dreaming that you see a little pond, signifies the love of a beautiful woman; if a woman have that dream, she shall have her design accomplished; to dream that your pond is dried up, signifies poverty or death; to dream that you are in a boat upon a pond of clear water, is very good, and signifies joy, and success in affairs.

Pot-herbs.—Dreaming of pot-herbs, especially such as have a strong smell, signifies discovery of hidden secrets and domestic concerns.

Precipices.—Dreaming that you see great precipices, signifies much injury to person and goods.

Prisoners.—To dream of seeing prisoners executed, is a good dream, as it signifies a boldness of courage, and a very clear conscience.

Paths.—

To dream, in paths both straight and fair,
You walk, doth happiness declare;
But crooked ways denote much ill
To those who have a headstrong will.

Peacock.—To dream of seeing this beautiful bird is a very good omen: it denotes great success in trade: to a man, a very beautiful wife, much riches, and a good place: to a maid, a good and rich husband: to a widow, that she will be courted by one who will tell her many fine tales, without being sincere: it also denotes prosperity by sea, and a handsome wife in a distant port.

Pictures.—To dream that you are looking at beautiful

pictures, foreshows that you will be allured by false appearances into some unprofitable concern, that you will waste your time on some idle project, and that you will always be in pursuit of happiness without attaining it; in love, it denotes great pleasure in the enjoyment of the beloved object; it promises a handsome wife, a good husband, and beautiful children.

Pomegranates.—To dream of pomegranates, foretells some very unexpected legacy, by which you will be enabled to make a fortune; they denote that your sweet-heart is of a good temper, sings well, and is very faithful; to the married, they show an increase of riches and children, and great success in trade.

Quagmire.—To dream one is falling into a quagmire, shows obstructions and difficulty in business.

Quails.—Dreaming of quails, signifies bad news.

Queen.—To dream of a queen, signifies that a change in your political sentiments will cause you an increase of power and importance, but not of happiness.

Quicksilver.—To dream of this mineral is a sign of trouble, discontent, and unhappiness in the married state; to the lover, it is a sure sign of a quarrel; to the sick, of a slow recovery.

Quartan.—To dream of having this complaint is good, particularly to married persons.

Quacks.—To dream that you are under the care of quacks, is unfortunate, and foretells to the person dreaming, that he should beware of these nuisances to society.

Quinces.—To dream of quinces is favorable to the dreamer; if you are in prison, you will be shortly liberated; if you are in trouble, a change will take place that will relieve you from it; if you are sick, you will recover soon; if you are in love, you will marry, and become rich and happy.

Quilting.—To dream you are quilting foretells to an unmarried female that she will soon be wedded; it is also a good and lucky dream to a man. To be at a quilting party is good.

Quiver.—For either sex, if unmarried, to dream of a quiver is prognostic of success in love; but to the married it is a token of uneasiness to the dreamer.

Quoits.—If a woman dreams she is playing at quoits, it denotes that she will have some disagreeable and laborious undertaking to go through; to a man it is a sign of quarreling; quoits were always conceived a harbinger of ill-luck by the gipsies.

Quarreling.—To dream you are quarreling, denotes that some unexpected news will reach you, and that your sweetheart is about to be married to another.

Radishes.—To dream of radishes signifies a discovery of secrets or domestic jars; to lovers they foretell misfortune.

Rain.—To dream of being in a shower of rain, is particularly favorable to lovers. It denotes constancy, affection and a sweet temper; if it be a very heavy rain, accompanied by thunder and lightning, then expect to be assailed by thieves.

Rats.—To dream of seeing rats is a sign of having many enemies; if you are attacked by them, and get the better, it betokens that you will overcome your difficulties; if they should tear you, and make you run away, then expect some heavy misfortune.

Riding.—To dream you are riding, if it be with a woman, is very fortunate; if you are in trade, business will decay.

Ring.—To dream of a ring is favorable, if it be on your finger; if you are in love, expect to be speedily united to the person on whom you have placed your affections; to dream your ring falls off your finger betokens evil, also the death of some dear friend; to a maiden it is a warning to beware of her present lover.

Roses.—To the married, foretell the loss of their mates and children; to the lover, infidelity in the sweet-heart.

Reading.—To dream you are reading an agreeable book, shows you will be successful in love, and that you will become rich; in trade it is propitious.

Ribs.—If one dreams he hath his upper ribs broken or sunk, he will have some dissensions with his wife. If he dreams his lower ribs are broken, he will be afflicted by his female relations and kindred. If one dreams his ribs are grown longer and stronger than ordinary, he will take delight in his wife.

Rice.—To dream of eating rice, denotes abundance of instruction.

Rasp.—Dreaming that you see a rasp, is unfortunate to the married; to the virgin it is a caution for her to beware of her lover; to the lover it denotes that he will travel by sea.

Rub.—To dream that you are rubbing any thing, denotes to the lover that he will marry a very industrious girl, and be successful in business.

Ruins.—To dream of walking amongst ruins denotes loss of fortune; if they are covered with verdure, happiness and old age are in store.

Rusk.—To dream that you are baking them, is good; but to dream that you see others bake them, is bad.

Racing.—To dream you are running a race, is a token of good, presages much success in life, and that you will speedily hear some joyful news; in love it denotes that you will conquer all your rivals, and be happy in a union with the object of your affections. To dream you are riding a race, shows disappointment and anger, bad success in trade and in love; to a married woman, it denotes the loss of her husband's affections, and that her children will be in trouble.

Rouse.—To dream that you rouse a person from sleep, is good.

Rainbow.—To dream you see a rainbow, denotes great traveling and change of fortune; it also foretells sudden news of a very agreeable nature; it announces that your sweet-heart is of a good temper and very constant, and that you will be very happy in marriage, and have great success in business through the means of trading with foreign parts.

Raspberries.—To dream of raspberries, forewarns you of success in your undertakings; of happiness in marriage; of fidelity in your sweet-heart, and some news from beyond the sea in your advantage.

Ravens.—To dream you see a raven is a very unfavorable token; it denotes mischief and adversity; in love, it shows falsehood; to the married, it forebodes much mischief; to the sailor, it betokens shipwreck, and much distress on a foreign shore.

River.—To dream you see a flowing river, and that the waters are smooth and clear, presages happiness and success in life. If the water appear disturbed and muddy, or has a yellow tinge, then it denotes that you will go to the sea, where you will acquire considerable riches.

Rhinoceros.—To dream of this East India animal, denotes success to the man of business, but disappointment in love matters; but to dream they injure you is unfavorable to the dreamer. If you dream you see one dead, you'll soon leave a relative.

Rhubarb.—If a person dreams that he handles good rhubarb, he will be taken into favor with those he was not on good terms with before; but to dream of the dried Turkey rhubarb denotes sickness.

Seat.—To dream one has fallen from his seat and would fain get into it again, signifies that whatever office or employment he is in, he shall be displaced from, and not be able to recover it again.

Serpent.—To dream you see a serpent turning and winding himself, signifies danger and imprisonment; it denotes also sickness and hatred. To dream you kill a serpent, is a sign that you will overcome your enemies. To dream of beating serpents is very good.

Strange Place.—To dream of being in a strange place, denotes a good legacy from a relation whilst in prison; to the lover, it shows inconstancy and want of affection in the object of your love; to the sailor, sickness on the next voyage.

Starching.—To dream you are starching linen, shows you will be married to an industrious person, and that you will be successful in life, and save money; it also shows that you are about to receive a letter containing some pleasant news.

Squirrel.—To dream of a squirrel, shows that enemies are endeavoring to slander your reputation. To the lover, it shows your sweet-heart is of a bad temper, and much given to drinking: if you have a lawsuit, it will surely be decided against you; if you are in trade, sharpers will endeavor to defraud you; and you will quarrel with your principal creditor.

Sleep.—To dream you sleep or slumber, is evil to all except those who are in doubt or expectation of some danger; for this delivers them from pain and care. To dream you sleep in a church-yard, is death to the sick, and hindrance to others.

Sold.—To dream of being sold, or set up for sale, is fair to those who wish to change their condition, and to those who are in poverty and servitude; but to the rich and the sick, and those who are placed in honor and authority, it is ill.

Soldiers.—To see soldiers in your dream, shows troubles, persecution, and lawsuits: to the lover they denote that the object of your affections will be obliged to quit his present place of residence by command of a father, on your account: to the tradesman, they presage loss of good, and quarrels with creditors. To dream they are pursuing you, shows that you will be imprisoned, and meet with heavy losses, and be much disliked by your rich neighbors. This is one of those dreams after which the dreamer is advised to change quarters.

Spinning.—To dream of spinning is good, and shows a person to be diligent and industrious.

Son.—To dream that a man talks with his son, signifies some damage that will suddenly accrue to him.

Statues.—To dream of seeing brazen statues moving, signifies riches; but to dream you see great statues moving like monsters, denotes terrors and perils.

Stings.—To dream of stings, signifies grief and care. To many they have signified loss, and injuries by wicked persons.

Shipwreck.—To dream you suffer shipwreck, the ship being overwhelmed, is dangerous to all, except those detained by force; to them it signifies liberty.

Single Combat.—To dream of a single combat signifies lawsuits and marriages.

Scratched.—To dream of being scratched, betokens to him that is in his debt, that he shall acquit himself; to others it foretells hurt.

Sisters.—To dream you see your deceased brothers and sisters, signifies long life.

Shaving.—To dream you are being shaved, or that your head has been shaved, is a very unfavorable omen; in love, it denotes treachery and disappointment. To the tradesman, it argues loss of goods and business; to the sailor, an unpleasant and stormy voyage; to the farmer, it prefigures bad crops, and diseases amongst his live stock.

Sheep.—To dream you see a flock of sheep feeding, is a very favorable omen; it denotes success in life. To dream you see them dispersing and running away from you, shows that pretended friends are endeavoring to do you an injury, and that your children will meet with persecution and great troubles. In love, such a dream shows your sweet-heart to be fickle, and little calculated to make you happy. To dream you see sheep-shearing, is indicative of loss of property, and the affections of the person you love; also of your liberty. To dream you are shearing them yourself, shows that you will gain an advantage over some person who meant to harm you, and that you will get the better of difficulties, and marry the object of your affections.

Supreme.—To dream you have supreme command over any place, is unfortunate, particularly if the person is sick and helpless.

Surprise.—To dream that you surprise any one, denotes good-luck to the dreamer, and great success in trade.

Sycamore.—To dream you see this tree, denotes jealousy to the married; and to the virgin, she shall shortly be married.

Strawberries.—To dream of strawberries, denotes to a maiden speedy marriage with a man who will become rich, and make her happy; to a youth, they denote that his wife will be sweet tempered, and bring him many children, all boys. They foretell riches to the tradesman and to the sailor; they are a very fortunate dream to the farmer.

Sun.—To dream you see the sun shine, shows acquisition of riches, and enjoyment of honorable· posts in the State; also success to the lover. To dream you see the sun rise, promises fidelity in your sweet-heart, and good news from friends: to dream you see the sun set, shows infidelity in your sweet-heart, and disgraceful news; to the tradesman, loss of business. To dream you see the sun under a cloud, foretells many hardships and troubles about to befall you, and that you will encounter some great danger.

Swallows.—To dream of these harbingers of summer is a very favorable omen; they denote success in trade, and riches to the dreamer; in love, they denote a speedy marriage with the object of your affections.

Swimming.—To dream you are swimming with your head above the water, denotes great success in your undertakings, whether they be love, trade, sea, or farming. To dream you are swimming with your head under water, shows that you will experience some great trouble and hear some very unpleasant news from a person you thought dead. In trade, it shows loss of business.

Shooting.—To dream you are out shooting is very favorable, if you kill much game: to the lover, it shows a mistress kind and good-humored, who will make him au excellent and notable wife; to the tradesman and farmer, success and riches; to the sailor, wealth acquired in a distant country; but if you dream you kill little or no game, then it presages bad-luck, and disappointment in love. To dream you are shooting with a bow and arrows, is a very favorable dream, particularly to lovers and tradesmen.

Silk.—To dream you see silk, either in pieces or for sewing, signifies prosperity and success in undertakings; to dream you are clothed in silk foretells that you will rise to honors in the State, and become rich, but that you will quarrel with a rich neighbor, who will endeavor to do you mischief. If a maiden dreams of it, she will speedily see her lover.

Snakes.—To dream you see snakes and serpents, shows that you will be imprisoned, and encounter many dangers; if you are in love, your sweet-heart will be false. To dream you kill a snake shows you will overcome difficulties and enemies, and be successful in love, trade, or farming, but unsuccessful at sea.

Swoon.—To dream you see a person swoon is unfortunate to the maid; to the married it is a sign they will become rich and prosperous; to those who are nervous it is bad.

Scabs.—To dream you are all over scabs is the sure forerunner of great success in riches.

School.—To dream you begin again to go to school, and yet cannot say your lessons right, shows you are about to undertake something you do not understand.

Sea.—To dream of walking upon the sea is good to him that would travel; as also to a servant, and to him who would take a wife, or who hath a lawsuit: to a young man, this dream is love of a delightful woman; to a woman it signifies she lives a desolate life. To dream you walk in the sea, or on the shore, or catch fish, is a bad dream.

Ship.—To dream of seeing ships freighted with goods denotes prosperity. If you dream of seeing ships endangered by a tempest, it signifies peril.

Shoes.—To dream of losing one's shoes and walking barefoot, signifies pain in the feet and sickness. It also denotes loss and reproaches to those of a sanguine complexion, and more especially if this dream comes to you in the first days of the moon.

Silver.—If one dreams he gathers up silver, it signifies deceit and loss: to see silver eaten, denotes great advantage; to eat silver signifies wrath and anger.

Spectre.—Few dreams are more certain of good-luck to the dreamer, than to dream of spectres. It prognosticates business to the merchant, work for the artist and mechanic, and marriage to the maiden.

Sepulchre.—To dream of a sepulchre is a sign of great good to the dreamer.

Singing.—If any one dreams he sings, it signifies he will be affected and weep; to dream you hear singing or playing upon instruments, signifies consolation in adversity, recovery of health to those who are sick: to dream you hear birds sing, signifies love, joy, and delight.

Small-pox.—To dream one is full of the small-pox, denotes profit and wealth without infamy.

Snow.—To dream you see the ground covered with snow is a good omen.

Soldiers.—To dream you see soldiers, to those of a sanguine complexion may prove literally true; but to the phlegmatic it bids them look for sudden dissolution.

Stars.—To dream you see stars clear and fair, is good for a traveler, for it shows prosperity and advantage in a voyage, or journey: also good news. But, on the contrary, to see them dusky and pale-colored, signifies all sorts of mischief. Seeing the stars vanish and disappear, signifies poverty, vexation, and disturbing cares to those that are rich, and death to those that are poor.

Tamarinds.—To dream of tamarinds, denotes vexation and uneasiness through a woman, bad success in trade, a rainy season, and news from beyond the sea that is disagreeable; in love, it denotes disappointment.

Teeth.—To dream you lose a tooth denotes the loss of some friend by death, and that troubles and misfortunes are about to attend you: to the lover, it shows the loss of his sweet-heart's affection. To dream you cut a new tooth, denotes the birth of a child, who will make a great figure in the world.

Thirst.—To dream of thirst, signifies that you are aspiring. If quenched with pure water, you will rise; but if with wine, loss of fortune will follow; if with impure water, danger and disgrace attend you. To quench another's thirst in sleep, will signify to be the means of bestowing benefits.

Thunder.—To dream of thunder signifies affliction to the rich, but to the poor repose.

Tradesmen.—To dream you see those you employ at work, signifies that they are honest in their dealings with you. To dream you work yourself, betokens a happy contented life.

Traveling.—If one dreams that he is traveling through a wood, and that he sticketh in the briers and bushes, it betokeneth many troubles and hindrances. To travel over high hills and mountains and rocky places, signifies advancement, but with much difficulty obtained.

Trees.—To dream that you fell trees signifies loss. To dream you are climbing them, signifies future honor. To see withered trees, deceit. To see trees bear fruit, gain.

Tempests.—To dream you are in a storm or tempest, shows that you will, after many difficulties, arrive at great happiness, that you will become rich and marry well. For a lover to dream of being in a tempest, denotes that he will have rivals, over whom, after a great deal of vexation, he will triumph. It also foretells that you will receive some good news from a long-absent friend, who will have overcome many difficulties.

Thunder and Lightning.—To dream you hear thunder and see lightning is a very good dream. It denotes success in trade, good crops to the farmer, and a speedy and a happy marriage to the lover. If you are soliciting a place, you will obtain it; if you have a lawsuit you will gain it: it also indicates speedy news from a far distant country.

Toads.—To dream you see these venomous reptiles, argues evil to the dreamer; it shows enemies and disappointment among friends. To the lover, it denotes infidelity in his sweetheart; in trade, loss by swindlers and spoiling of goods. To dream you kill a toad, denotes that you will overcome an enemy, and discover a person who is robbing you, and in whom you place great confidence.

Tombs.—To dream of being amongst the tombs, denotes a speedy marriage, great success in business, and the gaining of a lawsuit; also, the birth of children and unexpected news.

Trumpet.—To dream you hear the sound of a trumpet is a bad omen, and denotes troubles and misfortunes. To the tradesman it presages the loss of business; to the farmer, bad crops; to the lover, insincerity in the object of his affections.

Tarts.—To dream one makes tarts, signifies joy and delight.

Treasure.—To dream you find a treasure in the earth is very ominous; it shows that you will be betrayed by some one whom you make your bosom friend; that your sweet-heart is unfaithful, and grossly deceives you ; and should you not be able to carry it away, then it denotes that you will have some very heavy loss; and that you will be waylaid by robbers, who will ill-treat you.

Turnips.—To dream of being in a turnip field, or that you see this wholesome vegetable, denotes acquisition of riches, and high employments in the State; to the lover they argue great fidelity, and an exceedingly good temper in your sweetheart, and that if you marry you will be very happy, have fine children, and thrive in the world.

Turkey.—To dream you see a turkey strutting about, is a sign you will overcome your enemies ; to dream you see or are amongst a drove of turkeys, betokens success in your most important undertaking, about this time. To dream of dead turkeys denote that you will encounter trouble which you will soon surmount.

Tumbler.—To dream you break a tumbler is prognostic of secrets being discovered that have long remained a mystery; to drink from a clear tumbler, denotes health and activity; to drink from a dirty one, the reverse.

Tops.—To dream you are spinning tops is ill.

Teapot.—If a person dream of teapots, he will soon form new friendships.

Undertaker.—To dream of an undertaker, is a forerunner of a wedding. If he is in black, the union will be unhappy; if in white, happiness will follow.

Veil.—To dream of a convent veil, signifies that you will lose your liberty. If you dream of wearing a white veil, look for honors received secretly; if it be black, you will be noted for penetration.

Vines.—To dream of vines, denotes health and wealth to the dreamer.

Vow.—To dream that you have made a vow and broken it, is bad to all.

Velvet.—To dream you trade with a stranger in velvet and other fine silks, is a sign of profit and joy.

Vote.—To dream you are voting, is bad, particularly to a sick person; for a newly married woman to dream of voting, is a sure sign her first child will be a boy, who will come to great honors.

Victuals.—To dream of victuals, and that you eat a variety of them, signifies loss.

Vulture.—To dream of the vulture is unfortunate to all except sick persons, to whom it foretells a speedy recovery.

Vine.—To dream you see a vine, denotes abundance and fertility; for which we have the example of Astyages, king of the Medes, who dreamed that his daughter br   t forth a vine, which was a prognostic of the grandeur, ric.   , and felicity of the great Cyrus, who was born of her after this dream.

Vinegar.—To dream you drink vinegar, signifies sickness.

Violin.—To dream one plays, or sees another play upon the violin or other musical instrument, signifies good news, and concord between man and wife, master and apprentice, brother and sister, &c.

Vomit.—To dream of vomiting, whether of blood, meat, or phlegm, signifies to the poor, profit; to the rich, hurt.

Venison.—To dream about venison, denotes change n affairs; to dream you eat of it, signifies misfortune.

Volcano.—To dream about volcanoes, forebodes liberty to a person in prison, and peace and contentment to those out of it.

Walking.—To dream one is walking in the dirt, or among thorns, signifies sickness. To dream one is walking in the water, or some torrent, signifies adversity and grief. To dream you walk in the night, signifies trouble and loss.

Walnuts.—To dream one sees or eats walnuts, or hazlenuts, signifies difficulty and trouble.

War.—To dream of war, and affairs of war, signifies trouble and danger to all except captains and soldiers; and to such as live by it, it is gain.

Watch.—To dream of a watch, signifies content in your position and pursuit; if it is broken, look for change of fortune; if it falls and breaks, you will lose a dear friend by death.

Washing.—For a man to dream he washes or bathes himself in baths or hot-houses, signifies riches, prosperity, and health to the sick. But to dream he washes or bathes himself contrary to the common custom or use, or in his clothes, is evil, and betokens sickness and great danger. To dream that you wash in fountains, ponds, or running water, and in fair and clear floods, is good, but not that you swim, for that is a sign of danger and sickness: washing is a sure sign of a removal.

Wedding.—For a man that is sick to dream that he is wedded to a maid, shows he shall die quickly. If any dreams he is wedded to a deformed woman, it signifies discontent; if to a handsome woman, joy.

Wife.—If a man dreams he sees his wife married to another, it denotes change of affairs or condition. If a woman dream she is married to another man, it is the same.

Winds.—To dream of roaring winds, is a warning to draw in your business pursuits, as you are speculating on too extensive a scale. To dream of gentle breezes, denotes happiness in married life.

Woods.—To dream of walking alone in the woods, signifies that you will live unmarried. If you meet another, it is a sign that some one who secretly loves you, is watching for a chance of introduction, but is prevented, by your seclusion, from meeting you.

6

Water.—To dream you are drinking water, denotes great trouble and adversity; in trade, loss of business, and being arrested.   To the lover, it shows his sweet-heart is false, prefers another and will never marry him.

Water-mill.—To dream of being in a water-mill is a favorable omen; to the tradesman it denotes great increase of business; to the farmer, abundant crops; in love, success, a rich sweet-heart, and a happy marriage.

Wasps.—To dream that you are stung by wasps, signifies vexation and trouble by envious persons.

Weasel.—To dream of weasels, shows a man in love with some ill-natured woman, by whom he will be ensnared, or some domestic that will cajole his master by subtlety.

Whales.—If you dream you are sitting on a whale's back, it is good; as the whale is the greatest of the water animals, so the one dreaming will become a great person, and live in peace many years.

Wild Boar.—The wild boar in dreams, signifies a furious enemy, well-furnished with all things necessary. And thus, if any one dreams he has hunted or taken a wild boar, he will chase or take some enemy that has the same qualities as the wild boar.

Wrist.—To dream that your wrists are broken is very good; it foretells that you will marry your present lover and be happy.

Walls.—To dream you are walking on a crazy, old and narrow wall, denotes that you will engage in some very dangerous enterprise, that will cause you much trouble and vexation; if you get down without hurting yourself, or the walls falling, then you will succeed; if the wall should fall whilst you are upon it, you will be disappointed; if you are walking between walls, and the passage is very narrow and difficult, you will be engaged in some quarrel, or other disagreeable affair, from which it will require great circumspection and caution on your part to disengage yourself; but if you get from between them safe, you will settle well in life, marry an agreeable partner, have children, and become rich and happy.

Weeping.—To dream one weeps and grieves, whethei it be for a friend departed, or any other cause, is joy and mirth.

Wheat.—To dream you see, or are walking in a field of wheat, is a very favorable omen, and denotes great prosperity and riches; in love, it argues a completion of your most sanguine wishes, and foretells much happiness, with fine children, when you marry. If you have a lawsuit, you will gain it, and you will be successful in all your undertakings.

Wood.—To dream you are are cutting or chopping wood, clearly shows that you will be happy in your family, and become rich and respectable in life. To dream you are carrying wood upon your back, shows that you will rise to affluence by your industry, but that your partner will be of a bad temper, and your children undutiful. If you dream you are walking or sitting alone in an extensive wood, by a running stream, it denotes that you will quickly fall in love, and also that you will be often married. To dream that you are walking or sitting there with the worthy object of your affections, betokens your speedy union, which will prove so felicitous, that you will be called " The Happy Couple."

Wool.—To dream you are buying or selling wool, denotes prosperity and great affluence, by means of industry and trade. To the lover, it is a favorable omen; your sweet-heart is thereby shown to be of an amiable disposition, very constant, and deeply in love with you.

Will.—Dreaming of making your will signifies that you will still live a long time in uninterrupted happiness and joy.

Wren.—To dream of this little bird is good, as the wren is noted for its innocence; the person so dreaming is certain of having a noble friend; but to dream you kill it is bad.

Walnuts.—To dream of walnuts portends difficulties and misfortunes in life; if you have children, your eldest son will marry a woman who will make him very unhappy. In love, they foretell infidelity and disappointment; to the seaman, storms and shipwreck; to the tradesman, loss of goods and reputation through a confidential servant.

Well.—If a young man dreams that he draws water out of a clear well, it signifies a speedy marriage to a fair maid, who will bring him a portion; if the water be troubled, he will be disturbed by her, and suddenly fall sick. If he seems to give to others clear well water to drink, it signifies that he will enrich them; but if the water be troubled, he will afflict them. If he dreams that he sees a person fall into a well, it signifies that the person dreamed of shall die quickly.

Water.—To dream you drink dirty water, denotes great trouble and adversity: in trade, loss of business, and being arrested; to the lover, it shows your sweet-heart is false, prefers another, and will never marry you.

Wounds.—To dream you are wounded, is a very favorable omen, especially if it be with a sword; to the lover, it denotes success in your amours, and with an agreeable partner, who will be faithful and affectionate; to the tradesman, profit and increase of business; to the farmer, an increase in his cattle, and plentiful crops; to the sailor, a profitable voyage, with unexpected success in love.

> To dream of a wound is sorrow and grief;
> Of dressing a wound is cure or relief.

Writing.—

> Dreaming of writing ever means news;
> 'Twill grant or deny, will give or refuse.

Yew Tree.—To dream of a yew tree, is an indication of the funeral of a very aged person, by whose death the dreamer will derive some benefit, or a protecting hand among the relations of the deceased person.

Zodiac.—To dream of the twelve signs of the zodiac, shows to a man that he will be a great traveler, and sail once round the world : to a woman, that she will wed a foreigner who is deeply skilled in astronomy.

THE FORTUNE TELLER.

THE method of using the "Fortune Teller" is very simple. To each question there are twenty answers. Having selected the question which is to be answered, let the inquirer take twenty cards, or bits of paper, and put on them numbers from one to twenty; throw them promiscuously into a vase or hat, and draw out one. Then, turn to the pages containing the question and its twenty answers, and the answer to the questions asked will be found under the corresponding number. It will be observed that there is a set of questions to be asked by ladies, and another set to be asked by gentlemen.

QUESTIONS FOR GENTLEMEN.

1. Shall I marry, or live an old bachelor?
2. Where did, or where shall I meet my future wife?
3. Shall I marry the lady I now love?
4. Does the lady I love, love me?
5. Describe my future wife.
6. Shall I be happy in my domestic relations?
7. What profession shall I follow?
8. What misfortunes await me?
9. Shall I be rich or poor?
10. What is my destiny?

QUESTIONS FOR LADIES.

1. Shall I marry, or live an old maid?
2. Where did, or where shall I meet my future husband?

3. Shall I marry my present lover?
4. Does the gentleman I love, love me?
5. Describe my future husband.
6. Shall I be happy in my domestic relations?
7. What profession shall I follow?
8. What misfortunes await me?
9. Shall I be rich or poor?
10. What is my destiny?

ANSWERS TO QUESTIONS FOR GENTLEMEN.

1. Shall I Marry, or Live an Old Bachelor?

1.   You would not your unhoused, free condition
   Put into circumspection and confine,
   For the sea's worth.

SHAKSPEARE.

2.   On thee, blest youth, a father's hand confers
     The maid thy earliest, fondest wishes knew;
   Each soft enchantment of the soul is hers;
     Thine be the joys to firm attachment due.

ROGERS.

3.   Thou shalt seek
   Temple and priest right soon; the morrow's sun
   Shall see across thy barren threshold pass
   The fairest bride.

SIR E. L. BULWER.

4. You would be bored with the exertion of choosing: if a wife now could be had, like a dinner, for ordering, you might perhaps think of it.

CHARLES MATTHEWS.

5. You adore the sex—*collectively*, they are your idols; but to *one* individual of woman-kind, never will you bend the knee.

T. H. BAYLY.

6.   You're one who single is and snug,
    With pussy in the elbow chair—
    And Tray reposing on the rug.
    If you must totter down the hill,
    'Tis safest done without a clog.

THOMAS HOOD

7.   Before the altar you shall soon
    Repeat the marriage vow;
    Nor ever after deem the pledge
    Less holy, pure, than now.

C. JEFFRIES.

8. On the day when to Jove the black list was presented,
 The list of what Fate for your lot here intends;
At the long string of ills a kind goddess relented,
 And slipped in three blessings—Wife, Children, and
  friends.

R. W. SPENCER.

9. Close by thy side will move a form of beauty,
 Strewing sweet flowers along thy path of life,
And looking up with meek and love-lent duty:
 I call her angel, but *thou'lt* call her—Wife!

W. G. CLARK.

10. If thou art to have a wife of thy youth, she is now living on the earth.

M. F. TUPPER.

11. Because you will not do woman the wrong to mistrust any, you will do yourself the right to trust none; and the fine is (for the which you may go the finer) you will live a bachelor.

SHAKSPEARE.

12. Before a month is out, you'll leave your father's house,
    And hire yourself to work within the fields ;
    And half in love, half spite, you'll woo and wed
    A laborer's daughter.

TENNYSON.

13.   She is a winsome wee thing,
           She is a handsome wee thing,
           She is a bonnie wee thing,
           This sweet wee wife o' thine.

ROBERT BURNS.

14. Fate asks, sir, your hand,
    To gift it with a bride, whose dowry shall match
    Yet not exceed her beauty.

SIR E. L. BULWER.

15. An old bachelor ! there's a nickname to break a man's
heart with, old Nick's own invention. But you've borne it for
many a long year, and it's now too late to think of getting rid
of it.

T. H. BAYLY.

16. I fear it's too late for you to think of matrimony. "If
you will not when you may"—you know the proverb—young
bachelors who are too hard to be pleased, must make the best
of a life of single blessedness.

T. H. BAYLY.

17. All things are waiting for the ceremony,
    And, till you grace it, Hymen's wasting torch,
    Burns dim and sickly.

J. TOBIN.

18. Could you meet a reasonable woman,
    Fair without vanity, rich without pride,
    Discreet though witty, learn'd yet very humble,
    That has no ear for flattery, no tongue
    For scandal ; one who never reads romances ;
    Who loves to listen better than to talk,

And rather than be gadding would sit quiet,
You'll marry, certainly.

J. TOBIN.

19. You'll be a rare old bachelor, and prick you fingers
With sewing on your buttons.

L. C. CROWE.

20. I have wooed in thy name, and the fair —— is won.
I have broke with her father, and his goodwill obtained;
name the day of marriage, and God give thee joy.

SHAKSPEARE.

---

2. Where did, or where shall I meet my future Wife?

1.   You'll meet her at a country ball;
          There, where the sound of flute and fiddle
      Gives signals sweet through the old hall,
          Of "hands across," and "down the middle."

PRAED.

2. 'Twas late, and the gay company was gone,
    And light lay soft on the deserted room,
    From alabaster roses, and a scent
    Of orange leaves, and sweet verbena came
    Through the unshuttered window on the air;
    And the rich pictures, with their dark old tints,
    Hung like a twilight landscape, and all things
    Seemed hushed into a slumber.   Isabel,
    The dark-eyed, spiritual Isabel
    Was learning on the harp, and you had stay'd
    To whisper what you could not when the crowd
    Hung on her look like worshipers.

N. P. WILLIS.

3. You'll meet with a sly flirtation
      By the light of a chandelier—
   With music to play in the pauses,
      And nobody very near.

N. P. WILLIS

4. She did eloquently smile on thee,
   While handing up her sixpence through the hole
   Of an o'erfreighted omnibus.

N. P. WILLIS.

5. You passed her one day in a hurry,
      When late for the post, with a letter,
   I think near the corner of Murray,
      And up rose your heart as you met her.

N. P. WILLIS.

6. You had been feasting with your enemy;
   When, on a sudden, one hath wounded you—
   That 's by you wounded.

SHAKSPEARE.

7. 'Twas but for a moment—and yet in that time
      You crowded th' impressions of many an hour;
   Her eye had a glow like the sun of her clime,
      Which waked every feeling at once into flower!

MOORE.

8.   You'll meet in the very house you know,
      With ugly windows, ten in a row!
            Its chimneys in the rear.

T. HOOD.

9.   Presiding at the festive board,
         With many faces laughing round,
      Where melancholy is ignored
         And mirth and jollity abound.

" PUNCH."

10.   In the far Eastern clime, no great while since.

SCOTT

11. At Cheltenham, where one drinks one's fill
    Of folly and of water,
  You'll dance next year your first quadrille,
    With old ——— ———'s daughter.

PRAED.

12. Years, years ago, while all your joy
    Were in your fowling-piece and filly;
  In short, while you were yet a boy,
    You fell in love with ———.

PRAED.

13.   You'll meet her in storm,
      On the deck of a steamer;
    She'll speak in language warm,
      Like a sentimental dreamer.

" PUNCH."

14. The dew was falling fast, the stars began to blink;
  You heard a voice; it said: "Drink, pretty creature,
    drink;"
  And looking o'er the hedge before you, you espied
  A snow-white mountain lamb, with a maiden at its side.

WORDSWORTH.

15.   You have been friends together,
      In sunshine and in shade;
    Since first beneath the chestnut trees
      In infancy you played.

CAROLINE NORTON.

16. An August evening, on a balcony
  That o'erlooked a woodland and a lake;
  You sat in the still air, and talked with one
  Whose face shone fairer than the crescent moon.

W. C. WILLIAMSON.

17. From the forest shade advancing
    There will come a lovely May,
  The dew-like gems before her glancing,
    As she brushes it away.

Straight you'll rise and run and meet her—
  Seize her hand —————— the heavenly blue
Of her eye smiles brighter, sweeter,
  As she asks you, "Who are you?"
                            W. E. AYTOUN.

18.   Dost thou remember when with stately prance,
    Your heads went crosswise in the country dance.
                            W. E. AYTOUN.

19. You'll meet at the sea-shore, the whispering tide
At your feet in soft murmurs shall ceaselessly glide,
You'll press the white hand as it rests on your arm,
You'll whisper soft nonsense—pray where is the harm?
                            G. G. DAYLEE.

20.   When wandering in the glen at eventide
    With weary heart, and sad foreboding sight,
    Listen !   You'll hear her footsteps on the grass.
                            E. J. DOLMER.

————◄●►————

3. Shall I marry the Lady I now love ?

1. You don't object to wealth and land,
      And she will have the giving
    Of an extremely pretty hand,
      Some thousands and a living.
    She makes silk purses, broiders stools,
      Sings sweetly, dances finely,
    Paints screens, subscribes to Sunday-schools,
      And sits a horse divinely.
    But to be linked for life to her !
      The desperate man who tried it,
    Might marry a barometer
      And hang himself beside it.
                            W. M. PRAED.

2. She is a woman—therefore may be woo'd;
She is a woman—therefore may be won!

SHAKSPEARE.

3. I will break with her, and with her father,
And thou shalt have her.

SHAKSPEARE.

4. She'll be your true and honorable wife,
As dear to you as are the ruddy drops
That visit your sad heart.

SHAKSPEARE.

5. She'll be your own,
And you as rich in having such a jewel,
As twenty seas, if all their sands were pearl,
Their water nectar, and their rocks pure gold.

SHAKSPEARE.

6. She shall be thy bride,
If she were sworn a maid.

SCOTT.

7. She'll be your wife by every tie that's sacred.

J. TOBIN.

8. You'll take her for your wife,
For you have wished this marriage night and day
For many years.

TENNYSON.

9. She shall obey you, love you, and most honor you.

SHAKSPEARE.

10. You love in vain—strive against hope.

SHAKSPEARE.

11. She 'll break her vow, she 'll break your heart,
And you may e'en go hang.

BURNS.

12. A noble flame shall warm thy breast,
A loving maiden faithful prove,

Thy youth, thine age, shall yet be blest
In woman's love.

MONTGOMERY.

13   Thou wilt meet no more in the lighted halls
    Amid happy faces and gay young hearts;
Thou wilt listen in vain as each footstep falls
    Thou wilt watch in vain as each form departs.
There are loving voices, but one dear tone
    Its cheerful greeting hath ceased to pour;
Her form from the dancing train is gone,
    Thou wilt meet no more—thou wilt meet no more!

MRS. NORTON.

14.   I think there is a rival in the case,
    A very rich, and very stupid fellow.

SARGENT.

15.   No, sir! Your rival's so dear;
    The reason she's " out" when you call,
Is—his income 's five thousand a year,
    And your's, it is—nothing at all.

MRS. OSGOOD.

16.   You are forgotten—as old debts,
    By persons who are used to borrow;
Forgotten—as the sun that sets,
    When shines a new one on the morrow.

PRAED.

17. Do you believe she loves you? Mark her start
When on her ear *another's* footstep falls;
The quivering lip, soft blush, and tender sigh
With which she listens to *another's* voice:
Lay by your love for her, 'tis all in vain
You sigh, and woo, and strive to win her heart,
The place that you would fill is occupied.

E. J. SMITH.

18. Never! though you die of sorrow,
Never! though your heart should break.

E. J. SMITH.

19. No !   She with quiet air
    Of mild indifference, and with truthful words,
    Kind, yet determined, will withdraw herself
    To chosen solitude, intent to keep
    A maiden's freedom.

MRS. SIGOURNEY.

20. She said, she could love thee in want and in wealth,
    Through clouds and through sunshine, in sickness, in
        health ;
    Then why should'st thou fear when thy spirit is
        weak ?
    For the truth she has plighted she never will break.

E. NEALE.

---

4. Does the Lady I love, love me ?

1. Not less is she in heart affected,
    But that she masks it with a modesty,
    For fear she should of lightness be detected.

SPENSER.

2.   Wherefore do you follow her
    Like foggy south, puffing with wind and rain ?
    You are a thousand times a properer man,
    Than she a woman.

SHAKSPEARE.

3.   She'll never tell her love,
    But let concealment, like a worm i' the bud,
    Feed on her damask cheek.

SHAKSPEARE.

4. All fancy sick she is, and pale of cheer,
    With sighs of love.

SHAKSPEARE.

5.   I think there is not half a kiss to choose
      Who loves the other best.

SHAKSPEARE.

6.   I find she loves you much because she hides it.

DRYDEN.

7.   Her eyes wont lose the sight of thee,
      But languish after thine, and ache with gazing.

OTWAY.

8.   She feels your flame, but deep within her breast,
      In bashful coyness, or in maiden pride,
      The soft return conceals.

THOMSON.

9. Fain would she speak the thoughts she bears to thee,
   But they do choke, and flutter in her throat.

JOANNA BAILLIE.

10.   Then youth, thou fond believer
                 This wily siren shun ;
               Who trusts the dear deceiver,
                 Will surely be undone.

MONTGOMERY.

11. She loves—but knows not whom she loves.

MOORE.

12. Love not ! love not ! the thing you love will change,
      The rosy lip will cease to smile on you ;
    The kindly beaming eye grow cold and strange,
      The heart still warmly beat, and not for you.

MRS. NORTON.

13.   She'll not be hit
        With Cupid's arrow.

SHAKSPEARE.

14. From love's weak childish bow she lives unharm'd.
    She will not stay the siege of loving terms,
    Nor bide the encounter of assailing eyes.

7   SHAKSPEARE.

15.   ·   She, whom you love now,
      Doth grace for grace, and love for love allow.

SHAKSPEARE.

16. By this day, she's a fair lady; I do spy some marks of
love in her.

SHAKSPEARE.

17.   She is too disdainful,
      I know her spirits are as coy and wild
      As haggards of the rock.

SHAKSPEARE.

18. Love on, she will requite thee,
      Taming her wild heart to thy loving hand.

SHAKSPEARE.

19. Nature never framed a woman's heart,
      Of prouder stuff than that of —— ;
      Disdain and scorn ride sparkling in her eyes,
      Misprising what they look on; and her wit
      Values itself so highly, that to her
      All matter else seems weak: she cannot love,
      Nor take no shape nor project of affection,
      She is so self endeared.

SHAKSPEARE.

20. She cannot be so much without true judgment,
      (Having so swift and excellent a wit,
      As she is priz'd to have) as to refuse
      So rare a gentleman as Signor ————

SHAKSPEARE.

---

5. Describe my future Wife.

1. Grace is in all her steps, heaven in her eyes,
      In every gesture dignity and love.

MILTON.

2. Her graceful ease and sweetness, void of pride,
   Might hide her faults, if belles had faults to hide;
   If to her share some female errors fall,
   Look in her face, and you'll forget them all.

POPE.

3. Her glossy hair is clustered o'er a brow
   Bright with intelligence, and fair and smooth;
   Her eyebrow's shape is like the aeriel bow,
   Her cheek all purple with the beam of youth,
   Mounting, at times, to a transparent glow,
   As if her veins ran lightning.

BYRON.

4.   She is like
       A dream of poetry, that may not be
       Written or told—exceeding beautiful.

WILLIS.

5.   Her look composed and steady eye,
        Bespeak a matchless constancy.

SCOTT.

6.   She is timid as the wintry flower,
       That, whiter than the snow it blooms among,
     Droops its fair head, submissive to the power,
       Of every angry blast which sweeps along.

MRS. TIGHE.

7.   Her eye's dark charm 'twere vain to tell;
         But gaze on that of the gazelle,
       It will assist thy fancy well,
         As large as languishingly dark.

BYRON

8.   Astronomy finds in her eye
         Better light than she studies above;
       And music must borrow her sigh
         As the melody dearest to love.

MOORE.

9. So bright is her beauty, so charming her song,
    As had drawn both the beasts and their Orpheus along;
    But such is her avarice, such is her pride,
    That the beasts must have starved, and the poet have
        died.

POPE.

10. A gentle maiden, whose large, loving eyes,
        Enshrine a tender, melancholy light,
     Like the soft radiance of the starry skies,
        Or autumn sunshine, mellow'd when most bright;
     She is not sad, yet in her gaze appears,
     Something that makes the gazer think of tears.

MRS. EMBURY.

11. Pure in her aim, and in her temper mild,
     Her wisdom seems the weakness of a child;
     She makes excuses where she might condemn;
     Reviled by those that hate her, prays for them;
     Suspicion lurks not in her artless breast,
     The worst suggested, she believes the best;
     Not soon provoked, however stung and teased,
     And, if perhaps made angry, soon appeased;
     She rather waives than will dispute her right,
     And injured, makes forgiveness her delight.

COWPER.

12. An angel face! its sunny wreath of hair
     In radiant ripples, bathes the graceful throat
     And dimpled shoulders.

MRS. OSGOOD.

13. She's beautiful!   Her raven curls
     Have broken hearts in envious girls;
     And then they sleep in contrast so,
     Like raven feathers upon snow—
     And bathe her neck, and shade the bright
     Dark eye from which they catch their light,

As if their graceful loops were made
To keep that glorious eye in shade;
And holier make its tranquil spell,
Like waters in a shaded well.

WILLIS

14. She is knowing in all needlework,
And shines in dairy and in kitchen too,
And in the parlor.

BARKER.

15. A delicate, frail thing—but made
For spring sunshine, or summer shade.
A slender flower, unmeet to bear
One April shower—so slight, so fair.

L. E. LANDON.

16. Her voice is sweet as the voice of love,
And her teeth as pure as pearls;
While her forehead lies like a snow-white dove,
In a nest of nut-brown curls.

MRS. WELBY.

17. Coquette and coy, at once her air,
Both studied though both seem neglected;
Careless she is with artful care,
Affecting to seem unaffected.

CONGREVE.

18. As fair as the siren, but false as her song.

MRS. HALE.

19. Thy likeness, thy fit help, thy other self,
Thy wish exactly to thy heart's desire.

MILTON.

20. A perfect woman, nobly plann'd,
To warm, to comfort, to command.

WORDSWORTH.

5. Shall I be happy in my Domestic Relations ?

1. Your happy altar hearth 'll be bright
    And ever blazing, there
  Are cheerful faces round it met,
    In an unending prayer.

NICOLL.

2. Your low-roof'd cottage still will be a heaven,
Music is in it—and the song she sings,
That sweet-voiced wife of thine, arrests the ear
Of your young child awake upon her knee.
And with his calm eyes on his master's face,
Your noble hound lies couchant—and all here—
All in this little home, yet boundless heaven,
Are, in such love as life has power to give,
Blessed to overflowing.

N. P. WILLIS.

3. You will forage all over this joy-dotted earth
To pick its best nosegay of innocent mirth,
Tied up with the hands of its wisdom and worth,
    And lo ! its chief treasure,
    Its innermost pleasure
      Will be always at Home.

M. F. TUPPER.

4.   You will feel
  The solitude of passing your own door
  Without a welcome.

BYRON.

5. For you no blazing hearth shall ever burn,
  Or busy housewife ply the evening care ;
No children run to lisp their sire's return,
  Or climb your knee the envied kiss to share.

GRAY.

6. A home for comfort, refuge, hope and peace;
　　A spot by gratitude and memory blest!
　Where, as in brightest worlds, "the wicked cease
　　From troubling and the weary are at rest."
　And unfledged loves and graces have their nest;
　　And brightly all the varied virtues shine,
　And nothing said or done is seen amiss;
　　While sweet affections every heart entwine,
　And different tastes and talents all unite,
　　Like hues prismatic blending into white,
　In charity to man, and love divine:
　　This little kingdom of serene delight,
　Heaven's nursery and foretaste, shall be thine.

TUPPER.

7.　　　　　Your home is the resort
　Of love, of joy, of peace and plenty, where,
　Supporting and supported, polished friends
　And dear relations mingle into bliss.

THOMSON.

8. The touch of kindred and of love you'll feel;
　The modest eye, whose beams, on yours alone,
　Ecstatic shine; the little, strong embrace
　Of prattling children, twining round your neck,
　And emulous to please you, calling forth
　The fond paternal soul.

THOMSON

9.　　　　　You'll have
　A warm but simple home, where you'll hold
　With her who shares your pleasures and your heart,
　Sweet converse.

COWPER.

10.　　Your home shall be an Eden on this earth.

E. J. SMITH.

11.   Your wife will be a preacher
          Inspired when she's vexed !
       She'll never lack a sermon,
          And you will be the text !
       She 'll preach of all your faults and flaws,
          And pay them all in kind,
       But most she'll hate, aye, more than all,
          The faults she cannot find.

ELLIOTT.

12.   O ! none shall have a better home
             Or brighter lot than thine.

SWAIN.

13.   From the gay world you 'll oft retire
          To your own family and fire,
             Where love the hour employs.

COTTON.

14. The jessamine clambers in flowers o'er your thatch,
       And the swallow chirps sweet from the nest in the
          wall ;
    And trembling with transport, you 'll raise up the latch,
    And the voices of loved ones reply to your call.

DIMOND.

15.   Yours shall be a home, where discord, strife,
       And vexed contention lengthen hours to days.

OLD PLAY.

16.   You 'll, for a month's delirious joy,
             Buy a dull age of penance.

J. TOBIN.

17.   You 'll to the close of this frail life prolong
       The pure delights of a well-governed marriage.

J. TOBIN.

18. You 'll have employment for the mind, exercise for the
body, a domestic hearth, and a mind at ease.

C. MATTHEWS.

19. With every pleasure money can bestow,
With all a man desires here below,
You still will feel in long domestic strife
The inconvenience of a scolding wife.

E. J. SMITH.

20. Your family will be nothing but bills, dirt, waste, noise, tumbles down stairs, confusion, and wretchedness. You scrambling home; from week's end to week's end, like one great washing-day—only nothing washed.

DICKENS.

---

5. What Profession shall I follow?

1. Within a noisy mansion skilled to rule,
You 'll live *the master of a village school.*

GOLDSMITH.

2. A *soldier,*
Full of strange oaths, and bearded like a pard,
Seeking the bubble reputation,
Even in the cannon's mouth.

SHAKSPEARE.

3. A *Judge*—a man so learned,
So full of equity, so noble, so notable;
In the process of your life, so innocent;
In the manage of your office, so incorrupt;
In the passages of State, so wise; in
Affection of your country so religious,
Envy itself cannot accuse, or malice vitiate.

CHAPMAN & SHIRLEY.

4. A *farmer's* simple life!
How pure the joy it yields!
Far from the world's tempestuous strife,
Free 'mid the scented fields.

C. W. EVEREST.

5.   A *Man of Law*, a man of peace,
      To frame a contract or a lease.

CRABBE.

6.   A poor *player*,
    That struts and frets his hour upon the stage,
    And then is heard no more.

SHAKSPEARE.

7.   *Poet!* esteem thy noble part,
          Still listen, still record—
        Sacred historian of the the heart,
          And moral nature's lord.

MILNES.

8.   Maker of the dead man's bed,
    A *sexton*, hoary-headed chronicler.

BLAIR.

9.   No better than a poor and loathsome *beggar*,

SHAKSPEARE.

10.   A *mason*, and forbidden
    By oath to tell the secrets of thy trade.

HORACE SMITH.

11.   A *smith*—a mighty man you 'll be,
          With large and sinewy hands;
        And the muscles of your brawny arms,
          Be strong as iron bands.

LONGFELLOW.

12.   Your shop is a *grocer's*—a snug, genteel place,
       Near the corner of Oak street and Pearl.

HALLECK.

13.   A *Dyer:*
    A man of dark and very reputable calling.

MULLEN.

4.   You are a *traveler*, sir; know men and manners.

BEAUMONT & FLETCHER.

15.   You 'll be a *tailor* gay
                 As ever wore a thimble,
               Through life you 'll work away,
                 Your fingers always nimble.

DIBDIN.

16.   You are a nice young man,
                 A *carpenter* by trade.

OLD SONG.

17. A *shoemaker* — a pale, sickly-looking, black-haired man, the very model of sober industry

MISS MITFORD.

18. A *blacksmith*, with a gloomy dwelling, where the sun never seems to shine; dark and smoky; within and without like a forge.

MISS MITFORD.

19. A bell-ringer, a ballad-singer — a troller of profane catches—a fiddler—a bruiser—a loller on ale-house benches —a teller of good stories—a mimic—a poet !

MISS MITFORD.

20. A young sculptor—that rare thing, a man of genius, and of genius refined and brightened by cultivation.

MISS MITFORD.

---

8. What Misfortunes await Me?

1. One by one thy griefs shall meet thee,
     Do not fear an armèd band ;
   One will fade as others greet thee,
     Shadows passing through the land.

PROCTOR.

2.   You, on pain of death,
   Till twice five summers have enrich'd our fields,

Shall not regreet our fair dominions,
But tread the stranger paths of banishment.

SHAKSPEARE.

3.   The whips and scorns of time,
The oppressor's wrong, the proud man's contumely.

SHAKSPEARE.

4. An exiled, outcast, houseless, nameless object,
You 'll flee for life, and scarce by flight will save it.

MATURIN.

5.   Fortune
Shall be corrupted, changed, and won from thee.

SHAKSPEARE.

6.   To outlive your wealth,
To review with hollow eye and wrinkled brow,
An age of poverty.

SHAKSPEARE.

7. You 'll find the friendship of the world a show,
Mere outward show.

SAVAGE.

8. One woe shall tread upon another's heels,
So fast they follow.

HAMLET.

9.   A malady will
Prey on your heart that medicine cannot reach,
Invisible and cureless.

MATURIN.

10. Ingratitude ! the marble-hearted fiend,
More hideous   *   *   *   *
Than the sea monster.

SHAKSPEARE.

11. Lying, vainness, babbling, drunkenness,
And every taint of vice, whose strong corruption
Inhabits our frail blood.

SHAKSPEARE

12. The venom clamors of a jealous woman.

SHAKSPEARE.*

13. Public calamities and household ills ;
The due reward to just desert refused,
.Your trust betrayed.

PRIOR.

14. To live a slave, and die a coward.

HEMMING.

15. The world is not thy friend, nor the world's law.

SHAKSPEARE.

16.   A felon's cell,
The fittest earthly type of hell.

WHITTIER.

17. Toss'd on the billows of the main,
You're doom'd from zone to zone to roam.

PIERPONT.

18. Must'ring all her wiles,
With blandish'd parleys, feminine assaults,
Tongue batteries, your wife ceases not day or night
To storm you.

MILTON.

19.   You'll hear
On all sides, from innumerable tongues,
A dismal, universal hiss, the sound
Of public scorn.

MILTON.

20.   To abjure
Forever the society of men.

SHAKSPEARE.

9. Shall I be Rich or Poor ?

1. In tattered old slippers, that toast at the bars,
And a ragged old jacket perfumed with cigars,
Away from the world and its toils and its cares,
You 'll have a snug kingdom up four pair of stairs.

THACKERAY.

2.   You 'll own
A wigwam that would hardly serve a sow ;
Your landlord, and of middle-men two brace,
Will screw your rent up to the starving place ;
Your garment, sir, a top-coat, and an old one,
Your meal, sir, a potato, and a cold one.

SCOTT.

3. The ghastly duns shall worry your sleep,
  And constables cluster around you ;
And you shall creep from the wood-hole deep,
  Where their spectre eyes have found you.

O. W. HOLMES.

4.   Ev'ry labor sped,
You 'll sit you down, the monarch of a *shed*.

GOLDSMITH.

5. Be honest poverty thy boasted wealth,
So shall thy friendships be sincere, tho' few,
So shall thy sleep be sound, thy waking cheerful.

HAVARD.

6. A rich man's son, you will have lands,
  And piles of brick, and stone, and gold ;
You will inherit soft white hands,
  And tender flesh that fears the cold.

J. R. LOWELL.

7. Your house within the city,
Shall richly furnished be with plate and gold ;
Basins and ewers to lave your dainty hands ;
Your hangings all of Tyrian tapestry :

In ivory coffers you shall stuff your crowns;
In cypress chests your arras, counterpoints,
Costly apparel, tents, and canopies,
Fine linen, Turkey cushions, boss'd with pearls,
Valance of Venice gold in needlework,
Pewter and brass, and all things that belong
To house or housekeeping.

SHAKSPEARE.

8. You 'll wed a wife of richest dower,
  Who 'll live for fashion, and you for power.

WHITTIER.

9. You 'll use up life in anxious cares,
  To lay up hoards for future years.

GAY.

10.   Such a house broke !
  So noble a master fallen ! all gone ! and not
  One friend to take your fortune by the arm,
  And go along with you.

SHAKSPEARE.

11. You 'll not be long in fortune's power:
  He that is down can fall no lower.

BUTLER.

12. You will never war with misery,
  Nor ever tug with fortune and distress.
  Have no occasion, nor no field to try,
  The strength and forces of your worthiness.

DANIEL.

13. You a base miser starve amidst your store,
  Brood o'er your gold, and griping still at more,
  Sit sadly pining, and believe you're poor.

DRYDEN.

14. Sore pierced by wintry winds,
  You 'll shrink into the sordid hut
  Of cheerless poverty.

THOMSON.

15. Condemn'd on penury's barren path to roam,
    Scorn'd by the world, and left without a home.

CAMPBELL.

16. Shortly your fortune shall be lifted higher.

SHAKSPEARE.

17. You have outrun your fortune ;
    I blame you not that you would be a beggar—
    Each to his taste.

BULWER.

18.   Think not that the good,
    The gentle deeds of mercy thou hast done,
    Shall die forgotten all ; the poor, the pris'ner,
    The fatherless, the friendless, and the widow,
    Who daily own the bounty of thy hand,
    Shall cry to heav'n, and pull a blessing on thee.

ROWE.

19. A poor man served by thee, shall make thee rich.

MISS BARRETT.

20. Your purse is very slim, and very few
      The acres that you number ;
    But you are seldom stupid, never blue ;
    Your riches are an honest heart and true,
      And quiet slumber.

E. SARGENT.

---

10. What is my Destiny?

1.   I see
    In my mind's eye, the cold and grinning Death
    Hang o'er thy head the pall.

SIR E. L. BULWER.

2.   Ambition, Love,
   The twin-born stars of daring destinies,
   Sit in your house of life.

                                        BULWER.

3. The weariest and most loathest worldly life,
   That age, ache, penury, imprisonment,
   Can lay on nature.

                                        SHAKSPEARE.

4. No medicine in the world can do thee good,
   In thee there is not half a year's life.

                                        SHAKSPEARE.

5.   To die—to sleep—
   No more—and by a sleep to end
   The heartache, and the thousand natural shocks
   That flesh is heir to.

                                        SHAKSPEARE.

6. Alone in the dark, alone on the wave,
       To buffet the storm alone,
   To struggle aghast at the wat'ry grave,
   To struggle, and feel there is none to save,
       God shield thee, helpless one!

                                MRS. E. O. SMITH.

7. You shall one day receive a traitor's judgment,
   And by that name must die.

                                        SHAKSPEARE.

8. A little breath, love, wine, ambition, fame,
   Fighting, devotion, dust—perhaps a name.

                                        BYRON.

9. Unrivall'd as thy merit, be thy fame.

                                        TICKELL.

10. Upon the next tree shalt thou hang alive;
    Till famine cling thee.

                                        SHAKSPEARE.

8

11. The death of those
       Who for their country die ;
     And oh ! be thine like their repose,
       When cold and low they lie.

MONTGOMERY.

12. Blown into atoms by a bomb, or drill'd
     Into a cullender by gunshot.

BULWER.

13. Self-murder, that infernal crime,
     Which all the gods level their thunder at !

FANE.

14.   On every nerve
     Shall deadly winter seize ; shut up sense ;
     And o'er your inmost vitals creeping cold,
     Lay you along the snows, a stiffen'd corse,
     Stretched out and bleaching in the northern blast.

THOMSON.

15. All forsaken—forgotten—forgone !
     You—a lone exile remembered of none—
     Your high aims abandoned—your good acts undone,
     Aweary of all that is under the sun—
     With that sadness of heart which no stranger may scan,
     You 'll fly to the desert afar from man.

T. PRINGLE.

16. They 'll cast you in a dungeon deep,
       Where you can neither hear nor see ;
     For seven long years they 'll keep you there,
       Till you for hunger are alike to die.

ANON.

17.   Never again
     Shall home, love, or kindred, thy wishes repay ;
     Unblessed and unhonored, down deep in the main,
       Full many a fathom, thy frame shall decay.

DIMOND.

18. They 'll bury you darkly at dead of night,
    The sod with their bayonets turning,
    By the struggling moonbeam's misty light,
    And the lantern dimly burning.

' WOLFE.

19. Thou art a slave, whom Fortune's tender arm
    With favor 'ill never clasp

SHAKSPEARE.

20. To take arms against a sea of troubles,
    And, by opposing, end them.

SHAKSPEARE.

ANSWERS TO QUESTIONS FOR LADIES.

1. Shall I marry, or live an Old Maid?

1.   Marry! no, faith; husbands are like lots in
    The lottery: you may draw forty blanks
    Before you find one that has any prize
    In him.

MARSTON.

2. You have many employments—this week you devote to study and various amusements—next week, to being married —the following week, to repentance perhaps.

BOURCICAULT

3.   The ring is on your hand,
        The wreath is on your brow;
    Satins and jewels grand,
    And many a rood of land
    Are all at your command—
        Are you not happy now?

E. A. POE.

4.   · Oh! you will find, or soon or late,
       A noble, fond, and faithful mate;
       Who, when the spring of life is gone,
       And all its blooming flowers are flown
       Will bless Old Time, who left behind
       The graces of a virtuous mind.

                                          PAULDING.

5.   The duties of a wedded life
          Hath Heaven ordained for thee.

                                          SOUTHEY.

6.   So, what I but guessed, my Mabel,
            The bird hath told at will,
          That you 're going to marry the miller,
            And live beside the mill.

                                     MRS. M. N. McDONALD.

7.   They tell me you 're promised a lover,
            My own Aramenta, next week;
          Why cannot my fancy discover
            The hue of his coat and his cheek?
          Alas! if he looks like another,
            A vicar, a banker, a beau;
          Be deaf to your father and mother,
            My own Araminta, say No!

                                          PRAED.

8.   Oh! be not coy, but use your time,
            And while ye may, go marry;
          For having lost but once your prime,
            You may forever tarry.

                                     ROBERT HERRICK.

9. You 'll dream of love, and strive to fill,
   With wild and passionate thoughts, a craving void;
   And thus you 'll wander on, half sad, half blest,
   Without a mate for the pure, lonely heart,

That, yearning, throbs within your virgin breast,
Never to find its lovely counterpart.

A. B. WELBY.

10.   You are betroth'd !
Nay, more, your marriage hour,
With all the cunning manner of your flight,
Determined of.

SHAKSPEARE.

11.   Heaven preserve you ever,
From that dull blessing—an obedient husband.

J. TOBIN.

12.   I think, to be an honest yeoman's wife
You were cut out by nature.

J. TOBIN.

13.   You 'll live a maiden dreary
For forty years and more,
And wish you had not been so coy,
When you 'd lovers by the score.

E. J. SMITH

14.   Before another twelvemonth casts
Its shadow o'er your brow,
You 'll wed the gallant sailor boy,
Who 's sighing for you now.

R. MASTERSTON.

15. They say, you shall never marry; and if to all who
pop the question, you continue answering with that chilling
monosyllable *No*, why perchance you never may.

T. H. BAYLY.

16.   Get thee to a nunnery !

SHAKSPEARE.

17.   Early next Thursday morn,
A gallant, young, and noble gentleman,
*   *   *   *   at St. Peter's church,
Shall haply make thee there a joyful bride.

SHAKSPEARE.

18. You had rather hear your dog bark at a crow, than a man swear he loves you.

SHAKSPEARE.

19.   I can't tell the date—but you 'll marry, I know,
      Just in time to have game for the feast.

T. HOOD.

20.   No, no, no, no, you never will marry !
          To be single and happy 's your plan,
      For you 'd rather lead monkeys forever,
          Than be led by that ape called a man.

SPANISH SONG, (*translation*).

——◄●►——

2. Where did, or where shall I meet my future Husband?

1.   The last time, by the lattice
          Of the great staircase.

SIR E. L. BULWER

2.   Where the moonbeam flieth
                  O'er the lone sea,
              There a sweet voice crieth,
                  I wait for thee !

SISTERS OF THE WEST

3.   The festival was high and proud,
                  The lamps were dazzling clear,
              And pealing music long and loud,
                  Rush'd on the listening ear.

SISTERS OF THE WEST.

4.   You 'll see him as the sun
              Across the western wave

Is sinking slow,
In a golden glow.

R. H. BARHAM.

5.   You will from pensive walk return,
Whether in shady woods, or pasture green,
And wait his coming at the well-known gate.

GAY.

6. He wore a brace of pistols the night when first you met,
His deep-lined brow was frowning beneath his wig of
jet;
His footsteps had the moodiness, his voice the hollow
tone,
Of a bandit-chief, who feels remorse and tears his hair
alone;
You saw him but at half-price, yet methinks you see him
now,
In the tableau of the last act, with the blood upon his
brow.

"PUNCH."

7.   You met him on the cars,
Where resignedly he sat;
His hair was full of dust,
And so was his cravat;
He was furthermore embellish'd
By a ticket in his hat.

ANON.

8.   He came across the meadow-pass,
That summer eve of eves—
The sunlight streamed along the grass,
And glanced amid the leaves;
And from the shrubbery below,
And from the garden trees,
He heard the thrush's music flow,
And humming of the bees;

The garden gate was swung apart—
  The space was brief between;
But there for throbbing of his heart,
  He paused, perforce, to lean.
He leaned upon the garden gate,
  He looked, and scarce he breathed,
Within the little porch you sate,
  With woodbine over wreathed;
Your eyes upon your work were bent,
  Unconscious who was nigh;
But oft the needle slowly went,
  And oft did idle lie;
And ever to your lips arose
  Sweet fragments, sweetly sung,
But ever, ere the notes could close,
  You hushed them on your tongue.

ANON.

9.   Go seek in the wild glen,
  Where streamlets are falling!
Go seek on the lone hill
  Where curlews are calling!
Go seek where the clear stars
  Shine down without number,
For there shall ye find him,
  Your true love, in slumber.

CUNNINGHAM.

10.   In Summer, when the days were long,
  You walked together in the wood:
Your hearts were light, your steps were strong;
  Sweet flutterings were there in your blood,
In Summer, when the days were long.

ANON.

11. On the twentieth day of August, at the feast of false
    Mahoun.

W. E. AYTOUN.

12.   You 'll meet him near
The hawthorn bush, with seats beneath the shade,
For talking age and whispering lovers made.

> GOLDSMITH.

13.   Within the sun-lit forest,
Your roof the bright blue sky,
Where fountains flow, and wild flowers blow.

> E. ELLIOTT.

14.   He has by moonlight at your window sung.

> SHAKSPEARE.

15.   'Twas on an evening bright and still,
    As ever blushed on wave and bower,
Smiling from heaven, as if naught ill
    Conld happen in so sweet an hour.

> MOORE.

16.   On a blue summer's night,
        When the stars are asleep,
        Like gems of the deep,
    In their own drowsy light.

> JOHN NEAL.

17.   His steed beside thy cottage door,
    Shall stand at sunset's hour,
And the rider's eye shall rest on thee,
    The low cot's fairest flower.
And many days shall come and go,
    And find the steed still there ;
But the rider will sit in the vine-clad porch,
    Wooing the maiden fair.

> L. COTTIN.

18. You 'll meet in the country, you 'll meet in the street,
You 'll meet where gay music invites merry feet,
You 'll meet him at eve, you 'll meet him in the day,
You 'll meet him when saddest, you 'll meet him when
    gay.

You 'll meet at the altar, your friends standing near,
You 'll give him the sole right to call you " my dear."

E. J. SMITH.

19. In the wildering waltz, in the ball-room's blaze,
In the chivalrous joust, and the daring chase,
In the swift regatta and merry race.

S. J. HALE.

20. You 'll meet by the side of a murmuring rill,
Flowing tranquilly on at the foot of a hill,
And he 'll swear by the waters, the earth, and the sky,
To love you fair maiden.

E. J. SMITH.

3. Shall I Marry my present Lover ?

1. Across the threshold led,
And every tear kiss'd off as soon as shed,
His house you 'll enter, there to be a light,
Shining within, when all without is night;
A guardian angel o'er his life presiding,
Doubling his pleasures, and his cares dividing.

ROGERS

2. He 'll straightway up, this very day,
And ask thee of thy father;
And all the blessings life can give,
In wedded life you'll gather.

MARY HOWITT

3.   Nothing shall assuage
Your love but marriage.

LILLY.

4. From this day forth in peace and joyous bliss,
You 'll live together long without debate,

Nor private jars, nor spite of enemies,
Shall shake the safe assurance of your state.

SPENSER.

5.   Your nuptial hour
Draws on apace.

SHAKSPEARE.

6. He wooed thee with his sword,
And won thy love
Bnt he will wed thee in another key,
With pomp, with triumph, and with revelling.

SHAKSPEARE.

7. No, he is fickle as the sea, as wavering as the wind,
And the restless, ever-mounting flame, is not more hard
    to bind;
If the tears you shed were tongues, yet all too few
    they 'll be,
To tell of all the treachery that he will show to thee.

BRYANT.

8. Oh yes, you 'll be his lawful wife
    Your earthly bliss shall know no measure,
Your days will be a whirl of joy,
    In a circle of endless pleasure.
And if you scold, and turn a shrew,
    He 'll bear it with resignation,
But if you will not praise his songs,
    He 'll sue for a separation.

HEINE.

9. The holy marriage vow
Shall shortly make you one.

"PUNCH."

10. On you he shall ne'er put a ring,
    So miss, it is in vain to trouble,
For you were but eighteen in spring,
    While his age exactly is double;

His figure, I grant you, will pass,
  And at present he's young enough plenty;
But when you are sixty, alas!
  Will not he be a hundred and twenty?

HALPIN.

11. He flirts with others just for fun,
  Be sure that there is nothing in it;
You are the first, the only one,
  His heart has thought of for a minute.

PRAED.

12. Ay! for you love him tenderly,
  And he in turn loves you;
With such a sameness in your hearts,
  You'll marry, or be fou.

E. J. SMITH.

13. Love on! love on! the time will come
  When he in turn will give,
His life to win one answering word
To his low question, scarcely heard,
  If he, *for you*, may live.

S. C. STURMER.

14. When it snows in August weather,
  When needles from the magnet flee;
When two Sundays come together,
  That's the time he'll marry thee.

E. J. SMITH.

15. Your coldness he heeds not,
  Your frown he'll defy,
Your affection he needs not,
  The time has gone by.

MRS. OSGOOD.

16. His love has perished like the sound that dies,
  And leaves no echo.

T. K. HERVEY.

17. He 's lo'ed thee o'er truly to seek a new dearie,
    He 's lo'ed thee o'er fondly through life e'er to weary,
    He 's lo'ed thee o'er long at last to deceive thee,
    Look cauldly or kindly, but bid him not leave thee.
MACGREGOR.

18. Forever thine ! mid fashion's heartless throng,
    In courtly bowers—at folly's gilded shrine ;
    Smiles on his cheek—light words upon his tongue— .
    His deep heart still is thine—forever thine.
A. A. WATTS.

19.   You will marry him,
    He will be every thing to you: your sympathizing
      friend,
    To teach, and help, and lead, and bless, and comfort,
      and defend ;
    He will be tender, just, and kind, unwilling to reprove,
    He will do all to bless you by his wisdom and his love.
TUPPER.

20. He never will marry, I 'll tell you the reason,
    One love at a time is all he can control ;
    And he loves *himself* so, he would think it high
      treason,
    To give any woman a share in his soul.
E. J. SMITH.

---

4. Does the Gentleman I love, love me ?

1.   It were all one,
    That you should love a bright, particular star,
    And think to wed it ; he is so above you.
SHAKSPEARE.

2 You know you love in vain, strive against hope.
SHAKSPEARE.

3. For ——, and the trifling of his favor,
　Hold it a fashion, and a toy in blood;
　A violet, in the youth of puny nature,
　Forward, not permanent—sweet, not lasting,
　The perfume and suppliance of a minute,
　No more.

SHAKSPEARE.

4. Your beauty cannot please his eye,
　So weep what's away, and weeping, die.

SHAKSPEARE.

5. 　　　　　　　He, on his side,
　Leaning, half raised, with looks of cordial love,
　Hangs over you enamored.

MILTON.

6. He, full of bashfulness and truth,
　Loves much, hopes little.

FAIRFAX.

7. Love reigns a very tyrant in his heart,
　Attended on his throne by all his guard
　Of furious wishes, fears, and nice suspicions.

OTWAY.

8. Art thou not dearer to his eyes than light?
　Dost thou not circulate thro' all his veins,
　Mingle with life, and form his very soul?

YOUNG.

9. There's not a word or look of thine,
　　His soul hath e'er forgot,
　Thou ne'er hast bid a ringlet shine,
　Nor given thy locks one graceful twine,
　　Which he remembers not.

MOORE.

10. Love is to his impassioned soul,
　　Not as with others, a mere part
　Of his existence, but the whole—
　　The very life-breath of his heart.

MOORE.

11.   To say he loves,
   Is to affirm what oft his eye avouched,
   What many an action testified, and yet
   What wanted confirmation of his tongue.

                              J. S. KNOWLES.

12.   It were not good
   You knew his love, lest you make sport at it.

                              SHAKSPEARE.

13. If thou dost love, his loving shall incite thee
   To bind your loves up in a holy band.

                              SHAKSPEARE.

14.   Do I not in plainest truth
   Tell you ————, he does not, nor he cannot love you?

                              SHAKSPEARE.

15. Thou shalt fly him, and he shall seek thy love.

                              SHAKSPEARE.

16. You dote on him, that cares not for your love.

                              SHAKSPEARE.

17.   He loves thee, sweetest,
   With a proud dotage, almost worshiping
   The idol it hath framed.

                          MISS MITFORD.

18. He never sued to friend nor enemy;
   His tongue could never learn sweet, soothing words;
   But now thy beauty is proposed his fee,
   His proud heart sues, and prompts his tongue to speak.

                              SHAKSPEARE.

19. I pray you do not fall in love with him,
   For he is falser than vows made in wine;
   Besides, he likes you not.

                              SHAKSPEARE.

20. It may be said of him, that Cupid hath clapp'd him o'
the shoulder, but I warrant him heart whole.

                              SHAKSPEARE.

5. Describe my future Husband.

1. Age sits with decent grace upon his visage,
    And worthily becomes his silver locks,
    He wears the marks of many years well spent,
    Of virtue, truth well tried, and wise experience.

    ROWE.

2. His high, broad forehead, marble fair,
        Tells of the power of thought within
    And strength is in his raven hair—
    And when he smiles, a spell is there,
        That more than strength or power can win.

    MRS. HALE.

3. His talk is like a stream which runs
        With rapid change from rocks to roses;
    He slips from politics to puns,
        Passes from Mahomet to Moses;
    Beginning with the laws that keep
        The planets in their radiant courses,
    And ending with some precept deep
        For dressing eels, or shoeing horses.

    PRAED

4. On his bold visage middle age
    Has lightly pressed his signet sage,
    Yet has not quenched the open truth,
    And fiery vehemence of youth;
    Forward and frolic glee are there,
    The will to do, the soul to dare.

    SCOTT.

5.   He has honor
        And courage; qualities that eagle-plume
        Men's souls.

    BULWER.

6. Proud is his tone, but calm; his eye
    Has that compelling dignity,

His mien, that bearing haught and high,
Which common spirits fear.

SCOTT.

7. Upon his brow shame is ashamed to sit;
For it is a throne where honor may be crown'd
Sole monarch of the universal earth.

SHAKSPEARE.

8. He's a strange enigma:
Fiery in action, and yet to glory lukewarm;
All mirth in action—in repose all gloom.

BULWER.

9. Rare compound of oddity, frolic, and fun,
He 'll relish a joke, and rejoice in a pun.

GOLDSMITH.

10   No haughty gesture marks his gait,
No pompous tone his word,
No studied attitude is seen,
No palling nonsense heard;
He 'll suit his bearing to the hour,
Laugh, listen, learn or teach,
With joyous freedom in his mirth,
And candor in his speech.

ELIZA COOK.

11.   He is more than six feet high,
And fortunate and wise;
He has a voice of melody,
And beautiful black eyes.

PRAED.

12.   'Tis much he dares;
And to that dauntless temper of his mind,
He hath a mission that doth guide his valor
To act in safety.

SHAKSPEARE.

9

13.   He hath turned
      A bitter knave of late, and lost his mirth.

                                    MISS MITFORD.

14.   A sad, wise man, of daring eye, and free
         Yet mystic speech.

                                    MISS MITFORD.

15.   He is a man of mirthful speech,
         Can many a game and gambol teach;
         Full well at tables can he play,
         And sweep, at bowls, the stake away.

                                    SCOTT.

16. His forehead by his casque worn bare,
     His thin moustache, and curly hair,
     Coal black, and grizzled here and there,
        But more through toil than age;
     His square turned-joints, and length of limb
     Show him no carpet knight so trim,
     But, in close fight, a champion grim,
        In camps, a leader sage.

                                    SCOTT.

17.   He has a noble spirit—
     The trumpet's sound did never rouse a braver.

                                    BAILLIE.

18. His hat is brush'd; his hands, with woundrous pains,
     Are cleansed from garden mould and inky stains;
     His glossy shoes confess the lackey's care;
     And recent from the comb shines his sleek hair.

                                    BARBAULD.

19.   An honest gentleman,
     And a courteous, and a kind, and a handsome,
     And, I warrant, a virtuous.

                                    SHAKSPEARE.

20. Oh! what a deal of scorn looks beautiful
     In the contempt and anger of his lip.

                                    SHAKSPEARE.

5. **Shall I be happy in my Domestic Relations?**

1.   Your home a home of happiness,
            And kindly love will be,
        And many a dwelling-place for joy
            In future still I see.

                                        NICOLL.

2.   Home, kindred, friends, and country—these,
            Are ties with which you'll never part.

                                        MONTGOMERY.

3. Scene of disunion, bickering and strife,
        A curse shall make its native blessings die,
    Sharp broils shall aye imbitter daily life,
        And cold self-interest form the strongest tie.

                                        M. F. TUPPER.

4. Let the gay and the idle go forth where they will,
    In search of soft Pleasure, that siren of ill,
    Let them seek her in Fashion's illumined saloon,
    Where Melody mocks at the heart out of tune,
    Where the laugh gushes light from the lips of the maiden,
    While her spirit perchance is with sorrow o'erladen;
    And where, mid the garland, Joy only should braid,
    Is Slander, the snake, by its rattle betray'd.
    Ah no! let the idle for Happiness roam,
    For you—you will always be happy at Home.

                                        MRS. OSGOOD.

5.   No home! No home, oh weary one!
            Thou shalt be like the dove of yore
        Who found no spot to rest upon,
            Wandering the waste of waters o'er.

                                        SISTERS OF THE WEST.

6.   You'll have a home, to quiet dear,
            Where hours untold and peaceful move.

                                        MRS. OPIE.

7. You 'll scent the air
Of blessings, when you come but near your house.

MIDDLETON.

8. Your matrimonial Cupid,
Lash'd on by time, grows tired and stupid.

PRIOR.

9. Your home is stedfast hate,
And one eternal tempest of debate.

YOUNG.

10. You will have
An elegant sufficiency, content;
Retirement, rural quiet, friendship, books,
Ease and alternate labor, useful life,
Progressive virtue, and approving heaven.

THOMSON.

11. Mutual love, the crown of all your bliss,
Awaits you.

MILTON.

12. A white-washed wall, a nicely sanded floor,
A varnished clock that clicks behind the door,
A chest contrived a double debt to pay,
A bed by night, a chest of drawers by day—
This be your home.

GOLDSMITH.

13. A wire-drawn puppet you will make
The man you marry! I suppose, ere long,
You 'll choose how often he shall walk abroad
For recreation; fix his diet for him;
Bespeak his clothes, and say on what occasions
He may put on his finest suit.

J. TOBIN.

14. You 'll be a thing
For lordly man to vent his humors on;
A dull, domestic drudge, to be abused:

"If you think so, my dear," and, "As you please;"
And "You know best"—even where he nothing knows.

J. TOBIN.

15.   Why, when they talk of you
Darby and Joan shall be no more remembered.

J. TOBIN.

16.   You will be
A patient, drudging, most obedient wife.

J. TOBIN.

17. Your husband will be dull—stupid, if you like; but then, remember, he'll have none of those ridiculous pretensions, which most men set up, to a will of his own.   That is a great point!   You can do what you like with him, if you'll only take the trouble.

J. TAYLOR.

18. As happy as a woman with a drunken husband and nine unruly children, poverty, and hard labor, can be.

OLD PLAY.

19.   Happy and gay—
Your husband a jewel,
Your children all treasures,
Every hour of your lifetime
Will bring in new pleasures
Happy and gay.

E. J. SMITH.

20. Day will open to new joys, and night close in on past pleasures.

OLD PLAY.

6. What Profession shall I follow?

1. The land of song within thee lies,
 Water'd by living springs;
The lids of fancy's sleepless eyes
Are gates unto that paradise:
Holy thoughts, like stars arise,
 Its clouds are angel's wings:
Look, then, into thy heart, and write.

LONGFELLOW.

2. Work! work! work!
 Your labor never flags;
And what are its wages?—A bed of straw—
 A crust of bread—and rags.
That shattered roof—and this naked floor—
 A table—a broken chair—
And a wall so blank your shadow you thank,
 For sometimes falling there.

Work—work—work—
 From weary chime to chime;
Work—work—work—
 As prisoners work for crime!
Band, and gusset, and seam,
 Seam, and gusset, and band—
Till the heart is sick and the brain benumbed,
 As well as the weary hand.

T HOOD.

3. Thy hand is well skilled
 To touch with fairy fingers,
The harpsichord with music filled,
 As o'er it beauty lingers.

KEESE.

4. You'll feed your poultry and your hogs!
And when you stir abroad on great occasions,
Carry a squeaking tithe pig to the vicar;

Or jolt with higgler's wives the market trot,
To sell your eggs and butter !

J. TOBIN.

5. A milliner, earning your daily bread
    By adjustments of feather and bow,
And trying each bonnet on your own head,
    With a simper upon your lovely face,
    Will say to each one, with smiling grace—
"There, is it not pretty, just so !"

E. J. SMITH.

6. Your daily occupation, to inspect the dairy, superintend the poultry, make extracts from the family receipt-book, and comb your Aunt Deborah's lap-dog.

R. B. SHERIDAN.

7. There's genteel comedy in your walk and manner, juvenile tragedy in your eye, and touch-and-go farce in your laugh.

DICKENS.

8. Superintend the samplers and spelling-books two counties off.

MISS MITFORD.

9. A little shopwoman, not much taller than a china mandarin, remarkable for the height of your comb, and the length of your ear-rings.

MISS MITFORD.

10. You are a learned lady, famed
    For every branch of every science known.

BYRON.

11. You'll stitch ! stitch ! stitch !
    In poverty, hunger, and dirt ;
And still in a voice of dolorous pitch,
    You'll sing the song of the shirt.

HOOD.

12. An author! 'Tis a venerable name!
How few deserve it, and what numbers claim!
Yo

13. 'Tis a strange calling for a woman! You'll keep a store to open oysters, deal out small beer, and sell tobacco.
OLD PLAY.

14. With weary fingers and aching head,
You'll make fine dresses for a crust of bread.
E. J. SMITH.

'15. You'll live, for you were born to rule,
The mistress of a public school;
Teach every grace the arduous place demands,
And when a scholar's naughty, tie his hands.
MATTERN.

16. All the profession you will ever be called upon to move in, will be professions of love and duty to your husband.
OLD PLAY.

17.   Landlady of a bustling inn,
You'll govern all the household well.
E. J. SMITH.

18. Is music a fine art? You'll doubt it ere long,
When harkening to music banged out of all tune,
By pupils who literally *screeching* a song,
Make you wish in your anguish to fly to the moon.
SPARSET.

19.   Over a tub of hot soap-suds,
You'll stand and scrub all day,
Getting up ladies' and gentlemen's "duds"
In the whitest and smoothest way.
E. J. SMITH.

20.   A *cantatrice*—men will bow
Before your beauty's shrine,
And drawn by melody's sweet power,
Applaud from clime to clime.
METTIER.

8. What Misfortunes await Me?

1. Thy heart, wrung by sorrow, and outraged by those it
has loved, will perish beneath the torture; or, as a resource,
will petrify beneath the dripping well of life.

MRS. ELLIS.

2.   The pangs of despised love, the law's delay.

SHAKSPEARE.

3.   By foreign hands thy dying eyes be closed,
     By foreign hands thy decent limbs composed,
     By foreign hands thy humble grave adorned,
     By strangers honor'd, but by friends unmourn'd.

POPE.

4.   Voice after voice shall die away,
          Once in thy dwelling heard;
       Sweet household name by name shall change,
          To grief's forbidden word.

MRS. HEMANS.

5   See a hand now pass before thee,
          Pointing to *his* drunken sleep,
       To thy widow'd marriage pillows,
          To the tears that thou shalt weep.

TENNYSON.

6.   An exile, all in heart and frame,—
          A wanderer, weary of the way;
       A stranger, without love's sweet claim,
          On any heart, go where you may.

MRS. OSGOOD.

7.   O agony! keen agony!
          Your trusting heart shall find
       That vows believed, were vows conceived
          As light as summer wind.

MOTHERWELL.

8.   Ah ! doom'd indeed to worse than Death,
       To teach those sweet lips hourly guile ;
     To breathe through life but falsehood's breath,
       And smile with falsehood's smile.

                                    MRS. OSGOOD.

9.   A secret, that will haunt thee, as of old
       Men were possess'd of fiends.

                                    BULWER.

10.   Slander !
     Whose edge is sharper than the sword ; whose tongue
     Out-venoms all the worms of Nile ; whose breath
     Rides on the posting winds, and doth belie
     All corners of the world.

                                    SHAKSPEARE.

11.   The broken heart, which kindness never heals ;
        The home-sick passion.

                                    MONTGOMERY.

12.   In a moment, look to see
     The blind and bloody soldier, with foul hand
     Defile the locks of your still shrieking daughter ;
     Your father taken by his silver beard,
     And his most reverend head dash'd to the wall.

                                    SHAKSPEARE

13.   Sorrow worn and pale,
      Those sunken cheeks beneath a widow's vail ;
      Alone you 'll wander where with *him* you 've trod,
      No arm to stay you.

                                    O. W. HOLMES

14.   Thou shalt have cramps,
        Side stitches that shall pen thy breath up.

                                    SHAKSPEARE.

15.   You 'll be so lean, that blasts of January
        Will blow you through and through.

                                    SHAKSPEARE.

16.   Decay's effacing fingers
         Shall sweep the lines where beauty lingers

                                        BYRON.

17.   To lose hope, care not for the coming thing.

                                        BAILEY.

18.   Thou art wedded to calamity.

                                        SHAKSPEARE.

19.   Banishment to that grave
      Of human ties, where hearts congeal to ice,
      In the dark convents of everlasting winter.

                                        BULWER.

20.   It is not that your lot is low
            That makes the silent tear to flow;
            It is not grief that bids you moan.
            It is that you are all alone.

                                        H. K. WHITE.

9. Shall I be Rich or Poor?

1.   Thou shalt have a dowry, girl, to buy
         Thy mate amid the mightiest.

                                        BULWER.

2.   Famine be in thy cheeks,
         Need and oppression staring in thine eyes,
         Upon thy back hang ragged misery.

                                        SHAKSPEARE.

3.   A middle state,
         Neither too humble nor too great;
         More than enough for nature's ends,
         With something left to treat your friends.

                                        MALLET

4. You, wretched matron, forced in age, for bread,
      To strip the brook with mantling cresses spread,

To pick your wintry fagot from the thorn,
To seek your nightly shed, and weep till morn.

GOLDSMITH.

5. A home in the mansions of pride,
Where marble shines out in the pillars and walls.

ELIZA COOK.

6. Two thousand ducats by the year,
Of fruitful land, all which shall be your jointure.

SHAKSPEARE.

7. You on silver floors shall tread,
With bright Assyrian carpets o'er them spread,
To hide the metal's poverty;
You shall look up to roofs of gold,
And naught around you shall behold
But silk and rich embroidery,
And Babylonish tapestry,
And wealthy Hiram's princely dye;
And Ophir's starry stones meet everywhere your eye.

COWLEY.

8. You 'll have
A noble house and splendid equipage,
Diamonds and pearls, and gilded furniture.

J. TOBIN.

9. Near some fair bower you 'll have a private seat,
Built uniform, not little or too great;
It shall within no other things contain
But what is useful, necessary, plain;
A little garden, grateful to the eye,
While a cool rivulet runs murmuring by.

POMFRET.

10. A better cellar nowhere can be found;
The pantry never is without baked meat,
And fish and flesh, so plenteous and complete
It snows within your house of meat and drink,
Of all the dainties that a man can think.

CHAUCER.

11.   You 'll have never a penny left in your purse,
           Never a penny but three;
       And one is brass, and another is lead,
           And another is white money.

PERCY'S RELIQUES.

12.   Your crown is in your heart, not on your head;
       Not deck'd with diamonds, and Indian stones,
       Nor to be seen: your crown is called Content.

SHAKSPEARE.

13.   You 'll know full well the scanty meal,
           With small, pale faces round;
       No fire upon the cold, damp hearth,
           When snow is on the ground.

L. E. L.

14. Of Nature's gifts thou may'st with lilies boast,
     And with the half-blown rose; but Fortune, O!
     She is corrupted, changed, and won from thee,

SHAKSPEARE.

15.   You 'll own
       Sofas, 'twere half a sin to sit upon
       So costly are they; carpets, every stitch
       Of workmanship so rare, they 'll make you wish
       You could glide o'er them like a golden fish.

BYRON.

16. High built abundance, heap on heap.

YOUNG

17.   Your means shall lie
       Too low for envy, for contempt too high.

COWLEY.

18.   Fair child of poverty! Your only dower
       Is your transcendant beauty, and the gift
       Which nature throws but seldom in a vase
       Of such exquisite workmanship—a heart.

MRS. SCOTT

19. Horses and serving men thou shalt have,
     With sumptuous array, most gallant and brave.

                              PERCY'S RELIQUES.

20. Your riches shall weigh you down with their abundance ; yet illness and peevishness shall make you poorer than
the meanest peasant.

                              OLD PLAY.

----◄●►----

10. What is my Destiny?

1.   To die—to sleep—
        To sleep ! perchance to dream !

                              SHAKSPEARE.

2.   Happiness courts thee in her best array.

                              SHAKSPEARE.

3. You have many goodly days to see ;
    The liquid drops of tears that you have shed,
    Shall come again, transform'd to Orient pearls,
    Advantaging their loan with interest,
    Oftentimes double gain of happiness.

                              SHAKSPEARE.

4. You shall have ease, you shall have health,
        You shall have spirits light as air ;
    And more than wisdom, more than wealth—
        A merry heart that laughs at care.

                              MILMAN

5. Your joys, like men in crowds, press on so fast,
    They stop by their own numbers and their haste.

                              HOWARD.

6. After long storms and tempests overblown,
    The sun at length his joyous face shall clear.

                              SPENSER.

7.   Your wretched brain gives way,
And you 'll become a wreck at random driven,
Without one glimpse of reason or of heaven.

MOORE.

8.   O ! snatched away in beauty's bloom,
On thee shall press no ponderous tomb;
But on thy turf shall roses rear
Their leaves, the earliest of the year;
And the wild cypress wave in tender gloom.

BYRON.

9.   Alas, pretty maiden,
    What sorrows attend you !
I see you sit shivering,
    With lights at your window;
But long may you wait
    Ere your arms may enclose him;
For still, still he lies
    With a wreath on his bosom !
Far, far on yon wild,
    Where the dead tapers hover,
There, cold, cold and wan,
    Lies the corpse of your lover.

HOGG

10.   The world is cruel—the world is untrue;
Your foes will be many—your friends but few;
No work, no bread, however you sue !

BARRY CORNWALL.

11.   Eagerly you 'll wish the morrow,
Vainly shall you try to borrow
From your books surcease of sorrow.

POE.

12.   A mind at peace with all below,
    A heart whose love is innocent.

BYRON.

13.   All comfort go with thee.

SHAKSPEARE.

14. One woe shall tread upon another's heels,
So fast they follow.

SHAKSPEARE.

15. Coldly to yourself sufficing,
  You'll disdain the gentle arts,
Never know the bliss arising
  From an interchange of hearts.
Slowly from your bosom stealing,
  Flows the selfish current on,
Till by age's frost congealing,
  It will harden into stone.

SCHILLER.

16. No care or grief shall wave
  Its cold and blighting pinions o'er you,
For love shall guard thy spirit's hope,
  Till heaven dawn before you.

MRS. OSGOOD.

17.   Grief will
Have power to change the pulses of thy heart
To one dull throb of ceaseless agony,
To hush the sigh on thy resigned lip,
And lock it in the heart.

MATURIN.

18. Thy happy soul shall all the way
  To heaven have a summer's day.

CRASHAW.

19. Faint not! though on thy onward way
  Griefs rise to greet thee, day by day,
  Sorrows may come, but hourly rise
  Hopes of pure joy beyond the skies.

E. J. SMITH.

20. Your life shall be as it has been,
  A sweet variety of joys.

R. H. WILDE.

PANTOMIME CHARADES;

OR,

CHARADES IN ACTION.

INTRODUCTION.

THE French have made themselves singularly famous by
their "*petits jeux*" as they call them. Their inability to sit
still for more than half an hour has forced them to invent a
long list of amusing excuses for locomotion. They have
their "*Pigeon Vole*," and "*Main Chaude*" or "*Berlingue*,"
and "*Chiquette*," and a thousand other receipts for making
a long evening short.

But the most celebrated of all these *petits jeux*, are their
"*Charades en Action.*" *Pigeon Vole*, and all the rest, have
given way to these Acting Charades.   No birth-day is allowed
to pass without playing at them. The young and the old
both delight in the game ; and invariably choose it. The old
people lay aside their dignity with a look of jovial martyr-
dom, and laugh more than any one else ; whilst—as if to
apolgize for their apparently unbecoming levity—they tell
you "they do like to see young people enjoying themselves."

Some persons have even acquired a kind of reputation as
Charade actors, and are in such request that invitations

shower down from all quarters; and if they can only be engaged, it is looked upon as a kind of a certificate that the party is sure to be a good one.

Lately, the game has been introduced into the drawing-rooms of a few mirth-loving Englishmen. Its success has been tremendous. Cards have been discarded; and blind-man's buff, forfeits, and hunting the ring, been utterly abandoned. On Christmas-day, it has been looked forward to, and entered into with as much energy as the sainted plum-pudding itself. We have seen it played among literary circles with unbounded mirth. We have seen philosophers and poets either acting their parts with all the enthusiasm of school-boys, or puzzling their brains to find out how they could dress as Henry VIII., with only a great coat and a " gibbus "

This game is, as its name expresses it, a Charade, acted instead of spoken. The two most celebrated performers of the party choose "their sides," and, whilst the one group enacts the Charade, the other plays the part of audience. A word is then fixed upon by the *corps dramatique ;* and "my first, my second, and my whole" is gone through as puzzlingly as possible in dumb show, each division making a separate and entire act. At the conclusion of the drama, the guessing begins on the part of the audience. If they are successful, they in their turn perform; if not, they still remain as audience.

The great rule to be observed in Acting Charades, is—silence. Nothing more than an exclamation is allowed. All the rest must be done in the purest pantomime.

If, in the working out of the plot, there should be some sentence that it is impossible to express in dumb-show, and yet must be made clear to the audience, then, placards may be used. As Hamlet says, they must "speak by the card."

The license may also be taken advantage of in the scenic department. For instance, it would be utterly impossible for the audience to know that the drawing-room wall before them is meant to represent a "magnificent view on the Rhine," or "the Wood of Ardennes by moonlight," unless some slight hint to that effect is dropped beforehand. In this case it is better to follow the plan so much in vogue about Queen Elizabeth's time, and which, for simplicity and cheapness, has never been surpassed. At the commencement of each act, hang against the wall a placard stating the scene that ought to be represented.

The audiences now-a-days are no doubt quite as accommodating as in the sixteenth century. Then, the same curtain that had served for "Ye pavelyon of Kinge Richarde," could, in the waving of a placard, be changed into "Ye feildes of Bosworthe;" and, there is no doubt but that in these days, a fashionable drawing-room assembly would believe any thing you could tell them.

By this simple method, the most expensive scenery can be commanded at any time. The palaces can be golden without any additional cost, and lakes can be fairy-like at a moment's notice. There is also this advantage—as each spectator will be his own scene-painter, the views are sure of giving general satisfaction.

Another very important point with Acting Charades is the proper delivery of the gestures in the pantomimic readings of the parts. Every actor ought to study the different expressions and suitable actions of the passions. So much depends upon this, that under these circumstances, perhaps it would be better to draw up a kind of code of expressions, or laws for the better regulation of frowns, smiles, and gestures.

Love, one would think, is too well known to require many directions. The pressing of the left side of the waistcoat or the book-muslin, the tender look at the ceiling, and the gentle and elegant swinging of the body, have, since the days of Vestris, always accompanied the declaration of a true devotion in the upright and dumb individual. The flame may, perhaps, be made a little more devouring by the kissing of a miniature, or the embracing of a well-oiled ringlet or figure-of-six curl.

RAGE, like a mean husband, can only be managed by fits and starts. It may be, pictured to an almost maddening amount by the frequent stamping of the foot, and the shaking of the fist. Frowning, and grinding of teeth, should be accompanied by opening the eyes to their greatest possible size; and, if a great effect is desired to be produced, the room may be paced, provided the legs of the performer are of a sufficient length to enable him to take the entire length of the apartment in three or four strides.

In DESPAIR the action is slightly altered; there, the limbs must almost seem to have lost their power. The actor must sink into a chair, pass his hands through his hair, with his five fingers spread open, like a bunch of carrots, or else, letting his arms fall down by his side, remain perfectly still—like a little boy on a frosty day—either gazing at his boots or the ceiling. Despair is made more tragic by a slight laugh, but this must only be attempted by the very best tragedians, on the principle that laughter, like the measles, is very catching.

HOPE, like a sovereign sent by post, is seldom properly delivered. Here there must be no violent gestures—every thing must be soft and pleasant. The finger must be occasionally raised to the ear, and the performer's countenance wear a bright smile and a look of deep intensity, as if listening to the soft, still voice within. The ceiling may be looked at frequently, and the bosom pressed; but, if great care is not taken, and the hands are not frequently clasped at arm's length, the audience will be imagining you are in love — and in a state of love, of course, one is quite hopeless.

DISDAIN is perhaps the easiest passion to be expressed. The dignified waiving of the hand, and the scornful look, gradually descending from top to toe, are well known to all who have been mistaken for waiters at evening parties. The eyes should be partly closed, the nose, if possible, turned up, the lips curved, and the countenance gently raised to the ceiling.

If any embracing should be required in the course of the piece, it is—under the present arbitrary laws of society and mothers—better to leave this interesting process to husbands and wives.

The effect, from the sheer novelty of the situation, will be startling. If they should refuse, the old theatrical plan should be resorted to—press heads over each other's shoulders, and look down each other's backs.

Many pieces conclude with a blessing. This is simply done by raising both the hands over the heads of the kneeling couple; look steadily at the ceiling till the eyes begin to water, and move the lips slowly, as if muttering. At the conclusion, the tear can be dashed away, and always has a very pretty effect. Weeping is generally performed by burying the face in the handkerchief, bending the head to the breast, and nodding it violently.

The great difficulty to be overcome in Acting Charades is the absence of a theatrical wardrobe. Very often it is necessary to dress as a Roman, a Persian, or a Turk. Sometimes an ancient knight is wanted in full armor. We have known Louis XIV. called for in a full court dress, and only five minutes allowed for the toilet. In all these trials the mind must be exerted with high-pressure ingenuity. The most prominent characteristic of the costume must be seized and represented. In the Roman, a sheet will do for a toga;

in the knight, the coal-scuttle for helmet, and the dish-cover
for breast-plate, make capital armor; and in Louis XVI., the.
ermine victorine wig, for well-powdered peruke, and the dressing-gown for embroidered coat, would express pretty well the
desired costume.

Great coats, vails, whips, walking-sticks, aprons, caps, and
gowns, must be seized upon and used in the dressing-up of
the characters. No expense should be spared, and every sacrifice be made, even though the incidents of the piece should
include the upsetting of a tray of tea-things, or the blacking
of all the young ladies' faces.

COURTSHIP.

ACT I.

COURT—

DRAMATIS PERSONÆ.

Lord Chief Justice.	Counsel.
Prisoner (*a Sailor*).	Eight Ladies (*his Wives*).
Jurymen. Policemen.	Spectators. &c.

Time—*before Supper-time.*

Scene—*A Court of Justice. At back of Drawing-room the Lord Chief-Justice's easy-chair, and ottoman for Counsel. To the right, sofa for Jurymen. To the left, fire-screen for Prisoner's dock.*

Flourish of splendidly-imitated trumpets. Enter procession in following order:—The Usher, holding the carpet-

broom of office; his Honor, robed in gorgeous dressing-gown, and wearing a magnificent wig of ermine victorine; the Counsel, carrying carpet-bags, holding briefs of music, and properly wigged with night-caps; the wretched Sailor, who stands charged with the dreadful crime of polygamy, in the close custody of the Jailer, bearing the street-door key of office, and endeavoring to restrain his prisoner from dancing the hornpipe.*

As soon as Prisoner is safely secured behind fire-screen, he again breaks out in a hornpipe, when

---

* Unfortunately for the pantomimic art, the hornpipe is the only means left for proving that a gentleman in black continuations is a sailor.

Enter the eight PLAINTIFFS (ladies whom the inconstant Prisoner has respectively married in the several ports he has visited). They are natives of various countries, and dressed in their different national costumes.

At sight of the vile sailor they are deeply moved, and intimate a strong desire to get at him.

Enter JURYMEN, who are immediately packed into the sofa.

Counsel for prosecution, in the most electrifying dumb show, proves, by pointing and frowning at Prisoner, who is still dancing, what a villain the man is.  He shows the validity of each marriage by putting an imaginary ring on the third finger; and having referred to the case of "LACHI DAREM—in RE DON GIOVANNI," *Italian Duets*, Vol. II., demands, by a thump on the ottoman, that the scoundrel should be punished with the utmost rigor of the law.

 Judge, putting on the black hat, proceeds to pass sentence of death on the wretched Prisoner, who evinces the utmost callousness by doing the split in the hornpipe.

The Wives no sooner hear their joint Husband's doom, than an affectionate rush is made toward him, which the wretched man perceiving, he seeks safety in flight.

TABLEAU.

ACT II.

—SHIP.

DRAMATIS PERSONÆ.

CAPTAIN.   SAILORS.   PASSENGERS.   &c.

SCENE—*The deck of that fast-sailing craft, the Front Drawing-room.*

Enter CAPTAIN, with noble cocked-hat, made out of yester-day's newspaper, and hair-brushes for epaulettes.   He shouts through a set of quad-rilles when 

Enter several tight lads, who proceed to the music-stool to heave at the capstan and weigh the imaginary anchor : whilst others pulley-oi at the larboard bell-rope to let out gallant maintop ceiling.   Two more brave  boys take the wheel, and, by means of the arm-chair, steer the room beautifully. 

PASSENGERS on after-ottoman now begin, by wild gesticulations—the turning up of eyes, and the sudden application of handkerchiefs—to intimate that they have passed out to sea whilst others, leaning over the backs of their chairs, implore their neighbors, in the most affect-ing pantomime, to throw  them overboard.

Enter STEWARD with basins, at which the passengers make a simultaneous rush.   He also enables several poor creatures —who are walking about in the most extraordinary manner, and rolling from side to side of drawing-room—to reach their berths

Presently a fearful storm is supposed to arise. The Passengers, binding life-preservers of comforters round their waists, jump hurriedly from their berths, and, springing over the sides of the ship, strike out for the door, where *exeunt omnes*.

ACT III.

COURTSHIP.

DRAMATIS PERSONÆ.

OLD FATHER.   HIS DAUGHTER.   HER LOVER.
RETAINERS.   LAWYER.   &c. &c.

SCENE—*Apartment in mansion of Old Father.*

Enter DAUGHTER, who shows, by pressing her side and swinging about, that she is deeply in love. She commences laying a table for two, and, having set down a lovely round of cold bandbox, she again expresses her fondest devotion for one of the knives and forks.

Sweet plaintive sounds of a splendidly-executed whistle are heard without. She claps her hands, and

Enter LOVER in full uniform of the new police, richly silvered with chalk. He glances anxiously at the cold round of bandbox, and then gives vent to the wildest movements of joy. They advance to table, and feast commences. Just as he has helped himself to the lid, a loud and continued knocking is heard without. They become agitated; and Lover, endeavoring to avoid an angry parent's just wrath, seizes some bread, and plunges beneath table.

Enter OLD FATHER, suffering acutely from an attack of suppositious gout, and forced to use brooms whilst walking. He expresses his surprise at banquet, but is pleased when he learns it was intended for him. Lov-er, growing tired of bread, endeavors to snatch some meat off his angel's plate. Old Father alarmed on seeing the mysterious hand, and jumping from his seat, drags Lover from under the table. Grand exposure. He is about to curse the villain, when

Enter LAWYER with placard announcing that the scoundrel has just come into a coronetcy and £2,000,000. He crowns him with a ducal meat cover. Old Father relents, and blesses his children. Retainers and maid of all work rush in, and arrange themselves into the subjoined

GRAND TABLEAU.

FIREWORKS.

ACT I.

FIRE—

DRAMATIS PERSONÆ.

A LADY.   PARISH BEADLE.   TURN-COCK.   LITTLE BOYS.

SCENE.—*Outside of Lady's house.*

ENTER LITTLE BOYS, with paper frills round necks and long pinafores on. They begin dancing about, and pointing to ceiling in the direction of Lady's house, to intimate that the kitchen chimney is on fire.

Enter LADY in great state of alarm at the cries of "Fire." She looks up, and then exit Lady rapidly.

Enter PARISH BEADLE in his full uniform, wearing a lady's colored traveling cloak for coat, and the footman's gold lace band on his hat. In his hand he carries the man-servant's tall walking-stick.

Enter troop of LITTLE BOYS and GIRLS, in pinafores and frills, dragging by a comforter the music Canterbury for the parish engine.

Enter TURN-COCK, who turns on the water, at an imaginary plug, with the kitchen poker. Beadle and Turn-cock then advance to the door of Lady's house, and keep giving single knocks, but nobody will answer. Little Boys and Girls keep jumping about all the time, and putting their hands up to the sides of their mouths, as if they were shouting fire.

Enter Lady's head through half-opened door. Turn-cock demands his fee, and Beadle requests that he may be paid the expenses of bringing out the parish engine. Lady refuses to pay them. Turn-cock points to the palm of his hand several times in an energetic manner, but the Lady will not listen

to him, and keeps shaking her head.   Beadle attempts to enter, when Lady closes the door violently.

They, with much ceremony, take the number of the house, and exit Beadle and Turn-cock, followed by parish engine and Little Boys and Girls dancing.

ACT II.
—WORKS.

DRAMATIS PERSONÆ.

TAILORS.   BOOTMAKERS.   CARPENTERS.   MILLINERS.
DRESSMAKERS.   LADIES AND GENTLEMAN.

SCENE—*A large work-room.*

Enter TAILORS, who seat themselves cross-legged upon the

ottoman, and begin work-
ing at coats and waist-
coats, cutting out patterns
with the tongs for shears,
and ironing their work with a flat-iron for goose.

Enter BOOTMAKERS, who begin re-
pairing boots, putting the ends through
à la mode des cobblers, whilst others
hammer away at the soles, and some
cut out shapes on the pasteboard with
a table-knife.

Enter MILLINERS, who arrange bonnets
on umbrella-stand in supposed window,
whilst the DRESSMAKERS gather round,
and all of them begin working at the
same *robe*.

Enter CARPENTERS, who commence repairing a chair, whilst others are French polishing the boudoir.

Enter LADIES and GENTLEMAN.   The Ladies advance to the Milliners, and hold up their hands in admiration of the

bonnets in the hat-stand.   They try them on before the glass.
Others hand to the Dressmakers brown parcels of silks they
have brought with them, and describe by their actions the
exact style in which they wish them to be made up.   The
Gentleman requests the Tailor to show him his patterns, and
minutely examines a panorama of London that is held up
before him.   He fixes upon one, and desires to be measured.
Next he patronizes the Bootmaker, and is shown some Wellingtons, which he forthwith purchases.

The Carpenter also disposes of his chair, and a bargain is
struck for the boudoir.

Exit Ladies and Gentleman, followed by Tailors, Bootmakers, Milliners, and Carpenters, who bow them out into the
passage.

ACT III.

FIREWORKS.

DRAMATIS PERSONÆ.

Ladies and Gentlemen.   Waiters, &c.

Scene—*Vauxhall Gardens on a gala night.   At the end, window curtains
arranged as seats with table.   The countless lamps, statues, with fountains, and grottoes can only be imagined and not described.*

Enter Ladies and Gen-
tlemen, who walk about
the gardens with umbrel-
las up, whilst others seat
themselves under window
curtains.

Enter Waiters with dishes and glasses, which they place
on table bower of window curtains.

Suddenly a bell is heard to ring violently in the passage, by means of the tongs and the poker, and the ladies and gentlemen, with their umbrellas still up, form themselves in a ring round the door.

Then the well-imitated ascent of a rocket is heard ush-h-h-ee-ing without, and the crowd, looking toward the ceiling,

cry, 'Oh! oh! oh!' which is followed with a loud bang! This is repeated several times, until at last the quick succession of ohs! and bangs! tell that the grand display of rockets has gone off, and the Ladies and Gentlemen make for the door as quickly as possible.

BLACKGUARD.

ACT I.

BLACK—

DRAMATIS PERSONÆ.

ELDERLY BACHELOR. YOUNG WAGS.

SCENE 1—*Second floor back of elderly Bachelor.*

Enter ELDERLY BACHELOR, who seats himself in arm-chair, and commences reading *Sunday Times.* He turns to the advertisements, and reads intently. Suddenly he jumps up, and kisses the second column of the advertisements, then presses it to his heart, and, in impassioned dumb-show, informs the audience that he must hasten to meet some one in the passage, and, by holding his clasped hands toward the ceiling, intimates that he will force her to accept his love. He snatches up a pen, and writes a letter. Having folded it up, he seizes his hat and umbrella, and rushes forth.

SCENE 2—Waterloo Bridge by night.

Enter Young Wags with the letter written by Elderly Bachelor. Whilst one of them pretends to read it, the others lean one ear forward to show they are listening attentively; and, by holding their sides, intimate that they enjoy the contents marvellously.

Suddenly they point to the door to tell that the Bachelor is coming, and one of them runs out, whilst the others all retire behind the window curtains.

Re-enter Young Wag with friend dressed in a lady's gown, and a thick vail thrown over her head. The Young Wag also retires behind curtains, leaving Young Lady alone.

Enter Elderly Bachelor. He sees the Lady, presses his heart, and points toward her. She lets fall her pocket-handkerchief as a signal. Then elderly bachelor rushes toward her, and falling on his knees, declares his passion. Giggling heard behind window-curtains. He leads her to ottoman, and prevails upon her to be seated. He offers her his hand and well-filled purse. She consents. He then begs of her to show him her face. She refuses, but he pleads so earnestly that at last she is persuaded. On lifting the vail, he falls back in horror at finding she is—black. Wags rush out.

ACT II.
—GUARD.

DRAMATIS PERSONÆ.

HORSE-GUARD.   HIS CHARGER.   YOUNG LADIES AND OLD LADIES.

SCENE.—*The exterior of the Horse-Guards, with stall under window-pole for Guard and his Charger on duty.   The clock seen on the mantel-piece in the distance.*

A trumpet is heard, when enter GUARD, mounted on the back of his gallant CHARGER, which he guides to the sentry stall under window.   On his head is his helmet,* and on his shoulders are hair-brush epaulettes ; on his breast he wears a bright dish-cover cuirass, and his moustache is of the finest burnt cork, or bird's-eye tobacco.

No sooner has he taken his post than

Enter several LADIES, who gather round Guard.   Some of them express their admiration of his beautiful eyes ; others, in their love for him, stand for minutes with clasped hands, and intimate by their gestures that they are suffering from acute sideache.   Every moment the crowd round stall in-creases, and the last arrivals dart angry glances at the early comers.   The Guard smiles graciously at all, but in particular to an OLD LADY with a well-filled purse hanging from her arm.

Trumpet heard in distant passage, and exit Guard on his Charger.

Re-enter Guard.   The Ladies crowd round him.   Some

---

* The very best imitation helmet that can be made is the coal-scuttle. Some people object to it, and prefer the water-can; but it's nothing to the coal-scuttle.

present him with screws of full-flavored tobacco. He is gracious to those who give him any thing, but, above all, his admiration is riveted on Old Lady with heavy purse. The others perceiving that, despite their presents, he slights their love, grow jealous of Old Lady, each moment becoming more and more violent, and gathering menacingly round Guard.

At last enter small battalion of Guards, who try to disperse the small mob; but in vain. An imaginary Magistrate makes his appearance. He pretends to read the riot act from a piece of music, but without effect; the Ladies still cling to the Life-guardsman. At length, the Magistrate, by well-expressed gesticulations, directs the soldiers to present walking-sticks. They do so. At sight of this the Ladies scream, and run off in all directions.

ACT III.

BLACKGUARD.

DRAMATIS PERSONÆ.

Omnibus Conductor.   His Rival.   Old Lady and Family.
               Mob.   Policeman.

Scene—*Charing Cross. To the right are seen two of the opposition Conveyance Association Sofas, waiting, on their way to Bank, for passengers.*

Enter Omnibus Conductor and His Rival in great-

coats, and comforters round necks. On their breasts they wear their saucepan-lid badges. They each mount their sofas, and, holding up their fore-fingers, lean forward *à la Taglioni*, hailing the distant passers-by. Every now and then they turn round and shake their fists at each other, putting themselves into the much-admired attitudes of street disputants.

Enter OLD LADY and FAMILY of four sweet children in

great hurry, and all holding up their fingers to stop omnibus. The Conductor and His Rival descend, when a violent struggle to possess the fares takes place. Two of the children are carried kicking to one sofa, and two are thrust into the other, whilst Old Lady wrings her hands, and by her action intimates she is calling Police. The Conductor and His Rival return to Old Lady. Each seizes an arm, and endeavors to drag her to his omnibus. Old Lady resists, expressing the strongest indignation. All the time the men are abusing one another, and each insisting, in violent gesticulation, that the Lady called him first. At last one drags away her shawl, and the other her bag.

MOB gathers round, and insist on Conductor and His Rival "letting the Lady alone."

Enter POLICEMAN, who immediately releases Old Lady, liberates kicking family, and takes the numbers of Conductor and His Rival.

The Lady expresses great gratitude to the Policeman, and takes an ivory card-counter from her purse to give to him. Policeman turns his head away.

------◄●►------

MISCHIEF.

ACT I.

MISS—

DRAMATIS PERSONÆ.

OLD LORD.   ARCHERS.   MUSICIANS.   SERVANTS.   &c.

SCENE—*Splendid Turkey carpet lawn, surrounded by magnificently veneered woods. In the distance is seen (the music) Canterbury. At one end of scene, the window curtains pitched as tents. Chairs for Visitors.*

Enter OLD LORD, surrounded by SERVANTS, who cheer him. On his breast he wears the star of the oyster scallop.

Enter MUSICIANS, who forthwith commence tuning their bellows, and ascending the chromatic scale on their pokers-a-piston. (*Soft music.*)

Enter LADIES and GENTLEMEN, as merry foresters — the

Ladies with pea-jackets over their dresses, and large, bulgy umbrellas slung at back for quivers; the Gentlemen with their collars turned down, and their what-do-ye-call-'ems tuckered up above their Wellingtons; in their hands they carry their unstrung whips for bows. The Visitors are graciously received by the Old

Lord, who exhibits to them the splendid bright poker they are to contend for. (*Soft music.*)

Enter Servants, who arrange the loo-table as the target.*

The archery commences in a most spirited manner, the barbed walking-stick darting from the twanging whip as fast and as far as it is possible to throw it. Not one can hit the bull's-eye of the loo-table. At last the Old Lord takes his whip. All look on with anxiety. He shoots, and the sound of broken glass tells that the arrow has smashed the conservatory. All laugh, and call upon the only remaining Young Lady to show her skill. She advances, rebuking them for their want of talent. As she draws her walking-stick from its umbrella, betting begins. She takes her aim and fires, and immediately a piercing scream is heard from Old Lord,

who has been looking on, and who rushes about, holding up to his face the Young Lady's arrow, which, by some mistake, has hit his eye instead of the bull's. (*Soft music.*)

* Many ladies may object to have their loo-tables made targets of; but they should remember that the whole point of this Act lies in nobody hitting the mark.

ACT II.

—CHIEF.

DRAMATIS PERSONÆ.

OLD FATHER.   HIS DAUGHTER.
THE BRIGAND CHIEF.
BRIGANDS.   POSTBOY.   BRIGAND'S WIVES.

SCENE—*Imaginary cave, a little to the south of Rome.   The fearful roar of a neighboring water-fall is supposed to be heard.*

Enter BRIGANDS, who place their loaded brooms against the wall, and casting themselves on the floor, forthwith commence gambling with flour-dredging dice-box.

Enter WIVES in Italian costume, with flat napkins on their heads.   Some begin working with their distaffs of umbrellas, whilst others hand round wine.

Enter CHIEF splendidly dressed, with coat tails turned up, and wearing a hat made, peaked, with a copy of a newspaper, a spacious green baize table-cloth is thrown over his shoulders, and in his girdle are numerous double-barrelled hoop-sticks. He smokes.

Suddenly a shrill whistle is heard. The Brigands seize their brooms, and, following their Chief, hasten to attack the passage.

Re-enter Brigands, dragging in OLD FATHER, HIS DAUGHTER, (both in traveling costume), POSTBOY, and several port-

manteaus, bags and boxes, which the Wives proceed to rifle of their contents.* The Postboy is bound to the piano, whilst the Chief orders Old Father's boots to be taken off, and draws from them a purse heavily filled with card-counters. He distributes the counters among his men, and then, by laying his hand on his heart, and turning his eyes up to the ceiling, intimates his extreme love for Young Lady. All the Brigands do the same, and a scuffle to possess her takes place. Suddenly the Chief rushes in with two full-cocked hoop-sticks, and, by shooting two of his men, restores peace and harmony. Then taking the Young Lady's hand, he kneels with her before Old Father, who blesses them. The Brigands cheer, and throw their hats in the air.

GRAND TABLEAU.

ACT III.

MISCHIEF.

DRAMATIS PERSONÆ

A MEDICAL STUDENT. HIS FRIEND. THE DOCTOR.
POLICEMEN. CITIZENS. &c.

SCENE—*The outside of the Doctor's house, with lighted candle placed as lamp over door. On one of the posts is a placard, on which is written "Night Bell." Camphine lamps are lowered.*

Enter MEDICAL STUDENT and HIS FRIEND on tiptoe. They commence laughing and laying their fore-fingers on one side of their noses, to prove what a bit of fun they are going to have. By pointing at the Doctor's door, they show that he

---

* The fun here may be greatly increased by the production of several articles which form part of the mysteries of the toilet. A false front or a bustle is sure to produce a good three minutes' laughter. Grimaldi was the first to discover this.

is to be their victim.   After hu-sh-shing a little, they advance
cautiously, and having wrenched from the door the flat-iron
knocker, commence pulling the night-bell, which is made to
to ring violently by rattling a knife
in a tumbler in the passage outside.

Enter DOCTOR, with sheet thrown
round him as night-gown, and holding rush-light shade in his hand.

Medical Student pretends he is very bad in his interior from
having swallowed something deadly; and whilst Doctor is
feeling his pulse, he, by an act of legerdemain, brings the flat-
iron knocker out by his nose. His friend then closes the door,
and locks out the Doctor, who expresses his great alarm lest
any one should come.

A scuffle ensues, when enter the NEIGHBORS in haste, with

sheets thrown over them.   They, in pantomime, intimate their
great indignation at having been disturbed, and then gather
round Doctor, who forthwith re-commences his scuffle with
the Medical Student's Friend. During fight, Medical Student
creeps round, and after much blowing out of cheeks, stamping
on floor, and holding of sides to express fun, proceeds to pin
all the Spectators together. Doctor is knocked down, and all
the neighbors hasten to pick him up, but are held back by
their being fastened to each other. Medical Student and His
Friend decamp. Great confusion.

BRIDEGROOM.

ACT I.

BRIDE—

DRAMATIS PERSONÆ.

FATHER.   MOTHER.   BRIDE.   BRIDESMAIDS.
BRIDEGROOM.   BEADLE.   PEW OPENER.

SCENE—*Interior of church.   At one end the window curtains arranged as altar.*

ENTER BRIDEGROOM.   He walks about hurriedly, looks at his watch, and presses his heart several times.   Then, drawing from his pocket a ring, he gazes on it intently, when

Enter BRIDE, FATHER, MOTHER, and BRIDESMAIDS.   The

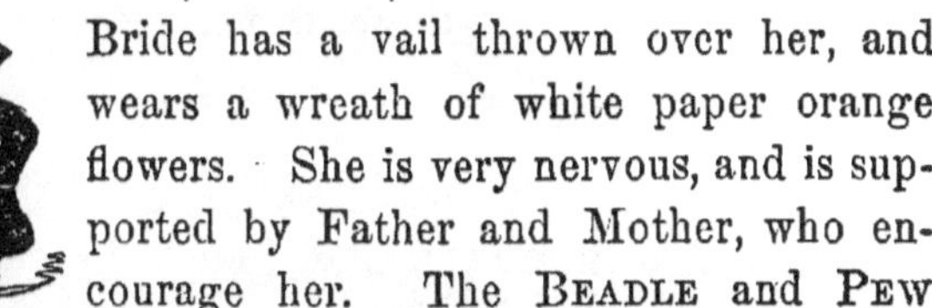

Bride has a vail thrown over her, and wears a wreath of white paper orange flowers.   She is very nervous, and is supported by Father and Mother, who encourage her.   The BEADLE and PEW OPENER wear huge favors of white paper in their bosoms. The Bridegroom rushes forward, and, by a declaration of his passion, gives fresh vigor to the bride.

Enter CLERGYMAN in robes of white sheet.   He advances to the window, and marriage party stand round.   He points to the Bride, and asks the Bridegroom by a look whether he will have her for his wife.   He nods in answer, and the Clergyman asks the same question of the Bride, but she is overcome

by her feeling, and faints away on the spot.   Great confusion, the Mother holding smelling-bottle to her nose, the Brides-maid slapping her hands, whilst the Bridegroom walks madly up and down the room.   At length she comes-to a little, and the ceremony proceeds, the Mother encouraging her daughter. After the Father has given her away, she once more faints off; and, at the conclusion, she is so moved that she swoons in the arms of her husband.   The Bridesmaids, losing all power over their feelings, faint away into the arms of Father, whilst Mother and Pew Opener fall upon the Clergyman, who with difficulty sustains the burden.

ACT II.

—GROOM.

DRAMATIS PERSONÆ.

NOBLEMEN.   HORSE-DEALER.   GROOM.   LITTLE FIVE-YEAR OLD.

SCENE—*The interior of Tattersall's.*

Enter HORSE-DEALER and GROOM in close conversation. The Horse-dealer drawing a purse from his pocket gives groom an ivory card-counter as a sovereign, at the same time winking, and holding finger up to his nose.   Groom lays his hand upon his breast in an attitude as if he was saying "upon his honor," and, hearing somebody coming, glides sway. •

Enter NOBLEMEN smoking cigars.   Horse-dealer bows to

them, and they bid him show them his Little Five-year-old. Horse-dealer again bows to them, and knocks loudly at the door, when

Enter Groom, leading in THE LITTLE FIVE-YEAR-OLD,  neighing. Noblemen gather round and examine him, at the same time expressing their admiration of its beauty. They bid the groom run the animal up and down, and show its paces. They are enchanted with its beautiful action, and offer a purse to the Horse-dealer as the purchase money. The Horse-dealer refuses the offer with an expression that shows how ridicu-  lously low it is, and again bids the Groom to run the Little Five-year-old up and down the court. They are still more de- lighted, and offer another purse. The Horse-dealer takes the two purses, and delivers over the Little Five-year-old. Exit Horse-dealer and Groom laughing.

Directly thy are gone, the Little Five-year-old commences kicking and plunging. Noblemen endeavor to approach him, but are kept back by his capering. At last they reach him, when exit Little Five-year-old dragging Nobleman after him.

ACT III.

BRIDEGROOM.

DRAMATIS PERSONÆ.

BRIDEGROOM.　　BRIDE.　　FATHER.　　MOTHER.
BRIDESMAIDS.　　FRIENDS.　　SERVANTS, &c.

SCENE—*The dining-room in mansion of Father. In the centre a table covered with wedding feast, in the midst of which is the large white bandbox wedding cake.*

Enter BRIDEGROOM, BRIDE, MOTHER, FATHER, BRIDESMAIDS, and FRIENDS, with handkerchiefs up to their eyes. They take

their seats at Bridal feast in a solemn silence. SERVANTS hand round dishes. The clatter of knives and forks alone disturbs the tranquillity.

Suddenly the Bride commences sobbing, and the whole party again fall to weeping. They force the Bride to take some wine, and the dead silence is again restored. The father rises to propose the health of the Bride, and everybody turns

round to listen to him. He turns his eyes up to the ceiling, and, holding his hands over his plate, invokes a blessing on her head. At this the sobs burst forth anew. Then he shakes his clenched fist at his alarmed Son-in-law, and, pointing to his Daughter, declares that the Bridegroom will be a scoundrel if he does not treat her as she deserves. Here the boo-boos burst out in great strength, and Bride falls into the arms of her Mother. The Bridegroom attempts to do a few pantomimic sentences, but is frowned down by the company; and it is only by his swearing by the soup-tureen to love her that harmony can be restored. The Bride rushes toward him, and he clasps her in his arms. Then the weeping once more commences, and ends in a violent blowing of noses.

At last all the SERVANTS rush in with their aprons up to their eyes, to announce that the fly is at the door, and the company escorts the happy pair to the door, their faces buried in their pocket-handkerchiefs.

PASSPORT.

ACT I.

PASS—

DRAMATIS PERSONÆ.

DUKE OF WELLINGTON.	HIS CHARGER.	BRITISH ARMY.
NAPOLEON.	FRENCH ARMY.	SENTINEL.

SCENE 1—*The Plains of Waterloo. The British Camp.*

ALARUM of Trumpets.

Enter the DUKE OF WELLINGTON at the head of the BRITISH ARMY. The Duke is mounted on his charger, and wears a

blue cloak, and a cocked hat made with a newspaper. The Army goes through its evolutions of presenting brooms, &c. The Duke addresses his men in a short pantomimic speech, and the troops, waving their hats in the air, swear to follow him to death.

Exit Duke of Wellington, his Charger, and the British Army.

SCENE 2—The Plains of Waterloo. The French Camp.

Alarum of Drums.

Enter NAPOLEON, leading on the FRENCH ARMY. To show that he is Emperor, he either stands with his hands behind him, or else looks through a sheet of music. He wears a cocked hat, and a cut-away coat, turned up with white paper facings. He has high boots of japan table-cover rolled round his legs.

He makes a short address to the Army, and they all kneel down to him and beg of him to believe in them. He is visibly

affected, and takes snuff repeatedly. He blesses them, and they rise. Having placed a SENTINEL at the window curtain, Exit Napoleon and the French Army.

SCENE 3—Night-time.

The Sentinel is on duty, pacing the room with shouldered broom.

Enter NAPOLEON, in deep thought. He walks up and down the room with his hands behind him.

The Sentinel perceives him, and presenting his arms, he challenges Napoleon. The Emperor hesitates, when Sentinel draws from his pocket a placard, on which is written "On ne passe pas."

Napoleon is delighted, and declares himself. The Sentinel kneels, and the Emperor gives him a "croix d'honeur."

Enter FRENCH ARMY.

ACT II.

—PORT.

DRAMATIS PERSONÆ.

SAILOR.   HIS SWEET-HEARTS.   COMPANIONS.

JEWS.   LANDLORD.

SCENE—*Portsmouth.   Outside of an Inn, with a placard of "The Jolly Tar," being a sign over the door.*

Enter SAILOR with bundle on the end of the stick on his shoulder.   He throws away his luggage and dances a horn-pipe.

Enter his SWEET-HEARTS (*music*), who take his arms, and dance round the room with him.   At the end of the dance, Sweet-hearts declare their love for Sailor, who untying his bundle, gives to one a shawl, to another a handkerchief, and to a third a necklace.

Enter LANDLORD, who bows respectfully to Sailor.   He asks him what he would like to drink.   The Sailor orders grog all round, which the Landlord immediately places on the table. The Sailor pulls from his pocket a heavy purse to pay Land-lord, and he is immediately surrounded by his sweet-hearts, who begin coaxing him.

Enter JEWS, dressed in dressing-gowns, and long beards of

tobacco gummed on their chins. They gather round the Sailor, and commence flattering him. One offers him a watch, and another a coat, whilst the remainder exhibit brace-lets and ear-rings for his Sweet-hearts.

The Sailor is captivated with the watch, and offers the Jew money for it, which is refused indignantly.   The Sweet-hearts press him to purchase the ear-rings, and Sailor is overcome and presents them with all the Jews have brought.   He also takes the watch.

Exeunt Jews laughing and jingling their money.

Enter LANDLORD with his bill. The Sailor has no more money and cannot pay him. The Landlord grows impatient, and demands the watch in payment. It is given to him.

Exit Sailor with his Sweethearts and the Landlord laughing.

ACT III.

PASSPORT.

DRAMATIS PERSONÆ.

ENGLISH GENTLEMAN.	HIS WIFE.	HIS FAMILY.
PASSENGERS.	GENDARMES.	HOTEL TOUTERS.

SCENE—*The Pier at Boulogne. A bell is heard ringing to announce the arrival of the Steamer.*

Enter GENDARMES, who stand in a file with drawn walking-sticks, waiting for the Passengers.

Enter PASSENGERS with carpet bags in their hands. Each one presents his Passport, and is allowed to proceed.

Enter HOTEL TOUTERS, who gather round Passengers and offer them their hotel cards, beseeching their patronage.

Enter ENGLISH GENTLEMAN, HIS WIFE, AND HIS FAMILY, who are stopped by the Gendarmes.

English Gentleman is disgusted at such behavior, and in strong action inveighs against such a want of hospitality. The Hotel Touters gather round his Wife, and with compli-

ments beseech her to patronize them. His Wife is overcome by their praises, and delivers to them the carpet-bags, cloaks, and umbrellas.

Exeunt Hotel Touters dancing.

The English Gentleman is unable to speak the French

language, though he understands it perfectly. The Gendarmes in vain endeavor to make him comprehend that they require his passport. They threaten to take him and his Wife and Children to prison, and he defies them to it. His Wife in her alarm delivers over to them several articles she had attempted to smuggle. The Gendarmes are not satisfied, and seize English Gentleman. His Wife and Family weep.

Enter GENDARME with placard, on which is written "*passport.*" The English Gentleman clasps his hands, whilst his Wife, pointing after the Hotel Touters, declares that it is in her carpet-bag.

Exeunt English Gentleman, his Wife and Family, in close custody of Gendarmes.

TABLEAU.

BIRTHDAY.

ACT I.

BIRTH—

DRAMATIS PERSONÆ.

| MOTHER. | HER CHILD. | MONTHLY NURSE. |
| HUSBAND. | LADY VISITORS. |

SCENE—*The street outside of Mother's house. To the right the door, with flat-iron for knocker.*

Enter MONTHLY NURSE dressed in showy gown, wth large  cap and clean apron on. She points to the house, and dangles an imaginary child in the air, to inform the audience that there has been a slight addition to the family. Then taking from her pocket

12

a white glove, she fastens it round the knocker.   Exit Mothly
Nurse dancing for joy, and still dangling child.

SCENE 2—*Interior of Mother's bed-chamber.   On the sofa is seen Mother in
a white jacket and cap, nursing her child.*

Enter Monthly Nurse leading in HUSBAND.   She shows to
him the CHILD, and by her actions
informs him that it is exactly like
him, having got his nose, his eyes,
and his mouth.   The delighted Father gives Monthly Nurse a card-
counter.

Enter LADY VISITORS, who rush up to Mother, and, in impassioned action, inquire after her health.   Monthly Nurse
shows them the Baby.   They are delighted with it, and clasp
their hands in admiration.   Each Lady Visitor requests to be

allowed to kiss it.   The delighted Mother smiles, and the
Monthly Nurse madly embraces the Child.

The Ladies are enchanted with the scene.   Caudle is handed
round and drank, and the Monthly Nurse, placing herself at
the door, ushers out each Lady, who slips into her hand a
supposed half-crown.

ACT II.

—DAY (Dey.)

DRAMATIS PERSONÆ.

THE DEY OF ALGIERS.   CAPTIVE ENGLISH LADY.   HER HUSBAND.
              SLAVES.   BRITISHERS.

SCENE—*The ramparts of Algiers.*

Enter the DEY of ALGIERS, dressed in his robes-de-chambre

of State, with a turban on his head.   He is followed by his
SLAVES, who arrange the ottoman for him to sit cross-legged
upon, and hand him his pipe.

Enter further SLAVES, bringing with them the ENGLISH

LADY, who has a vail thrown over her.   The Slaves salaam,
and the Dey orders them to remove the vail from their Captive.   They obey him, and the Dey is visibly moved with the
charms of the Lady.   He rises from his seat, and paces the
room.   Then advancing to her, he presses his heart and declares his passion.   She repulses him haughtily.   He draws

from his pocket a heavy purse, and offers it to her, but she
points to her wedding ring, and casts the purse at the feet
of the tyrant.

The Dey's love is then turned to rage, and he gives a signal
to his Slaves, who salaam, and bring in a cannon, made by
placing the sofa bolster on the music Canterbury.

The Slaves seize Captive English Lady, and bind her to the
mouth of loaded bolster.   The Dey once more offers his love,
and is once more refused.   The signal to fire is given, when

Enter HER HUSBAND at the head of a gallant band of
BRITISHERS.   A scuffle ensues, each Britisher engaging two
Slaves in combat.   The Dey is dethroned, and the English
lady is released, and rushes into the arms of her Husband.

The Britishers kneeling on prostrate Algerines.

ACT III.

BIRTHDAY.

DRAMATIS PERSONÆ.

OLD LORD.   HIS SON, *aged 21.*   TENANTS.   THEIR WIVES.
SERVANTS.   MUSICIANS.

SCENE—*Park on Estate of Old Lord.   In the centre is placed a table with
chairs on each side, in preparation a feast.*

Enter TENANTS and their WIVES, gayly dressed, and carry-

ing a flag made out of an old newspaper.   They form themselves into two rows, when

Enter OLD LORD and HIS SON.   The Tenants wave
their hats
in the air,

and their wives courtesy.   The
Old Lord bows to them, and
delivers a short speech, constantly pointing to his Son.   The
Tenants again wave their hats in the air, when

Enter SERVANTS, bearing a bandbox barrel of beer, which
they place on the table.   Glasses are handed
round, and the Old Lord, taking one, proposes the health of their young Squire.

Enter MUSICIANS, when the tenants all

stand up for a dance, his Son leading off with one of their Wives.

——◆——

CABBAGE.
ACT I.
CAB—

DRAMATIS PERSONÆ.

FOREIGN COUNT.		TWO FOREIGN COUNTESSES.
CABMEN.	CAB-HORSES.	&c., &c.

SCENE—*A Street.   Stand of one-horse arm-chairs ranged down centre.*

ENTER CABMEN with handkerchiefs round necks, great-coats on and whips in hand.   Each one leads his prancing CAB-HORSE, which he forthwith harnesses to his arm-chair with traces of shoe ribbon or string.   After a bag containing a feed of keys and pocket-handkerchiefs has been fastened round the neck of each steed, Cabmen collect in group, tossing commences, and several mugs full of foaming wool are discussed.

Enter FOREIGN COUNT escorting TWO FOREIGN COUNTESSES. The Count wears a splendid beard of bird's-eye tobacco, gummed on to his lips and chin.*   On each side of the face of the two Countesses is fastened an immense brown paper *acroche-cœur*, to mark their foreign extraction.   They carry in their hands carpet-bags labelled, in large letters, "France." The Count summons Cabmen.   They gather round, and he explains to them, by showing the label on his carpet-bag, that he wishes to be taken to the Dover Railway.   Then by pointing to the palm of his hand, to himself, and the Countesses, he asks how much they will charge to take him there.

The Cabman demands twenty fingers.   The Count refuses; but offers five fingers.

---

* A very nice beard may be made with burnt cork, but to our mind nothing can look more gentlemanly than tobacco.

As the train is on the point of starting he rushes madly about, appealing to each Cabman, but all, pointing to the carpet-bag—refuse, with a wink, to reduce their price even one finger.

At this moment the railway bell* is heard ringing violently in the passage, and Count, fearing to lose the train, dashing his hat on head, shakes his fist at Cabmen, and, with the Countesses, jumps into the first arm-chair, and so *exeunt.*

ACT II.

—AGE.

DRAMATIS PERSONÆ.

"Uncle Nunky-punky,"   "Aunty Panty-shanty,"
Age 98 years.   been 50 *for the last* 30 *years.*
Young Nephews and Nieces.   Musicians.

Scene—*Drawing-room in House of " Uncle Nunky-punky." In the centre, table laid out for a Grand Feast, plates containing an Apple and an Orange.*

Enter some of the actors dressed as Young Nephews, with their collars laid down and coat-tails turned up, and Young Nieces, with pinafores on and long sashes round waists. They romp about until seeing feast on table; they advance to

---

* The extreme difficulty of proving that the train is about to start must be the excuse for the Railway Bell being heard at this distance.

it, and by rubbing their hands up and down their waistcoats

and pinafores, whilst examining the orange and apple, show what a delicious treat they are going to have. Suddenly they hear somebody coming, and, replacing the delicate fruits, rush out to meet the visitor.

Enter "UNCLE NUNKY PUNKY" and "AUNTY PANTY-SHANTY," surrounded by Nephews and Nieces dancing for joy. The Uncle's long gray wadding locks fall about his shoulders. The wrinkles left by the burnt cork of Time, his

bent knees, and the stick he leans upon, tell how infirm he is. Aunty, with her huge brown-paper spectacles, dark false front, immense cap, and scarf of well-frilled toilet-cover, is a most affecting picture.

Enter MUSICIANS, who play a lively air upon the grand piano, and touch the rails at back of arm-chair as harp strings.

Nephews and Nieces invite the old couple to dance. At last they consent. They stand up, and, by their heavy panting and continued coughing, prove how fatiguing a process it is at their time of life. At last old Uncle kisses old Aunt, who screams, and faints into the arms of the Nephews and Nieces.

GRAND TABLEAU.

ACT III.

CABBAGE.

DRAMATIS PERSONÆ.

TOBACCONIST.   TAILOR.   STATUE OF HIGHLAND CHIEF.   A SAILOR.
A GENTLEMAN.   MOB.   POLICEMEN, &c.

SCENE—*The exterior of two Shops.   Over each is a placard—the one inscribed" Tailor," and the other " Cigars."*

Enter TAILOR and TOBACCONIST.   They shake hands, and each enters his shop.   Tailor, having taken off his pumps, threads his needle, and commences repairing a coat.   Tobac-

conist brings out STATUE OF HIGHLAND CHIEF, with muff and plumes on head, and tartan shawl round waist.   He places it before shop.   Then taking some cabbage-leaves from pocket, he rolls them into full-flavored Havannas.

Enter SAILOR with folded-up sheet under his arm, his long pig-tail of sable boa reaching down to his waist.   He enters Tailor's shop, and by pointing first to the sheet, and then to his legs, explains that he wants a pair of thing-o'-my's made.   He orders them to be made full by holding his hands a yard apart at his ancles.   Tailor takes sheet, and, by putting his fingers on one side of his nose, and winking, shows how fearfully his morals have been neglected.   As soon as the Sailor has gone, he jumps off his seat, and, cutting the sheet in two,* puts one half in his own pocket —all the time winking as before.

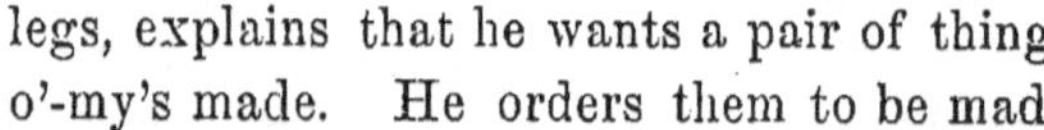

* This apparent destruction of property may be effected by having previously run two sheets together.

Enter Gentleman, who seeing the Statue of Highland Chief taking snuff, steps into Tobacconist's shop. He asks for a cigar, by slowly raising with a graceful motion his hand to his mouth and puffing. The Tobacconist hands him one of the cigars he has made with cabbage-leaves. The Gentleman lights it, and intimates, by opening his mouth and eyes, and pressing his waistcoat, that he is very ill. He flings cigar at Tobacconist, and exit rapidly.

Re-enter Sailor, who goes up to Tailor. He demands his trousers. Tailor bows and scrapes, and produces a pair of child's drawers, and invites Sailor to try them on. Sailor, in a great rage, jumps round Tailor in circles, squaring at him. Tailor draws his long shears or tongs. They fight.

Enter Mob with Policemen, when Sailor strikes the Tailor to the ground.

GRAND TABLEAU.

PIEBALD.

ACT I.

PIE—

DRAMATIS PERSONÆ.

NEIGHBORING LADIES AND GENTLEMEN.   A BAKER.

SCENE—*Baker's Shop.   The Sofa lengthwise as an oven.*

ENTER BAKER with a nightcap and footman's jacket and apron on. His face is white with best seconds. He lights an imaginary fire under the sofa, and, with the dust-pan tied to the end of a fishing-rod for his "peel," he awaits his customers.

Enter NEIGHBORING LADY bearing a delicious imitation leg of mutton,* which she hands over to Baker, who slips it into sofa oven, and gives in return card-counter as the customary tin check.

Enter NEIGHBORING GENTLEMAN, with the largest dish in the kitchen, covered with the largest tin cover. This he also hands over and receives a mother-o'-pearl check.

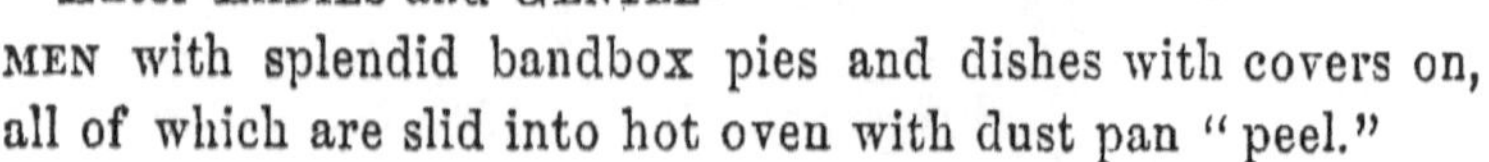

Enter LADIES and GENTLE-MEN with splendid bandbox pies and dishes with covers on, all of which are slid into hot oven with dust pan "peel."

When the customers are all gone, the Baker on tiptoe goes round the room to see that nobody is looking, and then, draw-

---

* It requires even more than the genius of a Udo to tell how the following joints and pies are to be made. Children's toy-boxes, cushions, bags, everything that the mind can think of, and the hands be laid on, must be put in requisition.

ing out all the dishes, he takes from a closet his own very small pie, and changes it for the largest, by "ringing the changes," and altering the tin checks upon every dish.

Re-enter Neighboring Ladies and Gentlemen with napkins to place over their dishes. They present their checks, and

demand their dinners. They are extremely shocked at seeing the great alteration in the size of their joints and pasties. The Baker shrugs his shoulders, and proves to them very clearly, by pointing to the ceiling, that the meat has shrunk by evaporation in the cooking. When they have a second time departed, Baker, bursting out laughing, takes his heavy dish and makes his exit, dancing for joy.

ACT II.

—BALD.

DRAMATIS PERSONÆ.

OLD GENTLEMAN.   MIDDLE-AGED LADY.   CHAMBERMAID.

SCENE.—*Supposed double-bedded room at an Inn not a hundred miles from Town. On one side an imaginary bed with window curtains, on the other the sofa ready turned down. In the centre a toilet table with looking-glass upon it.*

Enter CHAMBERMAID lighting in OLD GENTLEMAN, who

has just arrived from the passage.   He 
intimates, by leaning on his hands and
yawning, that he is very tired, and putting down his carpet-bag, he untwists
his comforter, and takes off his cloak.
Then taking his night-cap from his pocket, he puts it on,
hangs his coat and waistcoat on the back of a chair, turns in
behind the window-curtains, and in a few seconds is heard
snoring.

Enter MIDDLE-AGED LADY with her hair (by means of a pair
of luxuriant sable cuffs) dressed *en bandeau* at each side of her
face, and bulging out her well-filled cap.   Under
her arm she carries the warming-pan, with which
she begins warming her sofa-bedstead.   In the
midst of it she rouses the Old Gentleman from
his sleep.   He pokes his nightcap through the window curtains, and his face bears a look of intense horror at finding a
lady in his room.   As she continues warming the sofa, his
timidity leaves him, and he admires her beautiful hair, and
looks frequently up to the curtain poles to show that he is
deeply moved by her beauty.

Suddenly Middle-aged Lady advances to the looking-glass
on the table, and Old Gentleman rapidly with- 
draws his head.   She begins her toilet, and the
Old Gentleman reappears, and his face wears an
expression of ghastly astonishment as he sees her
unpin from each side of her face the lovely sable
cuffs that he had been admiring as her own luxuriant tresses.
At last she removes her cap, and he nearly falls backward on
perceiving that she is quite bald.*   In his horror the Old
Gentleman groans audibly, and Lady turns round quickly as

* Baldness can be imitated capitally with an oil-skin bathing cap.   At a
pinch, a baby's cap with pink lining might do; but Macassar Roland himself could not tell the oil-skin.

he disappears.   She throws her arms about her wildly for one moment, and then sinks into chair and faints from fright.

Old Gentleman, seizing his carpet-bag and clothes, taking advantage of the moment, hurries quickly from the room. WAITERS, CHAMBERMAIDS, &c., rush in.   They express surprise at Lady's baldness.   She revives, screams, and runs out; when *exeunt omnes.*

ACT III.

PIEBALD.

DRAMATIS PERSONÆ.

POOR NEGRO.   HIS ENGLISH WIFE.   THEIR THREE CHILDREN.
KIND LADIES AND GENTLEMEN.

SCENE—*Inside of Poor Negro's house.   In the centre deal table; on each side a kitchen chair.*

Enter POOR NEGRO.*   He has a white turban on, and a nightgown tied tightly round his waist.   In his hand he holds the broom he has been sweeping the crossing with.   He presses his forehead several times, to tell that he is in deep distress;   and, finally, drawing the kitchen chair to table, he flings himself into it, and buries his face in his hands.

* Unless there is a black man in the house, the easiest way of making one is by stretching a piece of dark silk across the face, and cutting out holes for the eyes and mouth.   Burnt cork, of course, is the true coloring matter of the real theatrical negro; but that is out of the question.

Enter his fair Wife, also in deep distress.   She sees Negro weeping, and turns her head away with a graceful attitude, and weeps also.   Then advancing to him, she taps him on the shoulder.   He starts up and embraces her.

He tells her, by pointing several times to his open mouth,  that he is very hungry, and wants something to eat.   She shakes her head slowly, and turns aside to hide her emotion.

Enter Kind Ladies and Gentlemen, who putting their glasses up, examine closely every thing in the room.   Negro and his wife bow to them. The ladies are shocked at the destitution of the place, and give them money.   Ladies then, by dandling imaginary baby in the air, ask if they have any children.   Wife nods her head several times joyfully, and rushes from the room.

Re-enter Wife with first one Child.   It is black.   The Visitors express, by pointing to the face of the little one and the Negro, that it is the image of its Father.   The Wife then introduces a second Child.   It is white.   The Visitors remark that it resembles its Mother.   At last the third is brought in.   It is a Baby in long clothes, and being like both Father and Mother, it is—Piebald.   Astonishment of Visitors, and

GRAND TABLEAU.

MISTLETOE.

ACT I.

MISTLE—(Mizzle.)

DRAMATIS PERSONÆ.

POOR TENANT.　　　HIS WIFE.　　　HIS FAMILY.
ANGRY LANDLORD.

SCENE—*House of Poor Tenant comfortably furnished.*

ENTER POOR TENANT in a state of extreme dejection. HIS WIFE, who follows him, endeavors to console him, but in vain, for he only stamps and presses his forehead the more. She clings to him and demands the cause of his sorrow. He pulls from his pocket a placard written, "RENT DAY TO-MORROW." She falls back in horror, and weeps.

Enter HIS FAMILY, who, seeing their Father and Mother's affliction, are overcome by their feelings. They turn aside their heads and sob audibly.

Poor Tenant addresses his family. He a second time ex-

hibits his placard, and the sorrow of the group becomes extreme. He tells them, by pulling his pockets inside out, that he has not a penny. He points to his comfortable furniture, and informs them that the Angry Landlord will seize it all for rent. Sinking into a chair, he is overwhelmed in his grief. His Wife and Family gather round him, and ask in what way they can assist him. They offer to bear away their goods that night, and carry them beyond the reach of the Angry Landlord. A gleam of joy passes over the countenance of Poor Tenant. He embraces his children, and His Wife blesses them.

His Family then seize the chairs, and carry them on tiptoe

into the passage. They return stealthily, until the whole room is stripped.' Then casting a long farewell look at the ceiling of their forefathers' home—they strike a touching tableau, and *exeunt* Poor Tenant, His Wife, and Family, mournfully.

Enter ANGRY LANDLORD, with a pen in his mouth and a ledger under his arm. He stamps loudly on the floor of Poor Tenant's house, but nobody comes. He stamps again and again, his face wearing an expression of surprise and disgust. In a great passion he raves about the room, expressing in action his indignation at all the furniture having been removed. He swears to be revenged, and draws a writ from his pocket.

Exit Angry Landlord, still swearing vengeance.

ACT II.

—TOE.

DRAMATIS PERSONÆ.

THE POPE OF ROME.	CARDINALS.	PRIESTS.
IRISH GENTLEMAN.	ENGLISH GENTLEMAN.	PAPAL SOLDIERS.

SCENE—*Interior of a Chapel at Rome.   Around it are hung pictures, and at the end is an arm-chair for the Pope's throne.*

Enter IRISH GENTLEMAN and ENGLISH GENTLEMAN arm-in-arm, to view the beauties of the chapel.   They are both delighted with the pictures, and while the Irish Gentleman kneels down, the English one carves his name on the door, to tell all further visitors that he has been there.

The solemen music of a piano is heard, and

Enter THE POPE OF ROME, dressed in full canonicals of red

table cover and lace cuffs.   He walks grandly, and is followed by CARDINALS in sacerdotal robes of bed-curtains, and devout PRIESTS in ladies' cloaks with the hoods over their heads. They tell their beads of coral necklaces.

The Pope seats himself in the arm-chair throne, and the Priests commence kissing his toe.   He blesses each one as he rises.   The Irish Gentleman advancing, beseeches by gestures Cardinals to allow him to take one fond embrace.   They are pleased with his earnestness, and consent.   He casts himself on his knees and kisses it madly.

They then invite the English Gentleman also to advance

13

and be blessed.   He folds his arms
and replies disdainfully.   The Pope
is enraged, and rises from his throne.
The Cardinals gather menacingly
round English Gentleman, and the 
Priests threaten him with wild gesticulations.   The Irish
Gentleman in vain endeavors to restore peace.   His friend is
once more besought to yield, but still refuses.   The Pope
beckons to his Priests, when

Enter PAPAL SOLDIERS, and surround English Gentleman,
 who still remains with his arms
crossed.   He refuses to stir, and
addresses the Pope, and his Court
in language of contempt.   The
Guards are ordered to do their
duty, and force English Gentleman away with the point of
their brooms.   (*Soft Music.*)   *Exeunt* Pope, Cardinals, and
Priests, solemnly, the Irish Gentleman cheering.

ACT III.

MISTLETOE.

DRAMATIS PERSONÆ.

GRANDFATHER.   HIS SON.
GRANDMOTHER.   HER DAUGHTER (*Wife to his Son*).
THEIR CHILDREN.   VISITORS.   SERVANTS.   MUSICIANS.

SCENE—*Old Hall in the Mansion of His Son.   Long table down the centre,
with chairs.*

Enter SERVANTS bearing grand feast, which they arrange
on the table.   They then stand behind the chairs.

Enter GRANDFATHER, GRANDMOTHER, HIS SON, HER
DAUGHTER, THEIR CHILDREN, and VISITORS in holiday costume.   Grandfather is so old that he can scarcely walk, and
is supported by His Son, whom he blesses.   Grandmother is

placed next to Her Daughter, and Their Children dance about with delight.   When they are seated at table, they eat.

Enter Servants bearing large dish with brown silk bundle in it for plum-pudding.   Their Children rise from the table and dance round it.

As soon as the dinner is removed, His Son gives a signal, when

Enter MUSICIANS with imitation instruments in their hands. Their Children serve them with wine and plum pudding. (*Affecting picture.*)   Grandfather goes out and fetches a bunch of Mistletoe, which he hangs to the lamp.   They all laugh, and are delighted with the wickedness of Grandfather. He laughs and coughs a great deal, and all Their Children thump him on the back to make him better.

The Visitors then take the Young Ladies, who appear

dreadfully bashful, and drag them screaming and tittering under the Mistletoe, where they embrace them theatrically, by crossing their heads over their shoulders.   Grandmother is delighted, and presses her sides with mirth, when one of Their Children takes her hand, and pulls her under the Mistletoe and kisses her.   Grandfather pretends to be jealous, and the fun increases.

Several of the Gentlemen are smitten with the charms of the Ladies, and after they have kissed them, proceed to the corners, where they fall on one knee and propose.   The Ladies weep, hesitate, and point to Grandfather.   The Gentlemen beseech the Grandfather to consent.　He weeps, and blesses them.

GRAND TABLEAU.

Musicians begin playing a court dance, all the party standing up.　The old Grandfather taking Grandmother's hand, leads off the dance.

CHARADE DRAMAS.

CHARADE I.

HOST-AGE.

DRAMATIS PERSONÆ.

COLONEL CLAYTON. HUMPHREY ALLRIGHT. NEHEMIAH GREATMAN.
SETH GREATMAN. CICELY ALLRIGHT. HANNAH ALLRIGHT.
Soldiers.

SCENE 1.—*The Bar in the Fox and Goose Hostel.* HUMPHREY, NEHEMIAH
and SETH *seated.* CICELY *moving about, occupied with some labor.*

Enter CLAYTON *without a hat, his clothes torn.*

Clayton.—Good man of the house, by the love thou bearest
to thy country and thy kind, bestow from your ample comforts a cup and a cake on an unlucky wight, down in the
world, and deucedly hungry. By the bright eyes of my fair
lady, I have tasted no food since I eat my breakfast from a
noble haunch the morning of yesterday.

Humphrey.—The fate of these disastrous times, friend ! I,
that once enjoyed moderately the comforts of life, am now
myself very sorely pressed down. My flesh is falling away,
my spirits are dull, my tongue is fettered, and my strong ale
is becoming sour, since men took to angry words and bloody
fights, instead of good-fellowship and sober enjoyment over
the ale-cup.

Clayton.—But if a man draw his sword in the right cause,
friend ; if he——

Humphrey.—Don't talk to Humphrey Allright about the
right cause or the wrong cause. I make it a point of conscience never to inquire on which side my customers choose to
fight. I shut my eyes and my ears, and no man living can
say that Humphrey Allright ever turns his back on a customer, or knows whether he be a Cavalier or Roundhead, as
it is the fashion to call all good Englishmen. All are wel-

(197) "

come to the Fox and Goose—that pay. And if it falls out, as God knows it oft happens, that they cannot pay, we have still a cup for the poor traveler, and no questions asked. Cicely, I charge thee to give to this poor man a cup of thin ale and a crust of last week's bread.

Clayton.—And add a slice of beef, my sweet Cicely, for charity, and by all thy hopes of seeing Roger back from the wars.

Cicely.—Roger, forsooth ! Take thy beef and bread, but talk not to me of men at the wars. I look for something better than a lame soldier.

Seth.—Aye, fair Mistress Cicely, I should be sorely grieved to see thee hold out thy hand to a profane ruffler like this needy vagabond. Thou art too comely a maiden to be cast away among the ungodly.

Cicely.—Nobody asked thy opinion, Seth Greatman ; and I warn thee no fair maiden will hold out her hand to thee, till thou lettest thy hair grow decently over thine ears, and trimmest thy beard more jauntily.

Clayton.—Dost thou hear that, Master Seth ? The fair Cicely is a damsel of good taste, and would rather be a Cavalier's lady and dance to the music of the merry viol, than the domestic drudge of a psalm-singing Roundhead, who would frown at her rosy smiles, and denounce damnation against a love-ditty. Let me place this gay knot of ribbons in thy smooth locks, pretty one—it is all I have to bestow on thee for thy beef and ale ; but the times may change, and I will not forget thee, sweet damsel.

Nehemiah.—Neighbor Humphrey, dost thou harbor and encourage traitors and vagabonds ? Beware, lest our pious magistrate should suspend thy license. Seest thou not, friend Humphrey, that thy light and worldly-minded daugh-ter, disregarding the sober addresses of Seth Greatman, my sin-hating son, listens eagerly to the false and flattering words of this curled and perfumed traitor to his country and his faith.

Clayton.—Why, thou canting varlet, was it not for thy years, I would cudgel thee, and pull the ears that stand out so temptingly uncovered at the sides of thy empty head. But if thou keepest not thy insolent tongue in better subjection, I will challenge thy son Seth to a bout of wrestling, and we will see which is the better man.

Nehemiah.—Hearest thou this man of evil words, friend Humphrey?

Humphrey.—I hear nothing, Nehemiah Greatman: it is not for me to hear or to see. Let every tub stand on its own bottom. I defy man living to say that Humphrey Allright was ever convicted of taking a part in any dispute, argument, quarrel, or fight. I am a man of no opinions, friend Nehemiah.

Nehemiah.—Nevertheless, this man of blood *has* opinions, and such opinions that it is expedient that he should be stopped, and if need be, let him be offered up a sacrifice. Seth, my son, follow me to the camp, that the chosen instrument, the godly Captain Cantwell, may learn from us what a dangerous malignant lurks in the neighborhood.

Seth.—Ay, father, I will visit with thee the tents of the Israelites who wage war against the idolatrous men of Moab Cicely, this wanton play-actor shall no longer beguile thee with his words of evil. He is delivered into our hands, and we accept the gift.

Exeunt NEHEMIAH *and* SETH.

Humphrey.—Now, behold, stranger what a kettle of fish thou hast cooked in my quiet hostel with thy mountebank tricks and vaunting speeches. Take my counsel, soldier, and ever rein thy tongue when thou knowest not thy listeners. I would fain urge thee to depart; but ere long, the swarm of the hornet will be roused by the zealous Nehemiah, and thy flight will be intercepted.

Clayton.—Nay, good Humphrey, the enemy are surely not so near us.

Humphrey.—I know no enemy; I speak of a reconnoitring party, commanded by a certain Round—*Hem!*—Parliamentarian captain, now encamped about a mile from this hostel, which has ever, I thank God and my own prudence, been neutral ground, until our unlucky charity toward thee.

Cicely.—God will never let us suffer for our charity, father; and it is our bounden duty to save this gentleman.

Humphrey.—Gentleman, girl! let not thy tongue run so glibly about gentlemen; such words become thee not. And take that flaunting knot from thy head, lest it be thought that we favor the cavaliers; moreover, such vanities might offend Seth Greatman, who is a youth well to do, and suited to be my son-in-law.

Cicely.—Thou shalt be obeyed, father; but of a surety, I will never lend an ear to the words of Seth, if this stranger in distress be not saved.

Humphrey.—I cannot help the man; by aiding him I might place myself in danger, which God forbid!

Cicely.—Leave it all to me, father; I would not have thy safety jeopardized. Let us all withdraw to grandmother in the kitchen, where I will show to ye both my skill in devices.

SCENE 2—*Kitchen of the "Fox and Goose."* CLAYTON, HUMPHREY, CICELY. HANNAH *seated near the fire in a deep arm chair.*

Cicely.—I will take grandmother for a few hours to good Martha Hall, who will tend her with all care. And mark well, father, thou must lead the stranger to thy chamber, and disguise him in the raiment of grandmother, which I have spread out for that purpose. Then must he seat himself in her chair to pass for her. The soldiers know that old Hannah Allright is stone deaf, and will not be at the trouble to put questions. Thou seest, soldier, what thy part is, and I doubt not will delude thy foes; thou hast the very look of a play-actor.

Clayton.—Thanks, fair and generous damsel; but shall I not need the aid of thy pretty hands to array me in such un-wonted garments; perchance, I may don my garb in some un-seemly fashion.

Cicely.—Then, after such unseemly fashion thou must wear thy garb; for thou wilt receive no aid from me. Behold thy model before thee : I'll engage thou canst carry it out. Come, grandmother, we will go to see worthy Martha Hall. (*Puts her on a cloak and hood.*)

Hannah.—To church, Circely ? God forgive me, I had nigh forgotten the Sabbath ! Where's Seth, to keep thee company ? I like none of yonder scowling vagabond. Give him a crust, and bid him begone, Cicely.

Cicely.—He's a stranger in need, grandmother.

Hannah.—What ! the bold-faced rascal that stole thy eggs at Easter ! He'll cut thy father's throat, girl, or perchance make off with my big china punch-bowl.

Cicely.—Come along, grandmother.

[*Draws her away with great difficulty. Exeunt* CICELY *and* HANNAH.]

Humphrey.—Thou hast head what Cicely Allright has said to thee, soldier. I like not the business, and verily I will know nothing of it. There lies the chamber she named to thee.

Clayton (aside).—An infernal, old, selfish, knave ! (*Exit.*)

Humphrey.—Verily, I am disturbed in mind ; that heedless damsel might entangle me in the snares of danger, but for my fair reputation. Woman, woman ! young or old, all alike ! vain, empty-headed, prone to evil, and looking not at the future. Yet Cicely is my child, a good child, though some-

what wasteful of the cakes and ale. Moreover, she helpeth
me greatly with her ready hands now, and will tend me carefully when I am aged. I will not chide her for this deed;
and verily I incline to do an act of charity, unknown to the
world, to these roystering Cavaliers. The times are strange,
and none can say what card may turn up trumps. But the
card must be turned, and then, whatever suit that card may
be of, that is Humphrey Allright's suit. Truly, this man deceives me; this is my mother, I affirm.

Enter CLAYTON, *disguised, with a short stick.*

Clayton.—Now, magnanimous Master Humphrey, shall I
pass muster? I have ever been reckoned no mean masque-
rader.

Humphrey.—I should truly judge as much, young brag-
gart. It seemeth to me that masquerading is thy proper calling. But I warn thee, there is yet danger.

Clayton.—Why, surely, old fellow, thou doth not mean to
denounce me?

Humphrey.—Denounce thee! How should I? I know
only that the stranger departed; and that my mother sitteth
as usual by the fire.

Enter CICELY.   *She dances laughing round the chair.*

Cicely.—Now, granny, remember thou art very deaf, and
very cross in speech; but speak little, and let me pull thy
hood over thy scented love-locks.

Clayton (in a tremulous voice).—My dutiful child, let me
embrace thee.

[CICELY *boxes his ears.*   *A loud knocking.*   HUMPHREY *trembles and runs
about; then lights his pipe and sits down by the fire.*]

Clayton.—And I have left my garments scattered about
the robing chamber!

Cicely.—Wiser heads than thine have been at work. I

have hidden thy trappings under my best hood and cardinal; and Seth himself, with all his suspicions, will not think to search for thee in a band-box.

Enter NEHEMIAH, SETH, Sergeant, *and two* Soldiers.

Nehemiah.—Friend Humphrey, behold these godly soldiers who come to remove from thy well-ordered hostel the malapert coxcomb and spy who hath intruded on thee; but I fear me he hath eluded justice.

Humphrey.—Verily, Nehemiah, I discharged him from my premises with powerful words, and found him no longer here when I returned from an errand to my cellar. Doubtless he absconded in fear of these valiant men.

Nehemiah (*to the soldiers*).—Depart speedily, in various directions, good men. Surely the malignant may yet be delivered into the hands of the righteous.

Sergeant.—My orders are written, Master Nehemiah: our first command is to search the house; and verily we will search it. Peradventure this comely damsel could aid us with some evidence against this Moabite.

Cicely.—Not I. The man came to eat and drink, and then ran away. I saw no harm in him, save that he was ugly, and poor, and hungry. Let wise Master Seth tell what raised his choler against a vagrant without a penny in his pouch; ye spend your time idly, soldiers, to search after such scarecrows.

Sergeant.—Nevertheless our orders are to search, and our duty is obedience. Old woman, didst thou mark whither this malignant wended?

Clayton.—A bad rheumatiz; God help me!

Seth.—Waste not thy words, sergeant, in discoursing with Granny Allright. She is an awful woman, stone deaf; and useth betimes sinful words.

Nehemiah.—Seth and I will conduct thy followers through

the chambers of the hostel, whilst thou resteth here, sergeant.
Depend on our zeal.

Sergeant.—I am not unwilling to rest. Follow the zealous
Nehemiah, soldiers.

Exit NEHEMIAH, SETH, *and* Soldiers.

Clayton.—Cicely, my child, give the worthy captain a seat;
also a cup of strong ale. I love the redcoats; good fellows
all. How fares the king? God bless him, and scatter the
Roundhead rogues; drink that, jolly boy! and spare not the
ale; 'tis good and wholesome.

Humphrey.—Heed her not good man; her years are many,
and she knows not the words she utters. Drink freely, and
tell us what news from the great army.

Sergeant.—The army is far from us now, friend Humphrey,
and verily our small party is in jeopardy, surrounded by the
idolatrous sons of Moab and Ammon. It behooveth us keenly
to search for the spies of the foe, lest we be scattered by the
craft of the scorners.

Clayton.—Lord send it! Humphrey, my son, I charge thee
to pray that this may fall true. My lads love not the sword
and the spear.

Humphrey.—She talks wilder than ever. Cicely, give thy
granny a cup of ale, and sign to her to hold her tongue, when
we are engaged in entertaining noble soldiers.

(*Cicely gives Clayton the ale.*)

Clayton.—Here's thy health, roving Jack. Thy grandsire
was like thee, a wild rogue, and courted and cast away scores
of merry damsels. God rest his soul! he sung a good song.
Thou singest, too, Humphrey, my son: give us a jolly stave;
the strong ale checreth me, and verily I will sing likewise
(*sings in a tremulous voice*), "And we'll keep the Round-
heads down, down, down!" (*she snores*).

Sergeant.—What an awful old woman! what a heavy burden for you, worthy Humphrey. Woman! forbear, at thy years, to sing the songs of the profane, and speak the words of the scorner.

Clayton.—Doth he ask me to dance with him, Cicely? Nay, nay, my dancing days are past. Seth wanted me to dance, too. Still, I'm very fresh yet (*sleeps*).

Humphrey.—Thou hast filled her with the strong ale, girl, and her weak head cannot stand its potency. It is well she sleepeth, for these quiet walls are unacquainted with such light words.

Enter NEHEMIAH, SETH, *and* Soldiers.

Nehemiah.—Friend Humphrey, thy words were veracious. The Philistine hath surely escaped our hands.

Sergeant (reading his orders).—I am next commanded to search diligently the out-houses.

Nehemiah.—Such proceeding will, I predict, be unfruitful; nevertheless, we will accompany thee.

Humphrey.—And even I, albeit my limbs are frail, will lead the search from granary to cellar. Cicely, put thy silly old granny to bed, and mind the bar.

[*Exeunt all but* CLAYTON *and* CICELY.

Cicely.—Now, granny, to thy chamber; doff this borrowed garb, and array thyself speedily in thy tattered finery. Then will I conduct thee through the plantation behind the house, while the soldiers search the offices in front. There thou wilt find my roan pony ready saddled; mount him and flee to the west, if thou wouldst avoid these disroyal knaves, and God be with thee. The pony is mine own, and I bestow it on thee; away!

Clayton.—Wilt thou not kiss thy poor old grandmother, Cicely?

Cicely.—Begone, Sir Cavalier. Thou art a bold coxcomb; and withal, an indifferent old woman.

[*Exeunt.*

Scene the Last.—Cicely *seated at work.*

An impatient, impudent fellow ! how he has rent it ! grand-mother's best gown, too !   Seth would have donned the gown and doffed it again, as carefully as if he had been arrayed in petticoats every day of his life.   Seth is a discreet youth ; but he did not well to bring down the soldiers on the gay and handsome Cavalier.   I should have served him right to have accepted the glittering ring pressed on me by the grateful soldier ; but father would have died outright to see the bauble. Well, by this time he is beyond pursuit, and Seth's jealous plots are scattered, and he has had his night's toil for nothing. Here they all come weary from their search through the vil-lage, and here comes father from his bed, now that all is safe.

Enter Humphrey, Nehemiah, Seth, *and* Sergeant.

Humphrey.—Is not then the knave taken, worthy and painstaking Christians ?

Sergeant.—Truly our search hath been in vain, though con-ducted with method and keenness.

Humphrey.—Be seated, friends, and Cicely will place be-fore ye a breakfast of beef and good ale, that you may be rested ere you depart with your ill-tidings.

Sergeant.—We have not yet fulfilled our duties, friend Humphrey : my instructions declare that I return not empty-handed.   The evil-minded stranger is suspected to be an im-portant officer in the service of the man Charles Stuart ; and should we fail to secure him, I am ordered to convey to the camp thy daughter, Cicely Allright, there to be detained in pledge, until we hear something of the fugitive.

Humphrey.—Cicely, my daughter ! nay, worthy sergeant, I cannot want her services ; moreover, we know nothing of the flight, nothing of the retreat of the dangerous delinquent. It cannot be necessary that my daughter should be carried off.

Sergeant.—Nevertheless, such are my orders, and they must needs be obeyed.

Humphrey.—My health and my business require the aid of my daughter. The damsel is well skilled in household matters. It is she that draweth the ale, serveth it out, discourseth with the guests, and marketh the score. Moreover, she prepareth for me the warm messes my failing health demandeth, and conducteth me in safety to my chamber, when, night after night, I am affected with dizziness of the head. I am unable to spare my daughter, good sergeant; and peradventure, my worthy friend, Nehemiah Greatman, will send his son Seth in place of the damsel. Seth is a stalwart youth, and will prove more useful in the camp than my daughter.

Sergeant.—We must obey our orders, which set forth that thy daughter must accompany us; therefore hasten, damsel, to make thy preparations.

Cicely.—I like not thy proceedings, soldier. What if I say I will not go with thee?

Sergeant.—Then, damsel, we must needs use force, and carry thee captive·to our tents.

Humphrey.—Nay, Cicely, resist not the law. The good man but fulfilleth his duty. Should contention arise, it might fall heavily on me—yield thee, child : this is a house of peace; go with the faithful soldier, and plead my cause before the saintly Captain Cantwell, that he may restore thee to thy helpless father.

Seth.—And verily I will also go. This mischief is of my making; but, damsel, I was wroth to hear thy light jests with that scented popinjay. My heart is sore and heavy to behold thee in captivity. Say thou wilt pardon me, Cicely?

Cicely.—Thou wert ever a simpleton, Seth; but thou hast a kind heart, and peradventure I may amend thy manners in good time. We will discourse the matter over as we follow unwillingly these——

Humphrey.—Good men, Cicely—good men, thou wouldst say.

Cicely.—Nay, father, these were not the words I was about to speak; but have it thine own way. I am ready, soldier, yet I warn thee to consider; but who.cometh now?

Enter CLAYTON, *in uniform, with* Soldiers.

Clayton.—Ah, friend sergeant, thou hast failed to bring down thy bird; and lo, now, thy myrmidons without' are my prisoners: therefore, friend, it will be well for thee to deliver up thy sword and join them. Thy sanctimonious captain and his crop-eared crew are also on the road to the army as our prisoners; and this pretty damsel, whom the pious Captain Cantwell intended to make a prize of, is free. Hearest thou' this, sergeant?

Sergeant.—Verily I do hear, and submit, for such is the chance of war. But though we be delivered up into the hands of the Philistines, yet will we not despair.

Clayton.—By no means, worthy sergeant, for thou wilt discover that thou mightest have done worse. The Philistines keep a good table, and are a jolly set of fellows; they will soon set thy face into a broader form. Begone!

Exit Sergeant.

And now, my pretty deliverer, how shall I thank thee for all thy kindness, in saving my life at the risk of thine own liberty. Above all, how canst thou pardon my falsehood when I confess to thee that I belong to another, and that all my pretty protestations to thee must be forgotten.

Cicely.—Didst thou really think, noble cavalier, that I heeded thy fine speeches, or admired thy love-locks? Didst thou not see that Seth and I were true and. betrothed lovers? and Seth is greatly more suited to my tastes than thou art. And now, that thou hast safely and honestly brought back my roan, and secured thy prisoners, if thou desirest to please me, depart speedily; for though I heed not thy speeches, Seth does, poor simpleton.

Clayton.—It is well ; I will pay thy father amply for his beef and ale ; but I will leave it to my fair lady to requite my pretty Cicely, by the offer of a wedding gift to her who chose rather to be a captive than to betray a brother in misfortune. Farewell, Cicely.

Humphrey.—And please, most noble Cavalier, if thou shouldst have to run away again in these parts, there is Peter Sourby's hostel lying about half a mile south, very commodious, where thou couldst have better attendance than in this poor place. I pray thee, sir, make Peter's thy place of refuge. I am fond of peace ; and if I had no longer my daughter to offer up, I myself, Humphrey Allright, a man of no opinions, might perhaps be torn away as a pledge ! Only think of that ! !

The scene closes.

———◦———

CHARADE II.

PAT-RIOT.

DRAMATIS PERSONÆ.

SIR JAMES ARUNDEL.   CAPTAIN O'BRIEN.   PATRICK O'BRALLAGAN.

LUCAS.   LADY ARUNDEL.   GERALDINE.   MARY.   COOK.

SCENE 1.—*A drawing-room.*   SIR JAMES, LADY ARUNDEL, GERALDINE.

Lady Arundel.—And now, my dear Geraldine, that you are restored to me, I hope you will forget speedily your Irish manners and customs.

Geraldine.—Never, mamma ; remember, that the seventeen years of my life have been passed almost entirely in dear Ireland.

Sir James.—And remember too, my lady, the drop of pure Milesian blood that runs in Geraldine's veins. My mother is proud of her country, and we can scarcely expect her adopted child should have dissimilar feelings.

14

Lady Arundel.—But I would not have the world believe she cherishes such feelings; Lord Dellington, whose attentions to her last night were gratifying, has, I know, a peculiar antipathy to Ireland.

Enter LUCAS.

Lucas.—A man, Sir James, about the footman's place; but I am afraid he is Irish.

Geraldine.—Do let him come up, papa.

Sir James.—Well, we are really in immediate need of a servant; we will see him at all events. Show him up, Lucas.

LUCAS *ushers in* O'BRALLAGAN *and retires.*

O'Brallagan.—God save your honors, and it's a beautiful parlor that ye 're havin' to yourselves. I'm the boy, sure, that 's come to take the place for want of a better; and by the same token, it's a capital servant your honors will get, musha!

Sir James.—You are premature, my friend.

O'Brallagan.—Will it be well-looking your honor is maning? arrah! and that's thruly what all the girls are saying.

Sir James.—I mean, young man, that I must hear something more of you, before I engage you.

O'Brallagan.—No offense in the world yer honor, and if agreeable to their honorable ladyships, I 'll tell the history of all the root and stock of the O'Brallagans.

Lady Arundel.—No, no, it is quite unnecessary, O'Brallagan, if that is your name.

O'Brallagan.—Is it the name that 's on me, yer ladyship? sure its Paitrick O'Brallagan; Terence, he 's the boy that comes next to me—and then there's Norah, our sister, a sweet purty girl, she that died i' the famine faver. Then——

Sir James.—You must not talk so much O'Brallagan, before the ladies. Be content to answer my questions. Where did you last live?

O'Brallagan.—It would be in the steerage, yer honor,

aboard of the steamer; and a very dacent place it was to lie down in, saving yer ladyship's presence.

Sir James.—You misunderstand me: I wish to know in whose service you have lived?

O'Brallagan.—Och! sure wasn't I at any gintleman's service that wanted a nate job done.

Sir James.—I am perfectly puzzled; I believe, Geraldine, I shall need your services to question the witness.

Geraldine (laughing).—Tell me, O'Brallagan, what can you do?

O'Brallagan.—And is it yer honorable ladyship asks me that with yer own beautiful mouth? Sure, ye might ask the thing that Patrick O'Brallagan is short of knowing; and if I don't answer yer honor, I have never seen the boy that will do that thing at all, at all.

Lady Arundel.—I do hope, Sir James, you will not think of engaging this ignorant Irishman. I am positively quite alarmed, he appears so eccentric.

O'Brallagan.—Not a bit of that same, yer honor. It's the quietest boy of the world ye'll find me, and that's the thruth; barring any spalpeen blackens me counthry, and thin me blood is riz, and no help for that, at all, at all.

Geraldine.—Oblige me, dear papa, by hiring O'Brallagan. He looks honest; Mary, who is a half-bred Irish girl, will teach him his duty; and in truth, papa, my heart warms to the brogue—it is home language to me.

Lady Arundel.—Geraldine, I quite shudder at your inelegant vehemence. I must entreat you to control this Irish impetuosity before the refined Lord Dellington.

Geraldine.—Oh, mamma! I hate to hear of Lord Dellington.

Sir James.—That is an improper expression my child. Lord Dellington is a good man in the world, a man of high rank, of large estates, and above all, he admires my little, wild Irish girl.

Geraldine.—But he is nearly as old as you are, papa; and I should really like to choose a husband myself.

Lady Arundel.—Sir James, I am in despair; this is indeed terrible.

Sir James.—We will discuss the matter afterward; in the mean time, we must endeavor to extract some information of Patrick's abilities. Can you perform the duties of a house-servant?

O'Brallagan.—Musha! is it the work? sure I'll do all the work of the house, beautiful! Will yer ladyship be kaping pigs, and won't I engage to make them so fat they'll bate the parson's?

Geraldine.—But we don't keep pigs, Patrick; we want a footman.

O'Brallagan.—And that's mighty lucky, my lady. Where will yer two beautiful eyes see a nater footman, if I was having but the fine coat? Would yer honor be agreable to me havin' a green coat, in regard of ould Ireland; may the sun never set on her! But, may-be yer honor would be wantin' a choice about the coat; and faith! I'm asy about the color; barring it wouldn't be orange, bad luck to it! And now, long life to your ladyship, will I go down to yer illegant kitchen and set to work?

Sir James.—However unpromising our first acquaintance is, I think I must oblige you, Geraldine, by giving this man a trial, as we really need a town servant. You may stay, O'Brallagan: Lucas and the maids will teach you your duty.

O'Brallagan.—Sure and they will! and my blessin' on yer honors, and the beautiful young cratur you own, and she that will be having the handsomest husband in Ireland, and free of his money. Long life to him, and not an honesther boy nor Patrick O'Brallagan ever darkened yer door, and quiet, barring the sup of whiskey, when the heart's heavy. And a good day this has turned up for us all, by the powers! (*Exit.*)

Lady Arundel.—I am by no means satisfied with your decision, Sir James. In this confined town-house, where we cannot have an establishment, we might surely have engaged a more respectable servant than this extraordinary savage.

Geraldine.—Do not think so harshly of him, mamma—you are not accustomed to the Irish; but believe me, they are true and faithful. (*Aside, with a sigh.*) Dear, dear O'Brien!

Sir James.—He is certainly a wild Irishman; but, with a little training, we may make a good servant of Patrick O'Brallagan.

[*Exeunt.*

Scene 2.—*A Kitchen.*—O'Brallagan, Mary.

O'Brallagan.—Faith and troth, it's an illegant place, and plenty to ate, and your purty face to comfort me, and long may it last. And didn't I tell you before, och! mavourneen, it would do yer bright eyes good to look on the fine grand captain, the thruest of lovers—when would an Irishman not be thrue?—one of the ould race, a raal O'Brien; the blood runs right down from the ould ancient kings, thrue for him! Isn't it all to see on paper and made out in Latin, as ould Corny O'Neil can show, musha! musha! So, darling of me heart, the captain comes to me and says,—Patrick O'Brallagan, you'll be the bachelor of purty Mary.

Mary.—What assurance indeed!—and what did you say to that, Mr. O'Brallagan?

O'Brallagan.—Wouldn't I tell the captain the thruth? how we came togither, and how I was proud to git a sight of yer face; and by the same token, it wasn't your fault, that ye were not knowen me, in regard that we had niver met sin we were born, at all, at all. Then says the captain, wouldn't your purty Mary be the girl to put the bit of paper to Miss Geraldine, and the mother that owned her niver be the wiser And didn't I spake for you, mavourneen, and give yer consint, and take the captin's illegant letther and the crown-piece, for you entirely. Few it is of them same crown-pieces iver rests with the O'Briens, in regard of their being remarkable free in parting wid them, blessins on them for iver and iver, it is them that are the raal thrue race. May the Heavens shower gold upon their heads.

Mary.—And must I give Miss Geraldine the letter, Patrick?

O'Brallagan.—In coorse ye will, my darlin; and when they are married, you are my choice to be Mrs. Patrick O'Brallagan, and then we will apply for the place of lady's maid to the captain and his bride, seeing that same would shute us entirely.

Mary.—Well, Patrick, I will do it, if you say it is right; but I feel rather shy about it, for Mr. Lucas has been watching us all along from his pantry window ; and Patrick, you know, he is jealous about you. Then Cook, she is jealous of him, and treats me like a slave, and I cannot help being better looking than she is.

O'Brallagan.—Not a bit of it, you beauty o' the world, and if ye wer' wishin' the fairies to make ye ill-lookin', they couldn't find in their hearts to do it. Here comes Mrs. Cook, so lave me to discoorse her nately, and go in it with the letther, ye good cratur.

[Exit MARY.

Enter COOK, with a plucked fowl.

O'Brallagan.—Sure, I knowed that would be your purty foot makin' the music on the flore. Och, by the powers, it is a wonderful woman ye are, Misthress Cook. I'm thinking, ye jewel, ye would asily make a roasted goose out of a prater, musha. A raal clever cratur ye are wi' the pans and gridirons.

Cook.—You says so, Mr. O'Brallagan, and you is haltogether a gentleman, but there's hothers that hought to be the first to speak them words that old their tongues, and runs hafter other girls as hought to be hashamed o' theirselves to be hinveggling hother people's sweetarts, and a making their hinnyhenders hagen them as is their betters.

O'Brallagan.—And, sure, it wouldn't be purty Mary ye would mane, Misthress Cook. Bad luck to him that would make her out to be a rogue, and me here to let that word be said, and Mary my own counthrywoman, and that's the thruth intirely.

Cook.—There hagen, Mr. O'Brallagan, you're a standin' up for her, and the girls hinsensed you as she's a Hirisher. No such a thing! My lady never ires no Hirishers, and she ave a sittyfittykit as ow as Mary wer' born hin Hessex.

O'Brallagan.—Och! only to see that same! But be asy, my jewel—isn't Mary my own lawful cousin? Leastways, her own born mother, which was Biddy O'Neil, was second cousin to my Aunt Honor Delany, which same was born at Kilfinane, and berred i' the thrubbles, God rest her soul! and it follows quite nat'ral that Mary would be cousin to me. And shure Biddy O'Neil was a Kilkenny woman, and any how her daughter would be a born Irishwoman.

Cook.—Really, Mr. O'Brallagan, you talk a deal of nonsense, you that's a man of heddication, and I cannot hunderstand your piggygrease; I stand to it as Mary's Hinglish, and old up er ed, and perk herself habout er beauty, sich has it his, and him encouraging er as hought to know better, and telling er he hadmire black heyes—more shame on im, when he knows my heyes is surilleen blue, hand that he swear with his hown tongue, till she tice im hoff, a himperent ussy.

O'Brallagan.—Be asy now, my fine woman, arrah what would you be havin? It's Patrick O'Brallagan that's her sworn bachelor, and will be thrue to her, and be the friend of her and hers for iver and iver, and bad luck to the spalpeen that lays his eyes on her at all, at all, without my lave from this day out. (*Sees Lucas enter behind.*) And you'd be hearing my words, Mr. Lucas, long life to you for a snake, stolen behind to listen to our discourse. May be it'll not be plasin you.

Lucas.—I hadvise you, O'Brallagan, not to disremember that you are speaking to a hupper servant, and to respect your betters and keep a civil tongue in your ed. I ear what you say of me and Miss Mary, and I hadvise you to mind your own haffairs.

O'Brallagan.—Shure now ! and a fine bit of advice it is ! and grand words; may be it would be the Masther that said them words to you, and you being sich a mighty fine gintle-man ! (*Enter Mary.*) Och ! Mary, mavournéen, it wouldn't be thrue that you'd be lettin him come round you with his grand discoorse; ye wouldn't be shaming them that came afore you. Shure ! it's not for your mother's daughter to de-mane herself to an Englishman.

Lucas.—What do you mean, you low Hirish feller ! I allays say you be quite inferiorer to us; and I take care that this ouse are too ot to old ye. I say to Sir James as ow you hin-sults the hupper servants, and as you conways cladderintestine letters to our Miss, which inference I'se make it my dooty to report to my lady, hin honnar.

O'Brallagan.—By the powers, and that's what ye mane to do ye ould rogue o' the world; and it 's a hullabaloo ye'll riz, ye will ! Arrah ! then what'll Patrick O'Brallagan be doing, musha ! musha ! To blazes wi' ye, ye schamer o' life, ye slave of a Saxon, may ye git yer desarvins, sooner or later. Hoorah ! for the rights of Ireland !

Cook (shrieks).—Pollis ! Pollis ! elp ! elp ! Oh the willun will murder poor hinnocent Mr. Lucas !

Lucas.—'Old im, Cook, 'old im ; get back to Hireland, you poor hignorant savage. Hall them Hirish is rogues and beg-gars.

O'Brallagan.—Whisha, girls, let me be. Arrah, you spalpeen, wait till we get our rights, and won't we driv' all ye venomous Saxons before us into the wide say, and clare you out of our own counthry outright, Whisha! whisha! (*Dances about, waving his arms; the women scream.*)

Enter SIR JAMES.

Sir James. What means this infernal noise? Are you all drunk, or mad? You have terrified the ladies into hysterics.

All together. Please, Sir James——

Sir James. I must understand the matter thoroughly: I command you all to follow me to the library, that I may learn the truth.

[*Exeunt.*

SCENE THE LAST—*The Library.* SIR JAMES, LADY ARUNDEL, GERALDINE *seated at a table; the* Servants *standing, the* Women *weeping,* LUCAS *and* O'BRALLAGAN *making gestures of anger.*

Sir James. Now, I must insist upon knowing the cause of this strange uproar. You appeared to be a quiet young man, O'Brallagan; what has thus provoked you to such violence?

O'Brallagan.—It's me counthry, yer honorable worship! that desaving thief of the world, what does he do but turn his black tongue to abuse me counthry! Ireland, yer honor, the fine ouldest counthry o' the world. Och! isn't it in me that our grand, ould ancient kings were uppermost ov' all the arth afore the black soil of England had riz from the bottom of the say. It wouldn't become yer beautiful ladyship to be larfing at my words anyhow, in regard of ould Corny O'Neil—that's him that bates the globe for larnin—and didn't he tache me and all the scholars the ould history that came down in Latin to him, that spoke Latin quite nat'ral. And didn't Corny insense us that the day was comin' for the thrue Irish boys to get their rights, and their ould ancient kings back agen.

And by the same token, isn't it every inch of the ground is blessed, in regard of St. Patrick himself that walked without a shoe to his foot from one end to another, and left it to us for iver and iver, that the boys would be the bravest, and the girls the purtiest of all the world, and that's thrue of it, and no lie at all, at all, as Corny know, and——

Lady Arundel.—Pray be silent, young man, your words are perfectly distracting to me.   .

O'Brallagan.—Ochone! see that now! what will I do at all, wisha? Sorra a bit would Patrick O'Brallagan be the boy to give the fear to her beautiful honorable ladyship; and the illegant young miss with the smile on her purty mouth, and one too that knows the Captain, him that's the thruest of lovers, and wanted to go off to the Crimmer to fight the Roosians, barring he wouldn't displase the jewel that owned his heart altogether. Wisha! wisha! what will I be saying now? That's the way wid me iver, the thruth always comes out; and if it wer' the killen' o' me, my heart gets the betther o' me.

Lady Arundel.—What does he man mean by these impertinent allusions to lovers?

Lucas.—Please, my lady, them were the very words I say which aggravate O'Brallagan. I think it my dooty, my lady, to infer, when I see O'Brallagan give Miss Mary a cladderin-testine letter to take to Miss Geraldine.

O'Brallagan.—Arrah, then, bad luck to yez for a maker-of-mischief; it's the saints themselves that ye would provoke, let alone a civil-spoken boy like me, that cannot put up with yer ways. Musha! Isn't it thrue for the master that ye're all alike, and it's divarsion from morn till night, and nothing else in the world ye think on, down below in the jintale kitchen, where there's plinty and no stint, and niver a pig durst show his purty face in it at all!

Sir James.—Do not look alarmed, my dear Lady Arundel,

The *cladderintestine* letter inclosed one to me, which Geraldine dutifully delivered, and told me the tale which she has yet been too timid to communicate to her mother. It was my mother who sanctioned and approved the addresses of Captain O'Brien, a gallant soldier, who has already earned laurels—the nephew and heir of our old friend, Lord O'Brien. The letter was from him, making such proposals for our daughter as I think even you will not reject, though the Captain is Irish. I expect the gentleman to call himself this morning—and probably that may be his knock. Go, Lucas, and usher in the visitor.

Lucas *retires, and returns, announcing Captain* O'Brien, Sir James *goes forward, shakes hands, and introduces him to* Lady Arundel.

Capt. O'Brien.—Truly, Sir James, an introduction to your gentle lady encourages me to hope. Who can behold her and not see at once that she must be the mother of the lovely Geraldine; if they did not decide that one so young and beautiful could only be her sister.

Lady Arundel.—You gentlemen of the sister Island certainly excel in the art of flattering the matrons, and winning the maidens.

Capt. O'Brien.—So the world says; but then, where are there such sons and such husbands as the true-hearted sons of Erin? Make me your devoted servant forever, dear lady, by granting me the hand of your fair image, my beloved Geraldine.

Lady Arundel:—I had other views for my daughter, but I leave all in the hands of Sir James; for though usually I have somewhat of prejudice against the Irish, there is a nobility about your manner, worthy of the nephew of Lord O'Brien, whom I knew well many years ago—in fact——I thought him too old!

Capt. O'Brien.—How fortunate, dear Lady Arundel! for if you had not thought so, the world would not have seen the flower of beauty, Geraldine Arundel, and I should not have been the heir of the O'Briens.

Sir James.—We will know you a little more, O'Brien, and then I think you need not despair.

Capt. O'Brien.—And blessed will be the day when I shall carry my little pearl of the world back to the land of love and beauty, dear Erin!

O'Brallagan.—And would ye be wanting a lady's maid, Captain?

Capt. O'Brien.—Arrah, Patrick, is that you? What in the world have you been brought up for?—you surely haven't been breaking the peace here?

O'Brallagan.—Wisha! wisha! What will I do? It was my blood was up! Wasn't it the innemies of our counthry, Captain, 'ud provoked me?

Capt. O'Brien.—And so you wish to go out as a lady's maid to Ireland?

O'Brallagan.—Plase your honor, that was in regard to purty Mary and Miss Geraldine, and she willin' to take me intirely if Miss Geraldine will want us for the lady's maid, or the lodge at the grand gate, when we would be havin' a pratey all the year round, and may-be a pig on the floor, and not a penny of rint to pay. And isn't Mary the girl that'll make me come home straight, niver looking at the shebeen, at all, at all.

Capt. O'Brien.—Well, O'Brallagan, I believe we Irish boys are best at home; so, if Sir James will allow it, and Lady Arundel will pardon your trespasses, you must return with me to the *ould counthry, good luck to it!*

O'Brallagan.—Hoorah! hoorah! for the thrue boys; ould Ireland for iver!

CHARADE III.

MIS-CHIEF.

DRAMATIS PERSONÆ.

GLENALLIN. M'LOMOND. JACOB HODGES.
JESSY. MARTHA WILLIAMS.

SCENE 1—*A room in a Highland Castle. Enter* JACOB.

"Thus far into the bowels of the land." And a very snug place is a Highland castle; "here would I rest." Well, "all the world's a stage," and decidedly my performances on its boards have for the last few days been uncommonly successful. A love affair! the aim of my life! All my experience before was but foil practice; now I am on the field of honor; on the path to victory. To speak simple truth, the whole affair may be called an artful dodge. First, I succeed in releasing the young lady's hawk unperceived and unsuspected; and then I recover it, of course at the peril of my life, and restore it to its fair mistress. How charmingly she thanked me for my rash and dangerous exploit; overcome by her matchless beauty, I remained long speechless with wonder; then crying out, "Oh, speak again, bright angel!" I involuntarily revealed my passion. Then I vowed that were she, as I hoped, some simple village maiden, I would abandon my father's halls, resign my high estate, and remain at her side, and "beyond all limit of what's i' the world, would love, prize, honor her." She blushed and trembled; then with the rich gift of speech which nature has so bountifully bestowed on me, I won her at length to answer my frantic demands. Unconscious that I had known and watched her long, she revealed to me, with a deep sigh, that she had the misfortune to be the heiress of Glenallin; which disclosure *naturally* filled me with grief and despair.   In my distraction, I threatened to terminate my wretched life ; but at her urgent entreaties, I consented to live for her sake.   *By accident,* we have met again and again ; and I have acted Romeo to the life, and I have, I trust, captivated my admiring Juliet.   It has become necessary to take a bolder step, and having *opportunely* to-day found the falcon's silver chain, I have ventured into the very den of the lion, in order to restore the young lady's property, but above all to have a peep into the interior of the establishment, to rub down the governor, and then, if the cards are in my favor, to present the happily worded letter of my Lord Glasgow.   Ah ! here comes the pretty little filly, neat in her paces, but I have seen freer action.—Poor Martha !

Enter JESSY.

Jessy.—Oh, Montague, rash and thoughtless man, how could you disobey me ? how could you venture to enter the castle uninvited ?   Glenallin is, fiery in temper, and you have all the pride and bravery of an English Knight.   I tremble to think on your meeting ; should you quarrel, what would be my misery !   Promise me, Montague, not to resent any hasty words my father may utter.

Jacob.—Rest happy, gentle maiden ! Your soft wishes will form a shield to protect your parent.   Could I, by word or act, create a pang in that valued heart ?   He is safe, though he insult me ; but though he should call out all his clan, he cannot stop me ; for, Jessy, "there lies more peril in thine eyes, than twenty of their swords."

Jessy.—" *O gentle Montague !*" it is very strange ! almost marvelous how all my dreams of fancy have been fulfilled. Would you believe it that when my sweet friend, Augusta Victoria Smith, and I used to speculate on our future prospects—for we shared the same dormitory at Mount Ida House, at Hampstead, and used to solace the long hours of our nocturnal watchfulness by planning charming romances of love—would you believe it that I then vowed I would tolerate no lover unless he was named Montague?"

Jacob.—Happy, prophetic inspiration! and did that ideal Montague resemble——

Jessy.—I must confess that my fancied adorer spoke very much as you do, and except for the uniform, the personal resemblance is striking. But alas! Glenallin wishes to betroth me to his constant ally and fast friend; and his name is unfortunately Alexander. Besides his accent is Scottish, and I am persuaded he would be laughed at and ridiculed at Mount Ida House. I allow that he is noble and rich, tall and handsome; but he has no sentiment, no romance in his character; he laughs so loudly that I am convinced Miss Primby would faint to hear him, and I fear many of his habits would be thought low at Mount Ida House Academy.

Jacob.—Then cast him from you, noble maiden, "Love is all gentle words, or sighs, or tears."

Jessy.—What would Augusta Victoria Smith think of such a rude and unfashionable *futur?* She is already betrothed; but sad to say, her lover, though a captain in the Hampshire Militia, is named John Thompson. This was ever a painful fact to her, till I suggested that we should always name him *Giovanni;* she was enchanted with the idea, and ever after addressed him *Il mio caro Giovanni.* Beloved, highly gifted Augusta Victoria!

Jacob.—Oh, say to your charming friend that Montague Fitz-Alan throws himself at her feet, entreating her to intercede with the peerless Jessy to accept the devoted love of her slave. Turn not away, light of my soul, from my bold words. "O Beauty! till now I never knew thee!"

Jessy.—I am weak and blamable to listen to your wild vows; besides, I cannot accept you; there is one insuperable objection; the hero of my school fancies was a soldier. Why,

Montague, with your noble nature, and distinguished figure, have you not adopted the graceful and honorable uniform that marks the defender of his country, in this her hour of need ?

Jacob.—Alas, fair maiden, family reasons have restrained my ardent desire to join the brave band who are gathering blood-stained laurels in strange lands. I am the sole representative of a noble and ancient family of high conservative principles. My proud father disdained to owe his son's commission to a commander-in-chief of opposite politics. The matter was even urged on him by high authority; but he firmly refused. But now, sweet Jessy, I am your slave; " Call me but love, I will forsake my name." I will accept rank in the army of the Whigs ! Decide for me, fair mistress of my fate; name your favorite regiment; and such is the influence of the name of Fitz-Alan, that my commission will be secured.

Jessy.—Not on any account, Montague: in truth, I fear I am wrong. I tremble at the thoughts of your meeting with Glenallin; that is, with papa. Miss Primley insisted on my always calling him papa at Mount Ida House ; she declared it was rude and ill-bred to speak so unceremoniously of my parent, and that I ought at least to say *Mister* Glenallin. I durst not address him thus for the world, and he forbids me to say papa; yet it would shock Augusta Victoria if I forgot the elegant manners of Hampstead. But you have no idea how absolute and imperious papa can be, Montague, and probably he will insist on knowing your business at the Castle.

Jacob.—And I am fully prepared to reply to him. Glenallin is no more formidable to me than Derby, Aberdeen, or any of my noble friends at the Court of England.

Jessy.—But I am not sure that I should like to appear at the Court of England, among your great friends. I am but a simple Scottish lassie, or at best a foolish English school·girl. And, then, papa is so anxious that I shall marry M'Lomond——

Jacob.—M'Lomond !   Is he in the Castle ?

Jessy.—No ; he is gone off on a hunting party ; and, besides, he was so offended with my indifference, that it will be
long before he comes here again.

Jacob (aside).—I trust it may.

Jessy.—But why do you ask ?   Do you know M'Lomond ?

Jacob.—I have hunted with him at Lord Glasgow's.

Jessy.—Glasgow is papa's great friend ;   therefore, his
name will be your introduction.   We will go to him in his
study.

[Exeunt.

SCENE 2.—*A room in the castle with books, trophies of the chase, &c.*
GLENALLIN *seated, with papers before him.*

What can have become of my bonnie spoilt lassie ?   Ah,
my lady Glenallin ! it was a dark day for me when you lay on
your death-bed, and urged me to promise to send my heart-
some lassie to learn English manners at a southron school.
And what has come of the deed ?   It will be long before she
bounds over the heath again with the free step of the Gael.
It will be long before she forget the mincing, sickening tongue
of the South ; nay, worse than all, I fear it will be long before
her wayward fancy will see the worth of the gallant, faithful
young M'Lomond.   My winsome Jessy ! I would not have
her to give her hand till he has won her heart ; but I have
again urged him to come, unknown to her ; and this day I
trust to see him at the head of his brave clansmen ; then I
ken little of a young lassie's fancy, if the bold M'Lomond,
towering above his clan, clad in his gray kilt and plaid, and
wearing his eagle plume above his noble brow, does not win
my Jessy.   I hear the music of her foot ; but who is this
stranger ?

Enter JACOB and JESSY.

Jessy.—Dear papa—Glenallin, I mean—this gentleman, an
English traveler, was so obliging as to secure my fugitive
15

falcon; and he has now kindly come to restore to me the silver chain which he has found.   This is Mr. Montague Fitz-Alan, papa.

Glenallin.—I thank Mr. Montague Fitz-Alan for his exploit, and I make no doubt that you have also thanked him, my daughter.   The halls of Glenallin are ever open to the stranger: he is welcome.

Jacob.—My lord, I come to claim more from you than your hospitality: I would not be a stranger in these honored halls.

I have long, unknown to her, admired and loved your fair daughter.   Deem it not presumption; I am the heir of a noble house, and I come forward boldly to beseech you to accept me as your son-in-law.   I have set my life upon the cast, yet dare not to urge my passion to the lovely maid without your sanction.   I rest all my hopes on your generosity—I ask but the maid; wealth I need not.   "My love, more noble than the world, prizes not quantity of dirty lands."   She, alone, is my attraction.   "That miracle!—that queen of gems!"

Glenallin.—But who, and what are you, young Englishman?   Your words are many, and beyond the comprehension of our northern simplicity.   You are welcome to the hospitality of my castle, as a stranger; but, as the wooer of my daughter, I would know more of you.

Jacob.—"I stand for judgment."   Know you not the highborn Lord Glasgow?

Glenallin.—Well I know the heroic Glasgow; but he is no longer in Scotland; ten days ago, at the head of the bravest of his clan, he sailed to fight the battles of his country in the East.   Even if you know him, he cannot appear to certify who you are.

Jacob.—"Doubt not mine honor."   The noble Glasgow has ever been my firm friend: we parted on the strand, and, at that anxious moment, I poured into his friendly bosom my tale of silent love.   He heard and pitied me; nay, more, he urged me to seek you his noble friend, and declare my passion;

he even wrote a few brief words before he left the shore, to advocate my cause. Behold the letter!

Glenallin.—I am satisfied that you are honorable by the sight of my friend's writing; it is scarcely needful to read his letter. (*Opens and reads it.*)

"Will you, for my sake, dear Glenallin, grant the bearer, if possible, the favor he asks from you; he will prove all you can wish. Ever yours,

"GLASGOW."

Truly, Mr. Fitz-Alan, this is high testimony, and had I not built my hopes on my little lassie becoming the bride of the brave M'Lomond, I should have proudly welcomed you as my son. Now, I must perforce disappoint you for——

Jacob.—Yet, stay, Glenallin. "Hear the lady!—let the lady speak!" I will abide by her decision.

"If she loves me not,
Let me be no assistant to a state,
But keep a farm and carters!"

Glenallin.—Young Englishman, it is not usual for Scottish maidens to dictate to their parents. I am the head of a clan, of which my daughter forms an individual. I require obedience, though I am no despot. My clansmen give me their services; I do not hold them in slavery. My daughter must yield me her duty; but I do not wish her to forfeit her happiness. Speak, then, my Jessy: is it true that you have so soon bestowed your heart on this stranger; and would you be his bride?

Jessy.—Oh, Montague, I cannot leave Glenallin. I believe I never meant seriously to leave home. But, papa, Augusta Victoria wrote to assure me you would compel me to marry M'Lomond; and I thought that would be terrible.

Glenallin.—And you thought your silly English correspondent knew your father better than you did yourself. No, Jessy; I would not force you to marry my friend, though I shall expect that the daughter of Glenallin wed only her equal. But you shall not decide hastily, my child. We will descend to the dining hall, and introduce the noble Saxon to Highland hospitality.

[*Exeunt.*

SCENE THE LAST.—*A hall in the castle. Table covered with jugs, glasses, &c. GLENALLIN, JACOB, JESSY, seated.*

Glenallin.—Leave us not yet, my Jessy. (*Aside*) I shal. weary of this stranger's fantastic words, if I am left alone with him. (*Aloud*) I have some hopes of a visit from an old friend to-day; when he arrives, you can seek your bower, and consider over the grand question.

Jacob.—(*Aside*) I should like to know who the old fellow expects; it would be advisable to *cut* in time. (*Aloud*) And I must tear myself awhile from all I love. I expect important dispatches from Government, and must be at my inn to receive them.

Enter Servant.

Servant.—There's a puir sonsie English lassie, clamoring for justice fra ye, Glenallin.

Glenallin.—Take her to my study, Andrew.

Servant.—But there's no hauding her, Glenallin, she is greeting just ahint me.

Jessy.—Let the poor woman come here, papa, if she be in sorrow. (*Exit servant.*)

Enter MARTHA, *who rushes up to* JACOB.

Martha.—Oh, Jacob Hodges, sham' on you! you're at your play-actor tricks again; gettin' into grand folks' houses wi' your rigmarole speechifying. How dar' ye lift up your head, man, after swearing to marry a poor lass, and then running off and leaving her altogether.

Jacob.—Woman, avaunt! I know thee not. "This is mere madness."

Martha.—Not know me, Martha Willans? God forgi' thee, Jacob! (*sobbing*) and oh, miss! sic a bonny quiet lad he was down i' Yorkshire, when we were bits of bairns together ; but nought wad sarve him but gang off wi' t' player folks ; and it was nobbit last Martinmas was a twelvemonth, that he settled down, and we cam' togither into yan house.

Glenallin.—Young man, what means this woman's violence ? Are you not a Fitz-Alan ?

Jacob.—"You are abused, my lord."

Glenallin.—I fear indeed that I am; and you must certainly have greatly imposed on Lord Glasgow.

Martha.—That he niver did, I'll stand to it. Jacob there, wi' all his bits of fine duds, and his silly ways, is as good a groom as ever rubbed down a horse, and that's what my lord couldn't but say on him.

Jessy.—A groom ! can it be possible ?

Martha.—Yes, miss, we baith lived wi' my lord, till he set off a soldering, and then Jacob, he had no mind for fighting, so my lord sits down, and writes him a character, to get him a good place. Then Jacob he ticed me on to gi' warning, and he telled me he would be sartain to meet me at Glasgow town-end last Monday was a week, and he would wed me. And I went like a fule that I was, and saw none on him, not I, and some folks we kenned tuik me in, and there I fell bad wi' crying and fretting, till our folks heard on him seeking for a place at Glenallin, and after him I cam, and——

Jacob.—*Amazing!* The woman labors under a strong mental delusion. Believe her not.

> "Mine honor is my life ; both grow in one ;
> Take honor from me, and my life is done."

Enter M'LOMOND.

M'Lomond (*taking Jessy's hand.*)—How fares my bonnie Jessy? What! in tears, my winsome lassie? What means this?

Jessy.—Oh, do not ask me, M'Lomond! I am ashamed to look on you.

M'Lomond.—I am in a mist. Speak, Glenallin, my good friend. You seem to be holding a court of justice in your banqueting hall. Who is this weeping woman and the gentleman?——Why, Hodges! what in the world has brought you in this gay attire to Glenallin.

Jacob.—" A truant disposition, good, my lord."

M'Lomond.—Oh, I see, then the lass you left behind you has followed to claim her property: a common case. But yet I cannot understand how Lord Glasgow's groom happens to be seated at Glenallin's board.

Jessy.—I will tell you all afterward, M'Lomond; my romantic folly has produced this vexatious scene. Entreat Glenallin to pardon his English school-girl, who promises in future to act like Glenallin's daughter.

Jacob.—Oh woman! woman! " Now could I drink hot blood." But, no, I will not. Would you please, Glenallin, to return me my character, " out of holy pity"? I must needs resume the duties of my profession. See, girl, what a pretty kettle of fish, thou hast made, but I forgive thee, and—

> " Mark not my fall, and that which ruined me!
> 'Martha, I charge thee, fling away ambition."

Let us leave the gorgeous palaces of the proud. " Not a frown more;" forgive my brief inconstancy, and

> " All my fortune at thy feet I'll lay,
> And follow thee, my love, through all the world."

[Exeunt Jacob and Martha.

M'Lomond (*laughing.*)—And now for explanations. I am anxious to discover the meaning of Martha's " kettle of fish."

TABLEAUX VIVANTS.

TABLEAUX VIVANTS, or Living Pictures, are, as their name
expresses, pictures formed within a frame by living persons,
in imitation of paintings. When well arranged and tastefully-
costumed, they may be made most effective and beautiful.

A frame about seven or eight feet high, and as wide as the
size of the room will permit, should be securely fastened, and
covered either with black net, or fine blue gauze, to harmonize
and subdue the colors in the dresses. Brackets for candles
should be arranged inside the frame, so as to throw the light
full upon the group forming the picture. The most beautiful
tableaux, and those which afford most pleasure to an intelligent audience, are either copies of well-known pictures or
scenes from popular dramas or poems. Of these we give a
few specimens, though the field thus opened to an enterprising manager of tableaux, is boundless.

No. 1.—THE LADY OF THE LAKE.

This scene is the last in Scott's celebrated poem, "The Lady
of the Lake." In the centre of the foreground stands James
Fitz James, beside him kneels Graeme, and at his right hand
Ellen stands. Fitz James is placing in Ellen's hand the clasp
of a gold chain which encircles Graeme's neck. At Ellen's
side Douglas stands, while the background is filled with cour-
tiers. The costumes must be Scotch. Ellen in white, with a

plaid thrown carelessly over her dress ; Fitz James in Lincoln green, and Douglas and Graeme in full Highland costume. The poem itself is the best guide for other details.

No. 2.—THE TRIAL OF CONSTANCE DE BEVERLY.

This scene from " Marmion," well arranged, makes a most exquisite and striking tableaux.

The light must be very dim, and the background should be a screen covered with a dull, stone-colored cloth. From the screen an iron lamp is suspended. A table stands in the centre of the picture, upon which are placed papers, a skull, and crucifix. Behind the table are seated the blind abbot of Lindisfarn, with white hair and black dress; and on either side of him are the abbess of St. Hilda and Tynemouth's prioress. On either side of these three, clad in rough dresses, are the executioners, with trowels and tools, standing back close to the screen. On the right of the foreground, is a man in frock and cowl, crouched as if in extremity of terror, on the ground. On the left of the foreground stands Constance De Beverly, with her profile to the audience. She is clad in a page's dress, with her head bare, and her hair flowing loosely over her shoulders. The moment chosen is as she is about to speak in her own defense. Again, for costume, and the proper expression of the faces, I must refer the reader to the poem. *Marmion, Canto* 2, verses xviii. to xxvi.

No. 3.—DRESSING THE MAY QUEEN.

The centre figure in this group should be a beautiful little girl dressed entirely in white, standing upon a chair, while round her are grouped three or four young girls. One on the left arranges a wreath upon the child's hair, a second near her presents a basket of flowers. A third, kneeling before the chair, is arranging the folds of the dress, while a fourth, on the right, stands off as if studying the effect. It adds very much to the effect of this picture to have a group of children gayly dressed and carrying flowers, grouped in the background, as if waiting to bear off their little Queen.

No. 4.—THE FORTUNE-TELLER.

The scene a room. A table in the centre is covered with papers, a skull, antique lamp, and some books. Seated behind the table, facing the audience, is a young, beautiful brunette, dressed in a gorgeous Eastern costume. Over a loose robe of white muslin, a short open jacket of crimson trimmed with jewels, and a loose long robe of crimson velvet, should be worn. The hair flowing free under a crimson velvet cap. Jewels should be worn. In her right hand the sorceress holds a scroll, while with her left she points a sceptre toward her visitor. In front of the table stands a young man in a rich dress, with a large cloak thrown carelessly over his figure, his cap is off, his face ghastly pale, and his eyes fixed with a malignant look upon a young girl kneeling near him. The girl should wear a simple white dress, her hair flowing, and look toward the sorceress, who, reading the scroll, seems about to pronounce some fearful doom upon this imploring figure. Behind the sorceress, a tall pedestal holds a colored globe, through which strikes a strong light, illuminating the group.

No. 5.—CONRAD AND MEDORA.

This scene is from Canto 1, verse xiv., of "the Corsair."

Medora, in a rich Greek dress, seated upon a pile of cushions, holds a guitar in her hands, and looks up with an expression of joyous recognition to Conrad, who, also in a Greek costume, is standing at the right of picture, as if just entering.

No. 6.—THE INTERCEPTED LETTER.

In the centre of the group stands a young girl in an attitude of bashful embarrassment, looking down. At her right, the mother, seated, reads with a perceptible frown the intercepted letter. Two young girls on the left, whisper together and point toward the culprit. The father stands a little back, reading the letter, looking over the mother's shoulder.

Hidden in the window, a curtain falling over him, his face just peeping out, is the audacious lover. The costumes should be modern, and according to the taste of the wearer.

No. 7.—OPEN YOUR MOUTH AND SHUT YOUR EYES.

A table at the right of the picture has upon it a large dish of cherries. Standing beside it is a young girl in a pretty peasant's dress, filling a boy's cap with the fruit. Her face is turned to a young peasant on her left, who holding a bunch of cherries over his own mouth with the right hand, points with the other to the open mouth of a lad, who is seated at his left, on a chair, his eyes closed and mouth open, waiting for the cherries. Prettily dressed and gracefully grouped, this makes an amusing and extremely graceful tableau.

No. 8.—THE JEALOUS LOVER.

A young lady lies asleep upon a sofa in the centre of the picture. Kneeling beside her is the jealous lover, softly disengaging from her hand an open letter. Dress must be left to the fancy of the performers.

As a companion to this may be given

No. 9.—WINNING THE GLOVES.

. A gentleman is asleep in an arm-chair, his head leaning upon a table, his face up and turned toward the audience. Beside the chair is a young girl, bending over the sleeping student as if about to kiss him. Another lady on the opposite side of the table, points laughingly to an open book before the sleeper; and a third young girl behind the student's chair, puts her fingers on her lip to silence the merry one. The costumes may be modern or not, according to the fancy of the performers.

No. 10.—THE CAPTIVES.

The scene is the inside of an Indian tent. In the centre of the picture is seated a young girl in full Indian dress, examining a miniature suspended by a chain from the neck of another girl, one of the captives, who wears white, with a shawl thrown round her. The owner of the miniature clasps her hands as she kneels before the young Indian, as though imploring her to spare the picture. To the right of this group is another, consisting of a tall Indian man, who stands in a threatening attitude over two lovers; the man in a soldier's dress, supporting the half fainting figure of the girl. To the left of the centre group, stands another Indian, his tomahawk raised over a woman kneeling, bending forward to protect two little children, crouched at her feet. Other Indians, as many as the resources of the company will permit, are grouped in the background.

The few tableaux given are merely as specimens, but the resources for this amusement are immense. Any person familiar with literature, will recall instantly various pictures painted by the pen which will make most effective Tableaux Vivants. I give the titles of a few, with their precise position in books, and leave to the reader the task of finding them, and adapting his company to the groups described, as the authors themselves are the best authority for costume and position.

No. 1. Charles the Second Leaving Woodstock.—*Scott's Woodstock*, Chapter 32.

No. 2. Ophelia's Madness.—*Shakspeare's Hamlet.*—Act 4, Scene 5.

No. 3. Portia's Defense.—*Shakspeare's Merchant of Venice*, Act 4, Scene 1.

No. 4. The Prisoner of Chillon.—*Byron's Prisoner of Chillon*, verse 8.

No. 5. Dressing Moses for the Fair.—*Goldsmith's Vicar of Wakefield*, Chapter 12.

No. 6. A Peruvian's Vengeance.—*Pizarro*, Act 4, Scene 3.

No. 7. The Sleep Walker.—*Shakspeare's Macbeth*, Act 5, Scene 1.

No. 8. The Living Statue.—*Shakspeare's Winter's Tale*, Act 5, Scene 3.

No. 9. The Sisters Jeannie and Effie Deans.—*Scott's Heart of Mid-Lothian*, Chapter 25.

No. 10. Rebecca Tried for Sorcery.—*Scott's Ivanhoe*, Chapter 37.

LEGERDEMAIN.

THERE is probably no amusement which excites more astonishment and interest in a youthful circle, than a series of
adroitly performed and humorous tricks of legerdemain, certainly none more harmless; and that we may add our quota
to the sports for a winter's night, we have carefully made a
selection of such tricks, as while they tend to promote

"Jest and youthful jolity,"

possess but little difficulty of execution, or require no great
quantity of apparatus.

WATER IN A SLING.

Half fill a mug with water, place it in a sling, and you
may whirl it around you without spilling a drop: for the
water tends more away from the centre of motion toward the
bottom of the mug, than toward the earth by gravity.

THE BALANCED STICK.

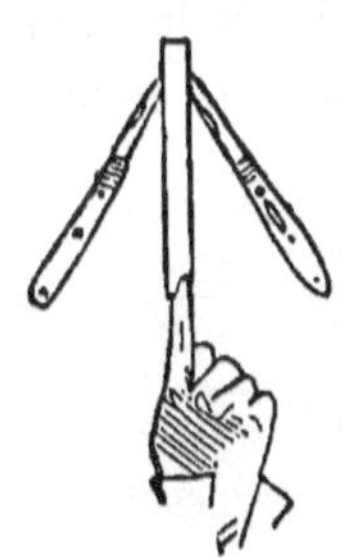

Get a piece of wood six inches in length and
about half an inch in thickness; and, near one
end of it thrust in the blades of two pen-
knives, in such a manner, that one of them incline to one side, and the second to the other,
as delineated in the illustration. Place the
other end of the piece of wood on the tip of the
forefinger, when it will remain perfectly upright,

without falling; and even if it incline to one side, it will instantly recover its perpendicular position, being, in reality, kept in equipoise by the weight of the knives.

THE LITTLE BALANCER.

A little figure may be made on the principles of the foregoing trick, so as to balance itself very amusingly. Get a piece of wood about two inches in length, cut one end of it 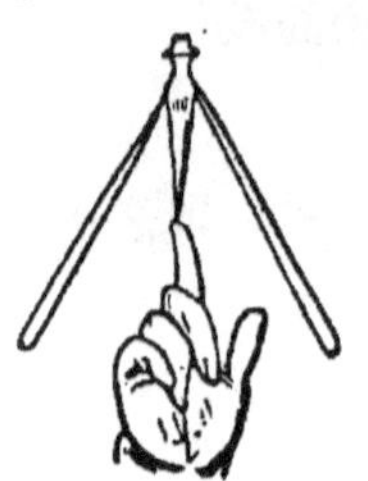 into the form of a man's head and shoulders, and let the other end taper off gradually to a fine point, as shown in the annexed figure. Next, furnish the little man with wafters, shaped like oars, instead of arms, which wafters may be somewhat more than double the length of his body; insert them in his shoulders, and he will be complete. When you place him on the tip of your finger, if you have taken care to make the point exactly in a line with the centre of his body, and have put the wafters accurately in their places, he will preserve his balance, even if blown about; provided he be not blown with so much force as to drive him off his perch. This little man will cause more surprise than the previous trick, in consequence of the fine point on which he oscillates.

EATABLE CANDLE ENDS.

The best time for exhibiting this trick is while the desert is on the table and the company are engaged in conversation. Cut a piece out of a large apple, as neatly as possible, into the shape of a candle end; next cut a slip out of the inside of a sweet almond, and make it nicely round and even, to imitate the wick of a wax candle; insert the wick into the apple-candle, light it for a moment to blacken the tip and to render the illusion more perfect; blow it out again, and the candle will be complete.   When showing the trick, light the candle, (the wick of which will readily take fire), put it into your mouth, masticate and swallow it with all the seeming relish you can possibly assume.

THE ANIMATED SIXPENCE.

If you pierce a very small hole in the rim of a sixpence and pass a long black horse hair through it, you may make it jump about mysteriously, and even out of a jug.   It is necessary, however, to perform this trick only at night time; and to favor the deception as much as possible, a candle should be between the spectator and yourself.

THE TRAVELING EGG.

Procure a goose's egg, and after opening and cleaning it, put a bat into the shell, and then glue a piece of white paper fast over the aperture.   The motions of the poor little prisoner in struggling to get free, will cause the egg to roll about in a manner that will excite much astonishment.

THE BALANCED EGG.

Lay a looking-glass face upward, on a perfectly even **table,** then shake a fresh egg, so as to mix up and incorporate **the** yelk and the white thoroughly ; with care and steadiness you may then balance the egg on its point, and make it stand upright on the glass, which it will be impossible to achieve when the egg is in its natural state.

TO MELT LEAD IN A PIECE OF PAPER.

Wrap a piece of paper very neatly round a bullet, so that it be everywhere in contact with the lead ; hold it over the flame of a candle, and the lead will be melted without the paper being burnt ; but when once fused, the lead will in a short time pierce a hole in the paper, and drop through it.

THE DANCING PEA.

Take a piece of a tobacco-pipe of about three inches in length, one end of which, at least, is broken off even ; and with a knife or file make the hole somewhat larger, so as in fact to form a little hollow cup. Next, get a very round pea, put it in the hollow at the end of the bit of pipe, place the other end of the latter in your mouth, hold it there in quite a perpendicular position, by inclining your head back, and then blow through it very softly ; the pea will be lifted from its cup, and rise and fall according to the degree of force with which the breath is impelled through the pipe.

TO MAKE A SHILLING TURN ON ITS EDGE ON THE POINT OF A NEEDLE.

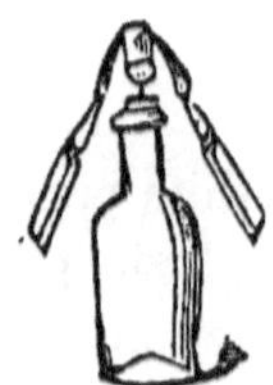

Provide a wine-bottle, and insert in the neck of it a cork, in which next place a needle in a perpendicular position. Cut a nick in the bottom of another cork, and fix a twenty-five cent piece in it, and into the same cork stick two common table forks, opposite to each other, with the handles inclining downward, as in the annexed engraving. If the rim of the coin be then placed upon the point of the needle, it may be turned round without any risk of falling off, as the centre of gravity is below the centre of suspension.

MAGICAL CARDS.

To perform this experiment, you must observe that there are many letters which may be transposed into others, without the alteration being very apparent ; for instance, *a* may be turned into *d*, the *c* into *e, a, d, g, o,* or *q*, the *i* into *b, d,* or *l*, the *l* into *t*, the *o* into *a, d, g,* or *q*, the *v* into *y*, etc., etc. Take a number of cards, suppose twenty ; on one of them write with sympathetic ink made of the juice of lemons, or a solution of salammoniac, the word *law*, but do not join the letters, and on another card, with the same ink, the words *old woman;* by holding them before the fire for a short time, the writing will become visible. Next alter (with the same ink) the *a* in the word law into *d*, place an *o* before the *l*, and add *oman* after the *w*, and the word will thus be turned into *old woman;* allow these alterations to remain invisible, that is, do not hold the card before the fire, and then write on the other cards whatever you think proper. Present the cards to two persons, contrive that one of them take the word *law*, and the other the words *old woman;* tell the former that the word *law* will vanish, and that words like those written on the other card will be substituted for it; to show them that you will not change the cards, request each one to write his name on the back of the card which he drew; you then place the cards together, and hold them before the fire, as if for the purpose of drying the names just written, and the action of the fire will bring out the sympathetic ink, and the word *law* will be changed into *old woman*, as you foretold.

<h3 style="text-align:center">THE BOTTLE IMPS.</h3>

Procure from a glass-blower's three or four little hollow figures of glass, about an inch and a half in height, and let there be a small hole in the legs of each of them. Immerse them in a glass jar about a foot in height, nearly full of water, and then tie a bladder fast over the mouth. When you wish the figures to go down, press your hand closely on the bladder, and they will instantly sink; and the moment you take your hand off, they will rise to the surface of the water.

<h3 style="text-align:center">TO TURN A GOBLET OF WATER UPSIDE DOWN, AND YET KEEP
THE WATER IN IT.</h3>

This is an exceedingly good trick when performed adroitly. Fill a goblet with water, lay a piece of paper on the top of

16

it, place the palm of your left hand flat on the paper, and press it closely down; then take hold of the foot of the goblet with the right hand, and invert the position of the glass, still pressing the paper close with the left hand. Hold it in this manner for a minute or two, and then withdraw the left hand, when the paper will remain attached to the glass, as shown in the illustration; for the pressure of air underneath, acting against the paper with a superior weight to that of the water, is sufficient to retain it in its position, and consequently to sustain the water in the goblet.

TO TAKE A SHILLING OUT OF A HANDKERCHIEF.

For this trick you must procure a curtain ring of exactly the size of a shilling. At first, put the shilling into the handkerchief; but when you take it out, to show that there is no deception, slip in the ring in its stead, and while the person is eagerly holding the handkerchief, and the company's eyes are fixed upon the form of the shilling, seize the opportunity of putting it away secretly. When the handkerchief is returned to you again, cautiously withdraw the curtain ring, and show the shilling.

A GOOD CATCH.

The following is a good catch : lay a wager with a person that to three observations you will put to him, he will not reply, "A bottle of wine." Then begin with some commonplace remark, such as, "We have had a fine, (or wet,) day today," as it may be; he will answer, of course, "A bottle of wine." You then make another remark of the same kind, as, "I hope we shall have as fine, or finer, to-morrow," to which he will reply, as before, "A bottle of wine." You must then catch him very sharply, and say, "Ah ! there, sir ! you've lost your wager;" and the probability is, if he be not aware of the trick, he will say, "Why, how can you make that out?" or something similar, forgetting that, though a strange one, it is the third observation you have made.

TROUBLE-WIT.

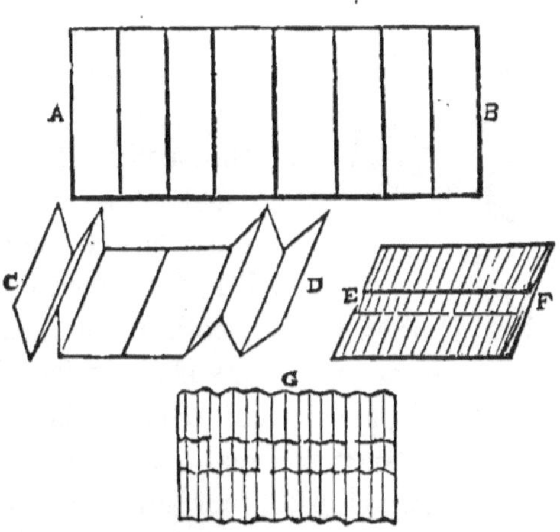

To make this exceedingly entertaining and ingenious puzzle, take a very large sheet of paper, either demy or cartridge, and divide it into eight parts, as shown in the piece A, B, in the above illustration; taking especial care to make the fourth and fifth divisions, (which are the two centre divisions of the sheet,) much wider than the others. In the illustration, the paper is shown as if it were only a half sheet, but it must be a whole sheet. Then plait the sheet as indicated in the piece C, D, and arrange the folds one over the other, as shown at E, F. Next, fold a series of small plaits, about a quarter of an inch in depth, across the paper, as delineated by the dotted lines across E, F, and it will appear as in the figure G.

Very numerous figures may be imitated by drawing out the paper and opening the folds, which are one upon the other;

and amongst them, the following :—A winding staircase, an oval table, a parasol, a Spanish hat, a Spanish ruff, a fan, a scraper to scrape a chimney with, a salt-cellar, a dark lantern, etc.   By exercising the ingenuity, TROUBLE-WIT may be turned into an infinity of figures, and be a source of great amusement.

THE EGG-BOX.

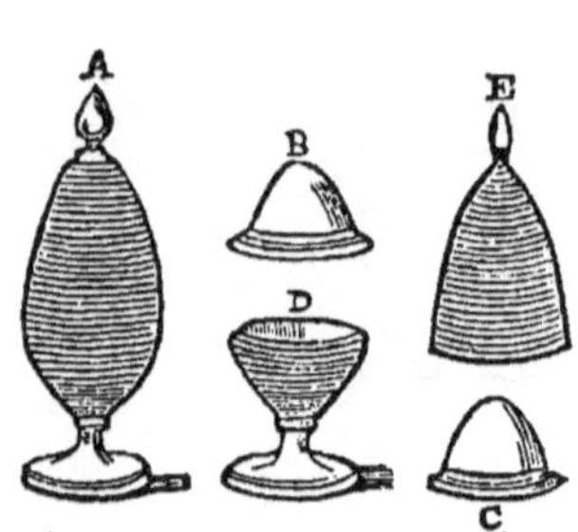

The egg-box is made in the shape of two bee-hives put together, as shown at A. B, an inner case, or box, is covered with half the shell of a real egg; another shell, C, is of the egg shape, but rather larger than the other; and E is the cover, or upper part of box, D. Put E upon C, and both upon B, and then all three upon D; when done, the box is ready for showing the trick. Then, call for an egg, and request the spectators to examine it, and see that it is a real one. Next, take off the upper parts, E, B, and C, with your forefinger and thumb; place the egg in the box, and say, "Ladies and gentlemen, you all see that it is fairly in the box;" uncover it and say, "You shall see me as fairly take it out;" suiting the action to the word, putting the egg in your pocket in their sight. Next open your box again, saying, "You perceive that there is nothing in it; place your hand about the middle of the box, and take C off, without B, and say, "There is the egg again;" it will appear to the spectators to be the identical one which you put in your pocket; and then, putting C on, and taking it, together with the inner shell B, off, exclaim, "It has vanished again :" which will really appear to be the case.

THE JUGGLER'S JOKE.

Take a little ball in each hand, and stretch your hands as

far apart as you possibly can, one from the other; then tell
the company that you will make both the balls come into
whichever hand they please, without bringing the hands into
contact with each other. If any of the lookers-on challenge
your ability of achieving this feat, all you have to do is to lay
one of the balls down upon a table, turn yourself round, and
take it up with your other hand. Both the balls will thus
be in one of your hands, without the latter approaching the
other, agreeably to your promise.

THE GLOBE-BOX.

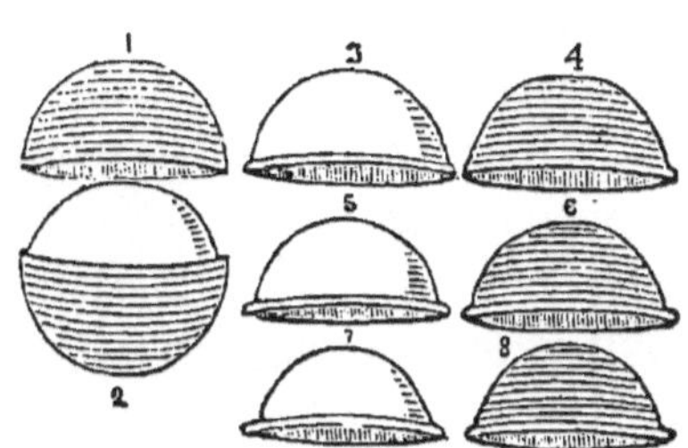

This trick is a very ex-
cellent one. It is performed
with a box made of eight
pieces, and a ball of ivory
or wood. The ball serves
to deceive the spectators,
and the trick should be
prefaced by throwing it down upon the table, for the
company to examine, and see that it is perfectly solid.
Then put the ball in the box, and close it up, with all the
pieces, one within the other; take off the upper shell with
your forefinger and thumb, and there will appear a ball in the
box, but of a different color to that which was put in. The
globe-like form thus displayed looks like a real ball, but in
reality it is no more than a very thin shell of wood, neatly
turned to that shape, and painted; and the other changes are
produced in the same way, as may be perceived by reference
to the illustration. No. 1 is the outer upper shell of the
box, taken off of the outer under shell No. 2, the top of which
represents an inner globe; 3 is an inner globe; 4, its cover;
5, another inner globe; and 6, its cover; 7 is a third globe;
and 8, its cover. These globe boxes may be made with as
many changes, and as varied in colors, as the performer pleases.

THE THREE SPOONS.

This is a most capital trick, but it requires a confederate's aid. Place three silver spoons crosswise on a table, request any person to touch one, and assure him you will find out the one he touches by a single inspection; although you will leave the room while he does so, and even if he touches it so gently as not to disarrange the order in which they are once put in the slightest degree. You retire; and when he gives you notice to enter, walk up to the table and inspect the spoons, as if trying to ascertain whether there are any finger-marks upon them, and then decide. Your confederate, of course, makes some sign, previously agreed upon, to give you notice which is the identical spoon; the actions may be, touching a button of his jacket for the top spoon, touching his chin for the second, and putting his finger to his lips may signify the lowest; but the precise actions are immaterial, so that the spoon they indicate be understood.

TO LIFT A BOTTLE WITH A STRAW.

Take a stout, unbroken straw, bend the thickest end of it into an acute angle, and put it into a bottle, so that its bent part may rest against the side of the bottle, as in the annexed figure; then take hold of the other end of it, and if you have managed the trick properly, you will be able to lift up the bottle without breaking the straw; and the nearer the angular part of the latter comes to that which passes out of the neck of the former, so much the more easy of accomplishment will be the experiment.

LOUD WHISPER.

Apartments of a circular or elliptical form are best calculated for the exhibition of this phenomenon. If a person stand near the wall, with his face turned to it, and whisper a few words, they may be more distinctly heard at nearly the opposite side of the apartment, than if the listener were situated nearer to the speaker.

TO BREAK A STICK PLACED ON TWO GLASSES.

The stick used for this trick must not be very stout; both of its extremities should be tapered off to a point, and they should be as uniform as possible in length, in order that its centre may be easily known. The ends of the stick must be rested on the edges of the glasses, which, of course, should be perfectly even in height, that the stick may lie in a horizontal position without any undue inclination, either to one side or the other; and if a smart quick blow be then struck upon its centre, proportioned (as near as can be guessed) to its size, and the distance the glasses are from each other, it will be broken in two without its supporters being injured.

THE BOTTLE CONJURER.

You must preface this trick by declaring to the company that it was formerly supposed to be impossible to set the *Thames* on fire; and that it was demonstrated some years ago, at the *Haymarket* theatre, that for a person to crawl into a quart bottle was an utter impossibility, but the progress since made in all kinds of knowledge has proved it is possible to set the Thames on fire, and that any one may crawl *in to* a pint bottle. This statement will, of course, be doubted; but to prove your assertion, get a pint bottle, and place it in the middle of the room; then slip outside the door, and in a minute or two return, creeping upon all-fours, saying : " Ladies and gentlemen, this is crawling *in to* the pint bottle !"

THE MYSTERIOUS WAFERS.

In the presence of the company, place on each side of a table-knife three wafers; take the knife by the handle, and turn it over several times, to show that the wafers are all on.

Request one of the party to take a wafer from one side of the blade, turn the knife over two or three times, and there will seem to be only two wafers on each side ; take off another wafer, turn the knife as before, and it will appear as if only one wafer were on each side; take the third wafer off, and again turn the knife dexterously twice or thrice, and it will appear as if all the wafers had disappeared from each side. Next, turn the knife once or twice more, and three wafers will appear on each side, as at the first.   In performing this trick, use wafers all of one size and color, and always have one side of the knife uppermost, so that the wafers may be taken one by one from that side ; three wafers will thus be left untouched on the other side ; and after you have made it appear that there are no wafers on either side, you may, to all appearance, show three on each.   When turning the knife, you must, as you lift it up, turn it completely round with your finger and thumb, so as always to bring the same side uppermost.

ADVANTAGEOUS WAGER.

Request a lady to lend you a watch.   Examine it, and give a guess as to its value ; then offer to lay the owner a wager, considerably below the real value of the watch, that she will not answer to three questions which you will put to her consecutively, "My watch."   Show her the watch, and say, "What is this which I hold in my hand ?" She, of course, will not fail to reply, "My watch."   Next, present to her notice some other object, repeating the same question.   If she name the object you present, she loses the wager ; but if she be on her guard, and remembering her stake, she says, "My watch," she must, of course, win ; and you, therefore, to divert her attention, should observe to her, "You are certain to win the stake, but supposing I lose, what will you give me ?" and if, confident of success, she replies for the third time, "My watch," then take it, and leave her the wager agreed on.

THE SMOKE-SNAKE.

To construct this pretty little toy, take a square piece of stiff card, or sheet copper or brass, about two-and-a-half or three inches in diameter, and cut it out spirally, so as to resemble a snake, as in the engraving. Then paint the body on each side of the card the colors of a snake; take it by the two ends, and draw out the spiral till the distance from head to tail be six or seven inches, as in the figure. Next, provide a slender piece of wood on a stand, and fix a sharp needle at its summit; push the rod up through the spiral, and let the end of the spiral rest upon the summit of the needle. Now place the apparatus as nearly as possible to the edge of the mantle-shelf above the fire, and the snake will begin to revolve in the direction of its head; and if the fire be strong, or the current of heated air which ascends from it be made powerful, by two or three persons coming near it, so as to concentrate the current, the snake will revolve very rapidly. The rod should be painted so as to resemble a tree, which the snake will appear to climb; or the snake may be suspended by a thread from the ceiling, over the current of air from a lamp. Two snakes may be made to turn round in opposite directions, by merely drawing out the spiral of one from the upper side, and the other from the under side of the figure; and fixing them, of course, on separate rods.

THE RING AND THE HANDKERCHIEF.

This may be justly considered one of the most surprising deceptions; and yet it is so easy of performance, that any one may accomplish it after a few minutes' practice.

Previously provide yourself with a piece of brass wire, pointed at both ends, and bent round so as to form a ring,

about the size of a wedding-ring. This conceal in your hand.
Then commence your performance by borrowing a silk pocket-
handkerchief from a gentleman, and a wedding-ring from a
lady ; and request one person to hold two of the corners of
the handkerchief, and another to hold the other two, and to
keep them at full stretch. Next exhibit the wedding-ring to
the company, and announce that you will make it pass through
the handkerchief. Then place your hand under the handkerchief, and substituting the false ring, which you had previously
concealed, press it against the centre of the handkerchief, and
desire a third person to take hold of the ring through the
handkerchief, and to close his finger and thumb through the
hollow of the ring. The handkerchief is held in this manner
for the purpose of showing that the ring has not been placed
within a fold. Now desire the persons holding the corners of
the handkerchief to let them drop ; the person holding the
ring (through the handkerchief as already described) still re-
taining his hold.

Let another person now grasp the handkerchief as tight as
he pleases, three or four inches below the ring, and tell the
person holding the ring to let it go, when it will be quite evident to the company that the ring is secure within the centre
of the handkerchief. Then tell the person who grasps the
handkerchief to hold a hat over it ; and passing your hand
underneath, open the false ring, by bending one of its points
a little aside, and bringing one point gently through the handkerchief, so as easily to draw out the remainder ; being careful
to rub the hole you have made in the handkerchief with your
finger and thumb to conceal the fracture.

Then put the wedding-ring you borrowed over the outside
of the middle of the handkerchief, and desiring the person
who holds the hat to take it away, exhibit the ring (placed as
described) to the company ; taking an opportunity, while
their attention is engaged, to conceal or get rid of the brass
ring

TO CAUSE WINE AND WATER TO CHANGE PLACES.

Fill a small narrow-necked bulb with port wine, or with water and colored spirit of wine, and put the bulb into a tall, narrow glass jar, which is then to be filled up with cold water; immediately the colored fluid will issue from the bulb, and accumulate on the surface of the water in the jar, while colorless water will be seen accumulating at the bottom of the bulb. By close inspection, the descending current of the water may also be observed, and the colored and the colorless liquids be seen to pass each other in the narrow neck of the bulb without mixing. The whole of the colored fluid will shortly have ascended, and the bulb will be entirely filled with clear water.

THE MAGIC CIRCLE.

Assure the company that it is in your power, if any person will place himself in the middle of the room, to make a circle round him, out of which, although his limbs shall be quite at liberty, it will be impossible for him to jump without partially undressing himself, let him use as much exertion as he may. This statement will, without doubt, cause some little surprise; and one of the party will, in all probability, put your asseverations to the test. Request him to take his stand in the middle of the room, then blindfold him, button his coat, and next with a piece of chalk draw a circle round his waist. On withdrawing the bandage from his eyes and showing him the circle you have described, he must at once perceive that he cannot jump out of it without taking off his coat.

THE GLASS OF WINE UNDER THE HAT.

Place a glass of wine upon a table, put a hat over it, and offer to lay a wager with any of the company that you will empty the glass without lifting the hat. When your proposition is accepted, desire the company not to touch the hat;

and then get under the table, and commence making a suck-
ing noise, smacking your lips at intervals, as though you were
swallowing the wine with infinite satisfaction to yourself.
After a minute or two, come from under the table, and address
the person who took your wager with, "Now, sir." His curiosity being, of course, excited, he will lift up the hat, in order to see whether you have really performed what you promised; and the instant he does so, take up the glass, and after
having swallowed its contents, say, "You have lost, sir, for
you see I have drunk the wine without raising up the hat."

THE MIRACULOUS APPLE.

To divide an apple into several parts, without breaking the
rind :—Pass a needle and thread under the rind of the apple,
which is easily done by putting the needle in again at the same
hole it came out of; and so passing on till you have gone
round the apple. Then take both ends of the thread in your
hands and draw it out, by which means the apple will be divided into two parts. In the same manner you may divide it
into as many parts as you please, and yet the rind will remain
entire. Present the apple to any one to peel, and it will immediately fall to pieces.

AN OMELET COOKED IN A HAT, OVER THE FLAME OF A CANDLE.

State that you are about to cook an omelet; then you break
four eggs in a hat, place the hat for a short time over the flame
of a candle, and shortly after produce an omelet, completely
cooked, and quite hot.

Some persons will be credulous enough to believe that by
the help of certain ingredients you have been enabled to cook
the omelet without fire; but the secret of the trick is, that the
omelet had been previously cooked and placed in the hat, but
could not be seen, because the operator, when breaking the
eggs, placed it too high for the spectators to observe the con-

tents. The eggs were empty ones, the contents having been previously extracted, by being sucked through a small aperture; but to prevent the company from suspecting this, the operator should, as if by accident, let a full egg fall on the table, which breaking, induces a belief that the others are also full.

THE IMPOSSIBLE OMELET.

Produce some butter, eggs, and other ingredients for making an omelet, together with a frying-pan, in a room where there is a fire, and offer to bet a wager, that the cleverest cook will not be able to make an omelet with them. The wager is won by having previously caused the eggs to be boiled very hard.

NEW PERPETUAL ROTATORY MOTION.

By an accidental occurrence, it has recently been discovered that a piece of rock-crystal, or quartz, cut in a peculiar form, produces, upon an inclined plane, and without any apparent impetus, an extraordinary rotatory motion, which may be kept up for an indefinite period of time. The curiosity of this philosophical toy having excited general interest in the scientific world, Professor Leslie, in his lecture, thus explains the phenomenon:

"The crystal has six sides, and being cut accurately from the faces to a perfect convex surface, if placed upon a wetted smooth surface, and held parallel, no motion will take place, because the centre of gravity of each face is balanced and supported in this position of the plain surface; but if a slight inclination is given to the plane, a rotatory motion commences, in consequence of the support being removed from the centre of gravity. The impetus once given, the centrifugal force increases the rotatory motion to such a degree, as for an observer to be unable to distinguish the form of the crystal.

"*To produce the effect.*—Place the crystal on a piece of plate or common window glass, a china or glazed plate, or any smooth surface, perfectly clean, as grease or a particle of dust would impede its motion. Wet the surface, and give the plane a slight inclination, when, if properly managed, a rotatory motion will commence, which may be kept up for any length of time by giving alternate inclinations to the plane surface, according to the movements of the crystal; to heighten the pleasing effect of which, a variety of paper figures, harlequins, waltzers, &c. may be attached. The first trial of the experiment had better be made by giving a slight rotatory motion to the crystal."

VENTRILOQUISM.

The main secret of this surprising art simply consists in first making a strong and deep inspiration, by which a considerable. quantity of air is introduced into the lungs, to be afterward acted upon by the flexible powers of the larynx or cavity situated behind the tongue, and the trachea, or windpipe: thus prepared, the expiration should be slow and gradual. Any person, by practice, can, therefore, obtain more or less expertness in this exercise; in which, though not apparently, the voice is still modified by the mouth and tongue; and it is in the concealment of this aid, that much of the perfection of ventriloquism lies.

But the distinctive character of ventriloquism consists in its imitations being performed by the voice *seeming* to come from the stomach: hence its name, from *venter*, the stomach, and *loquor*, to speak. Although the voice does not actually come from that region, in order to enable the ventriloquist to utter sounds from the larynx without moving the muscles of his face, he strengthens them by a powerful action of the abdominal muscles. Hence, he speaks by means of his stomach; although the throat is the real source from whence the sound proceeds. It should, however, be added, that this speaking distinctly, without any movement of the lips at all, is the highest perfection of ventriloquism, and has but rarely been attained. Thus, MM. St. Gille and Louis Brabant, two celebrated French ventriloquists, appeared to be absolutely mute while exercising their art, and no change in their countenances could be discovered.

It has lately been shown, that some ventriloquists have acquired by practice the power of exercising the vail of the palate in such a manner, that, by raising or depressing it, they dilate or contract the inner nostrils. If they are closely contracted, the sound produced is weak, dull and seems to be more or less distant; if, on the contrary, these cavities are widely dilated, the sound will be strengthened, the voice become loud, and apparently close to us.

Another of the secrets of ventriloquism, is the uncertainty with respect to the direction of sounds. Thus, if we place a man and a child in the same angle of uncertainty, and the man speaks with the accent of a child, without any corresponding motion in his mouth or face, we shall necessarily believe that the voice comes from the child. In this case, the belief is so strengthened by the imagination; for if we were directed to a statue, as the source from which we were to expect sounds to issue, we should still be deceived, and refer the sounds to the lifeless stone or marble. This illusion will be greatly assisted by the voice being totally different in tone and character from that of the man from whom it really comes. Thus, we see how easy is the deception when the sounds are required to proceed from any given object, and are such as they actually yield.

The ventriloquists of our time, as M. Alexander and M. Fitz-James, have carried their art still further. They have not only spoken by the muscles of the throat and the abdomen, without moving those of the face, but have so far overcome the uncertainty of sound, as to become acquainted with modifications of distance, obstruction, and other causes, so as to imitate them with the greatest accuracy. Thus, each of these artists has succeeded in carrying on a dialogue; and each, in his own single person and with his own single voice, has represented a scene apparently with several actors. These ventriloquists have likewise possessed such power over their faces and figures, that, aided by rapid changes of dress, their personal identity has scarcely been recognized among the range of personations.

Vocal imitations are much less striking and ingenious than the feats of ventriloquism. Extraordinary varieties of voice may be produced, by speaking with a more acute or grave pitch than usual, and by different contractions of the mouth. Thus may be imitated the grinding of cutlery on a wheel, the sawing of wood, the frying of a pancake, the uncorking of a bottle, and the gurgling noise in emptying its contents.

CONCLUSION.

The following hints are of considerable importance to the amateur exhibitor.

1. Never acquaint the company beforehand with the particulars of the feat you are about to perform, as it will give them time to discover your mode of operation.

2. Endeavor, as much as possible, to acquire various methods of performing the same feat, in order that if you should be likely to fail in one, or have reason to believe that your operations are suspected, you may be prepared with another.

3. Never yield to the request of any one to repeat the same feat, as you thereby hazard the detection of your mode of operation; but do not absolutely refuse, as that would appear ungracious. Promise to perform it in a different way, and then exhibit another which somewhat resembles it. This manœuvre seldom fails to answer the purpose.

4. Never venture on a feat requiring manual dexterity, till you have previously practiced it so often, as to acquire the necessary expertness.

5. As diverting the attention of the company from too closely inspecting your manœuvres is a most important object, you should manage to talk to them during the whole course of your proceedings. It is the plan of vulgar operators to gabble unintelligible jargon, and attribute their feats to some extraordinary and mysterious influence. There are few persons at the present day credulous enough to believe such trash, even among the rustic and most ignorant; but, as the youth of maturer years might inadvertently be tempted to pursue this method, while exhibiting his skill before his younger companions, it may not be deemed superfluous to caution him against such a procedure. He may state, and truly, that every thing he exhibits can be accounted for on rational principles, and is only in obedience to the unerring laws of Nature; and although we have just cautioned him against enabling the company themselves to detect his operations, there can be no objection (particularly when the party comprises many younger than himself) to occasionally show by what simple means the most apparently marvellous feats are accomplished.

I7

TRICKS WITH CARDS.

Although proficiency in games with cards is, in our opinion, a most pernicious accomplishment for youth, and one which cannot be too severely reprobated, we do not consider SLEIGHT-OF-HAND-TRICKS with a pack of cards at all objectionable, but rather as a source of much harmless amusement; and, under this impression, we do not hesitate to insert the following series of excellent deceptions and sleights-of-hand.

Playing cards are believed to have been invented in Spain as early as the fourteenth century; for, in 1378, John the First, king of Castille, forbade card-playing in his dominions, in an edict which is anterior to any similar legislative measure in other parts of Europe. The figures upon the cards themselves add to the strength of the supposition; for the suits answering to those of spades and clubs have not the same inverted heart and trefoil shape which ours of the present day display, but *espadas,* or swords, and *bastos,* or cudgels, or clubs; so that, in fact, we retain their names though we have altered the figures. At the present time, too, cards are a favorite diversion of the Spaniards, and the monopoly of selling them is vested in the hands of the sovereign.

In the reign of Henry the Seventh, card-playing was a very fashionable court amusement in England. The cards then used, differed materially in their figures from those now in vogue, as instead of clubs, spades, diamonds, and hearts, they

(258)

had rabbits, pinks, roses, and the flowers called columbines, upon them ; as also bells, hearts, leaves, and acorns, and deer, &c. Let us now turn to the tricks that can be played with cards.

TO TELL THE CARD THOUGHT OF IN A CIRCLE OF TEN.

PLACE the first ten cards of any suit in a circular form, as in the annexed figure ; the ace being counted as one. Request a person to think of a number or card, and to touch also any other number or card ; desire him to add to the number of the card he touched the number of the cards laid out, that is, ten ; then, bid him count that sum backward, beginning at the card he touched, and reckoning that card as the number he thought of ; when he will thus end it at the card or number he first thought of, and thereby enable you to ascertain what that was. For example, suppose he thought of the number three, and touched the sixth card, if ten be added to six, it will of course make sixteen ; and if he count that number from the sixth card, the one touched, in a retrograde order, reckoning three on the sixth, four on the fifth, five on the fourth, six on the third card, and so on ; it will be found to terminate on the third card, which will therefore show you the number the person thought of. When the person is counting the numbers, he should not, of course, call them out aloud.

TO GUESS THE CARD THOUGHT OF.

To perform this trick, the number of cards must be divisible by 3, and it is more convenient that the number should be odd. Desire a person to think of a card ; place the cards on the table with their faces downward, and, taking them up in order, arrange them in three heaps, with their faces upward, and in such a manner that the first card of the pack shall be first in the first heap, the second the first in the second heap, and the third the first of the third; the fourth the second of the first, and so on. When the heaps are completed, ask the person in which heap the card he thought of is, and when he tells you, place that heap in the middle; then turning up the packet, form three heaps, as before, and again inquire in which heap the card thought of is; form the three heaps afresh, place the heap containing the card thought of again in the centre, and ask which of them contains the card. When this is known, place it as before, between the other two, and again form three heaps, asking the same question. Then take up the heaps for the last time, put that containing the card thought of in the middle, and place the packet on the table with the faces downward, turn up the cards till you count half the number of those contained in the packet; twelve, for example, if there be twenty-four, in which case the twelfth card will be the one the person thought of. If the number of the cards be at the same time odd, and divisible by three, such as fifteen, twenty-one, twenty-seven, &c., the trick will be much easier, for the card thought of will always be that in the middle of the heap in which found the third time, so that it may be easily distinguished without counting the cards; in reality, nothing is necessary but to remember, while you are arranging the heap for the third time, the card which is the middle one of each. Suppose, for example, that the middle card of the first heap be the ace of spades; that the second be the king of hearts; and that the third be the knave of hearts: if you are told that the heap containing the required card is the third, that card must be the knave of hearts. You may therefore have the cards shuffled, without troubling them any more; and then, looking them over for form sake, may name the knave of hearts when it occurs.

TO TELL THE NUMBER OF CARDS BY THE WEIGHT.

Take a pack of cards, say forty, and privately insert amongst them two cards rather larger than the others; let the first be the fifteenth, and the other the twenty-sixth, from the top. Seem to shuffle the cards, and cut them at the first long card; poise those you have taken off in your hand, and say, "There must be fifteen cards here;" then cut them at the second long card, and say, "There are but eleven here;" and poising the remainder, exclaim, "And here are fourteen cards." On counting them, the spectators will find your calculations correct.

THE ODD TEN.

Take a pack of cards, let any person draw one and put it back again into the pack, but contrive so that you can find it at pleasure, which, by a little practice, you will be able to do, with the greatest facility. Shuffle the pack, and request another of the party to draw a card, but be sure that you force upon him the card which was drawn before; go on in this way, until ten persons have drawn the same card; then shuffle the cards, and show the one you forced, which, from its having been so managed, must of course be the one which every person drew.

THE QUEEN GOING TO DIG FOR DIAMONDS.

To perform this trick neatly, proceed as follows:—Tell the company that here are four queens in search of some diamonds (laying down the four queens in a row, and putting four common cards, of the suit of diamonds, separately upon the queens); to aid them in the search, they, of course, require a spade (laying down four common cards, of the suit of spades, upon the queens). Their husbands send with them, as an escort, a guard of honor, (laying down the four aces); notwithstanding which they are waylaid by knaves (laying down the four knaves), who had formed a conspiracy to kill, and afterward to rob them; for which purpose they had each provided themselves with a club (putting down four common cards of the suit of clubs). The kings hearing of this plot, resolve to follow and protect their queens (laying down the four kings); and, like chivalrous princes, taking good heart, proceed after them (laying down four common cards of the suit of hearts). Now gather the four heaps into one, beginning at the left hand, and allow several persons to cut them; and when a common card of the suit of heart comes to the bottom of the pack, lay all out again in four heaps, and the cards will follow in the same order as when you laid them down at first.

THE KNAVES AND THE CONSTABLE.

Select the four knaves from a pack of cards, and one of the kings to perform the office of constable. Secretly place one of the knaves at the bottom of the pack, and lay the other three with the constable, down upon the table. Proceed with a tale to the effect that three knaves once went to rob a house; one got in at the parlor window (putting a knave at the bottom of the pack, taking care not to lift the pack so high that the one already at the bottom can be seen); one effected his entrance at the first floor window (putting another knave in the middle of the pack); and the other, by getting on the parapet from a neighboring house, contrived to scramble in at the garret window (placing the third knave at the top of the pack); the constable vowed he would capture them, and closely followed the last knave (putting the king likewise upon the top of the pack). Then request as many of the company to cut the cards, as please; and tell them that you have no doubt the constable has succeeded in his object, which will be quite evident, when you spread out the pack in your hands; as the king and three knaves will, if the trick is neatly performed, be found together. A very little practice only is required to enable you to convey a knave or any other card secretly to the bottom of the pack.

TO HOLD FOUR KINGS OR FOUR KNAVES IN YOUR HAND, AND TO CHANGE THEM SUDDENLY INTO BLANK CARDS, AND THEN TO FOUR ACES.

It is necessary to have cards made on purpose for this trick: half cards, as they may be properly termed, that is, one half kings or knaves, and the other half aces. When you lay the aces one over the other, of course nothing but the kings or knaves can be seen; and on turning the kings or knaves downward, the four aces will make their appearance. You must have two perfect cards, one a king or knave, to put over one of the aces, else it will be seen; and the other an ace, to lay over the kings or knaves. When you wish to make them all appear blank, lay the cards a little lower, and by hiding the aces, they will appear white on both sides; you may then ask which they wish to have, and may show kings, aces, or knaves, as they are called for.

THE FIFTEEN THOUSAND LIVRES.

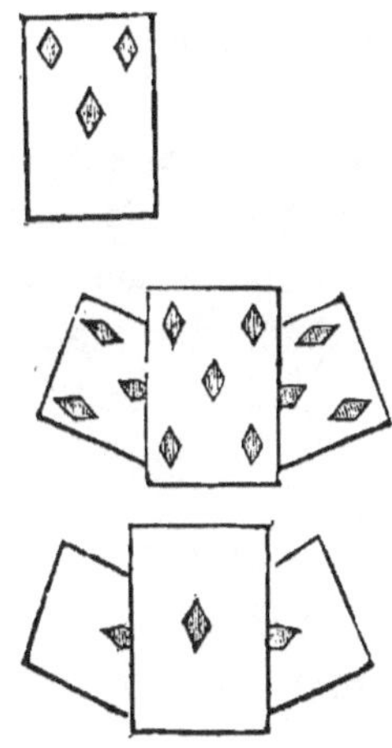

For this trick, prepare two cards like the accompanying engraving; and have a common ace and five of diamonds. Hold down the five of diamonds and the two prepared cards, as shown in the next engraving; and say, "A certain Frenchman left fifteen thousand livres, which are represented by these three cards, to his three sons; the two youngest agreed to leave their five thousand, each of them, in the hands of the elder, that he might improve it." While you are telling this story, lay the five on the table, and put the ace in its place; at the same time artfully change the position of the other two cards, so that the three cards appear as in this engraving. Then, resuming the tale, relate that "the eldest brother, instead of improving the money, lost it all by gaming, except three thousand livres, as you here see (laying the ace on the table, and taking up the five). Sorry for having lost the money, he went to the East Indies with these three thousand, and brought back fifteen thousand." Then show the cards in the same position as at first. To render this deception agreeable, it must be performed with dexterity, and should not be repeated, but the cards immediately put in the packet; and you should have five common cards ready to show, if any one desires to see them.

SEVERAL CARDS BEING PRESENTED IN SUCCESSION TO SEVERAL PERSONS, TO GUESS WHICH EACH HAS THOUGHT OF.

Show as many cards to each person as there are persons to select; that is to say three, if there be three persons. When the first has thought of a card, lay aside the three from which he has made his choice. Present the same number to the second person to think of one, and lay aside those three cards also. Having done the same with the third person, lay out the three first cards with their faces uppermost, above them the next three cards, and above these also the last three; so that all the cards may be disposed in three heaps, each consisting of three. Then ask each person, in which heap the card is which he thought of; that being known, it will be easy to tell these cards; for that of the first person will be the first in the first heap, that of the second the second of the next heap, and that of the third person will be the third of the last heap.

THE CARD DISCOVERED BY THE TOUCH OR SMELL.

Offer the long card, or any other that you thoroughly well know; and, as the person who has drawn it holds it in his hand, pretend to feel the pips or figures on the under side, with your fore-finger, or smell it, and then sagaciously declare what card it is.

If it be the long card, you may give the pack to the person who drew it, and allow him either to replace it or not. Then take the pack, and feel whether it be there or not; shuffle the cards in a careless manner, and, without looking at it, decide accordingly.

THE CARD IN THE EGG.

To perform this feat, provide a round, hollow stick, about ten inches long and three quarters of an inch in diameter, the hollow being three-eighths of an inch in diameter. Also, have another round stick to fit this hollow, and slide in it easily, with a knob to prevent its coming through. Our young readers will clearly understand our meaning, when we say, that in all respects it must resemble a pop-gun, with the single exception that the stick which fits the tube, must be of the full length of the tube, exclusively of the knob.

Next steep a card in water for a quarter of an hour, peel off the face of it, and double it twice across, till it becomes one-fourth of the length of a card, then roll it up tightly, and thrust it up the tube till it becomes even with the bottom. You then thrust in the stick at the other end of the tube till it just touches the card.

Having thus provided your magic wand, let it lie on the table until you have occasion to make use of it, but be careful not to allow any person to handle it.

Now take a pack of cards, and let any person draw one; but be sure to let it be a similar card to the one which you have in the hollow stick. This must be done by forcing. The person who has chosen it will put it into the pack again, and, while you are shuffling, you let it fall into your lap. Then, calling for some eggs, desire the person who drew the card, or any other person in the company, to choose any one of the eggs. When he has done so, ask if there be any thing in it? He will answer, there is not. Place the egg in a saucer;—break it with the wand, and pressing the knob with the palm of your right hand, the card will be driven into the egg. Then show it to the spectators.

A great improvement may be made in this feat, by presenting the person who draws the card with a saucer and a pair of forceps, and instead of his returning the card to the pack, desire him to take it by the corner with the forceps and burn it, but to take care and preserve the ashes; for this purpose you present him with a piece of paper (prepared as hereafter described), which he lights at the candle; but a few seconds after, and before he can set the card on fire, it will suddenly divide in the middle and spring back, burning his fingers if he do not drop it quickly. Have another paper ready and desire him to try that; when he will most likely beg to be excused, and will prefer lighting it with the candle.

When the card is consumed, say that you do not wish to fix upon any particular person in company to choose an egg, lest it might be suspected he was a confederate; therefore, request any two ladies in company to choose each an egg, and having done so, to decide between themselves which shall contain the card; when this is done, take a second saucer, and in it receive the rejected egg, break it with your wand, and show the egg round to the company; at the same time drawing their attention to the fact of those two eggs having been chosen from among a number of others, and of its not being possible for you to have told which of them would be the chosen one.

You now receive the chosen egg in the saucer containing the ashes, and having rolled it about until you have blacked it a little, blow the ashes from around it into the grate; you then break the egg with the same wand, when, on touching the spring, the card will be found in the egg.

The method of preparing the paper mentioned in the above feat is as follows:—Take a piece of letter paper, about six inches in length and three-quarters of an inch in breadth, fold it longitudinally, and with a knife cut it in the crease about five inches down; then take one of the sides, which are still connected at the bottom, and with the back of the knife under it, and the thumb of the right hand over it, curl it outward as a boy would the tassels of his kite; repeat the same process with the other side, and lay them by for use. When about using them (but not till then, as the papers will soon lose their curl if stretched), draw them up so as to make them their original length, and turn the ends over a little, in order that they may remain so; when set on fire, they will burn for a minute or two, until the turn-over is burnt out, when the lighted ends will turn over quickly, burning the fingers of the holder: this part of the trick never fails to excite the greatest merriment.

THE CHANGEABLE CARDS.

Having shuffled a pack, select the eight of each suit, and the deuce of diamonds; hold the four eights in the left hand, and the deuce in the right, and having shown them, take in the deuce among the four in the left hand, and throw out one of the eights; give them to be blown upon, when they will be turned into four deuces; you now exchange one of the deuces for the eight, and giving them again to be blown upon, they will appear all black cards; you again take in the deuce, and discard the eight, when, by blowing on them, they will all turn red; you now, for the last time, take in the eight, and throw away a deuce, when they will be found to be four eights and a deuce, as they were at first.

To perform this ingenious deception, you procure five plain cards the size of playing cards, which you paint to resemble the five cards as follows :—

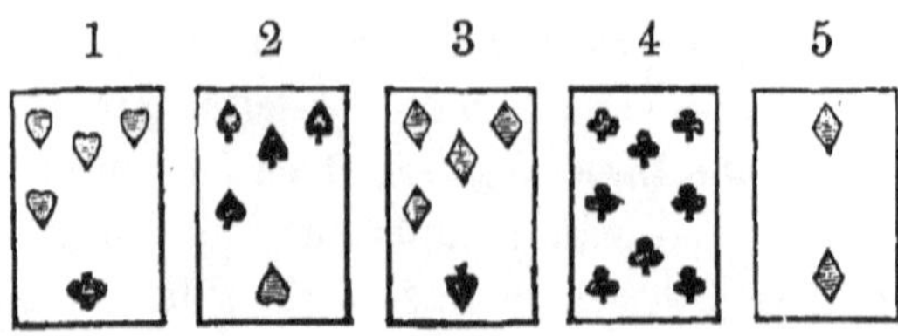

Then, mixing them with a common pack, you next, under the pretense of selecting the eight of each suit, and the deuce of diamonds, take out your false cards (Nos. 1, 2, 3, 4), which you hold as under; and taking No. 5 in your right hand, you show your company that there are the four eights and the deuce of diamonds; you should likewise hold them up to the light, to let them see that they are not double, which you may do without fear of detection, as the lower parts of the cards will be so opaque, that the deficiency of spots will not be perceived: you now place the deuce of diamonds between Nos. 3 and 4, the latter of which you withdraw and throw on the table, but take care not to do so until you have first taken in No. 5 (the deuce of diamonds), else the deficiency of spots on No. 3 will cause the trick to be discovered; you then close those four cards together, and taking them by the top, with

the fingers and thumb of the right hand, having the thumb on the face of the cards and the fingers on the back, hold them out with their faces turned toward the floor, and desire some person to blow upon them; when this has been done, give your wrist a turn, so that the top part of the cards will now be the bottom; in fact, you turn the cards upside down; hold them up to your mouth, pretending to breathe on them, which not only tends to deceive your company, but gives you time to arrange your cards, which you do by opening them out to the right hand, when they will appear to be four deuces, in the order represented in the following figure; you may again hold them up to the light, to show that they are single cards.

The next change, although rather more difficult to accomplish, is decidedly the best of the whole, inasmuch as the cards are never shut up, nor removed for one moment from under the eye. Having shown them to be four deuces, you take in the eight of clubs, and place it between Nos. 3 and

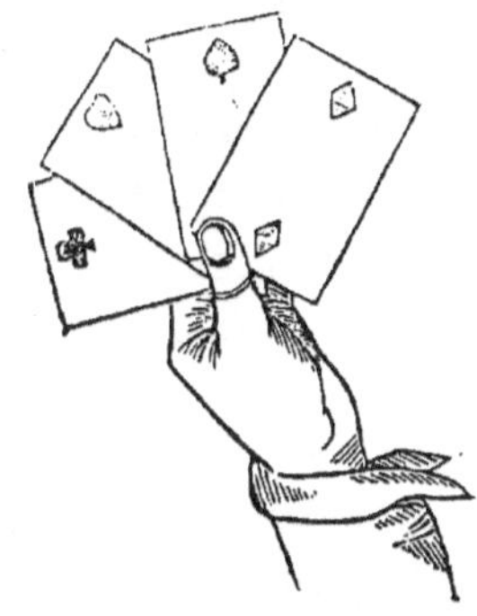

5; withdraw No. 5, and holding it up to the light, you desire the company to observe that the cards are not double, and while all eyes are turned to this card, turn your left hand, containing the other four, with its back toward the ceiling, and the faces of the cards toward the floor, keeping them in a horizontal position; throw down the deuce of diamonds, and continue your remarks on the cards not being double, by saying, "You perceive any of them will bear examination;" at the same time take hold of the card next but one to your right hand, with the fingers and thumb of that hand, taking care to have the thumb above and the fingers underneath the card, take it out, still keeping it in a horizontal position, and while making the above observation, turn it round with the fore-finger of the right hand, until you have got hold of the other end, when, before anybody has time to take hold of it, return it to the situation from which you took it, taking care that you put it exactly in the same angle.

Now hold those cards out, with the backs upward, to be blown upon; but you have no occasion to shut them up at this change, as, if you turn them over, it will be perceived that they are all black; you now take in the deuce of diamonds, as you did at the first change, and discard the eight of clubs, close them up, and taking them *by the top*, hold them out to be blown upon, give your wrist a turn as before, open them out to yourself while pretending to breathe on them, when, on showing them to your company, they will be all red ; you now again take in the eight of clubs, throwing out the deuce of diamonds on the table, with its face downward, and taking hold of the card next but one to your right hand, throw it down in the same manner ; whilst performing this latter part, you should say, "I take in the eight, and I throw out the deuces—Oh ! I beg pardon—only one of the deuces ;" at the same moment take up the last card you threw out, by the opposite end to that which you formerly held it by, and return it to its own place again, taking particular care of the angle ; let them be blown upon, when they will be found to be four eights and a deuce, as they were at first.

Should any persons now desire to examine the cards, tell them you can only give them one at a time, breathe upon the deuce of diamonds and present it to them ; when they have returned it to you, and before they have time to ask for another, hand them the eight of clubs, saying, that perhaps they would like to examine a black card ; they seeing you so confident, will scarcely ask for any more.   We recommend our young friends to practice this trick well before they attempt to show it, as it is too good a one to hazard its discovery by impatience, which is too frequently the case.

The two preceding tricks have been extracted from the very amusing manual, entitled, "Parlor Magic."

OPTICAL AMUSEMENTS.

"Hail, holy light! Offspring of heaven, first-born.
————— ————— —————Before the sun,
Before the heavens, thou wert; and at the voice
Of God, as with a mantle didst invest
The rising world of waters dark and deep."
MILTON.

"Oh, what a noble, heavenly gift is light!
By light, that blessed being, all things live."
SCHILLER'S WILLIAM TELL.

THE branch of natural philosophy denominated OPTICS treats of the nature of Light; the laws by which, under certain circumstances, it is ruled; and the beautiful effects which it produces.

The nature of light has not yet been defined; but, of its principles we know many interesting facts; some few of which are continually displayed in every-day life, whilst most of the others can be proved by very easy experiments. These facts are, its amazing *velocity;* its always moving in *straight* lines; that it may be thrown out of its straight course, and be either *reflected* or *refracted;* that it is not *white;* and that it is the cause of *all* color.

The VELOCITY of LIGHT is truly wonderful; for, according to the calculations of astronomers, it progresses at the rate of 192,000 miles in a second of time—which, as our youthful readers well know, is nearly the smallest portion of time which can be measured, being but the sixtieth part of a minute; consequently, its fearful rapidity is lost upon us, being impossible for the imagination, however fertile it may be in forming conceptions of the vast and wonderful, to picture to itself any thing like such a degree of swiftness; for, as Sir John Herschel asks: "What mere assertion will make any man believe that in the one second of time, in one beat of the pendulum of a clock, a ray of light travels over 192,000 miles; and would therefore perform the tour of the world in less time than the swiftest runner could make one stride?" Experiments have proved the accuracy of this calculation, and therefore the statement can be relied upon.

That LIGHT invariably moves in STRAIGHT LINES, unless some obstacles intervene to throw it out of its course, is a fact easily proved by simple experiment. A bent tube affords a good illustration of this part of optics; for, on looking into one, we shall find that its shape hinders the straight passage of the light, and consequently prevents our seeing through it. Another experiment may be made by taking several cards, piercing a small hole in each, and then placing them in a right line one behind the other, when we shall not be able to see through them, unless they be so arranged that the apertures coincide exactly with each other. Another proof that light moves in straight lines, is within the reach of every one's observation: it is, that the shadow from any object or body, when cast upon a plane or level surface, has a form exactly like the section of the body which throws it; of the truth of this our readers may satisfy themselves when the sun peeps out, and casts shadows from houses, trees, &c.

The REFLECTION of LIGHT is its being hindered in its outward course, and thrown back in a direction contrary to that which it was originally pursuing: this is caused by its falling upon very smooth and highly-polished surfaces, such as mirrors, whether of looking-glass or metal, whether of plane or flat surfaces, or convex, *i. e.* the surface rounded *outward;* or concave, or rounded *inward;* and according to the form of the surface from which the reflection takes place, so is the effect produced. With respect to the two last-mentioned forms of mirrors, there are some effects which invariably occur: these are, that when the rays are reflected from a convex body they *diverge*, that is, the further they proceed from the body reflecting, the wider they spread; and when they are reflected from a concave body, they *converge*, or come to a point at a distance from the reflecting object.

LIGHT is refracted, or bent out of its course, when it passes obliquely through a medium of greater density than that through which it has been traversing, so as to fall quite in a different place to what it would have done, had it not passed into that medium; and the amount of this refraction or bending of the light is always governed by its obliquity, and the nature of the substance through which it progresses. There are some substances or media which are of greater density, and refract light better than others: for instance, alcohol refracts light more than water, oil more than alcohol, and glass even more than oil. Amongst the many useful inventions which the progress of civilization and knowledge has brought forward, there are few which are of so much utility as those which depend upon the refractive powers of glass for their effect; and these are the telescope, microscope, camera-obscura, magic lantern, &c. &c. The pieces of glass used in these instruments are termed *lenses* from their being made in the shape of a flat bean or lentil; this shape, from being rounded outward on both sides, forms what is called a convex lens, and in addition, the concave, or *hollow* on both sides, with the various modifications of both kinds of lenses, employed for optical purposes. The convex lenses cause the different rays which pass through them, from any given point or object, to bend and unite together again at another point beyond them. The more convex the lens is, the nearer is its focus; for it has been ascertained that the focus of a double

18

convex lens is exactly where the centre of the sphere would be, of which the surface of the lens is a portion; consequently, in proportion to the convexity of the lens, so will the nearness of its focus be, as it then forms a part of a smaller sphere. When the light proceeding from all points of any object placed before a lens, is collected at a certain point beyond it, and received on a white screen or other medium in a darkened room, it produces the well-known effects of the magic lantern, the solar and oxy-hydrogen microscopes, and the camera-obscura; and when the image beyond a lens is viewed in the air, in a particular direction, it then shows the disposition of parts which form the telescope, common microscope, &c. The concave lens acts exactly the reverse of the convex: that is, instead of converging the rays to a point, it expands them, and causes them to fill a space considerably larger than the size of the lens itself.

Some of the most striking celestial appearances, and which are of very frequent occurrence, are the result of the reflection and refraction of the rays of light. The serene, mild glow of twilight, which so softly ends the day, and diminishes the transition from the burning glare of the sun to the cold hues of night, is owing to reflection; and so also is that beautiful many-colored arch, the rainbow. The varied tints of the clouds, from the gray, pearly, morning dawn, to the brilliant crimson-and-gold glories of sunset, are produced by a combination of causes—absorption, reflection, and refraction. The deceitful mirage is another effect owing to refraction. It is occasioned by unequal refraction, that is, when the rays of light enter a medium of different densities; and is a phenomenon of rare occurrence in temperate climates, occurring chiefly in those subject to the extremes of temperature, whether of heat or cold. In the arid deserts of Africa, the mirage frequently presents the appearance of a delightful tract of country stretching across the wide plain, in which the traveler fancies he may refresh himself and his camels, sheltered by lofty palm-trees from the scorching rays of the sun; but as the wanderer pursues his onward course, he finds the unsubstantial forms vanish before his eager gaze, making the dreary way still more desolate from the bitterness of disappointment. In the Arctic regions, also, the mirage presents forms of great interest and beauty, but of a different character from those in the torrid zone; displaying lofty towers and pinacles, high battlemented walls and aërial palaces, from the refracted forms of the icebergs.

It was formerly supposed that SOLAR LIGHT was a WHITE substance; but that opinion has been exploded since Newton discovered, by means of a prism, that light is composed of seven elementary colors—red, orange, yellow, green, blue, indigo, and violet. Dr. Wollaston considered there was but four primitive colors: red, green, blue, and violet; whilst, according to the analysis of Dr. Young, three only—red, yellow, and blue—can be reckoned; this last opinion is supported by Sir David Brewster, from the results of his own experiments. To our young readers it may seem a startling matter to consider the transparent body called *light* as being composed of seven colors; but if they try the simple and pleasing experiments at page 282, they will find that by decomposing and afterward recomposing a beam of solar light, that it is by no means that colorless medium they would otherwise be disposed to imagine it.

LIGHT is the cause of all COLOR; for color does not belong naturally to any substance, but is entirely regulated by the peculiar rays which the substance reflects and absorbs. Those objects which appear *white* to us, reflect *all* the primitive colors; whilst those which seem black, *absorb all* and *reflect none;* whatever appears *green*, absorbs the red ray, and reflects the *blue* and *yellow* rays only, which, blending together, produce the compound color *green*. Thus, bodies seem to be of those colors which are formed from the reflected rays; for the reflected elementary rays combining, produce another kind of color, which is the one our visual organs take cognizance of. The varied colors which we see around us, and the harmonious tints displayed upon every object within our notice, are produced by combinations of the elementary rays of color; and are to be accounted for on the principles of reflection, refraction, and absorption.

We shall now proceed to enumerate a few practical illustrations.

OPTICAL AUEMENTATION.

Take a large conical-shaped drinking-glass, put a shilling into it, and fill it about half-full with water. Place a plate upon the top of the glass, and turn it very quickly over, so that the water may not escape, and a piece of silver as large as half a crown will immediately appear on the plate; whilst, some little way up the glass, another piece will present itself, about the size of a shilling. This effect is caused by refraction.

REFRACTION OF LIGHT.

Put a piece of money at the bottom of an empty basin, and then retire a few steps backward, till the edge of the basin screen the money from your sight. Keep your head steady, and request some one to fill the basin very gently with water; as the water rises, the coin will come gradually into view; and when the basin is nearly full of water, it will be completely visible.

THE THAUMATROPE, OR WONDER-TURNER.

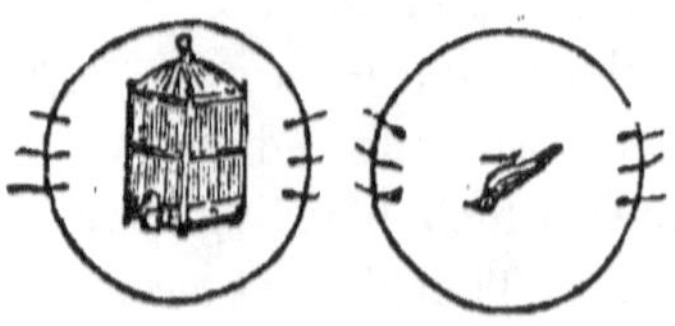

The Thaumatrope is an exceedingly amusing toy, of very simple construction and pleasing effect. It is made in the follow-

ing manner :—Cut out a piece of car figures correspond exactly
and affix to it six pieces of string, th of tone, as much of the
lineated in the margin. Paint on one upon accuracy in this
and on the other a cage ; being caref
down to each other, otherwise the de
produced. When showing the toy, t
strings between the forefinger and thu it of card-board, placed
to the card, and twist or twirl the card rapidly round ; when
lo ! the bird will appear snugly ensconced in its cage. The
principle on which this pleasing toy acts, is, that the image of
any object received on the retina or optic nerve, which is at
the back of the eye, is retained in the mind for about eight
seconds after the object causing the impression is withdrawn ;
consequently, the impression of the painting on one side of
the card is not obliterated ere the painting on the other side
is brought before the eye ; it therefore follows that both sides
are seen at once. The subjects suited to the Thaumatrope
are very varied : amongst others, the following are well calculated for display ; a juggler throwing up two balls may be
drawn on one side of a card, and two balls only on the other,
and according to the pairs of strings employed, he will seem
to toss two, three, or four balls ; the body and legs of a man
on one side, and his head and arms on the other ; a candle
and its flame ; a mouse and a trap ; and a horse and his rider ;
this last is a very good one, as by using the different pairs of
strings, the relative positions of man and horse may be varied
most singularly.

THE STOBOSCOPE OR PHENAKISTISCOPE.

This is a most amusing instrument, and in its principles resembles the Thaumatrope ; its effect depending, like that, upon
the continuance of the image of an object upon the retina.

of those colors which ar
the reflected elementary
of color, which is the
of. The varied colors
monious tints displayed
are produced by combin
and are to be accounted
         absorptio

consists of a disc made of stout card-
ard, upon which, toward the edge, a
ies of figures in eight or ten different
sitions is painted; thus, if it be wished
produce the illusion of a man running,
e first position should be quiescent,
anding upright, the second advancing

forward a little, the third stepping out still more, and so on
to the sixth figure, which should be drawn as if running at
full speed; the remaining attitudes should show the person
gradually returning to the first quiet attitude. Between each
figure, a slit must be made about three quarters of an inch in
length, and a quarter, or less, in width; running in a parallel
direction with the radii of the disc, and extending to an equal
distance from the centre, as in the illustration. This disc, 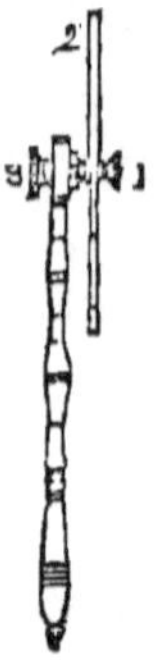
when completed, should be put upon a handle as in
the annexed figure; Fig. 1 shows a little nut, which
must be unscrewed ere the disc can be placed on its
axis, and which keeps it in its proper place, so that it
cannot lean forward and spoil the experiment; 2 is
the disc, and three is a nut fixed to the axis by which
the rotatory motion is given to the disc. When trying the effect of this instrument, stand before a looking-glass, and hold the painted face of the machine
toward the glass; cause it to revolve on its axis, and
look through the slits, when, instead of beholding a mass of
confusion, as might naturally be expected, and as would undoubtedly be the case, were the disc viewed in the ordinary
way, the figures will seem to be running as fast as possible,
and with very natural movements, their velocity being, of
course, proportioned to the rate at which the disc is impelled.
The number of subjects adapted for this species of exhibition
is considerable; and if they be well drawn, they may be made
the source of much merriment. Especial care must be taken,

when drawing them, to make the figures correspond exactly with each other in shape and depth of tone, as much of the good effect of the display depends upon accuracy in this respect.

OPTICAL DECEPTIONS.

If two equal cog-wheels be cut out of card-board, placed upon a pin, and wheeled round with equal velocity in opposite directions, instead of producing a hazy tint, as one wheel would do, or even as the two would if revolving in the same direction, there is presented an extraordinary appearance of a fixed wheel. Again, if one move somewhat faster than the other, then the spectral wheel appears to move slowly round ; if the cogs be cut slantwise on both wheels, the spectral wheel in like manner exhibits slant cogs ; but if one of the wheels be turned so that the cogs shall point in opposite directions, then the spectral wheel has straight cogs. If wheels with radii or arms be viewed when moving, then similar optical deceptions appear ; and though the wheels move ever so fast, yet the magic of a fixed wheel will be presented, provided they move with equal velocities. If they overlap each other in a small degree, then very curious lines will be seen.

Perhaps, the most striking deception is the following : A pasteboard wheel has a certain number of teeth or cogs at its edge ; a little nearer the centre is a series of apertures resembling the cogs in arrangement, but not to the same number ; and still nearer the centre is another series of apertures, different in number, and varying from the former. When this wheel is fixed upon an axle, its face held two or three yards from an illuminated mirror, and spun round, the cogs disappear, and a grayish belt, three inches broad, becomes visible ; but on looking at the glass through the moving wheel, appearances entirely change ; one row of cogs appears as fixed as if the wheel were not moving, while the other two give an opposite result; shifting the eye a little, other and new ap-pearances are produced.

With the two wheels mentioned in the first experiment, if only one be turned in the sunlight, a shadow corresponding to its appearance will be produced; but if both be turned in opposite directions, the shadow is no longer uniform, but has light and dark alternately, and resembles the shadow of a fixed wheel.

Prick a hole in a card with a needle; place the same needle near the eye, in a line with the card-hole, look by daylight at the end of the needle, and it will appear to be behind the card, and reversed.

Prick a hole with a pin in a black card, place it very near the eye, look through it at any small object, and it will appear larger as it is nearer the eye; while, if we observe it without the card, it will appear sensibly of the same magnitude at all parts of the room.

Cut out a disc or circle of pasteboard, and cover it with paper, half green and half black : cause the disc to be rapidly turned round (like the shafts of a toy windmill), and the colors will combine and produce white.

COLORS PRODUCED BY THE UNEQUAL ACTION OF LIGHT UPON THE EYES.

If we hold a slip of white paper vertically, about a foot from the eye, and direct both eyes to an object at some distance beyond it, so as to see the slip of paper double, then, when a candle is brought near the right eye, so as to act strongly upon it, while the left eye is protected from its light, the left-hand slip of paper, will be of a tolerably bright *green* color, while the right-hand slip of paper, seen by the left eye, will be of a red color.   If the one image overlap the other, the color of the overlapping parts will be white, arising from a mixture of the complementary red and green.   When equal candles are held equally near to each eye, each of the images of the slip of paper is white. If, when the paper is seen red and green by holding the candle to the right eye, we quickly take it to the left éye, we shall find that the left image of the slip of paper gradually changes from *green* to *red*, and the right one from *red* to *green*, both of them having the same tint during the time that the change is going on.

THE STANHOPE LENS

Is a very simple, portable, and economical kind of microscope, invented by the late Earl of Stanhope. It is a cylinder of glass, about half an inch in length and a quarter of an inch in diameter, and is generally mounted in white metal, silver, or gold. Both ends are ground convex, one rather more so than the other; and as its focus does not exceed its length, it is only necessary to put the object to be viewed either upon, or in immediate contact with, the end which has the slighter degree of convexity, to hold the instrument up to the light and look through it, when the object will be seen considerably magnified, to the extent, we believe, of 4096 times; its magnifying power is, therefore, nearly equal to that of many compound microscopes. The animalculæ in stagnant water, the mites in cheese, the farina and delicate leaves of flowers, the beautiful down upon the wings of butterflies and moths, human hair, the hairs of different animals, are amongst the objects which this lens developes in a lucid manner; as likewise the exquisitely minute crystallization of salts, if a drop of a solution of a salt be lightly spread over one end of it, and viewed instantaneously ere the moisture evaporates.

TO MAKE A PRISM.

Provide two small pieces of window glass and a lump of wax; soften and mould the wax, stick the two pieces of glass upon it, so that they meet, as in the cut, where *w* is the wax, *g* and *g* the glasses stuck to it, (Fig. 1.) The end view

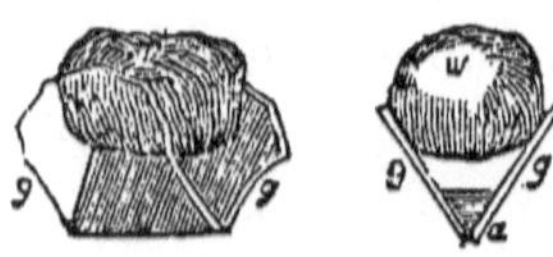

Fig. 1.   Fig. 2.

(Fig. 2,) will show the angle, *a*, at which the pieces of glass meet; into which angle put a drop of water.

To use the instrument thus made, make a small hole, or a narrow horizontal slit, so that you can see the sky through it, when you stand at some distance from it in the room.   Or a piece of pasteboard placed in the upper part of the window-sash, with a slit cut in it, will serve the purpose of the hole in the shutter.   The slit should be about one-tenth of an inch wide, and an inch or two long, with even edges.   Then hold the prism in your hand, place it close to your eye, and look through the drop of water, when you will see a beautiful train of colors, called a spectrum; at one end red, at the other violet, and in the middle yellowish green.

The annexed figure 3, will better explain the direction in

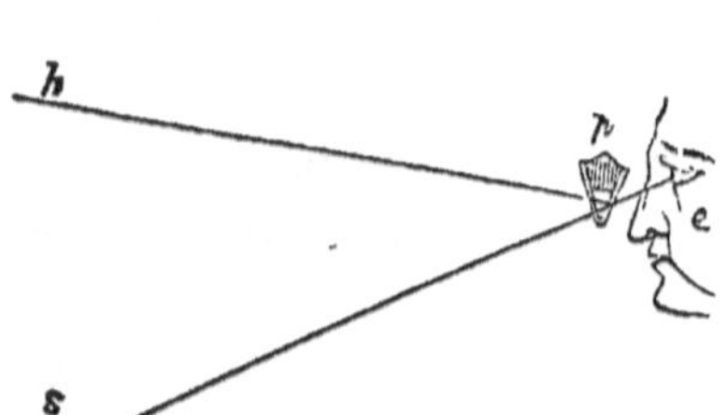

Fig. 3.

which to look : here, *e* is the eye of the spectator, *p* is the prism, *h*, the hole in the shutter or pasteboard, *s*, the spectrum.   By a little practice, you will soon become accustomed to look in the right direction, and will see the colors very bright and distinct.

By means of this simple contrivance, white light may be analyzed and proved to consist of colored rays, and several of its properties be beautifully illustrated.

THE PRISMATIC COLORS.

Our young readers will find these three experiments upon the colors in a ray of light, of great interest and beauty.

Close the shutters of a room into which the sun is shining; and if there be not an aperture in the shutters, then bore a little hole. Hold a prism at a short distance from the aperture, so as to allow the slender stream of sunlight to pass through, and be decomposed by it; when, instead of a little round spot on the opposite wall of the room, an oblong image will be displayed, consisting of the seven colors of the rainbow, red, orange, yellow, green, blue, indigo, and violet. This image is called the solar spectrum.

If the hole in the shutter be exceedingly small, and no prism be employed, then only four colors will be evident, and these are red, green, yellow, and violet.

The above experiments show by decomposition, that light is a compound color; and to confirm them, it is only necessary to recompose the seven colors, and produce the pure sunlight effect as follows :—

Take another prism corresponding in every respect with the first, and placing them both together, so as to form a parallelogramic figure, the seven rays will be reunited, and form a single spot of light.

THE CAMERA-OBSCURA.

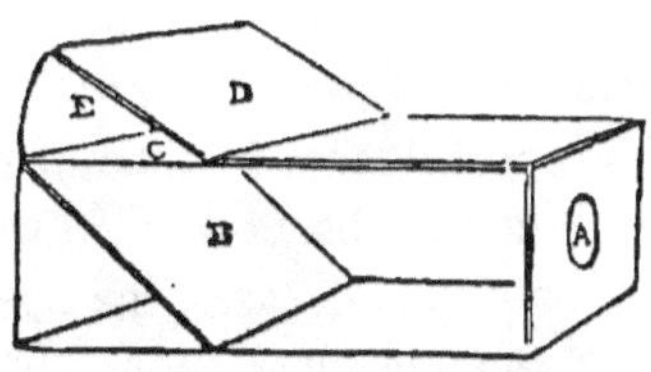

Provide a box about twelve inches in length, four in depth, and six in width; in the middle of one end of it let a hole be bored, as at A, in the annexed diagram, in which put a double convex lens; and at the other end, inside the box, place a piece of looking-glass, as at B, inclining it at an angle of 45°, or in less technical phrase, in a position midway between the horizontal and perpendicular, so as to reflect objects upward. Part of the top of the box must be made so as to serve as a lid, upon hinges, as D; and the space beneath be filled up by a piece of ground glass C, upon which medium the objects are reflected from the looking-glass with the utmost exactness and beauty, so as to appear like an exquisite picture in miniature. Sides are usually added to the lid, as at E, to keep off as much of the circumambient light as possible. In some cameras, instead of a fixed lens, a sliding tube, with a lens at the extremity, is employed. The inside of the box should be covered with lamp-black and water, or stained with ink.

MULTIPLYING THEATRES.

Place in a box two pieces of looking-glass, one at each end, parallel to one another; and looking over, or by the edge of one of them, the images of any objects placed on the bottom of the box, will appear continued to a considerable distance.

Or, line each of the four sides of the box with looking-glass, and the bottom of the box will be multiplied to an astonishing extent, there being no other limitation to the number of images but that which is owing to the continued loss of light from reflection. The top of the box may be almost covered with thin canvas, which will admit sufficient light to render the exhibition very distinct.

The above experiments may be made very entertaining, by placing on the bottom of the box some toy, as two persons playing at cards, sentry soldiers, &c.; and, if these be put in motion, by wires attached to them, or passing through the bottom or side of the box, it will afford a still more entertaining spectacle. Or the bottom of the box may be covered with moss, shining pebbles, flowers, &c.; only, in all cases, the upright figures between the pieces of looking-glass should be slender, and not too numerous, else they will obstruct the reflected light.

In a box with six, eight, or more sides, lined with looking-glass as above, the different objects in it will be multiplied to an almost indefinite extent.

THE COSMORAMA, OR SHOW-GLASS.

Improved portable Cosmoramas, complete, may be purchased of any optician; but the ingenious may construct them with little difficulty, if they provide themselves with the glass and prints.

In forming the Cosmorama, place the picture about two inches within the focus of the lens. Then place a piece of scenery about four inches before the marginal parts of the picture, which by scene-painters is called the wings, and may consist of a balcony and a few trees, rocks, etc., according to your taste. This will be similar to the public Cosmoramas; for, by cutting off or hiding the marginal parts of the picture, as above described, the spectator cannot calculate the dimensions of the view.

This, if properly managed, with lights placed behind, and well painted scenery, affords a source of great amusement to young persons. If the bright lights in moonlight subjects be washed over with a composition of equal parts of linseed oil and spirits of turpentine, very pleasing transparencies may be formed.

The Cosmorama may be formed at less expense and trouble than, perhaps, any other public exhibition, while it may be varied to infinity.

It consists merely of a picture, seen through a magnifying glass, exactly in the same manner as in the common shows exhibited in the streets for the amusement of children; the difference not being in the construction of the apparatus, but in the quality of the pictures exhibited. In the common shows, coarsely colored prints are sufficiently good; in the Cosmorama, a moderately good oil painting is employed. The construction will be readily understood by the following description: In a hole of a door or partition, insert a double convex lens, having about three feet focus. At a distance from it rather less than the focal distance of the lens, place, in a vertical position, the picture to be represented. The optical part of the exhibition is now complete; but as the frame of the picture would be seen, and thus the illusion be destroyed, it is necessary to place between the lens and the view, a square, wooden frame, formed of four short boards. The frame, which is to be painted black, prevents the rays of light passing beyond a certain line, according to its distance from the eye; the width of it is such that upon looking through the lens, the picture is seen as if through an opening, which adds very much to the effect; and if that end of the box, or frame, next the picture, have an edge to it, representing the outlet of a cave, a Gothic ruin, or a rocky archway, which may be partially lighted by the top of the box being semi-transparent, the beauty and apparent reality of the picture will be very much enhanced.

Upon the top of the frame should be placed a lamp. It is this which illuminates the picture, while all extraneous light is carefully excluded by the lamp being contained in a box, open in the front and at the top.

OPTICAL INVERSION.

Put a little clear syrup into a square, white glass bottle, and then pour into it, upon the syrup, about an equal quantity of water. Then place a printed card about an inch behind the bottle, and, if you look through the syrup, or through the water, the letters on the card will appear *erect;* but, when they are seen through that part where the two fluids are gradually mixing together, the letters will appear equally distinct, but *inverted.* A similar effect may be produced with hot and cold water; or even by two portions of cold and heated air. To show the latter, place two chairs back to back, and about a foot apart; connect the tops of the chairs with two pieces of strong wire, and on the wires lay the kitchen poker, the square end of which has been made red hot. Exactly in the direction of the poker, pin a large printed letter upon the wall, say at about ten feet distant ; then, by looking along the heated poker, you will see *three* images of the letter, the middle one being inverted, and the two others erect.

KALEIDOSCOPIC CIRCLES.

Put on a piece of white paper a circular piece of blue silk, of about four inches diameter; next, place on the blue silk a circular piece of yellow of three inches diameter; on that, a circle of pink, two inches in diameter; on that, a circle of green, one inch in diameter ; then, one of indigo, of half an inch in diameter, and finish by making a small speck of ink in the centre. Place it in the sunshine, look on the central point steadily for a minute or two, and then closing your eyes, and applying your hand at about an inch from them, so as to prevent too much light from passing through the eyelids, you will see the most beautiful circles of colors the imagination can conceive ; differing widely from the colors of the silks, and also adding to the richness of the experiment by changing in kaleidoscopic variety.

SIMPLE MICROSCOPES.

Get a piece of thin platinum wire, and twist it round the point of a pin, so as to make a very small ring, with a handle to it. Next break a piece of flint glass into pieces about the size of mustard seeds, or somewhat larger ; put one of the pieces upon the ring of wire, and hold it in the point of the flame of a candle ; when the glass melts, it will become of a completely globular form, and serve, when mounted, every purpose to which microscopes can be applied. The simplest mode of mounting these diminutive lenses, is either to put one between two pieces of brass, which have holes made in them of just the size to retain the edge of the lens; or they may be fastened to a single piece of brass by the aid of a little gum. It is to be observed, that the smaller the drop of glass, the more globular it will remain, and consequently possess greater magnifying power.

PORTABLE MICROSCOPE.

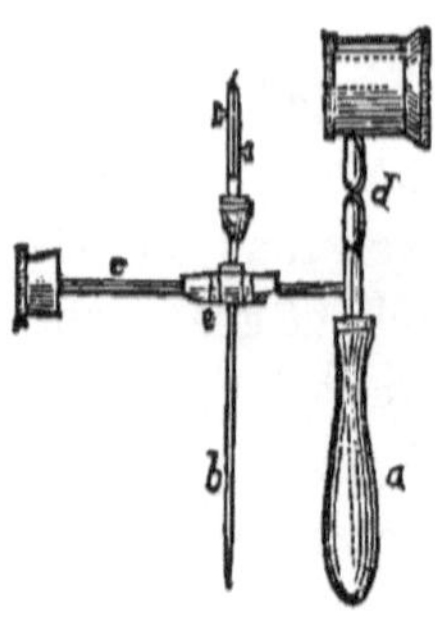

This cheap and useful instrument consists of a handle of hard wood, *a*, which is screwed into a brass piece, *d*, having, at its top, a ring, with screws on back and front, into which are to be screwed two cells with lenses of different foci. There is also a projecting piece formed on the side of the brass piece, *d*, in which is a hole to receive the screwed end of a cylindrical rod of brass, *c*. Upon this rod a spring slit socket, *e*, slides backward and forward, and is also capable of being turned round. This socket has affixed to it, on one side, a projecting part, with a screwed cavity in it, to receive a short screwed tube, with a small hole in its centre, made to fit the steel stem of the spring forceps; a corresponding hole being made at the bottom of the screwed cavity, where is lodged a piece of perforated cork; which, being pressed upon by the action of the screw, closes upon the steel stem of the forceps, and steadies them, and the objects held in them. The stem of the forceps being removed from its place in the short tube; the handles and lenses, and the rod, *c*, and the sliding socket upon it being unscrewed from its place in the handle; they can all three be packed in a black paper case, which is only three and a half inches long, one inch broad, and half an inch thick.

This microscope possesses three different magnifying powers, namely, those of two lenses separately, and the two in combination.

Microscopes of a still simpler nature are small globules of glass formed by smelting the ends of fine threads of glass in the flame of a candle; and small globular microscopes of great magnifying power, made of hollow glasses about the size of a small walnut, may be purchased very cheap of the opticians.

WATER LENSES.

Temporary microscopes of considerable distinctness may be very easily made, by piercing a hole about the size of a pin's head in a piece of brass, and carefully placing a minute drop of water on the hole, where it will assume a globular shape. These lenses, as may be imagined, are rendered useless by the slightest movement.

AN OPTICAL GAME.

Give a ring to a person, or place it at a little distance, in such a position that the plane of it shall be turned toward his face; then desire him to shut one of his eyes, and endeavor to push a crooked stick through the ring; when, to his surprise, he will seldom succeed. The reason is evident: being unaccustomed to use one eye only, he cannot judge of the distance correctly, and, of course, errs; but a person having only one eye, would not fail of achieving the trick.

THE MAGIC LANTERN, OR PHANTASMAGORIA.

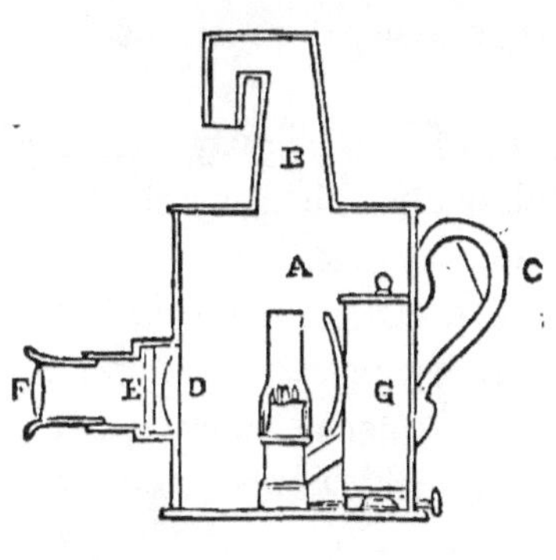

The magic lantern, one of the most amusing of optical instruments, was invented by Kircher, about the middle of the 17th century: it was of the greatest service to the magicians of those times, by enabling them to work upon the credulity of the ignorant and superstitious, with the utmost

19

facility. As a vehicle of amusement, it contributes in no small degree, in the shape of a gallantee-show, to the hilarity of a party in a long winter's night; and as a means by which lectures on astronomy can be elucidated, it arrests the attention of graver spectators.

The instrument, the construction of which demands our attention first, is represented in the margin. A, is a box made of wood or tin, about eight inches square, having a bent funnel or chimney, B, at the top; a handle, C, renders it a portable instrument, and holes are made near the bottom to feed the flame of the lamp with the air which is requisite for its combustion; in the front of the box is a tin tube, furnished at the end near the light with a plano-convex lens, D—which, indeed, is affixed to the lantern itself—and at the other, a doubly convex lens, F; this tin tube is fixed to the lantern by a square foot, the sides of which are open, as at E, to admit the sliders, and the end of the tube, in which the doubly convex lens is fastened, is made to slide in and out for convenience when adjusting the focus; a third lens is occasionally employed when the space is very confined, as a larger field of view can be obtained by its aid than in the ordinary method. The lamp, G, is a common argand burner, furnished with a concave tin reflector, to concentrate the intensity of the light; and if the lamp be made to slide backward and forward by means of a wire, it will be so much the more useful.

The Phantasmagorial Lantern varies but slightly from the foregoing; the chief points in which it differs being in the form of the tube containing the doubly convex lens, which is made to project further beyond the lens, F; and in the lens itself being contrived so as to move readily backward and forward, either by a rack and pinion, or studs fastened on each side; in a flap to shut off the light abruptly, which may be either a tin slider to run into the groove, or else a piece of tin fastened in the front of all ; and in the top of the square chamber, in which the sliders run, being made so as to open occasionally.

TO PAINT THE SLIDERS.—The sliders are made of pieces of glass, surrounded by a slight frame, and in dimensions are of course regulated by the depth of the aperture intended for them in the lantern. Few hints can be given for painting them beyond naming the colors, and the mode of preparing them ; as taste is the best guide, and practice the most impressive instructor, in all matters relative to painting. The proper colors are only such as are transparent, and as follow : Gamboge, scarlet lake, Prussian blue ; a green made of distilled verdigris and a quarter of its bulk of gamboge ; burnt sienna, burnt umber, and lampblack. A few implements, such as a glass muller and slab, which last may be about six inches square ; a palette-knife, and some small bottles to put the colors in after they are ground, are also requisite. The colors should be ground up with Canada balsam and turpentine, equal parts of each ; or, if in that proportion they be too thick for grinding freely, rather more turpentine may be added ; thus mixed, they require about a week to dry, and have a very beautiful appearance ; but to have them harden in less time, mastic varnish may be employed instead of the above. When painting, take a very little color at a time out of the bottles, as it soon hardens ; and if too thick, temper it with turpentine. A piece of glass will serve as a palette, and a bit of stick as a means of getting the color out of the bottles. The black pigment used in darkening the surface of the glass round the figures of the Phantasmagorial sliders, is composed of lampblack and asphaltum, dissolved in turpentine.

The subjects intended for the sliders must be carefully drawn upon a piece of paper, which should be placed under the glass, and then painted from ; too much attention cannot be paid to the drawing of the subjects, for when they are thrown upon the wall, all their defects, however minute, are enlarged to an astonishing extent.

Those parts of the subjects which are to appear white, must be left entirely destitute of color, as flake, and all other whites are opaque pigments. The mixed colors are produced by blending the colors before-mentioned : thus greens are made by means of yellow and blue, orange by means of yellow and carmine, &c.; this last, although not an exact orange, is near enough for the purpose, since the red which composes the proper tint is opaque, and consequently useless. The shadows may be obtained either by stronger tints of the same colors, or by shadows of brown or blue, as may be requisite. The sky tints must be darker than they are intended to appear, for as the yellow light of the lamp throws a yellowish tone upon the colors, they would lose their effect were they not so managed ; for the same reason, the green of trees and grass should be painted bluish-green ; the reds be but very slightly used, and never shaded with blue ; purples should also be but sparingly employed, for the yellow tone of the lights uniting with the blue and lake colors used in the purple, forms a decidedly neutral tint, or blackish purple, much too dark and unintelligible for the purpose. As it is often necessary to remove some parts which do not harmonize, even after they have well dried, a penknife will be found of great assistance ; when bright lines are required upon a dark ground, the effect is easily managed, by scratching the color away with a needle, or any other pointed instrument ; and if the lines are to appear faintly colored, it is only necessary to point them delicately after the scratching is completed.

The sliders for the common magic lantern are transparent: that is, the figures are painted on a piece of plain glass ; whilst, on those used in the phantasmagorial lantern, the figures are

surrounded by an opaque, black tint, as in the illustration: the figures of the former are usually shown upon a wall, familiar doubtless to most of our readers, and invariably have a circle of light around them; whilst those in the latter are thrown upon a semi-transparent screen, which is placed between the spectators and the lantern; and in consequence of no circle of light accompanying them, they have a very beautiful appearance.

Almost magical effects of light, shade, and motion may be produced by means of different glasses; and the sliders so adapted are termed "movable sliders."

Landscape-glasses are glasses on which several views are painted, divided from each other by some slight foreground object, as a tree, or a building, or guide-post. Various effects, from the brightest mid-day to the deepest tints of night, may be produced in these, by means of double sliders, and these contrivances may be thus applied. Cut away the frame of the slider at each end, nearly even with the glass, and fasten two narrow strips of wood along the glass, one at the top, and the other at the bottom; the piece of glass which is to be moved, should exactly fit the space between the upper and under frames, and act upon the slips; and to keep it steadily in its place, two or three pins may be driven into the slips.

Storm-glasses, which are very ingenious representations of the effects developed by a change from a calm to a thunder-storm, require two glasses, as in the former slider. Fig. 1, in the annexed illustration, shows a com-

mon slider painted at one end to represent a calm of sea and sky, and the sun setting in splendor; toward the centre the clouds appear threatening; and a gentle undulation of the water breaks its repose; further on, a still greater agitation of the clouds and water is shown; and at the other end, the lightnings flash, and the sweeping wave tells of the war of elements. The effect is materially heightened by means of the second slider, fig. 2, having several ships painted on it; and these, of course, must correspond to the action of the water, from the bark sailing in quiet majesty to the tempest-torn and shattered hulk.

The effects of moonlight and sunrise may also be imitated by double sliders; and by a third one, figures may be introduced upon the scenes to add to their beauty.

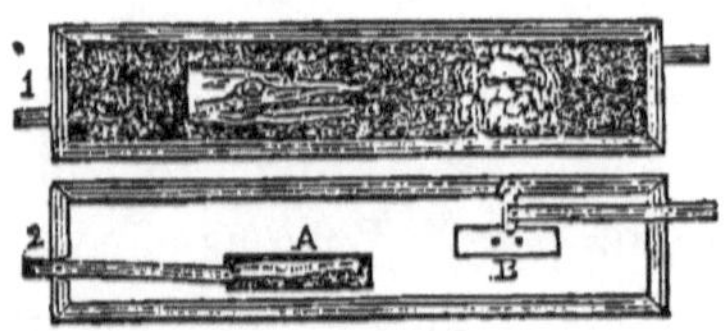

The eyes and mouths of figures and animals may be made to move, and produce a most singular, nay almost frightful effect; and by referring to the marginal illustration, the modes by which these are managed will be clearly understood. In fig. 1 the heads of a crocodile and lion are delineated, and in fig. 2 the contrivances for moving the jaw of the one and the eyes of the other. A, represents a piece of talc having the lower jaw painted upon it and surrounded with black, which fills up a space of corresponding size left blank in the perfect slider; a slight lever should be fastened to this piece of talc, to act upon a pivot on the frame, which projects a little beyond it; and as it moves up and down, so will the crocodile's mouth appear to open and shut. The eyes of the lion must be painted black upon a transparent piece of talc, as at B, from which a side lever should be carried, as in the former case, to a little beyond the frame; and to prevent the talc from shifting too far either backward or forward, a drop or two of sealing-wax, or a little knob of wood fastened to the glass on each side, either of the talc or lever, will be found sufficient.

SCREENS FOR THE LANTERNS.—As we before briefly stated that different media were required, on which to show the effects of the Magic-lantern and Phantasmagoria, we must, in concluding this article, give some directions respecting them. Although any white surface will do very well to receive the objects from the Magic-lantern, yet a clean sheet, stretched tightly upon a wall, is by far the best, as the chief point is to have a medium of perfect whiteness and quite flat. The screen for the phantasmagoria may be made of tissue paper strained upon a frame. Some persons recommend oiled paper as the best medium; but we consider paper so prepared to be too transparent, the plain tissue being thin and translucent enough for any purpose.

Wetted muslin and waxed muslin are also recommended by some persons; but for a screen suited to the pockets of young experimentalists, nothing can be better than the one we recommend; or, for the Phantasmagoria, instead of the figures being reflected on a white wall, or sheet, as by the Magic-lantern, they are thrown on a transparent screen or curtain. The most desirable situation is, where there are folding-doors from one room to another; the curtain should be hung in the doorway, and the spectators placed at the opposite end of the room. The exhibiter, or person who manages the lantern, is then to place himself in the adjoining room behind the curtain; the lantern should be fastened round the waist, so as to leave the hands at liberty; then holding the slide with one hand, he should adjust the tube with the other. He should now go pretty close to the curtain or screen, and draw out the tube until the image is perfect, which of course will be very small—then walking slowly backward, and sliding the tube in at the same time, to keep the image distinct, as it increases in size, it will appear to the spectators on the other side of the screen to be coming toward them; and then again, by the exhibitor walking toward the screen, to diminish the image, it will appear as if the figure was moving backward. Before changing the painting, the darkening door of the lantern may be pushed down, to shut out the light, or the hand may be placed before the lens.

It will also be necessary to observe the following instructions.

If the lamp do not burn brilliantly, the image will be faint, and very likely the darker parts will not appear at all. The argand lamp must be raised or lowered, so as not to smoke, but to enlighten the field all over, before the slides are put in.

2. If the lenses or the paintings be soiled or dusty, the images will be proportionally faint.

3. In holding the lantern under the arm, or when fastened to the waist, care must be taken to keep it upright, otherwise one side of the figure will be faint, or perhaps disappear altogether.

4. In exhibiting the Phantasmagoria, the spectators should not stand directly before the screen, or they will see the light of the lantern; but they should be stationed a little on one side, and as far off as is convenient.

To give motion to the figures, a variety of movable slides are made for this purpose, many of which produce very singular appearances; but with the plain slides the figures may be made to move in a circular, elliptical, or any other way, by moving the lantern in a corresponding direction, which will of course produce the like motion in the images. A curious effect is produced by drawing out the tube, and slipping it suddenly to the focus; this is easily done, by holding the tube tight at the proper place. A shivering motion may be given to the figures, by giving the lantern a sudden shake, or a skeleton made to tumble to pieces by means of a slide made for that purpose. By standing at the bottom of the stairs, a figure may be made to appear going up. The figure of a skeleton is a very good one for this purpose. In the same way, this figure may be made to lie on the floor, and rise up in a sitting or standing position. By applying movable slides to the lantern, an immense variety of curious effects may be produced, particularly on the transparent screen; many of these are often exhibited in public. Those who take delight in the apparatus will soon be able to produce the whole of them.

THE KALEIDOSCOPE.

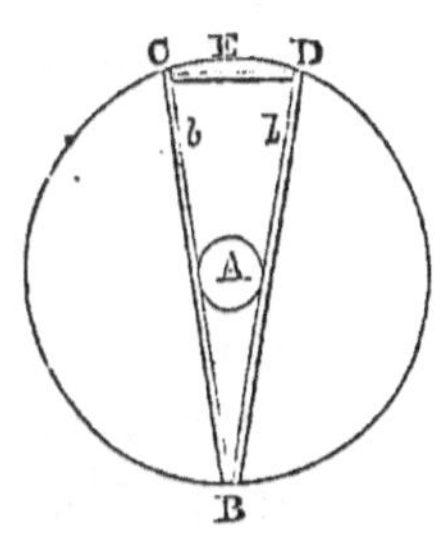

This intellectual instrument is of modern invention, and forms a toy of exhaustless amusement. Rough, but effective, kaleidoscopes may be purchased for a very moderate price at most toy-shops; but for those of our readers, who would like to make them, we proceed to give some information by which they may construct tolerably good specimens for a trifling expense. Get a tube of tin or pasteboard of eight or ten inches in length, and one and a half or two inches in diameter; have one end stopped up with a piece of tin firmly soldered in, and let there be a slight hole made exactly in the centre of this end-piece. Next, procure two pieces of looking-glass of nearly the length of the tube, for reflectors; but if looking-glass be not easily obtained, strips of good new crown-glass will answer the purpose, if the lower surfaces be blackened with lampblack or black wax. These plates of glass must be put into the tube in the manner shown at B C, B D, in the marginal figure; they must be quite parallel and close to each other at the lower part B, and kept asunder at the upper part by a piece of cork or any other substance E ; the polished sides of the glasses must be uppermost, as at *b b ;* A indicates the sight-holes at the further end, and close to this the reflectors must be fitted. The reflectors being put in, a piece of glass, of the same diameter as the tube, is to be pushed into the tube so as to touch the reflectors; sundry bits of different colored glass are to be laid on it, a ring of brass or copper placed round its edge, and then another piece of glass, one side of which has been ground with fine emery, laid upon that ; the edges of the tin tube are then to be burnished round the last-mentioned piece of glass, by which plan the glasses are firmly secured in their places, and the instrument completed. If a piece of marbled or tinted paper be afterward nicely pasted over it, the Kaleidoscope will have a very neat and workmanlike appearance.

THE MYRIAMOSCOPE.

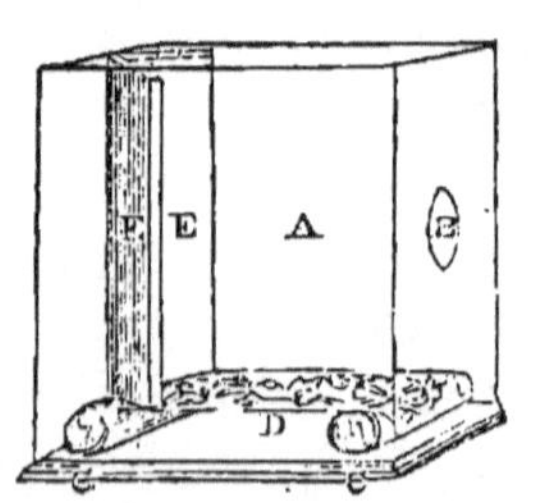

This instrument is a variation of the Kaleidoscope, possessing much of the beautiful effect of that pleasing invention, without its liability to be affected by a shake, so as to derange the elegant forms which it produces. A is a square box, in the front of which the sight-hole, B, is made; two rollers, C C, are placed at the bottom of the box; and in order that they may be made to move round with facility, knobs or handles should be fixed to the ends of their axles at sides of the box. On these rollers, a piece of calico, D, must be wound ; and upon it, fanciful borders, flowers, and ornaments ; cut out from pieces of paper hangings, must be pasted. Two plane mirrors, E E, joined together by a strip of leather, hinge-fashion, are then to be put on the calico, as shown in the margin ; and, of course, all the objects thereon make a very pretty display in the glasses when viewed through the sight-hole, B. The mirrors must be so constructed that they may be put to any inclination, by means of two small pieces of wood fastened to them, and passing through the sides of the box. An opening should be made in the box for the conveni-ence of renewing the subjects, and the top of it be covered with strained muslin, or some other semitransparent medium.

CHINESE SHADOWS (OMBRES CHINOISES).

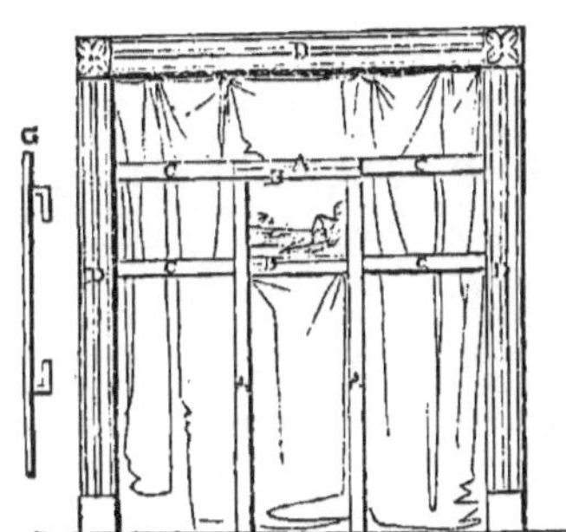

These can be best shown in a room which communicates with another apartment by means of folding-doors, so that the spec-tators may be in one room, and the operator in another. Have a frame of wood made about seven feet in height and four in breadth, as shown at A A A, in the annexed figure; and at B B have two grooves made in the frame, about two feet apart, taking care that the lowest of them be five feet from the ground; these grooves should be half an inch in width, and an inch in depth, as indicated by the small diagram G, which represents a section of the frame. Provide also several frames of four feet in width by two in depth, and cover them with white Italian gauze, varnished over with gum copal; on the gauze, then, paint various scenes, buildings, or landscapes, in which the figures are to appear. The woodwork of these gauzed frames must not be more than an inch in depth, nor quite half-an-inch in thickness, in order that they may slide with facility into the grooves, B B. When exhibiting the shadows, the frame A A A, may be supported by slightly nailing the pieces of wood, C C C C, affixed to it for the purpose, to the framework of the door D D D, as shown in the illustration; and the whole of the framework and its supports should be hidden by hanging drapery on the outside, so as completely to screen all movements and the lights in the room, from the spectators, yet not hide the aperture where the shadows are to appear; in the figure above, the drapery is slightly defined, as also a scene on a gauzed frame. Having prepared and painted scenes, next proceed to get the figures ready; they should be made of pasteboard, and that their shadows may have a better effect, the different figures ought to be movable. To make them act easily, small iron wires must be affixed to their limbs, bent back, and made to terminate in rings, through which rings put the fingers of the right hand, whilst with the left, support the figure by means of another iron wire. By these contrivances, the figure may be made to advance, retire, or gesticulate, without the spectators perceiving the principle on which they act; and as the shadows of the figures are not visible on those parts of the scenes where the colors are dark, they may be held in reserve until the proper time at which they should appear. The painted slides should receive their light from a reverberating lamp, which may be placed about four or five feet from the screen, but so that it is exactly in the centre of the painting.

You must pay particular attention to the carrying on a kind of dialogue, and also to the actions of your figures, to see that they make the corresponding movements of their arms and legs; and it adds materially to the amusement if you can contrive to imitate the shutting of a door, or the sounds uttered by animals, the barking of a dog, crowing of a cock, &c.

AMUSEMENTS IN CHEMISTRY.

HEAT.

1.—Put some water into a glass or cup, and pour upon it about half its quantity of sulphuric acid; upon stirring them together, the temperature will rise to many degrees above boiling water. In mixing the acid with the water, the greatest care should be taken not to do it too suddenly, as the vessel may break from the sudden, intense heat, and the acid be spilt on the hands, clothes, &c. The greatest caution is also necessary in using it, as it will burn every thing it is dropped on.

2.—The expansive force of spirit of wine when heated, may be shown by placing a glass bulb of the size of a pea, filled with it, into the wick of a candle; the liquid will in a short time expand so much, that it will burst the bulb, and put out the light. It is necessary to retire as far from the candle as possible, as when the globule explodes, the pieces are scattered about in all directions.

3. The great expansion of bulk which takes place when water is converted into steam, may also be shown by placing a glass globule like that represented in the preceding experiment, half filled with water, into the wick of a candle; the instant the steam is produced, a violent explosion takes place; it is of course necessary to get out of the reach of the little fragments of glass ejected by the explosion.

(301)

4.—If a piece of iron is hammered smartly on an anvil, its latent heat will be evolved in a short time to such a degree, that the iron will become almost red hot.

5.—Put a little calcined or pure magnesia in a tea-cup on the hearth, and suddenly pour upon it as much concentrated sulphuric acid as will cover it: in an instant sparks will be ejected, and the mixture will be completely ignited.

6.—Put a small quantity of pulverized charcoal into a warm tea-cup, and pour upon it some nitric acid; ignition will instantly take place, and sparks will be thrown out in all directions.

7.—Pour a little clear water into a small glass tumbler, and put one or two pieces of phosphuret of lime into it. In a short time, flashes of fire will dart from the surface of the water, and terminate in ringlets of smoke ascending in regular succession.

8.—Add a grain or two of chlorate of potass to a tea-spoonful of alcohol, and let fall upon it a few drops of strong sulphuric acid; the mixture will immediately burst into a flame.

9.—Thinly spread some dry nitrate of copper on a piece of tin foil, three or four inches square, and wrap it up; there will not be any effect produced. Unfold the tinfoil, and sprinkle a very small quantity of water on the nitrate of copper, wrap it up again as quickly as possible, and press down the edges closely. Considerable heat, attended with fumes, will now be evolved; and if the experiment be dexterously managed, it will ignite. This shows that nitrate of copper has not any effect on tin, till in a state of solution.

10.—Mix together two grains of chlorate of potass, and about three of sulphur, both in fine powder; if a little of the mixture be dropped into a wine-glass containing a small quan-tity of sulphuric acid, a beautiful column of flame will burst out.

11.—Put three or four grains of chlorate of potass into a mortar; reduce it to a powder with a pestle, and then add a little flour of sulphur, very finely pulverised. On rubbing the two materials together, a sharp, crackling detonation will ensue, unattended with danger. This experiment may be repeated several times with the same materials.

12.—Fill a saucer with water, and drop a small piece of potassium into it; the instant it touches the water, it will burst, with a slight explosion, into a brilliant violet-colored flame. It will continue burning for a short time on the surface of the water, darting from one side of the vessel to the other with great violence, like a beautiful fire-ball. Or, if the potassium be thrown upon ice, it will likewise instantly take fire.

13.—Pulverise separately one ounce of crystallized muriate of ammonia, an equal quantity of nitrate of potash, and two ounces of sulphate of soda; mix them together in a goblet with four ounces of cold water, and immediately immerse in the mixture a thin glass tube, containing cold water; in a short time it will freeze, even in a warm room, or in the midst of summer.

14.—Take a very thin glass bulb, half filled with water, and continue to drop ether so slowly upon it, that it may evaporate, and not fall from the surface of the glass; the water inside will quickly be frozen, and this effect will take place sooner if the bulb be held in a current of air.

15.—Put into a wine-glass a few tea-spoonsful of a concentrated solution of silicated potash, and add to it gradually, drop by drop, sulphuric acid. If these two liquids be stirred together with a glass rod, they will become converted into an opaque, white, and almost solid mass.

16.—Pour a small quantity of water in some muriate of lime, just sufficient to saturate, not liquefy it; then let some concentrated sulphuric acid fall gradually upon this solution, and a solid compound, called sulphate of lime, will be produced.

HEAT PASSING THROUGH GLASS.—Heat a poker bright-red-hot, and having opened a window, apply the poker quickly very near to the outside of a pane, and the hand to the inside; a strong heat will be felt at the instant, which will cease as soon as the poker is withdrawn; and may be again renewed, and made to cease as quickly as before. Now, it is well known, that if a piece of glass be so warm as to convey the impression of heat to the hand, it will retain some part of that heat for a minute or more; but, in this experiment, the heat will vanish in a moment. It will not, therefore, be the heated pane of glass that we shall feel, but heat which has come through the the glass, in a free or radiant state.

MAGIC OF HEAT.—Melt a small quantity of sulphate of potass and copper in a spoon over a spirit-lamp: it will be fused at a heat just below redness, and produce a liquid of a dark green color. Remove the spoon from the flame, when the liquid will become a solid of a brilliant emerald-green color, and so remain till its heat sinks nearly to that of boiling water; then, suddenly, a commotion will take place throughout the mass, beginning from the surface; and each atom, as if animated, will start up and separate itself from the rest, till, in a few moments, the whole will become a heap of powder.

RUPERT'S DROPS.—Glass is an extremely bad conductor of heat, and the reason why tumblers and other vessels made of glass crack when hot water is suddenly poured into them, is, that the interior of the glass expands before the heat can penetrate through the particles on the outside, which are consequently then riven asunder. Small glass toys, called Prince Rupert's drops, which may be obtained at a glass-blower's, show very clearly the effect of heat on bad conductors: They are made by dropping a small quantity of glass, while almost in a liquid state, into water, by which means a globule with a spiral tail is instantly formed; the outside of the globule cools and solidifies the instant it comes into contact with the water before the inner part changes, and this portion would contract, were it not retained and kept in its form by its adherence to the outer crust. If the tail be broken off, or any other injury done to the globule, it will burst with a slight noise and fall to pieces. In order that glass-ware may be durable, it is annealed; that is, it is put into an oven, the temperature of which is allowed to decrease gradually.

ATTRACTION AND DECOMPOSITION.

1.—Add a little water, impregnated with carbonic acid, to a wine-glass of clear lime-water: these two liquids will combine and form a white substance called carbonate of lime.

2.—Throw a piece of copper into a wine-glass, and pour upon it some nitric acid; these two substances will combine, and a solution of a clear blue color will be produced. If you plunge into it a piece of iron, (the blade of a knife will answer,) the acid will combine with this new body, and the copper will be precipitated on the blade of the knife in its original state. Should the solution be allowed to remain undisturbed for some days, it will crystallize, and salts of copper will be produced.

3.—Pour a little of the infusion of litmus, or of red cabbage, into a wine-glass, add to it a single drop of nitric or sulphuric acid, and it will be instantly changed into a beautiful red color.

4.—Take a little of the liquid mentioned in the above experiment, either before or after it has been converted to red, add to it a few drops of the solution of potash, or soda, and upon stirring it up, a fine green color will be produced.

5.—Let a drop of nitrate of copper fall into a glass, then

20

fill it up with water, and it will be perfectly colorless; but upon putting a drop of liquid ammonia, which is also without color, into the glass, the liquid will change to a beautiful deep blue.

6.—Take some of the blue liquid left by the former experiment, let a drop or two of nitric acid fall into it, and it will become clear as crystal.

7.—A drop of nitrate of copper poured into a glass of water will not produce any change in the color of the water; but if a small crystal, or a drop of the solution of prussiate of potash be added, the water will become a dark brown.

8.—Mix a little powdered manganese with a little nitre, throw the mixture into a red-hot crucible, and a compound will be obtained possessed of the singular property of changing to different colors, according to the quantity of water that is added to it. A small quantity gives a green solution, while a greater quantity changes it to a beautiful rich purple. The last experiment may be varied by putting equal quantities of this substance into separate glasses, and pouring hot water into the one, and a portion of cold water into the other. The hot solution will assume a beautiful green color, and the cold one a deep purple.

9.—By pouring lime-water into the juice of beet-root, a colorless liquid is obtained; but if a white cloth be dipped in the liquid and dried, in a few hours it will become quite red, by the mere contact of the air.

10.—Spirit of hartshorn dropped into a solution of copper so weak as to be almost colorless, will produce an intense blue, which disappears by adding an acid.

11.—Mix some lime with muriatic acid, and the substance called muriate of lime will be produced. Then add to the mixture some potassa; the acid will combine with this, and the lime will be precipitated in a state of powder.

12.—Mix some magnesia with muriatic acid, and from this combination muriate of magnesia will be produced; if you add to this some potassa, the acid will quit the magnesia, which will consequently be precipitated, and muriate of potassa will result.

13.—To make soap.—Pour a little water into a phial containing about an ounce of olive oil, shake the phial, and if the contents be narrowly examined, we shall find that no union has taken place; but if some solution of caustic potass be added, and the phial then shaken, an intimate combination of the materials will be formed, and a perfect soap be produced.

14.—Pour a little nitro-muriatic acid upon a small piece of gold, or gold-leaf: in a short time it will be completely dissolved, and the solution assume a beautiful yellow color.

15.—Pour a small quantity of nitric acid upon a little bit of pure silver, or silver-leaf, and it will dissolve in a few minutes.

16.—Pour a little sulphuric acid, diluted with about four times its bulk of water, upon a few iron filings; a strong effervescence will take place, and in a little time the filings will disappear.

17.—Pour some diluted nitric acid on a piece of copper, and in a short time the copper will be dissolved, and the solution will become of a beautiful blue tint.

18.—Pour a little diluted nitric acid upon a piece of lead; it will first convert it into a white powder, and then dissolve it.

19.—Into a solution of nitrate of silver, immerse a small bar of polished copper; on withdrawing the bar, it will be found covered with a fine coating of metallic silver.

20.—A small bar of polished iron immersed in like manner in a solution of nitrate of copper will receive a coating of metallic copper.

21.—A piece of silver immersed in the above solution will remain unchanged; but if immersed in contact with a piece of iron, both, when withdrawn, will be found to be coated with metallic copper.

22.—Pour half an ounce of diluted nitro-muriate of gold into an ale-glass, and put to it a piece of very smooth charcoal. Expose the glass to the rays of the sun, in a warm place ; and in a short time the charcoal will be covered over with a beautiful golden coat. Take it out with a pair of pincers, and inclose it in a glass for show.

23.—Immerse a silk riband in phosphorised ether ; when the ether has evaporated, which will be known by the smoking of the phosphorus, dip it into a diluted solution of nitrate of silver, and the metal will appear revived on the surface of the silk.

SYMPATHETIC INKS.

All writings or drawings executed with Sympathetic Inks are illegible until, by the action of some chemical agents upon a peculiar acid or substance which forms the basis of the ink, a change is effected, and a color produced from that which was before colorless.

1.—Write with a weak solution of sulphate of iron, and it will be invisible ; when dry, wash it over with a solution of prussiate of potash, and the writing will be restored, and turned blue.

2.—Write with some of the above solution, and it will, as before stated, become invisible ; but if a brush which has been dipped in a decoction of oak bark, or tincture of galls, be slightly passed over it, it will turn black.

3.—Write with the nitro-muriate of gold, and brush the letters over with muriate of tin in a diluted state. The writing, before invisible, will then appear of a beautiful purple color.

4.—Dissolve oxyd of cobalt in acetic acid, to which add a little nitre ; write with this solution, hold the writing to the fire, and it will be of a pale rose color, which will disappear on cooling.

5.—Dissolve equal parts of sulphate of copper and muriate of ammonia in water; write with the solution, and it will give a yellow color when heated, which will disappear when cold.

6.—Dissolve nitrate of bismuth in water; write with the solution, and the characters will be invisible when dry, but will become legible on immersion in water.

7.—Dissolve, in water, muriate of cobalt, which is of a bluish-green color, and the solution will be pink; write with it, and the characters will be scarcely visible; but, if gently heated, they will appear in brilliant green, which will disappear as the paper cools.

8.—Write with a diluted solution of muriate of copper, and the writing will be invisible, when dry; but on being held to the fire, it will be of a yellow color.

MAGIC LANDSCAPE.—A landscape may be drawn on paper with Indian ink, representing a winter scene; the foliage may be painted with muriate of cobalt, muriate of copper, and acetate of cobalt, so that by gently warming the picture, the trees, flowers, &c., will display themselves in their natural or verdant colors, which, however, they will only preserve so long as the paper continues warm: this may be repeated as often as required.

AMUSEMENTS IN ELECTRICTY, GALVANISM, AND MAGNETISM.

ELECTRICITY is one of the most active principles in nature. It exists in all bodies, and is exhibited by various means, one of which, and the most generally employed, is friction; but the bodies rubbed together must consist of different substances; for, if they are alike, electricity will not be evolved Some substances, such as soot, charcoal, iron, gold, silver copper and other metals, water, &c., are called *good conductors*, because they transfer with great facility, to other bodies, the electric fluid which glides over the surfaces with the velocity of light: whilst others, such as silk, wool, hair, feathers, dry paper, leather, glass, wax, &c., are called *non-conductors*, because they absolutely resist the progress of the fluid, which accumulates all the time the friction continues. It is from these media that are obtained the usual phenomena of electricity, as exhibited in the experiments which we shall hereafter describe. Its effects are felt in almost every part of nature: the awful lightning is the exhibition of the electrical fluid, which accumulates in the clouds, and which is discharged when the heavy, lurid masses come in conflict with each other; the mysterious, sweeping whirlwind, the terrific rising and rolling of the sand in the desert wilds of Africa, and the beautiful yet evanescent Aurora Borealis of the northern climes, are amongst a few of its effects.

The next branch of the science of Electricity is GALVANISM, or, as it is sometimes called, Voltaic Electricity; it is obtained through the simple contact of different conducting

(310)

bodies with each other. It was first discovered at Bologna in the year 1791, by the lady of Louis Galvani, an Italian philosopher of great merit, and professor of anatomy; indeed, from whom the science received its name. His wife being possessed of a penetrating understanding, and passionately loving him, took a lively interest in the science which so much occupied his attention. At the time the incident we are about to narrate took place, she was in a declining state of health, and taking soup made of frogs by way of restorative. Some of these animals, skinned for the purpose, happened to be lying on the table of Galvani's laboratory, where also stood an electrical machine, when the point of a knife was unintentionally brought into contact with the nerves of one of the frog's legs which lay close to the conductor of the machine, and immediately the muscles of the limb were violently agitated. Madame Galvani having observed the phenomenon, instantly informed her husband of it, and this incident led to the experiments and interesting discoveries which will transmit his name to the latest posterity.

The uses of Galvanic Electricity for scientific purposes are incalculable; and its phenomena are so various and extraordinary, as to render the study of this science exceedingly interesting. Through means of a galvanic battery, substances are decomposed, colors changed, water is made inflammable, and motion is given to lifeless bodies.

The experiments we give on galvanism show the effect of the combination which forms what is called a simple galvanic circle, by means of two metals, zinc and silver, or zinc and copper, and water.

Galvanic action is always accompanied by chemical action, and all that is necessary to disturb the galvanic fluid, is to unite two metals together, and subject them to the action of a fluid, which will act chemically upon one of them, differently to what it does on the other.

A galvanic circle may also be formed of one metal, and two different fluids, which have a different action upon the other.

MAGNETISM is a modification of Electricity; at least, there is sufficient evidence that these causes are intimately connected, if not identical; but philosophers are as yet ignorant of its nature.

The property designated by the word Magnetism, is found in an iron ore of a certain composition, and of a dark gray color and peculiar lustre. This ore alone is the local habitation of Magnetism, whilst all others are subject to its influence, or to be attracted by it. Still, so little difference is there between the Magnetic ore, or loadstone, and those which do not possess the property, that only practiced mineralogists can discern one from the other; and an experienced eye may see two ores join each other by the principle of attraction, without knowing in which resides the power, until another ore, non-magnetic, is brought within the sphere of attraction, when it will adhere only to that which contains the principle.

This singular property of the loadstone is imparted to other metallic substances, by rubbing and keeping them close together for some length of time: if the metal be of a hard texture like steel, it retains the magnetic principle permanently; but if soft, it loses the power as soon as separated from the magnet. The metals thus prepared, acquire the same directive and attractive power as the loadstone or natural magnet, and are employed for purposes of the utmost importance.

We proceed to give the youthful amateur the opportunity of exemplifying the principles of Electricity, Galvanism, and Magnetism, by several simple experiments.

EXPERIMENTS IN ELECTRICITY.

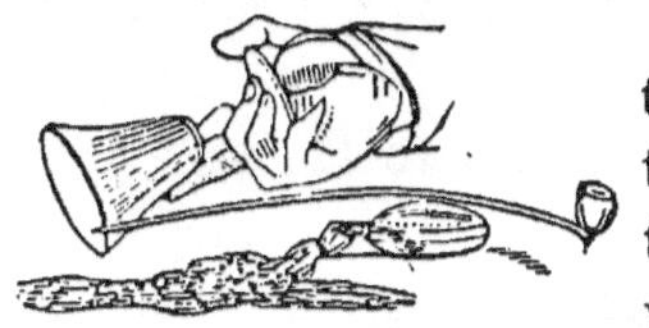

1.—Lay a watch down upon a table, and on its face balance a tobacco-pipe very carefully. Next take a wine-glass, rub it quickly with a silk handkerchief, and hold it for half a minute before the fire; then apply it near to the end of the pipe, and the latter, attracted by the electricity evolved by the friction and warmth in the former, will immediately follow it; and by carrying the glass around, always in front of the pipe, the latter will continue its rotatory motion; the watch-glass being the centre or pivot on which it acts.

2.—Warm a glass tube, rub it with a warm flannel, and then bring a downy feather near it. On the first moment of contact, the feather will adhere to the glass, but soon after will fly rapidly from it, and you may drive it about the room by holding the glass between it and the surrounding objects; should it, however, come in contact with any thing not under the influence of electricity, it will instantly fly back to the glass.

3.—A stick of sealing-wax rubbed against a warm piece of flannel or cloth, acquires the property of attracting light substances, such as small pieces of paper, lint, &c., if instantly applied at the distance of about an inch.

4.—Suspend two small pith balls, by fine silken threads of about six inches in length, in such a manner, that when at rest they may hang in contact with each other; on applying a piece of sealing-wax, excited as in the former experiment, they will repel each other.

5.—Take a piece of common brown paper, about the size of an octavo book, hold it before the fire till quite dry and hot, then draw it briskly under the arm several times, so as to rub it on both sides at once by the coat. The paper will be found so powerfully electrical, that if placed against a wainscotted or papered wall of a room, it will remain there for some minutes without falling.

6.—And if, while the paper adheres to the wall, a light, fleecy feather be placed against it, it will be attracted to the paper in the same way as the paper is attracted to the wall.

7.—If the paper be again warmed, and drawn under the arm as before, and hung up by a thread attached to one corner of it, it will hold up several feathers on each side; should these fall off from different sides at the same time, they will cling together very strongly; and if after a minute they be all shaken off, they will fly to one another in a very singular manner.

8.—Warm and excite the paper as before, lay it on a table, and place upon it a ball made of elder-pith about the size of a pea; the ball will immediately run across the paper, and if a needle be pointed toward it, it will again run to another part, and so on for a considerable time.

9.—Support a pane of glass previously warmed, upon two books, one at each end, and place some bran underneath; then rub the upper side of the glass with a black silk handkerchief, or a piece of flannel, and the bran will dance up and down under it with much rapidity.

10.—Place your left hand upon the throat of a cat, and, with the middle finger and thumb, press slightly the bones of the animal's shoulders; then, if the right hand be gently passed along the back, perceptible shocks of electricity will be felt in the left hand. Shocks may also be obtained by touching the tips of the ears after rubbing the back. If the color of the cat be black, and the experiment be made in a dark room, the electric sparks may be very plainly seen. Very distinct charges of electricity may also be obtained by touching the tips of the ears, after applying friction to the back, and the same may be obtained from the foot. Placing the cat on your knees, apply your right hand to the back; the left fore-paw resting on the palm of your left hand, 'apply the thumb to the upper side of the paw, so as to extend the claws, and by this means, bring your fore-finger into contact with one of the bones of the leg, where it joins the paw; when, from the knob or end of this bone, the finger slightly pressing on it, you may feel distinctly successive shocks, similar to those obtained from the ears. It is, perhaps, unnecessary to add, that, in order to this experiment being conveniently performed, the experimenter must be on good terms with the cat.

ELECTROTYPE APPARATUS.

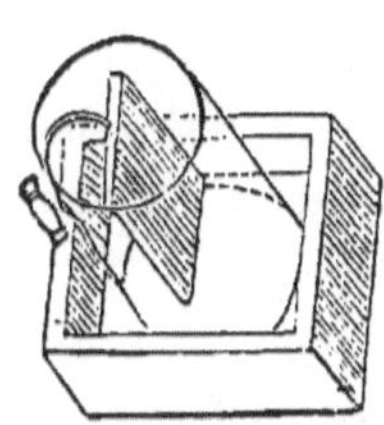

By this simple apparatus may be procured, by galvanic action, perfect facsimiles of engraved copper-plates, however elaborate; also, correct copies of medals, and all kinds of metallic ornaments. The apparatus may be purchased for half-a-dollar, or upward.

It consists of a trough for holding a solution of sulphate of copper, and an inner vessel for the acid and water. The medal to be copied should first be moulded in fusible metal, and a wire attached to the mould to connect with the binding screw. A piece of zinc, amalgamated by washing it with a little dilute sulphuric acid, and rubbing the surface with mercury, is then suspended in the acid by another copper wire, and attached to the binding screw; which, after the lapse of a few hours, will produce a perfect facsimile of the medal.

To copy copper-plates for printing, as they cannot be moulded, a reverse must first be taken from the plate, and this reversed again, which will produce an exact copy of the original plate.

ELECTRICAL SHOCK FROM A SHEET OF PAPER.

Place an iron japanned tea-tray on a dry, clean beaker glass; then take a sheet of foolscap writing-paper, and hold it close to the fire until all its hygrometric moisture is dissipated, but not so as to scorch it; in this state it is one of the finest electrics we have. Hold one end down on a table with the finger and thumb, and give it about a dozen strokes with a large piece of india rubber from the left to the right, beginning at the top. Now take it up by two of the corners and bring it over the tray, and it will fall down on it like a stone; if one finger be now brought under the tray, a sensible shock will be felt. Now lay a needle on the tray with its point projecting outward, remove the paper, and a star sign of the negative electricity will be seen; return the paper, and the positive brush will appear. In fact, it forms a very extemporaneous electrophorus, which will give a spark an inch long, and strong enough to set fire to some combustible bodies, and to exhibit all the electric phenomena not requiring coated surfaces. If four beaker glasses are placed on the floor, and a book laid on them, a person may stand on them insulated; if he then holds the tray vertically, the paper will adhere strongly to it, and sparks may be drawn from any part of his body, or he may draw sparks from any other person, as the case may be; or he may set fire to some inflammable bodies by touching them with a piece of ice.

LIGHT UNDER WATER.

Rub two pieces of fine lump sugar together in the dark, and a bright electric light will be produced. The same effect, but in a more intense degree, may be produced with two pieces of silex or quartz, the white quartz being much the best for this purpose. The same effect may also be witnessed by rubbing the pieces of quartz together, *under water*.

EXPERIMENTS IN GALVANISM.

1.—Place a thin plate of zinc upon the upper surface of the tongue, and a half-dollar or other piece of silver, on the under surface.   Allow the metals. to remain for a little time in contact with the tongue, before they are made to touch each other, that the taste of the metals themselves may not be confounded with the sensation produced by their contact.   When the edges of the metals, which project beyond the tongue, are then suffered to touch, a galvanic sensation is produced, which it is difficult accurately to describe.

2.—Place a silver teaspoon as high as possible between the gums and the upper lip, and a piece of zinc between the gums and the under lip.   On bringing the extremities of the metals into contact, a very vivid sensation, and an effect like a flash of light across the eyes, will be perceived.   It is singular, that this light is equally vivid in the dark and in the strongest light, and whether the eyes be shut or open.

3.—Put a silver cup or mug, filled with water, upon a plate of zinc on a table, and just touch the water with the tip of the tongue ; it will be tasteless so long as the zinc plate is not handled, for the body does not form a voltaic circle with the metals.   Moisten your hand well, take hold of the plate of zinc, and touch the water with your tongue, when a very peculiar sensation, and an acid taste, will be immediately experienced.

4.—Take a piece of copper of about six inches in width, and put upon it a piece of zinc of rather smaller dimensions, inserting a piece of cloth, of the same size as the zinc, between them ; place a leech upon the piece of zinc, and though there appears nothing to hinder it from crawling away, yet it will not pass from the zinc to the copper ; because its damp body acting as a conductor to the fluid disturbed, as soon as it touches the copper it receives a galvanic shock, and of course retires to its resting-place.

5.—Plunge an iron knife into a solution of sulphate of copper, (blue-stone); by chemical action, only, it will become covered with metallic copper.   Immerse in the same solution a piece of platinum, taking care not to let it touch the iron, and no deposition of copper will take place upon it; but if the upper ends of the metals be brought into contact with each other, a copious deposition of copper will soon settle upon the platinum likewise.

EXPERIMENTS IN MAGNETISM.

1.—We have said that the agency of the magnet can be imparted to hard metallic bodies; this may be done in a very easy way. If you pass a magnet, (which may be either natural or artificial,) over a sewing-needle several times from the eye to the point, the needle will acquire the principle, and attract iron filings in the same manner as a natural magnet would do. But the part of the magnet which you apply to the needle must be the north pole; and you must not pass it over the needle backward and forward, but lift it always from the point and again begin from the eye. Suppose you wish to impart the principle to a small bar of tempered steel, tie the piece to be magnetised to a poker with a piece of silk, and hold the part of the poker to which it is attached in the left hand; take hold of the tongs, a little below the middle, with the right hand, and rub the steel bar with them, moving the tongs from the bottom to the top, and keeping them steadily in a vertical position all the time. About a dozen strokes on each side will impart sufficient magnetic power to the bar to enable the operator to lift up small pieces of iron and steel with it. The lower end of the bar should be marked before it is fastened to the poker, so that the poles may be readily distinguished from each other when it is taken off; the upper end being the south pole, and the lower the north.

2.—Scatter some iron filings upon a piece of paper, and hold a magnet underneath it. The instant the contact takes place, the filings will raise themselves upright, and fall down as soon as the magnet is withdrawn. The effect is singular, and indeed very amusing ; the diminutive iron particles rising and falling, as if by supernatural agency.

3. MAGNETIC SWAN.—Form a swan of cork, and place within its beak a little bit of steel strongly magnetised ; then cover it with a thin coating of white wax, and to render the illusion more complete, beads may be put in its head to represent the eyes. The swan being thus made, you must provide it with a lake to swim in. A basin of water may supply this ; and when your lake is ready, and the swan placed in it, the next object is to make it swim about. This you may easily accomplish by holding in your hand a magnet bar, on which the north and south poles are marked. Show the north pole of the wand to the swan, and the little creature will immediately follow it, moving very gently over the water : you may thus lead it about, and when you wish it to retire, present the south pole of the wand to it, and, like an obedient bird, it will readily recede, and turn back.

If you wish to make a magnetic wand, you may do so by procuring a hollow cane, eight or nine inches in length, and half an inch thick, and a small steel bar well magnetised. Put this bar in the cane, and close it at both ends by screwing on small ivory tops, differing in shape, or having some marks by which you may in an instant recognize the north and south ends of the rod. With this wand you may direct the course of any floating figure.

4. MAGNETIC ANGLING.—A small piece of wood, with a silken thread attached to it, and an iron hook attached to the other end of the silk thread, will constitute your rod, line, and hook, though a somewhat indifferent-looking apparatus. The hook must be powerfully magnetised, and with it you may easily take the fish, to be bought, not at the fishmonger's, but

at the toy-shops. They are made of lead, cast hollow, and very light, with fins and scales, and form altogether very tolerable imitations of fish. In the mouth of each of these little fish, a piece of iron wire, which has been well rubbed with a magnet, is inserted. Throw the fish into a pond, or more properly speaking, basin of water; hold the hook near them, and they will be immediately attracted by its magnetic influence, and ultimately attach themselves to it.

5. The Obedient Watch.—Conceal in one of your hands a piece of loadstone, and in the other hold a well-going watch. Suppose that your friends are standing around you, to observe the obedience of the watch, hold it close to the ear of the first person, and desire his testimony that the watch is going; then pass it to the hand in which the loadstone is concealed, commanding it to stop, and hold it up to the ear of the next person; having obtained his word that the watch is silent, pass it to the other hand, shake it gently, and again command it to go; and so on, through all the company. The cause of the watch stopping, as you may have guessed, is its coming in contact with the loadstone.

6. To show the effect of the Magnetical Agency by means of a Balance.—Suspend a magnet in one of the scales of a very delicate balance, and carefully adjust it by putting weights into the other scale; when thus counterpoised, hold a piece of iron under the scale to which the magnet is attached, and it will immediately descend. If instead of the magnet, a piece of iron be attached to the scale, and the magnet held under the iron, the scale will descend as before.

7. To show that the Power of Attraction resides chiefly at the Poles.—Place some iron filings upon

a table, and then put amongst them a magnetic rod or bar. The filings will immediately adhere to the ends of the bar or rod, but not to the middle or centre, where the power of attraction is very little exerted, if at all.

8. To show the Repulsion of the Poles.—The north poles of two magnets repel each other, and the same happens with the south poles, for the magnetic attraction is exerted only between the contrary poles. Thus, if you fix two magnetised needles in two pieces of cork, and place them in a basin of water, and they are in a parallel position with the same poles together, that is north to north, or south to south, they will mutually repel each other; but if the contrary poles point to one another, then they will be attracted and draw close together.

9. To show the Directive Power of the Magnet.—If you balance a bar of iron, or an untouched needle, horizontally upon a pivot or centre, it will remain stationary; but magnetise the same, place it again on its centre, and you will see that it turns round, and does not stop until its north pole is in the direction of the north pole of the earth.

CONCLUSION.

The preceding experiments in Electricity, Galvanism, and Magnetism, we have selected for the simple yet clear expositions which they offer of the fundamental principles of those branches of philosophy; more elaborate experiments we have refrained from inserting, as although, perhaps, more astonishing and impressive in their effects, the costly and cumbrous apparatus which they require, raise them far above the means of most boys, for whose instruction and amusement we cater.

21

PUZZLES AND PARADOXES,

THOUGH in themselves "trifles light as air,"—Puzzles and Paradoxes are undoubtedly the result of much ingenuity on the part of the contrivers, and certainly the cause of much patient investigation on the part of those who attempt to solve them; and since we have assumed the task of catering for *every* taste, we proceed to lay before our readers a selection of some of the most amusing and intricate puzzles we have been able to gather.

In the arrangement of them, at least of most of them, we have adopted a different system to that usually followed; for, instead of giving the solutions of the puzzles immediately after the propositions, we have classed them under a distinct head, that of "The Key to the Puzzles and Paradoxes;" and we would suggest that our readers should try to unravel the problems ere they seek the aid of the authentic explanations.

1. How many kings have been crowned in England since the Norman conquest?

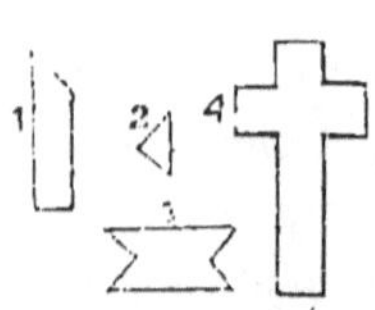

2. Cut out of a piece of card, five pieces, similar in shape and size to the annexed figures, viz. one piece of fig. 1, three pieces of fig. 2, and one like fig. 3. These five pieces are then to be so joined as to form a cross, like that represented by fig. 4; but of course larger in size.

(322)

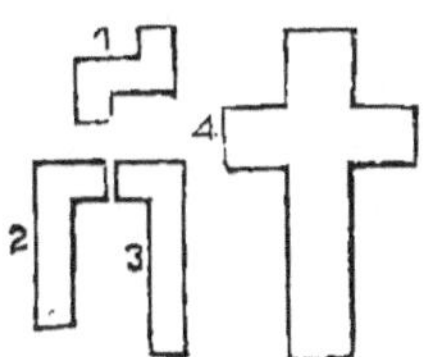

3. This is a variation from the preceding puzzle, and is much more complex in its different parts. Cut out of a stiff card three pieces, in shape like fig. 1, and one like fig. 2, and be very careful to make them in exactly the same proportion to each other; next cut out one piece like fig. 3, and then endeavor to arrange them so as to form the cross shown in fig. 4.

4. A gentleman sent his servant with a present of nine ducks, in a hamper, to which was affixed the following direction :—

"To Alderman Gobble, with IX ducks."

The servant, having more ingenuity than honesty, took out three of the ducks, and contrived it so, that the direction on the hamper corresponded with the number of the ducks. As he neither erased any word or letter, nor made a new direction, how did he manage it?

5. Cut twenty triangles out of ten square pieces of wood; mix them together, and request a person to make an exact square with them.

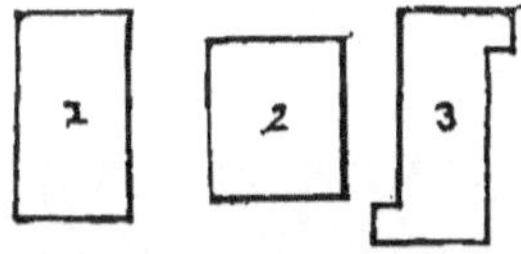

6. A parallelogram, as in the illustration, fig. 1, may be cut into two pieces, so that by shifting the position of the pieces, two other figures may be formed, as shown by figs. 2 and 3.

7. Two men, A and B, went to C, to purchase some spirits. A had a five-gallon keg, B a three-gallon keg, and C had no other measure than an eight-gallon keg; now, as A and B only want four gallons of liquor each, I wish to know if it is possible for C to measure the desired quantity to his two customers, and also how he does it?

8. Cut a piece of apple or turnip into the shape of a horse-shoe, stick six pins in it for nails, and then by two cuts divide it into six parts, each containing one pin.

9. Take one from nineteen,—the remainder you'll see,
    Is twenty exactly; pray how can this be?

10. Mathematicians affirm that of all bodies contained under the same superficies, a sphere is the most capacious, but surely they have never considered the amazing capaciousness of a body whose name is now required; and of which it may be truly said, that supposing its greatest breadth is four inches, length nine inches, and depth three inches, yet in these dimensions it contains a solid foot.

11. A lady met a gentleman in the street: the gentleman said "I think I know you;" the lady said he ought, as his mother was her mother's only daughter. What relation was he?

12. If from six you take nine, and from nine you take ten,
    Ye wits now the puzzle explain;
    And if fifty from forty be taken, there then
    Will just half a dozen remain.

13. Is it possible to place twelve pieces of money in six rows, so as to have four in each row?

14. THE BEAD PUZZLE.—This puzzle may be procured at many toy-shops. The part A is made of ivory; a cord fastened to the end B, is passed through the hole D, in such a manner that it forms a loop there, capable of being drawn out at pleasure, and is afterward fastened off at C. Two beads are put on the string, as delineated here, and the object of the puzzle is to play both balls on to one string.

15. A MAZE, OR LABYRINTH.—This maze is a correct

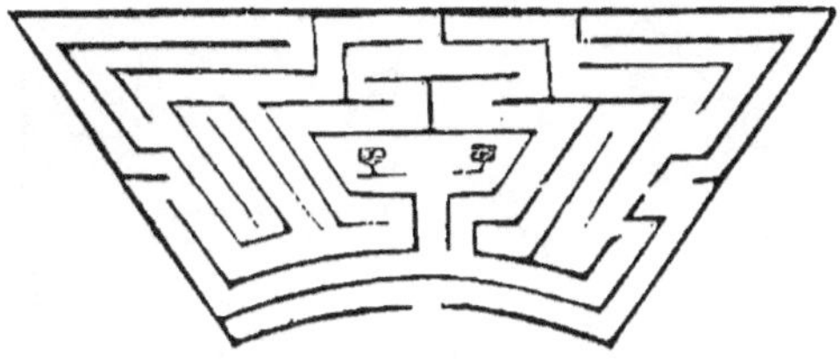

ground-plan of one in the gardens of the Palace of Hampton Court. No legendary tale is attached to it, of which we are aware, but its labyrinthine walks occasion much amusement to the numerous holiday parties who frequent the palace grounds. The partitions between the walks are hedges of clipped hornbeam, and are about five feet in height. The puzzle is to get into the centre, where seats are placed under two lofty trees; and many are the disappointments experienced before the end is attained: and even then, the trouble is not over, it being quite as difficult to get *out* as to get *in*.

16. THE CHINESE PUZZLE.—This puzzle, being one for the purpose of constructing different figures by arranging variously-shaped pieces of card or wood in certain ways, requires no separate explanation. Cut out of very stiff card-board, or thin mahogany, which is decidedly preferable, seven pieces, in shape like the annexed figures, and bearing the same pro-

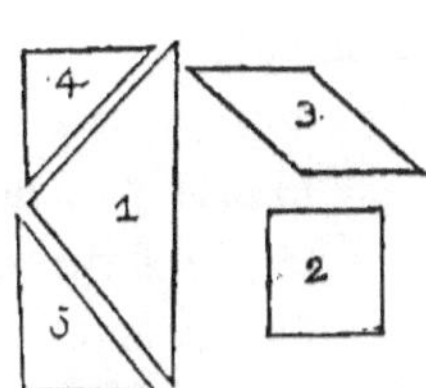

portion to each other; one piece must be made in the shape of figure 1, one of figure 2, and one of figure 3, and two of each of the other figures. The combinations of which these figures are susceptible, are almost infinite; and we subjoin, on the next page, a representation of a few of the most curious. It is to be borne in mind, that all the pieces of which the puzzle consists, must be employed to form each figure.

17. The Circassian Puzzle.—This is decidedly the most interesting puzzle ever invented; it is on the same principle, but composed of many more pieces than the Chinese puzzle, and may consequently be arranged in more intricate figures. Houses, fortifications, monuments, and even perfect geometric forms, are some of the many things which may be imitated with success.

18. The Mosaic Puzzle is a very pleasing and ingenious one. It consists of sixty-four small squares, each composed of triangular pieces of white and black wood. Exceedingly pretty and gay imitations of mosaic pavement may be formed by the judicious arrangement of these tesserulæ, and some very elegant forms have been published in the books which accompany the puzzles.

KEY TO THE PUZZLES AND PARADOXES.

1. One, only: James I., who was king of Scotland before he ascended the English throne.

2. A simple inspection of the annexed figure will show how the pieces must be arranged to form the cross.

3. To form this cross, the pieces must be arranged in the manner shown in the annexed representation.

4. The servant merely put the letter S before the two Roman numerals IX. The direction then read as follows:—

"To Alderman Gobble, with SIX ducks."

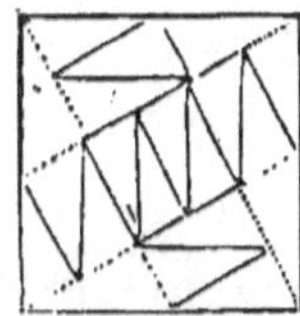

5. The solution of this puzzle may be easily acquired by observing the dotted lines in the engraving; by which it will be seen that four triangles are to be placed at the corners, and a small square made in the centre. When this is done, the rest of the square may be quickly formed.

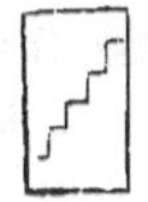
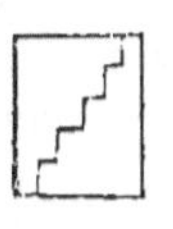

6. Divide the pieces of card into five steps, and by shifting the position of the pieces, the desired figures may be obtained.

7. C first filled the three-gallon keg out of the eight, and then poured the three gallons into the five-gallon keg; he next filled the three again out of the eight, and poured two

out of the three into the five. He thus filled the five, and left one gallon in the three; he then emptied the five into the eight, and the one out of the three into the five. He then filled the three again, and poured it to the one in the five, and thus contrived to pour four gallons of liquor into the five-gallon keg, and four into the eight, the exact quantity A and B required.

8. By cutting off the upper circular part, containing two of the pins, and by changing the position of the pieces, another cut will divide the horse-shoe into six portions, each containing one pin.

9. XIX make nineteen; therefore, if you take I away, XX must remain.

10. A Shoe.

11. Her Son.

12. From SIX take IX, and S ⎫
    "   IX "   X,   " I ⎬ will remain.
    "   XL "   L,   " X ⎭

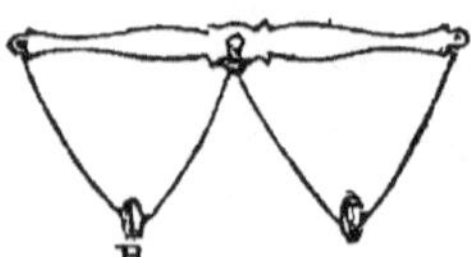

13. By forming a figure like the annexed, and putting a piece of money at each angle and each point where the lines intersect each other, the query will be resolved.

14. Draw down the loop, and pass one of the beads (say B) through it. Still holding the ivory in the same position, pull all the strings at the centre hole toward you, till two loops are drawn through; pass the same ball through both of these, and pull the strings back again. It will then be seen that by passing the ball through one remaining loop, it will be brought on to the same string with the other. It may be played back again, in a precisely similar manner.

THE MYSTERIOUS CIRCLES.

Cut from a card two discs or circular pieces, about two inches in diameter. In the centre of one of them make a hole, into which put the tube of a common quill, one end being even with the surface of the card. Make the other piece a little convex, and lay its centre over the end of the quill, with the concave side of the card downward, the centre or upper card being from one-eighth to one-fourth of an inch above the end of the quill—attempt to blow off the upper end by blowing through the quill, and *it will be found impossible.*

If, however, the edges of the two cards be made to fit each other very accurately, the upper card will move and sometimes it will be thrown off; but when the edges of the cards are, on two sides, sufficiently far apart to permit the air to escape, the loose card will retain its position, even when the current of air sent against it be strong. The experiment will succeed equally well, whether the current of air be made from the mouth or from a pair of bellows. When the quill fits the card rather loosely, a comparatively light puff will throw both cards three or four feet in height. When, from the humidity of the breath, the upper surface of the perforated card has a little expanded, and the two opposite sides are somewhat depressed, those depressed sides may be seen distinctly to rise and approach the upper card, directly in proportion to the force of the current of air.

Another fact to be shown with this simple apparatus, appears equally inexplicable with the former. Lay the loose card upon the hand with the concave side up; blow forcibly through the tube, and, at the same time, bring the two cards toward each other; when within three-eighths of an inch, if the current of air be strong, the loose card will suddenly rise, and adhere to the perforated card. If the card through which the quill passes has several holes made in it, the loose card may be instantly thrown off with the least puff of air.

For the explanation of the above phenomenon, a gold medal and one hundred guineas were offered, some years since, by the Royal Society of England. Such explanation has been given by Dr. Robert Hare, of Philadelphia, and is as follows :—

Supposing the diameters of the discs of card to be to that of the holes as 8 to 1, the area of the former to the latter must be as 64 to 1. Hence, if the discs were to be separated (their surfaces remaining parallel) with a velocity as great as that of the air blast, a column of air must, meantime, be interposed, 64 times greater than that which would escape from the tube during the interim ; consequently, if all the air necessary to preserve the balance be supplied from the tube, the discs must be separated with a velocity as much less than that of the blast, as the column required between them is greater than that yielded by the tube ; and yet the air cannot be supplied. from any other source, unless a deficit of pressure be created between the discs, unfavorable to their separation.

It follows, then, that under the circumstances in question, the discs cannot be made to move asunder with a velocity greater than one sixty-fourth of that of the blast. Of course, all the force of the current of air through the tube will be expended on the movable disc, and the thin ring of air, which exists round the orifice between the discs; and since the movable disc can only move with one sixty-fourth the velocity of the blast, the ring of air in the interstices must experience nearly all the force of the jet, and must be driven outward, the blast following it, in various currents, radiating from the common centre of the tube and discs.

EASIER TO CARRY TWO WEIGHTS THAN ONE.

A boy carries a single dumb-bell with difficulty, owing to his body being overbalanced, and he stretches out the opposite arm to bring himself again upright. But, two bells, one in each hand, are carried with much greater ease, because they balance each other.

TWO SOUNDS AT ONCE FROM THE SAME MOUTH.

The power of producing two simultaneous sounds from the mouth has been strikingly shown by the experimenter whistling airs, first as solos, and then as duets. It appeared that, at the time, the mouth was divided into two parts by the tongue, and that each portion of air was thrown into a separate state of vibration by the embouchure formed at the mouth.

PARLOR GAMES.

HOT COCKLES.

FORTUNATELY, the principles of this game of our ancestors are more easily explained than its title, whose origin is lost in the mists of antiquity.

A player kneels down before a lady, concealing his face in her lap, as for the crying of forfeits. He then places one hand, with the palm uppermost, on his back. The rest of the company advance in turns, each administering to the open hand a slap. The task of the kneeler is to discover (without looking) who it is that has given the slap. Should he succeed, the detected player takes his place; if not, he continues to occupy it himself, till such time as he shall make a more fortunate guess.

The impatience of the victim, who having received several slaps without divining the operator, hears ironical suggestions offered to him, such as, "the loan of a pair of spectacles," "a bedroom candle, as he really ought not to go to sleep *there*," a promise to "hit harder next time, that he may recognize the hand," &c.—is very delightful indeed—*to the spectators.*

THE BUNDLES.

This is the only variety of the class of games known as "Touch," or "Tag," worthy of distinction.

The players, who must be of an even number, are formed into a double ring, their faces to the centre—a lady being placed in front of each gentleman—each pair forming what is termed a *bundle*. The *bundles* being arranged, two of the players are chosen—one to run after and touch the other. The pursued has the right of crossing the ring in any direction (for which purpose the *bundles* must be sufficiently far apart from each other to afford an easy passage), and when tired and not wishing to be touched (and consequently become *pursuer* in his turn), may rest himself by standing in front of one of the *bundles*. The *bundle* is then composed of three persons—which is not allowable. The outside one of the three must therefore run away to avoid being touched. If touched he takes the place of his pursuer (who is chased in his turn); or if he likes it better, places himself in front of one of the *bundles*, thereby compelling another player to run away,—as the first. The fugitive can, however, resign his post at any moment, by placing himself in front of a *bundle*, the "outsider" of which invariably becomes the fugitive. The more frequently this is done, the greater the perplexity of the pursuer;—and, in consequence, the animation of the game.

An an in-door amusement, this game is out of the question, from the space required for its exercise.

THE FEATHER.

One of the players takes a bed feather, a bit of cotton-down, or any light substance coming under the comprehensive denomination of "fluff," which he tosses up in the centre of the assembled circle (who should be seated as closely together as convenience will admit of). He then blows upon it to keep it floating in the air. The individual to whom it comes nearest does the same, in order to prevent its falling on his knees, or, indeed, any part of his person—an accident which would subject him to the payment of a forfeit.

One of the chief advantages of this simple but highly amusing game is, that steadily serious people may be induced to engage in it. The gravity of their faces, blowing and puffing away at the contemptible feather, as if all their hopes were centred in evading its responsibility, is truly edifying. Sometimes it happens (it being impossible to blow and laugh at the same time) that the "fluff" drops into the player's mouth at the very moment when he is concentrating all his energies in the effort to get rid of it. This is the signal for shouts of laughter, and for a forfeit demanded in just expiation of the player's greediness. We recollect seeing an eminent college dignitary in such a predicament—a spectacle not without its instructive tendencies.

~JACK'S ALIVE!

The players pass, from one to another, a lighted match or twist of paper, of which the flame has been blown out, saying (as they present it), "*Jack's alive!*"

The player in whose hands the last spark dies out, pays a forfeit: for which reason, when "Jack" appears in a tolerably lively condition, you do not hurry yourself to give it up. When, on the contrary, the sparks seem inclined to die out, you lose no time in handing it to your neighbor, who is bound to receive it directly after you have pronounced the requisite words.

This very simple game affords considerable amusement, without in the least degree taxing the intellectual resources of the players.

THE WOLF AND THE LAMBS.

In this game, all the ladies of a company may participate, but only one gentleman at a time—who should be a man of dauntless courage and great powers of endurance.

This latter personage is called the *Wolf*. The principal lady takes the part of the *Shepherdess*. The others stand behind her in a single file, and constitute the *Flock*.

The aim of the Wolf is to catch the innocent lamb who may happen to be at the extremity of the flock. He, however, manifests his hostile intentions by the following terrible announcement:

"I am the Wolf! the Wolf! come to eat you all up."

The Shepherdess replies, "I am the Shepherdess, and will protect my lambs."

The Wolf retorts, "I'll have the little white one with the golden hoofs!"

This dialogue concluded, the Wolf attempts to make an irruption in the line of the flock. But the Shepherdess, extending her arms, bars his passage. If he succeeds in breaking through, the lamb placed at the end abandons her post before he can catch her, and places herself in front of the Shepherdess, where she incurs no risk; and so on with the others in succession, till the Shepherdess finds herself the last of the row.

The game then finishes. The unlucky Wolf pays as many forfeits as he has allowed lambs to escape him.

If, on the contrary, he has contrived to seize one of them, he does not eat her, but has the privilege of saluting her, and compels her to pay a forfeit.

This game, in company with cricket, skittles, steeple-chasing and others, is more adapted to the open air than the precincts of an expensively furnished drawing-room.

HUNT THE SLIPPER.

This well-known game, or rather "romp," is usually played in a circle seated on the ground, in which case, it is more adapted to the lawn or park than the drawing-room.

It may, however, be played in-doors, the company being seated on chairs. It is advisable that there should be an uneven number of players. The one fixed on to commence the game, remains standing. The rest form a circle (a lady and a gentleman being placed alternately), in the centre of which all their toes meet. The legs, however, should not be stretched out quite straight, but bent a little at the knee, so as to form a sort of circular gallery for the passage of the slipper. When all have taken their seats, the player standing up throws the slipper into the centre of the circle. A hand seizes it and passes it round under the gallery. It is the *hunter's* duty to keep his eyes about him, to watch where it goes, for it often travels a long way before he can catch a trace of it. From time to time, when he is observed to be completely *off the scent*, one of the players draws the slipper from its hiding-place, and raps the heel of it three times against the floor; then, while the hunter is trying to catch it, passes it quickly round again to his neighbors, who, whenever they see a fitting opportunity, repeat the same ceremony. Frequently there is no time to pass it round the circle; in which case, the holder throws it into the centre, when it is caught by the most alert, and put in circulation as before.

If the hunter, tired of ducking and leaping around the circle, renounces so fatiguing a chase of his own free will, he pays a forfeit, and receives from each player a rap from the heel of the slipper on the head, or (if considered invulnerable in that quarter, from the known thickness of the material) on the knuckles. If, on the contrary, he succeeds in catching the slipper, he takes the place of the player who has suffered him to do so, and who, in turn, has to give chase,—of course, after having paid a forfeit.

This game being, as we have already said, nothing more or less than a downright romp, it should only be played in family parties, or among the most intimate friends, where the bounds of gentleness and propriety are sure not to be exceeded.

THE DRILL SERGEANT.

A deserving individual is promoted from the ranks of the company to the above honorable position.   He selects a lady, and conducts her to the centre of the room.   The remaining "gallant fellows" in the company follow his example, and range themselves in a line facing the first couple.   The sergeant then proceeds to put the troops through their exercise. He advances toward them, and with a rigid look, expressive of unflinching discipline, and in a stern voice, gives the following words of command:—"Attention!"—"Take ladies' hands!"—"Arms round waists!"—"Right about face!"— "Make ready!"—"Present!"—"Fire!"   The sergeant himself, considering, like an able (though non-commissioned) officer as he is, that example is better than precept, executes every movement as he commands it; and at the last order, which is no sooner expressed than understood, salutes his lady — the manœuvre being imitated by the rest of the troops.

BIRDS FLY.

A very simple game, in which all the players place a finger on a table, or on the knees of the conductor of the game, to be raised in the air, when the conductor says, "*Birds fly*," "*Pigeons* (or any winged object in natural history) *fly*."

If he names a non-winged animal, and any player raises his hand in distraction, the latter pays a forfeit—the same in case of his neglecting to raise it at the name of a bird or winged insect.

THE ELEMENTS.

The players form a semicircle round the king of the game, who holds in his hand a ball of thread partially unrolled and

22

fastened by a knot, leaving a length of thread sufficient for the ball to *reach* one of the players he may choose to throw it to, and enable him to draw it back immediately. The names of three animals—each inhabiting a different one of the three elements, EARTH, AIR, or WATER—must be first decided on; such as *dog, salmon, pigeon.* When the king touches a player with his ball of thread, saying, EARTH, AIR, or WATER, the player must respond immediately with the name of the animal inhabiting the element cited.

For instance, if the king says WATER, the person he touches immediately replies *salmon.* Should he reply *dog* or *pigeon,* he pays a fine—neither of these animals inhabiting the water.

The king may also say FIRE. A dead silence must be observed when he does so—fire not being inhabited by any animal yet discovered. Should he say THE ELEMENTS, all the players together must pronounce the names of the three animals, in quick succession.

The game may be played without fixing on the names of any particular animals; in which case, when the king names an element, the player he touches must respond immediately with the name of an animal known to inhabit it, and not mention the same animal twice, on pain of a forfeit.

The former, however, is the most amusing method—the frequent repetition of the three names generally leading to great confusion.

THE BOX OF SECRETS.

This game, which is very popular in France, under the name of *la boîte d'amourette,* is simply a means of collecting forfeits. It is played as follows:—

The player who commences the game, presents a box to his neighbor on the right, saying, "I sell you my box of secrets; it contains three—*whom I love, whom I will kiss, and whom I will send about his (or her) business.*"

The neighbor replies—

"Whom do you love? whom will you kiss? whom will you send about her business?"   (We assume the giver of the box to be a gentleman.)

The first speaker names, in answer to each question, the one of the players whom he loves, the one he intends to kiss (why these should not be one and the same it is not our business to inquire into), and the one he intends to send about her business.

The person he intends to salute is compelled to submit to the operation on the spot.   The one to be sent about her business pays a forfeit.   No notice whatever is taken of the loved one, which we are at a loss to account for, except as a satire upon professions of affection generally.   In candor, however, we are compelled to confess that we do not believe any thing of the kind was ever intended—which is a pity.

COME OUT OF THAT.

This game is not complicated, being confined to the following dialogue :

"Come out of that !"

"What for ?"

"Because you have such or such a thing, and I have not."

Care must be taken not to name any thing you really possess yourself, or that has been mentioned by a previous player ; that is, unless you wish to pay a forfeit.

PINCH WITHOUT LAUGHING.

In this game each player pinches the nose of his neighbor, who must submit to the operation without laughing.   If he as much as smiles, he pays a forfeit.   Of course the most strenuous exertions are made by the operators to cause him to lose his gravity.

We have heard of some designing persons in this game,

blackening the tips of their finger and thumb with burnt cork, which leaves a very agreeable impression on the pinched nose. If two or three unsuspecting individuals happen to be victimised in this way, they laugh heartily *at each other*, neither suspecting that he is an object of equal ridicule—which is not only a fine moral lesson, but also leads to the great accumulation of forfeits.

MY GRANDMOTHER'S GARDEN.

A circle is formed, and the player best acquainted with the game addresses his nearest neighbor as follows :—

"I have been to my grandmother's garden. My grandmother's garden is a beautiful garden. In my grandmother's garden there are four corners."

Each player, in succession, repeats the same phrase, not adding or omitting any thing, on pain of a forfeit ; the next player always taking up the word before he can have time to correct an error. When the turn of the first speaker comes round again, he repeats what has been previously said ; adding to it, "in the first corner there is a rose-tree. I love you to distraction."

The others repeat not only this, but also the original phrase, paying a forfeit for each mistake.

The turn finished a second time, the leader repeats the whole ; adding, "In the second corner there is a sun-flower. I would kiss you, but I am afraid."

After the third turn he adds, "In the third corner there is a peony. Tell me your secret."

Each player then whispers whatever he pleases in the ear of his preceding neighbor.

The fourth repetition over, the leader makes another addition.

"In the fourth corner there is a poppy. Repeat aloud what you whispered to me just now."

As the oration (which has now reached its full growth)
goes round the circle, each player is compelled to divulge the
secret he had previously imparted to his neighbor in confidence—rather an embarrassing condition sometimes, for people
not prepared for such an arrangement—for the company are
equally amused at the secrets which are not very clear, as at
those which are rather too much so.

This game will be recognized as only another version of the
old *House that Jack built,*—on the model of which endless
games may be formed, the leader relying upon his own invention for the sayings to be repeated.

THE SCISSORS.

A pair of scissors, or any other object to represent one, is
passed from hand to hand—each player saying, as he presents
it to his neighbor, " I make you a present of my scissors, open
or shut" (as he may choose).

In the first case the player must cross either his arms or legs
carelessly, so as not to attract attention; in the second he must
take care to keep them separate.

Many people, from the want of attention, are made to pay
forfeits for a long time without knowing why, their surprise
and perplexity being the chief amusement of the game.

HOT COCKLES FOR TWO.

This game is executed *apparently* in the same manner as
Hot Cockles, only that there are two *confessors,* who receive
on their laps the heads of two patients. One of these must
be acquainted with the trick of the game; the other without
the slightest suspicion of it. The former (when both have
concealed their faces) quietly gets up, and strikes the hand of
his companion with his own; then returns to his place, and
appears to rise at the same time as the other.

It will be believed that the victim may go on guessing for

ever, without hitting upon the right person. The other, at the end of a few turns, names, according to his own choice, any member of the company, who immediately affects to be detected fairly, and takes his place. This is done to avoid awakening suspicion. The game is continued till the victim gives it up in despair, and declares himself at the mercy of the company, who ruin him in forfeits for his want of perception.

THE WHISTLE.

A whistle is attached to the skirts of an unsuspecting individual. He is then placed in the middle of the players (all standing up), having been previously shown another whistle, which he is told is to be passed round the company, and sounded while his back is turned—his office being to detect the player. The person on whom he has turned his back adroitly takes hold of the whistle attached to him, and blows on it. The victim turns round quickly at the noise. The other, no less quick, has let go the whistle, and—while he is watching closely to detect its presence in this quarter—he hears it sounded at his back. He turns round again—whenever he looks for the whistle it is sounded behind him. It is as well to put a stop to the game at the first signs of insanity exhibited by the bewildered victim. This, however, is quite optional.

THE MOLE IN THE FARMER'S FIELD.

One player addresses another :—"Have you seen the mole in the farmer's field ?"

The other replies,—

"Yes, I have seen the mole in the farmer's field."

"Do you know what the mole does ?"

"Yes, I know what the mole does."

"Can you do as he does ?"

The secret is to *shut your eyes* every time you answer (all the answers being echoes of the questions in the affirmative). Failing in this, you pay a forfeit.

THE PORK BUTCHER.

The enterprising individual who has purchased the stock and goodwill of the Pork Butcher's business—in other words, the conductor of the game—says, "I have just killed a pig; who'll take some of it from me?" then addressing one of the players, "Will you?"

The latter replies in the affirmative. The pork butcher then asks him, what part he will take? The answer is according to the taste of the purchaser; as a hand, a leg, a cheek, the feet, &c.

This is merely a forfeit trap for the unwary. The secret is, that whatever part of the pig you name, you must touch the corresponding part of your own person. Failing in this you pay a forfeit.

THE COOK WHO DOESN'T LIKE PEAS.

The leader of the game puts the following question to the assembled players in succession :—

"My cook doesn't like peas; what shall we give her to eat?"

A player suggests "turnips," "potatoes," "a piece of bread," "chops," "a penny roll," "pork," &c.

To all these the questioner replies, "She don't like them (or it)—pay a forfeit."

Another proposes "carrots," "dry bread," "beef," "mutton," &c., the answer to any of which is,—

"That will suit her," and the *questioner* pays a forfeit.

If only two or three are in the secret, the game proceeds for some time to the intense mystification of the players, who have no idea what they have said to incur or escape the penalties. It depends upon a play of words. The cook not liking "*P's*," the players must avoid giving an answer in which that letter occurs. As the same proposition must not be repeated twice, those even who are in the plot are sometimes entrapped; the answer they had resolved on being forestalled by another player, they have no time for consideration.

I'VE BEEN TO MARKET.

The company being formed into a circle, one of the players says to his neighbor on the left—

"I've been to market."

The neighbor inquires—

"What have you bought?"

"A coat, a dress, a nosegay, a shoe:" in fact any thing that may come into the head of the *customer*, provided he be able, on pronouning the word, to *touch* an article such as he has named. Whoever neglects or is unable to perform this ceremony, pays a forfeit. Naming an article previously indicated is similarly punished.

THE END.